WILDS OF AGGAR

by **Skye Montague**

set in a universe by
Chris Anne Wolfe

BLUE FORGE PRESS
Port Orchard * Washington

Wilds of Aggar (Book 6, Amazons of Aggar)
Copyright 2017
by Skye Montague and Chris Anne Wolfe

First Print Edition July 2017
Second Print Edition January 2023

ISBN 978-1-59092-933-9

For information about film, reprint or other subsidiary rights, contact: blueforgegroup@gmail.com

Blue Forge Press is the print division of the volunteer-run, federal 501(c)3 nonprofit company, Blue Forge Group, founded in 1989 and dedicated to bringing light to the shadows and voice to the silence. We strive to empower storytellers across all walks of life with our four divisions: Blue Forge Press, Blue Forge Films, Blue Forge Gaming, and Blue Forge Records. Find out more at www.BlueForgeGroup.org

Blue Forge Press
7419 Ebbert Drive Southeast
Port Orchard, Washington 98367
blueforgepress@gmail.com
360-550-2071 ph.txt

Before her death from cancer in July 1997, beloved lesbian-feminist author Chris Anne Wolfe published two of her four classic Amazon adventure novels — *Shadows of Aggar* and *Fires of Aggar*.

Wolfe left her literary estate to friend and publisher, Jennifer DiMarco. After releasing Chris Anne's *Sands of Aggar* and *Oceans of Aggar*, as well as *Roses & Thorns: Beauty and the Beast Retold*, *Annabel & I*, *Talismans & Temptations*, and the *Amazons Across Aggar* card game, Jennifer finally opened the world to authors passionate about Aggar who want to help continue Chris Anne's legacy.

Wilds of Aggar is the second of this new generation of adventures.

To become a writer for Amazons of Aggar, write to Jennifer at blueforgepress@gmail.com

More by Chris Anne Wolfe

Amazons of Aggar

Book 1: Shadows of Aggar
Book 2: Fires of Aggar
Book 3: Sands of Aggar
Book 4: Oceans of Aggar
Book 5: Bonds of Aggar
Book 6: Wilds of Aggar

Annabel and I

Roses and Thorns

Talismans & Temptations

www.BlueForgePress.com

WILDS OF AGGAR

by **Skye Montague**

set in a universe by
Chris Anne Wolfe

PART ONE

ON THE TRAIL

RIXTON: BEHIND THE WALLS

Elana sat astride her horse, staring down the winding trail to the town spread across the valley below. Rixton had been built into the hills separating the Ramains from the southern deserts. A nondescript settlement held by a wealthy minor Ramains nobleman. It was neither famous nor crumbling. It was a jot on the map. Somewhere Elana never expected to go. She pursed her lips and held tight to Leggings' reins. Sometimes the darkest secrets hid where they were least expected.

They'd traveled quickly from the Council's Keep, winding their way through the wilds of Aggar further south to the foothills of the Ramains mountains. They had made a similar journey not even a season ago to find special ingredients to cure the Mistress of the Keep – Elana's grandmother – from poison. Elana had expected to be off-world by now. She'd expected to be off-world a season ago. But her journey to the planet of the Amazons to live on Di'Nay's homeworld had been put off indefinitely.

So much had changed in such a short time. Elana's grandmother was dead. Many of the adepts and Council members were dead. The seers were in seclusion. Young adepts who weren't yet qualified to lead were suddenly in positions of power. The Keep had been attacked – ripped apart from the inside, upending what had once been Elana's home.

And children were missing. Seer children, kidnapped on their way to the Keep. The most vulnerable of Aggar were at risk and Elana and Di'Nay had been sent to find them. Elana had to concentrate on that. She couldn't think of her loses. There was only the children, and the Order of Blindness that had stolen them.

Di'Nay rode toward her, her face buried in her map.

Sunlight painted her short, blonde hair with platinum highlights. Elana smiled at the woman she loved as she studied their location. Sometimes the elements seemed to catch on the Amazon and make her radiant.

"This looks like the place. Rixton. Held by Baron Anton Skalde and his wife Isande." Di'Nay glanced up from the map.

"Their child was a seer."

Di'Nay nodded. "They sent their son to the Keep when they realized his true nature. They seemed very grateful when they learned we rescued him."

"Do they expect us?"

"Telias sent word we were visiting. It'll be nice to have a warm reception."

Elana shifted, her gaze falling once more on the town. It looked plain, almost idyllic. But with her Blue Sight she sensed something else. "Tristan thinks there may be cult presence here?"

Di'Nay cocked her head to the side, studying her lover's face. "You sense something dangerous?"

"No. But unsettling. There's no reason the Order of Blindness would target a young child from such a small town. The Ramains court didn't even know he existed. They must have some connection to the Skalde family. The Marshals wouldn't have sent us here if they didn't think there was something to find."

Di'Nay tucked her map away and pulled out the folded piece of paper Tristan had given them. Elana still didn't know what to make of Tristan and the Royal Marshals, a secret organization dedicated to protecting the Ramains through information and stealth. He had never lied to them. He had helped save the Keep. But he was unpredictable. Elana was a shadow. She had drawn her strength from the darkness since she first came to the Keep. She didn't trust anyone who lived deeper in the shadows than she did.

"All his leads are hearsay."

"He didn't want to send his own agents on so little evidence."

"It makes sense to start with the first place we knew a child was targeted. Telias thought so."

Elana frowned. Telias was a good leader. She'd been training to lead the Keep eventually, but she wasn't ready. No one imagined the entire line of succession would be killed off in battle. Still, Elana still paid allegiance to the Council, and she trusted their guidance.

"I don't understand why a family that may have ties to the Order would send us their child."

"Maybe they angered the Order somehow? They aren't in league with them?" Di'Nay suggested.

"I hope so."

Di'Nay tucked the paper away into her belt pouch. "Any lead is more than we had before."

"I don't think Tristan is telling us everything he knows," Elana grumbled.

"Probably not. But we're good at finding the truth."

Elana clenched her jaw. The truth she was most interested in had more to do with Tristan than the Skaldes, but she wouldn't let seer children suffer because she didn't trust her informant. "Let's present ourselves to the Skalde family."

Di'Nay smiled. "It would be rude not to."

Elana laughed. "You're just hungry from the ride."

Di'Nay shrugged. "How often do we get to work where we're invited?"

"I don't know if it will help or hinder our investigation. I'd rather they didn't know we were there."

"Let me handle diplomacy, Soroi. I'll distract them while you move through the shadows."

Elana chuckled. "I'll hold you to it."

Di'Nay clucked to her horse and Kaing set out at a trot toward Rixton. Elana hesitated a moment before following, steeling herself for what was to come. She shook off the unsettling energy lingering across her skin like a thin slime. Di'Nay glanced back at her in concern.

"Elana?"

Elana shook her head. "I'm fine." She rode forward to join her lover and they rode down the winding path cut through the steep hills toward town.

Di'Nay chose her words carefully. "Do you want to change plans? The last time we ignored your instincts we were kidnapped."

Elana shook her head. "It's not apprehension about our actions, there's just something about the environment that puts me on edge."

Di'Nay nodded and returned her attention to the trail.

Elana smiled softly to herself. In the past, her older lover might have tried to coddle her, but not anymore.

The trail to Rixton was thin, but well-worn and flat. They must not have many merchants, but the few they had did a good amount of trade. The grass was long and vibrant green, tall, pristine white daisies growing in clusters just off the trail. There was a rich, earthy scent of upturned soil and cut grass. Elana checked the sky. It probably rained a good deal in the spring and autumn, keeping the landscape vibrant.

The town gates were simple and wooden, manned by a single sentry who barely glanced at them as they passed. The theme continued through the town. The homes were simple and well-maintained, made of stone and wood. The market was small but Elana could see all the basic necessities for sale.

Elana settled back just enough behind Di'Nay to be able to follow her without thought. She instead used her attention to take in her surroundings. She noted the minor changes in architecture and the narrow alleys. Rixton was older than she'd expected, and either hadn't changed much over time or they took great care to keep buildings uniform. Elana didn't doubt most of the families in town had lived there for generations.

She used her Sight to dull her blue eyes to a dark gray to not attract attention. She wasn't an exceptional woman by Aggar's standards. She barely garnered a glance from the townspeople. Most who took the time to note their arrival were drawn to Di'Nay for her obviously off-world heritage. Still, they blended well in the small town. It comforted Elana some to see that she could move easily without attention.

"Skalde manor is just ahead." Di'Nay indicated a large house on a nearby hill overlooking most of the town. In the distance, she could see orchards surrounding the property.

Elana smiled at the gentle scent of apples and the crisp tang in the back of her mouth, more transferred through her Sight than the air. They were the kind of apples she'd loved most as a child, tart and a bit sour, more flavorful than the sweeter apples that grew closer to the Keep. The sensation grew stronger the closer they came to the manor and Elana clung to it, savoring it as she pushed aside her apprehension.

An elderly servant jogged out of the house to greet them. "Greetings, travelers. What brings you to Skalde manor?"

"Diana n'Athena and Min Elana, representatives of the Council's Keep to see the Lord and Lady of the house," Di'Nay introduced.

"Ah!" the man clapped his hands. "We've been expecting you! I'll tell the Baron and Baroness of your arrival. There are stables to the right if you wish to care for your mounts."

Di'Nay nodded and smiled. "Thank you, Tad."

The servant returned to the manor and Di'Nay turned Kaing toward the stables. "First impressions?" she questioned in a low voice.

"He was sincere."

Di'Nay clapped her hands together with a beaming smile. "Perhaps this won't be so bad."

Elana glanced back at the manor, the taste of apple momentarily growing bitter and acidic in her mouth. The taste of blood. "Perhaps."

Skalde manor was standard for a small-town noble keep – a spacious home of wood and stone, simple in design but decorated with fine family heirlooms. Diana stood before a large, woven tapestry depicting servants in the orchards and smiled. The strong scent of apples wafted in from the kitchen and orchards. She'd had an aunt who cared for a fruit orchard. She'd worked many summers helping with the harvest as a child. She had so many fond memories of those sunny days turning to warm nights, eating as much as she picked, her hands smelling of citrus and berries for days afterward.

She glanced at Elana and wondered what she'd think of food on Yemaya. Diana had spent much of her life off the Amazon homeworld. As a member of house n'Athena, she had dedicated herself to diplomacy and exploration. Elana, however, had never left Aggar. Elana's thoughts were always distracted about policy, gender politics, and the more complicated aspects of moving to another planet, but it was the small things that always went overlooked. Food, the scent of flowers, the texture of clothing, and the colors of nature – she wondered if Elana had even considered how different life would be. It was always the small things that made one feel at home or completely out of place.

Elana touched Diana's arm, drawing her attention. "Soroi?"

Elana smiled. "I like when you're thinking about Yemaya."

Diana blushed lightly and placed her hand on her lover's. "I'm thinking about you."

"I know." Elana dropped her hand a moment before Diana heard footsteps approaching.

"Min Elana? Min Diana?" A servant stepped out into the hallway, her hands tucked behind her back. "My Lord and Lady Skalde will see you now."

"Thank you, Min."

The servant led Diana and Elana upstairs to a small study and left, closing the door behind her. The Baron and Baroness Skalde were dressed in conservative black garments, the Baron in a black and silver brocade coat and the Baroness in a full, black gown with long sleeves and a corseted waist. They were both middle-aged, their hair painted with gray and silver streaks. Diana considered them closely. They were older than she'd expected. Many on Aggar didn't have very young children at such an advanced age.

"Welcome to my house, Min Diana and Min Elana," Baron Skalde greeted, standing and offering his hand to each of them. Diana smiled at his lack of hesitance to greet her as she shook his hand – it was always a risk that male noblemen on Aggar would turn up their noses at female diplomats, especially those from off-world.

"Thank you for having us," Diana responded.

Baroness Skalde joined her husband. "We can't thank you enough for saving our child. It's good to know he's with people who can take care of him."

"He's loved and cared for," Elana promised.

"With his own kind," the Baron agreed.

Elana shifted. Diana felt her discomfort at his comment radiate between the connection of the lifestones in their wrists. The opaline stones set into their skin not only bound their life forces together, but also occasionally their strong emotions. Standing so close together, it was hard not to sense Elana's wariness.

"I heard you're traveling Aggar in search of the people who attempted to kidnap our son. Have you found any leads? We're happy to help you," the Baroness offered.

"We have a few, but this is our first stop along our journey. Just having a safe place to rest is very valuable," Diana remarked.

"Why would you start here? I guarantee no one in Rixton

would attempt to hurt our child. If there were, he wouldn't have made it as far as the capitol."

"We wouldn't think it, and we aren't here looking for suspects," Diana assured him. "It just makes sense to start here – to gather as much information about the child and where he came from as possible."

"What do you need to know? Our son wasn't anything special. He never spoke to us. He barely looked at us."

Diana drew a slow breath and studied the Baron more closely. There were cracks around his calm facade. Something he wasn't saying. Or perhaps he could tell there was much Diana wasn't saying?

The Baroness placed her hand on her husband's arm. "You're welcome to ask any questions that would help. Now that he's at the Keep, we want our son to stay safe. If he's being targeted, finding the people responsible is our highest priority."

"Thank you, Baroness. We'll do our best to ease your worries."

The Baroness nodded, her eyes focused on Diana's mouth instead of looking her in the eyes. For a moment, Diana saw tension around her eyes, wrinkles that held years of exhaustion and worry.

"Melanda!" The Baron called out into the hall and after a moment the study door was opened. The maid who'd led Elana and Diana to the study bowed. Diana made a point to remember her name.

"My Lord?"

"Would you see Min Diana and Min Elana to their room?"

Melanda bowed again. "Of course."

"Please feel free to ask Melanda for anything you need or if you need to reach the Baron or me. You're welcome to join us for dinner at dusk or take a meal privately."

"Thank you," Elana and Diana spoke together before following Melanda out of the study.

They were led to the western wing of the house to a set of rooms, each containing a bed, bureau, nightstand, and wardrobe.

"Will these do?" Melanda questioned.

"Perfectly. Thank you," Diana answered.

Melanda nodded deeply. "Please let me know if I can help you with anything else."

"Is there anything you can tell us about the household? Anything we should be aware of?"

Melanda's cheeks grew dark with sudden tension. Diana cocked her head, the maid's emotional shift was surprising. "There's nothing unusual about the Skalde household, Min. We're very happy to have you here."

"I didn't mean to imply otherwise," Diana assured her. "I just want to make sure we keep to house rules."

Melanda settled a bit. "You'll be fine, Min. We're here to help with anything you need."

Elana placed a hand on Diana's arm. "I'm sure you're very busy. Thank you for your help. We'll see you at dusk."

The maid bowed again and rushed down the hallway. Once she disappeared around the corner, Elana shot Diana a knowing glance. "She's terrified."

"Of what?" Diana questioned.

"I don't know." They entered Diana's room and shut the door. Elana sat on the bed, leaning against the thick wooden post of the canopy. She stared out the window on the opposite wall to the orchard beyond. "It seems my fears before were justified."

Diana sighed and sat beside her. "I sense it, too. Did you sense malice in anyone in particular?"

Elana shook her head. "Only discomfort. We're not as welcomed as they want us to believe, but they aren't going to push us away."

"Maybe Tristan's rumors were right. Maybe they do have ties to the Order."

"Many things can create discomfort in an Aggar household. Both of us alone could cause concern. A Shadow from the Keep and an Amazon? We draw attention. You don't have to be part of the Order of Blindness to be wary of the unknown in Aggar."

"The Baron didn't show any sign of discomfort around me," Diana defended.

Elana's voice was suddenly acidic. "The Baron is a bigot."

Diana sighed and leaned back on her elbows. "Let's get some sleep before dinner. I'm tired from traveling."

Elana turned, her thoughts drawn from her concerns about the household to Diana's needs. "Perhaps that would be best. You look tired."

Diana smiled. "Do I, Love?"

Elana chuckled. "I'm sure I do, too."

"You look beautiful."

Elana leaned down and kissed her, the simple touch of intimacy soothing the lingering tension from their meeting with the Baron and Baroness.

It took only a moment for them to remove their boots and outer layers and climb into bed. It had initially been a ploy to lighten Elana's mood, but as her head hit the pillow, the exhaustion from traveling sank into Diana's bones and she was grateful for a moment of rest. She closed her eyes as Elana rested her head on Diana's chest and she quickly slipped into dreams.

Diana woke to the sound of a rapping echoing through the room. She shifted, glancing out the window. Was it dusk already?

"A moment!" she called as she eased out of Elana's arms and shuffled to the door. When she opened it, however, there was no maid waiting on the other side. She closed the door slowly, unsure if the sound had been part of a lingering dream. The knocking echoed again. Diana tensed, tracing the sound. It wasn't coming from the door, it was coming from the walls.

She followed the wooden walls, listening intently. Were they hollow? Could an animal have gotten inside? She tapped along the boards, hoping to scare off the vermin, but instead the tapping started to echo her own. She tapped twice and was answered. She tapped three times and the taps were echoed back to her.

"Hello?"

An animalistic shriek rebounded behind the walls. Diana shouted and fell back, hitting the ground hard. Elana sat straight up in bed, her eyes wide in shock.

"Di'Nay?"

Diana released a breath she hadn't realized she was holding. "There was something in the walls. Do you feel anything?" Elana shook her head and Diana's eyes grew wide. "Not even an animal?"

"I don't sense anything."

Diana tried to shake off her lingering fear. There had to be an explanation for what had happened. Old stories from her childhood echoed in a tangled weave her mind. Stories of ghosts and spirits. She'd had nightmares of Onryo every night for a year when she first heard about them.

"You didn't hear anything?"

Elana touched Diana's shoulder apologetically. "Only you. But I was sleeping very soundly."

"It must have been an animal."

"I'll keep listening for it. Perhaps we can tell Melanda?"

Diana smiled at her. "I know you can feel my thoughts. You don't have to humor me over some childhood fears. If I hear it again, I'll be sure to wake you. Then we can decide what to do."

Elana mirrored her smile and helped her stand. "Thank you for letting me sleep."

"It did us both a world of good."

Another knock echoed and Diana jumped. Elana laughed and moved to answer the door.

"Mins, dinner is served if you'd like to join us."

Elana glanced over her shoulder at Diana, concerned about how startled she'd been. Diana nodded to Melanda. "Thank you. We'll be down in a moment."

"I'm fine," Diana protested as Elana closed the door. "I promise."

Elana kissed her gently. "I trust you." There was teasing in her eyes.

"There must be silly things you feared as a child that still linger with you!"

"*Soroi*, I'm what everyone else in Aggar feared."

Diana felt a rush of heat dance up her spine at Elana's use of Yemayan words. She would never stop loving her lover embracing even small bits of Amazon culture. "We should get dressed for dinner."

"If you're settled."

"Mother save me from brazen women!" Diana exclaimed, invoking Elana's goddess.

"The Mother may take pity on you, but I fear your Yemayan goddesses have a tender spot for brazen women."

"You're probably right."

Elana kissed her again. "I won't tease you anymore."

"Tease all you like, my Love. You only give me permission to return the favor someday."

Elana kissed her once more, the mischief still in her eyes. "Now. To change for dinner."

Elana ate slowly, her eyes darting between the Baron and Baroness and the servants that stood at the back of the dining hall. Diana entertained them, her charm and diplomacy more than enough to sway the Skalde household, allowing Elana to keep more to herself and study.

The household already knew she was a Blue Sight, but she continued to dim her irises to gray. She found the cloak made people more comfortable around her. She wasn't just teasing Di'Nay earlier – she really was the childhood nightmares for many people in Aggar, particularly those who had been raised outside of larger cities. She wouldn't get any answers if she was a walking reminder of their nightmares.

She was already so unlike the standard woman of Aggar. Most were buxom and golden, either of hair or darker complexion. Elana was a willow branch, slender and boyish in comparison. Her ebony hair fell wild down her back, thoroughly untamable. For those sensitive to different people, she stood out already. She didn't need to add her Sight to the mix.

She kept her head tipped down toward her soup, letting her eyes linger over people through her lashes and hair. No one sensed her, most enthralled with Diana's story of the rescue of the Skaldes' seer child. Elana allowed herself a moment to smile over Di'Nay. She could have been a storyteller if her heart had been less inclined to politics.

She returned her attention to the servants. She didn't sense malice in any of them, but that darkness was still there, seeping over every bit of the house like thick tar or oil. She constantly felt the need to bathe.

"Min Elana, you're a Shadow of the Keep, yes?"

Elana was startled by the Baroness's question, but hid it well. "Yes."

The Baroness sipped at her tea. "I've always been fascinated by the Council's Keep. So mysterious."

Elana could sense more behind her question than what she was saying. She took a guess at the meaning. "The mystery is more out of necessity than secrets. In many ways it's a sanctuary for those that couldn't live well outside its walls. The seers are very happy."

She smiled faintly and Elana knew she'd allayed some of

the Baroness's fears. "What's it like, their home?"

Elana took a moment to choose her words, deciding how much she wanted to say. "Seers are like honeybees or ants. They have a kind of psychic network that binds them together. They aren't happy being disconnected from that hive mind – they don't know how to exist alone. At the Keep they stay close together. They dream and have visions. They see all of time and space. They're where they want to be. It's very comforting to be near them."

The Baroness smiled into her teacup. "My boy was always unhappy. I don't think there was a day when his cries didn't echo through the house until we sent him to the Keep."

"He hasn't cried once since he joined the seers," Elana answered honestly. "You did the right thing."

Elana felt a warmth from the Baroness that nearly wiped away the darkness until her husband spoke. "It better have been the right choice. We paid enough for it." He didn't look at anyone in particular as he carved at a hunk of meat on his plate. "Still, it was worth it to have some peace and quiet here again."

Elana frowned at his callousness as his wife's joy dampened and her eyes lowered back to her tea. Surprisingly, his statement seemed to affect the servants as well. Many shifted, casting glances at each other. It was barely noticeable, but Elana could feel the emotions swelling off them. Fear. Something was going unspoken.

"I promise your money was well spent." Di'Nay tried to turn the conversation pleasant again. "Baron, I noticed your beautiful apple orchards. Has the season been good to you?"

The Baron finally showed interest in the conversation as he began to wax poetic about crops and Skalde cider. It wasn't long until he started trying to broker sales with Di'Nay for serving Terran military bases. Di'Nay had no power to make such a deal, but the merchant in her found the conversation amusing.

Di'Nay didn't seem to notice the anger in him, or if she did she played it close to the chest. The Baroness, however, kept casting short glances at Elana, her lips trembling and her amarin whispering that there was so much she desperately wanted to say but wouldn't. Of everyone in the room, she seemed the least nervous of Elana's abilities. Elana made a mental note to try to speak with the woman alone.

Dinner ended without another incident. Elana thanked her hosts with as much grace as Di'Nay, but her smile died on her lips the moment they left the dining hall to return to their room.

"I don't trust him."

Di'Nay eyed her with surprise. "Did you sense something?"

"He doesn't like the Council."

"The Keep saved his son."

"He hated his son."

Di'Nay turned away, uncomfortable. "I've lived here a long time, but sometimes I feel like I'll never fully understand the subtleties you do."

Elana took her hand. "You don't have the Sight, Di'Nay. Most on Aggar wouldn't See what I do. It has nothing to do with being from another world."

"I feel like you're trying to humor me again."

Elana squeezed her hand, trading teasing for sincerity. "You see more than most. I couldn't have sensed what I did tonight without your charm."

Di'Nay was truly grateful. "I do what I can."

They returned to Di'Nay's room and Elana set about changing out of her dinner clothes.

"Do you want to go into town tomorrow?" Di'Nay questioned. "Investigate?"

"I'd rather explore the household a bit," Elana remarked. "I think whatever answers we seek are here."

Di'Nay sighed sadly. "I hate to think the seer child's parents could be behind the attack."

Elana slipped out of her dress, letting the weight of it fall to the floor as she stood in her lighter underdress. She ran her fingers through her hair. "Unfortunately, most threats to seer and Blue Sight children come from their families."

She felt the warmth of Di'Nay coming to stand behind her, resting her hands on her shoulders. "That's the second time today you've mentioned Blue Sights in such a way. Are you feeling threatened? I won't let anyone hurt you."

Elana turned and smiled sadly, cupping lover's cheek. "I'm fine. But the situation weighs heavily on me. The Order of Blindness, the attack on the seer children... it's made me more aware than ever that I'm not wholly welcome among my people."

Di'Nay turned to kiss her palm, closing her eyes a moment as she savored the intimate touch with Elana. "Someday I'll take you where everyone will love you."

Elana felt her stomach twist at the promise. As much as she longed to be on Di'Nay's planet with her beloved, far from the pain and suffering of Aggar, it didn't assuage the pain of being rejected by her homeworld. And she didn't wholly trust that Yemaya would be as kind to her as Di'Nay seemed to expect. Still. It was a beautiful dream.

"I know you will."

Di'Nay's smile faded and she turned to move away. She had sensed the pain and doubt in Elana's words. Elana shook her head and kissed Di'Nay, pressing tighter against her, not allowing her to turn away with such doubts in her mind. She didn't want to talk about darkness and fear. Di'Nay would never fully understand and Elana would never want her to. Instead, she would cover the fear with love.

As Di'Nay pulled her closer and laid her back in bed, all thoughts of rejection and loneliness disappeared for them both.

Diana washed her hands in the basin of warm water and gazed out the window of her room at the apple orchard of Skalde manor. She sighed. Elana was bathing and, due to the traditional Aggar sensibilities in the Skalde household, Diana couldn't join her. She was glad Elana had the small comfort of a warm bath. She had looked pale all morning, almost sickly. They needed to find what they were looking for quickly and leave.

She dried her hands on a soft towel by the basin and set it aside. She didn't know how long Elana planned to soak, but she was sure it was long enough to do some investigating of her own. Whatever she could do or find while Elana rested the better. It seemed interacting with the residents of the manor drained her more than anything else.

She grabbed a shirt from her traveling bag. The garment, which had been folded the night before, was now a crumple ball. As she shook it out she noticed three buttons missing. She searched her bag and the ground around it for the button but found nothing. Her brow furrowed. If anything valuable had gone missing she would have assumed it to be household staff stealing, but buttons?

She glanced around the room, paying more attention to see if anything else was missing. She didn't see anything right away, but a few oddities stood out. A vase of fresh flowers had been moved to the opposite side of the bureau. The canopy on the bed was more lopsided than before. Nothing that couldn't be explained away by Elana getting ready in the morning, but she still felt unsettled.

Diana froze as she heard another rush, as if someone were running in the walls. She shook her head. She was being childish. Letting the fears of her youth play tricks on her.

Elana was right – it had to be some kind of animal. It would even explain her missing buttons, bitten away by some rodent.

She heard a sharp knock on the wall. She tensed. "Hello?"

There was no response. She crept forward, listening intently for any other sounds of physicality. She didn't hear breathing or steps. She didn't hear skitters or grunts like she'd expect from a woodland creature or the flap of wings of a trapped bird.

She hesitated, then knocked on the wall. An answering knock echoed from behind her bed. She moved to the sound and knocked again. She heard another shuffle and her breath caught in her throat. Faintly in the distance she could hear a gentle weeping. It didn't sound like any animal she'd ever heard.

"Hello?" she repeated.

She fell back as another shriek filled the room. Her heart raced as she rushed out into the hall. She paused to catch her breath just outside Elana's door and wondered if Elana would tease her too much if she asked to change rooms.

Her breathing calmed and she closed her eyes. She didn't see herself as superstitious, but childhood fears were hard to shake. She also wasn't prone to hearing things, and she was sure Elana would be able to tell if she was losing her mind in some way, but as far as she knew, she was still the only one who ever heard the activity in her room. She clenched her jaw. If there were any answers for her, the staff should have them.

She moved swiftly through the hallways. She paused as she reached the lobby, waiting patiently for any sign of a servant who would talk with her. There were a few who seemed unphased by her presence, but many of them avoided her, either out of manners or fear.

After a while, Melanda strode toward her from the parlor. "Min, can I help you with anything?"

"I've been hearing sounds in my room."

Melanda's cheeks grew dark. "Sounds?"

"Scuffling and knocks. Sometimes shrieks."

Melanda met Diana's eyes as she spoke and the color in her cheeks faded to normal. "This house is very old and the wooden base creates pockets between walls that sometimes attract small animals from the orchard. I'll have someone investigate your sounds this evening. I'm sorry you've been disturbed."

Diana didn't let her surprise reach her face, but there was something new in Melanda – a boldness she hadn't expected. Either her response about animals or her signs of fear were well rehearsed. Diana was no longer sure which.

"Thank you."

Melanda bowed. "Is there anything else?"

"No."

"Let me know if you need anything else."

She disappeared back into the parlor. Diana stood still for a moment, processing what had happened. She would have to ask Elana to pay more attention to their assigned maid. Until then, she was suddenly sure the answers she was looking for wouldn't be found from staff so close to the house.

Diana walked outside, bound for the stables. Kaing was restless as she reached his stall. He was never one for being pampered too long. She would have to take him for a run soon or he'd stop behaving for the handlers.

"You his owner?" A stable hand left a nearby stall, a brush and stool in his arms. He was young, nondescript with dusty hair and the ropy muscles and broad shoulders of a lifetime servant. His skin was a bit ruddy for one of Aggar, but if she'd seen him on the street she wouldn't have looked twice. "I was just about to start his grooming."

Diana shook her head. "It's fine. I can do it." He offered her his brush and she smiled. "He's behaving?"

He nodded. "He's a fine beast, Min. Both your mounts are. Could fetch a fortune in town."

Diana ran the brush over Kaing's back and felt him start to relax under her hand. "Unfortunately, he wouldn't behave as well for another owner."

"I don't doubt it."

Diana glanced at the young man. He watched her, seeming

to want to say something but hesitating. "You can talk to me."

"What's it like staying in the manor?" The question leapt from his mouth with all the force of youthful curiosity.

"You don't stay there yourself?"

"Nah. Don't think I'm brave enough. Most of us live past the orchard."

Diana regarded him out of the corner of her eye, her hand never pausing her grooming. He was naïve, even eager to speak. She could take a few chances being bold. "Brave? Is there something frightening about the manor?"

"You haven't heard the stories? The place is cursed. My aunt works in the kitchen. Says things disappear and dead birds and rodents show up on the kitchen table all the time. Something moves through the walls. She thought it was the spirit of that demon baby, but the kid is gone and the ghosts are still there."

"The child was a seer, not a demon."

"Couldn't quite tell the difference, the way the Master treated him."

"The Baron was cruel to him?"

"Not physically, but everyone knows he hated the kid. Poor thing never stopped screaming, no matter what his mother did to try to calm him."

"She was kind to him?"

"Nearly died when the baby was taken to the capitol. My aunt says she prayed to the Mother every day for a child. To her, even a broken one was better than nothing. You heard the ghosts?"

It took a moment for Diana to process his shift in subject. "No. Not ghosts."

"But you've heard something?"

"Just animals or pests in the wood."

"Pests? Nah. It's something from the Fate's Cellar for sure. Sometimes in the middle of the night you can hear it screaming. Don't know an animal that sounds like that."

"What do you think it is?"

"I think it's the poor souls of those dead and buried in the orchard."

"Is there a graveyard there?"

"There's a reason the Skaldes have so much money."

"You think they've killed people?"

A bell clanged in the distance and the boy looked out the

barn door. "That's midday meal. You got everything you need?"

Diana nodded and he rushed out the door toward the orchard. She watched him leave, his words racing through her mind. If she hadn't heard the sounds on her own, she wouldn't have believed him. But she'd heard the tapping and scuffling, and whatever it was had definitely given an intelligent response to her knocking. Had the Skaldes really been involved in murders?

Something was going on. Something Elana couldn't sense with her Sight, which should be connected to every living thing on Aggar. Could a Blue Sight sense the dead?

Elana pulled herself from her bath with a sigh. Her muscles ached from the effort, but they weren't as strained as earlier in the day. She sat on the rim of the tub, letting her feet and calves continue to soak in the warm water. The bathing room was simple – just tile and a large wash tub – but hot baths were often more healing for Elana than sleep. And she needed something to soothe her mind.

There was something about Skalde Manor – something she couldn't sense – that was slowly eating away at her. She was exhausted. Her body ached. She had a headache. She had hoped she was just getting sick, but it was started to affect Di'Nay as well. She insisted she was hearing things and feeling the presence of a creature that Elana couldn't sense with her Sight. It was amusing at times to tease her lover about childhood superstitions, but the reality of their situation was that Di'Nay was genuinely hallucinating or once again Elana's abilities were proving unstable.

Elana had been unable to save her home from attack when the Order of Blindness proved they could hide from her Sight. She'd spent her entire life relying on her abilities to guide her through the world. She had no experience being unable to trust her senses – to trust the amarin of every living things around her. The Order hadn't just attacked her, they'd made her acutely aware of her own limitations. She'd never felt like more of a liability. The thought that it could be happening again left her cold.

What was she missing? She was sure the Baron was a bigot and the Baroness was absorbed in her grief. The staff were hiding something – something they didn't even dare think about. But she had no proof of wrongdoing, nothing that could tie anyone at the Manor to the Order or the attempted kidnapping of the seer child.

She finally left the tub and dried herself with a soft towel, her thoughts spinning as she combed her hair and donned a simple cotton dress. The lifestone in her wrist was warm and connected to Di'Nay more strongly than earlier. Her Amazon was thinking of her as she moved through the manor. She was investigating, wanting to take the burden of conversing with the staff off Elana's shoulders.

Elana smiled softly to herself. Perhaps if Di'Nay was tackling one of her stressors, Elana could investigate one of Di'Nay's.

Elana walked to Di'Nay's room and closed the door. If something was moving behind the walls, Elana should be able to find it. Skalde manor was more wooden than Elana was used to. The Keep was entirely made of stone and even her childhood home had been largely framed in stone. It wouldn't surprise her if animals regularly became trapped in a wooden framework, like birds caught in a chimney. She laughed softly to herself, imagining Di'Nay's face if Elana found a woodpecker or rat making the disturbing noises.

She moved along the walls, running her hands over the panels and listened. She could feel a very faint amarin off the wood panels, the ghosts of the energy they'd had as trees. She could feel the residents of the manor and the gentle presence of the orchard.

As she moved and focused she felt the amarin of tiny insects in the narrow hollows between the walls. They seemed at rest, used to their dark abode, but there was an anxiety that clung to them as if they'd been recently disturbed.

She circled the room multiple times, her brow knitting tightly with every pass. Nothing seemed out of place. There were no scraping or rushing sounds like Di'Nay described. She didn't feel the presence of anything larger than a spider.

She tried to move the furniture, but it was too heavy to shift alone. She thought a moment before sliding onto her belly and easing herself under the bed. She moved along the walls, pressing her hands against the boards and paused as she reached the patch of wall behind the headboard. The panels shifted under her palm.

The space seemed to be a patch in the siding, boards cut short to fit between the floor and the longer panels above. She pushed harder and they fell back, creating a small opening into the space between the walls. She squeezed through the small opening, barely getting her narrow hips through the hole. It wasn't large enough to rise above the headboard – it would be invisible to the rest of the room even when the boards were removed.

She pushed herself to her feet, waving her hands around her face to knock aside the numerous spider webs that clung to her skin and hair. She sent a soothing feeling to the surprised insects. She wouldn't disturb their homes wherever possible, but it was best if they retreated for a time further up the walls.

The space was narrow and pitch dark, but there were enough insects to fill her mind's eye with their amarin and guide her through the shadows. They stood out like lights, illuminating the walls and angles of the twisting pathways that seemed to travel through the entire house.

Elana walked carefully, feeling for sudden drops or broken boards with her feet. There were dips and chutes as the pathways dropped to lower levels. It was a labyrinth. Were all wooden homes like this? It seemed unusual and impractical.

Elana's path stayed even for a time and then slopped upward. As she reached the outside wall, Elana grabbed the wooden beams and climbed until she felt a stable floor again. She hadn't realized there was another story above her own. The house was bigger than it looked.

She took a few steps forward along the new floor and then hesitated. She could smell blood. She took another step forward and heard a brittle snap as she stepped into some kind of nest. She fell back a step and crouched low, feeling for whatever she'd broken.

She felt dried hay and dirt. Her stomach turned as she felt the broken remains of rat skeletons and the feathers of a bird. Perhaps it was a cat stuck in the walls, leaving the remains of its dinners in one place. She stood again, using the wall to steady herself. She froze, a new lingering amarin flooding through her fingers. Blood was dried to the wood, grimy and caked like dirt. She prodded the nest with her foot again. No cat was big enough to splatter rodent blood on the walls at Elana's shoulder level.

She heard a scuffle in the distance and closed her eyes, trying to focus on what was making the noise. Nothing. She couldn't feel anything but death. Her hands trembled and her heart pounded. What was it? Why was she suddenly blind again? She felt like she was being watched. She always felt like she was being watched when she thought too long about the Order and her flagging Blue Sight. She was blind. She felt helpless.

"Hello?"

She jumped, nearly falling to the floor as a piercing, raging shriek echoed through the corridor followed by the pounding of running feet and a searing pain in her side as something ran past her. She gasped in shock, reaching for what felt like a dagger in her side, but there was no hilt and what stuck out of her was too slender to be a knife. Elana turned, falling back, ready to defend herself from another attack, but the creature continued forward, ignoring her.

Elana squeezed her eyes shut, pushing back tears as she pulled the weapon free and ran after the creature as fast as she dared. Whatever had attacked her sounded swift, moving as if it knew every twist and turn of the channels between the walls of Skalde manor. By the time Elana reached the opening into Di'Nay's room again, there were no signs of the creature. The spiders were in a panic. This wasn't the first time the creature had come through the spiders' domain and they were afraid.

Elana crawled back under the bed and pulled the boards into place. She rolled out from under the bed and grabbed at her side, now wet with blood. It wasn't as deep a wound as she'd feared, but she needed to bind it. With the light of day, she looked down at the object in her hand. It was a slender bone, sharpened to a point. As her mind calmed, Elana sensed bits of life that had once clung to it. It had come from a large rat, probably a rib. She saw a flashing memory – a moment of terror etched forever into the bone during the rat's last moments. The pain and fear of being ripped apart and devoured.

She trembled as she forced herself to stand, letting the bone drop onto the bed. She tried to remember which bag held their medical kit. Knowing the weapon's crude origins made her even more wary of infection.

She cleaned her wound with trembling hands. Diana wasn't hallucinating, but this clearly wasn't a ghost. It had form. It had weight. And it had intent to kill.

Diana reached the lobby of the manor when she felt Elana's emotions burning through her lifestone like living fire. She grabbed her wrist in shocked panic. Elana was hurt.

She raced to their room, listening for any sounds of attack

or cries for help. She burst into her room, surprising Elana as she finished bandaging her waist. Diana sighed loudly in relief seeing Elana whole and safe, but her eyes instantly darted to the bandages and the pallor of Elana's cheeks.

"What happened?"

Elana was trembling. Diana closed the doors and reached out to her, wary of touching her without knowledge of her injuries. Elana sank into her arms and tried to collect herself, but Diana's lifestone still throbbed.

"I found your creature."

"What?" A dozen jumbled thoughts sped through Diana's mind, everything from an animal attack to vengeful spirits.

"It's not a ghost."

Diana pulled away just enough to look down at Elana's face. "It attacked you?"

Elana nodded to the bed and Diana saw a bloody bit of bone on the blanket. The end had been sharpened into a very crude blade.

"Stabbed me in the side. The wound isn't vital. I think it's too shallow to have been a treat to my organs. But I don't know if it will become infected."

"What happened?"

Elana walked to the bed. "Help me move it? There's a space here. A hole in the wall."

Together Elana and Diana moved the massive bed frame, sliding it forward just enough to reveal an uneven patch of smaller boards extending to the floor. Shoddy craftsmanship – probably the reason for the bed placement – and easy to compromise.

Elana walked forward and nudged the boards free with her foot, revealing a small hole. "I went back there. Into the walls."

Diana's eyes widened. Elana must have crawled on her stomach to get through. "What did you find?"

"The house is built around a labyrinth of narrow corridors. None of them finished, but wider than I expected. There's a story above ours. It was covered in animal blood and filth. Something came at me in the darkness. Something I couldn't sense. It stabbed me and ran away."

"You couldn't sense it with your Sight?"

Elana shook her head, her lips tight and her skin growing darker in fear. "I thought only the Order could hide from me."

"Elana…" Diana didn't know what to say. For the first time she hoped they *would* find something supernatural. Elana didn't need another reason to doubt her abilities with the living.

"Do you see your attacker?"

Elana shook her head. "It's very dark, but it was very small. I thought at first it was a cat or other animal. It doesn't move like a human. But that bone was fashioned into a weapon with intention and I don't know of any animal that could stab me like that."

Diana considered. "You said it ran away?"

"Yes. It was gone by the time I reached the room again."

"Then we should go back in. Bring lights and weapons. See what we find."

"That makes sense."

Diana felt Elana's relief at the suggestion of going together and it gave her some peace. "You'll be safe to investigate?"

Elana nodded. "The wound hurts, but it isn't dire."

Diana grabbed an oil lamp from the bureau and lit it. She then grabbed her long knife and handed it to Elana. "I have my dagger." Elana took the blade and her hands steadied. "Thank you."

Elana crouched down beside the hole in the wall, half expecting to see eyes shining at her from the darkness, but everything seemed peaceful. She eyed the hole and glanced up at Elana with a raised brow.

"I don't think my hips will fit."

Elana cracked a smile and the show of humor eased the rest of Diana's worries about her young lover. "They will. If you squeeze hard enough." Diana mocked offense and Elana laughed aloud.

Diana took a chance and attempted to pull herself through. It was tight and took some wiggling, but Elana was right that she just barely fit through.

Elana called to her through the wall. "Be careful of the spider webs. The spiders have been traumatized today."

Diana imagined all the insects that must find shelter in the dark, still spaces of the walls and paled. "Z'ki saks, Diana!" Diana growled the declaration to Yemaya's goddess and Elana laughed.

"I knocked most of them down already."

Diana stood and instinctively swiped at the cloud of webs. "I'm taller than you, Soroi."

The darkness lit as Elana slid through with the lantern.

"True."

The small corridor was unfinished to the point Diana couldn't tell if it was intentional or a side-effect from the building of the house. The beams were bare and many other hollows and offshoots led above and around other rooms.

The space had truly become a home for small creatures. Insects scuttled away from them as Elana led her forward. Diana spotted rat droppings and the occasional feather, though she didn't see any spaces were the creatures could be entering.

At points the floor either gave way or became dangerously narrow as it dropped to the floors below between support beams. Diana felt sick thinking of Elana navigating the space in complete darkness and she was thankful for the spiders and their amarin which must have acted as guides for Elana.

"Here." Elana stopped beside what Diana assumed to be the outer wall of the house, as it was more stone than wood. Elana shone her light higher, revealing an entry way above. "I climbed up there, and was attacked."

"There must be an attic," Diana guessed. "It's not too far up. I'll climb then reach back down for the lantern." Elana hesitated. "Neither of us can climb with it. I'll be fine."

Elana nodded and Diana climbed up the beams to the floor above. She reached down and was barely able to grab the lantern from Elana's outstretched hand. As the Blue Sight climbed up to join her, Diana turned. She paled and nearly vomited.

The lantern illuminated what looked like a wild animal's den. Blood smeared the walls and floors. Animal bones, stripped of all flesh, littered the ground in little nests. Scat, urine, and the remains of animal hair and feathers were clustered in corners and around the walls. Diana studied some of the bones in one of the nests. There were gouges across them – teeth marks. They'd been eaten.

"You sure it wasn't an animal?" Diana questioned.

Elana shook her head. "It's not as frightening in the light."

Diana's face twisted in disbelief. "This is disgusting."

"Yes. But very animalistic."

Elana stood before a set of streaks of blood on the wall. "This isn't human blood. It's animal. I Don't see any water. Maybe the creature was trying to clean its hands."

Diana forced herself to ignore the filth and think more

clearly. "I kept mice as a child. They always designated a single area for waste."

Elana nodded. "This isn't a living space."

Diana gestured to the bones. "I don't know any animals that eat where they defecate."

Elana shook her head and pointed out more nests. "I don't think anything is eaten here. Look at the nests. They're planned."

Diana's brows rose as she saw the pattern. Every nest was spaced out in neat lines, each seemingly obsessively the same distance from the one before. The bones in the nests further down the walls seemed wrapped in bits of cloth.

"There's order here. And some kind of respect for the dead in the building of those nests. The bones are cleaner than anything else here."

Once Elana pointed it out, it was all Diana could see. Her heart settled at the signs of care gleaming through the gore. She said a silent prayer of thanks to her goddess for Elana's keen eyes. "Then whatever attacked you doesn't live here."

Elana shook her head. "I don't think so. Maybe it attacked me because I surprised it."

"But *what* is it? This isn't human."

Elana clenched her jaw, her face grim. "We need to find its home."

They continued through the room, finding another corridor in the shadows at the back of the space. It was far narrower than before, forcing Elana and Diana to navigate it sideways. Diana's muscles cramped and jumped at the tight, enclosed space and she forced herself to breath slowly and not imagine becoming trapped.

Elana finally slipped out of the corridor ahead of Diana into a larger space. Diana nearly ran into her lover as she squeezed through. Elana had frozen in place as she'd exited.

The lantern illuminated what had to be an attic space, the massive room paneled and finished like the rest of the house. The space they'd entered through had been created by tearing through the wall panels like in Diana's bedroom.

There were no animal carcasses or blood on the walls. There were no windows and Diana couldn't see any doors or exits. There were trunks stacked along the walls like hidden away storage. A bed stood against one wall, the posts covered in claw marks and scratches. The sheets, once white, were filthy and torn.

Old cider jugs were lined along one wall filled with water.

There were wet stains near the water that smelled of wine and something else, something sweeter. Diana tried to remember where she had smelled it before. After a moment it returned to her: it was a sedative, a concoction she'd been given by a healing woman during her first journey with Elana. Whoever lived in this space had been drugged. It seemed by the stains on the walls that was no longer effective.

Elana moved slowly through the room, inspecting everything. Diana stayed close, neither of them speaking a word. The claw marks weren't just on the posts of the bed but the walls as well. In many sections Diana couldn't tell if they'd been made with nails or knives.

Elana opened one of the trunks. It held child's clothes and a few toys. She opened another and paused. A woven cradle, frayed with age but obviously once a well-crafted toy, held a small doll without a head. The baby had been wrapped in what looked like scraps from the dirty sheets. Diana's missing buttons were placed in the cradle with other odds and ends – pale stones, buttons, feathers. Trinkets and treasures gathered in a nest.

"Like the rat bones," Elana whispered.

Diana rested her hand on Elana's shoulder, fearing the worst and knowing through her connection with Elana that she feared the same things. "Are there any exits?"

"I would be surprised." Elana's voice was faint and pained. They walked around the and eventually found what looked like an old entryway into the attic, but it had been sealed. There were more claw marks here than anywhere else. Diana could see bits of dried blood in the crevices.

Elana threw one of the trunks down in a rage, its contents spreading across the floor. Elana was trembling and clenching her free fist. Diana could only watch her as she mourned. She knew instinctively to touch her was the wrong choice.

She moved to gather what had scattered across the ground and placing them back in the fallen trunk. She paused as she righted it. A portrait was stuck in the base of the trunk, the frame too wide to fly out with the other papers. It was old. The Baron and Baroness were younger, no gray yet in their hair. The Baroness held a child. There was no way it was painted for the child they'd recently sent to the Keep.

"Why…" Diana's words trailed off, swallowed by the silence of the attic.

Elana turned sharply and strode back toward the narrow corridor that led back into the walls. Diana quickly set the trunk back against the wall and followed the dwindling light as her lover left.

Elana tore through the passageways back toward her room. She couldn't feel her injury anymore. She couldn't feel anything but rage.

She had enough awareness to make sure Di'Nay was able to keep up with her. Thoughts and questions buzzed through the back of her mind. Why hadn't she been able to sense the child's presence? Why hadn't the child been drawn to her? If it was a seer or blue sight, it would immediately sense her presence.

Where had the child gone?

She reached the hole in the wall that led into Diana's room and crawled through. She sensed Melanda's presence even before she left the walls. The maid stood in the middle of the room, staring at the space revealed by the moved bed. She held her hands over her mouth and wept silently. Her skin was nearly black with terror and grief.

"Did you find her?"

Elana clenched her jaw, standing rigid and imposing over the smaller woman. She didn't attempt to dim her eyes. She didn't care if anyone else was comfortable around her. She was a walking accusation. A reminder of what the residents of Skalde manor had done.

Melanda cowered. Elana felt her guilt like bile in her throat. It was bitter and old. She'd known for many tenmoons.

"I try to help her. I bring her food and water. I… I never wanted…"

"You knew."

"From the beginning. Yes. Please don't hurt me!"

"Who else knows?"

"My Lord and Lady. No one else. There are rumors, but the Baron sent away everyone who ever knew of the child. That's why he asked me to watch you. To make sure you didn't find her."

"No one knew the Baroness had a child? No one in town?"

"It was thought my Lady was barren. When the child was

born... broken they kept it a secret."

"Elana." Di'Nay took Elana's shoulder, her voice soft, but Elana pulled away.

"You could have saved her."

"I did save her! She'd be dead without me caring for her!"

"You should have gotten her to the Keep!" Elana's shouts rang through the room. Elana rarely screamed or berated. Even Di'Nay took a step back in surprise. "You let this happen!"

Melanda was so terrified she couldn't speak through her tears. Di'Nay took Elana's arm again, more tentatively. Di'Nay turned to Melanda, speaking gently. "What happened to the child? Where is she? She wasn't in the walls."

"I don't know. I was looking for her. She didn't come to the pantry for dinner. I can always get her scraps at night. She never misses it. I was so afraid... you didn't find her body?"

Elana started to calm a bit toward the maid at the genuine care in Melanda's amarin, but the sensation only frustrated her more. If she cared so much, the child should never have been hurt.

"She ran away, possibly through this hole in the wall. Maybe she escaped?"

Melanda started to breathe more evenly, her color becoming less intense, bolstered by Di'Nay's kindness. "She can't be too long in sunlight. It hurts her eyes."

"She came out at night. Stole my buttons."

Melanda glanced at Di'Nay in confusion. "She never leaves the walls."

"Maybe she got sick of being your victim," Elana spat.

"Has anyone in the house been hurt?"

Melanda shook her head as she grew dark again with worry. "What if she got out of the house? What if she's been seen?"

"Maybe someone will help her," Di'Nay suggested.

"You don't understand. No one will help her. She's wild. She'll be killed at best."

Elana glanced out the window. Night was already falling. "If she meant to escape and can't travel by daylight, she's probably already gone."

"Elana, I think Melanda is genuine," Di'Nay insisted, shocked at Elana's callousness.

Elana glanced at the maid. "What's the child's name?"

Melanda's face blanked. "Excuse me?"

"The child. What's her name?"

"She has no name."

"You didn't give her one? You see her every night and you didn't once think to find something to call her?"

Melanda shuddered. "She wouldn't understand me if I did. What would be the point?"

Elana sneered. "The point is that she's a *human*, not a pet and not an animal. If you really felt for her, you would see that."

Di'Nay and Melanda exchanged glances, some of Di'Nay's empathy draining away.

Melanda shook her head. "I have to find her."

She turned and ran from the room. Elana and Di'Nay followed quickly as she sprinted into the yard toward the orchard. Elana stopped as they stepped just inside the tree line, letting Di'Nay and Melanda continue ahead. They wouldn't find her by shouting into the darkness. The child would be hiding. Scared. Even if Elana couldn't feel her, she would be able to sense the disturbance she caused the trees.

She walked slowly, trying to calm her rage enough to focus on her Sight without her fire tainting the apple trees. The scents were soothing, dark and sweet. The earth was fragrant from being well nourished. The top branches fluttered with birds coming home to roost. It wouldn't surprise her if the child would come here after a lifetime closed in darkness with rodents and insects.

As she reached the back of the orchard where it started to meet a more wild copse of trees she felt a shift in the network of amarin created by the trees. They were used to humans wandering their rows and plucking their fruits, so someone new caused no alarm. But there was a disconnect, like a cold spot that seemed to block the of living energy Elana could sense with her Sight.

She followed it quietly, using her Shadow abilities to not make a sound. She paused as she saw her. A young girl, no more than five tenmoons laid in the foliage, her knees curled to her chest and her face buried in her arms. She trembled and grunted in short, animalistic bursts. In the moonlight Elana could see she was incredibly pale, even her hair a snowy white as if she were made of starlight herself. She was dirty and dressed in rags. She was overwhelmed.

Elana approached slowly. The child looked out at her over her arms, her eyes glinting in the darkness, angled in a warning glare, but she didn't move. She likely no longer had the strength.

"I won't hurt you," Elana promised, wondering if the child even spoke.

As Elana knelt beside her, she used all her effort to be as intimidating as possible, moving with unbelievable speed to sit up, supporting herself with her arms as she nearly fell over again. Her eyes weren't blue, but she was surprisingly cognizant for a seer.

Elana blinked away tears when she saw a small metal medallion at her throat. An amulet from the Order of Blindness. A talisman that not only robbed her of her own Seeing abilities, but hid her from any Blue Sight. Perhaps the talisman had bound her abilities so long she'd learned to survive without them.

Elana reached for the necklace and the child snapped at her, nearly biting her hand. Elana pulled back and fixed the child with her blue eyes, asserting gentle dominance. "You don't like that on your neck, do you? You want it gone?"

The child watched her for a long moment, but then seemed to understand. She whimpered like a dog and bowed her head, one hand clawing at the metal band as she'd probably done for most of her life.

Elana brushed the child's hair aside and found a twisting clasp. She fought the sickening influence of the amulet. Just being in contact with the metal baring it was enough to make her Sight flicker and jump. Once the band was free she tossed it aside, happy to never touch it again.

The instant the amulet had been removed, the child's amarin came at Elana like a wave, overwhelming her with pain, fear, confusion, and frustration. The child started to scream, the return of her abilities ten times what Elana was feeling.

Elana pulled the child into her arms, letting her seer abilities feed on her energy and connection with the world. Blue Sights and seers were related – their abilities linked in some way – and while she couldn't be what the child needed, she could give more comfort than anything or anyone else until she was home with the hive.

The child's screams stilled and she wept, clinging desperately to Elana until her jagged nails bit at Elana's skin beneath her clothes. Elana hushed her softly, hummed to her and rocked her like an infant. It didn't escape her that it was probably the first touch of affection the child had received since infancy.

"You're safe now," she said the words aloud and fed the intent of them – the emotion behind them – into the child. "I'll protect you. You'll never go back in that room. You'll never have to hide in the walls again. You'll never have to eat the living rats again – or kill any living thing to eat."

A single image rose in Elana's mind, the first image from the child. It was an image of the doll in the cradle, surrounded by found treasures. Elana felt the tenderness the child had for her treasures. "I'll get them for you," Elana promised.

The child calmed and eventually fell asleep. It was only then that Elana allowed herself to cry silently, holding a hand to her face to keep her tears from trailing onto the child's face. She wept and held the child close – practically a cousin – and mourned for the life she could have had, the pain she's suffered, and ever Blue Sight and seer she couldn't save.

Diana watched Elana as she ran a comb through the young seer's hair. After the child had calmed, Elana had spent the next two days cleaning her in a nearby stream, finding new clothes for her, and easing her through regular anxiety attacks. She'd taken to calling the girl Silver for her pale complexion and the way she reminded Elana of the silverpine trees near the Counsel's Keep – pale and beautiful, but unbelievably strong.

They'd taken shelter in the thickest parts of the small forest behind the orchard, where Silver had the shade of the trees to slowly adjust to sunlight. She spent most of the day sleeping as Elana used her Sight to calm her, but Diana noticed her becoming more curious, wondering more at the stars, the moonlight, and the dapples of sunlight across the forest floor.

Diana had made regular trips back to the manor to keep from arousing suspicion. None of the servants nor even the Baron and Baroness seemed to have noticed Silver's absence. Melanda had disappeared, but with a note saying she had to go care for a sick relative. Diana was sure it was a ruse to get a few days ahead of the Skaldes before they decided she shouldn't be out from under their thumbs for long.

In that time Diana had returned to Silver's attic and recovered her treasures as Elana directed. Silver had calmed considerably when her things were returned and she slept with her doll every night.

Silver didn't speak and rarely made eye contact, but she could sit still and allowed Elana to clean her. The child seemed more aware of her surroundings than her brother had been, less lost to her seer abilities. Elana was convinced if she'd been properly trained and cared for she might have even been able to exist outside of the seer's cellar in the Keep. She'd survived for so long on her own. She'd discovered the sedatives Melanda had been sneaking into her meals at night. She'd planned her own escape. She was obviously incredibly intelligent.

Without the amulet from the Order of Blindness binding her, however, Silver seemed to be slipping more and more into her connection with Aggar. It was clear she'd be best served with the other seers and her brother. Diana hoped the connection gave her comfort, tied her to other living and happy things.

Elana wept ever morning when Silver slept as she told Diana what she had learned about the girl through her Sight as they became closer. All Diana could do was hold her.

As Diana thought, Silver pulled away from Elana's brush and turned to crawl silently into Elana's arms like a child demanding attention. It was a common occurrence, a way for the child to draw comfort from Elana's Sight and calm her anxiety. Elana set the brush aside and patiently held her until Silver pulled away once more and crossed the camp to hold her doll. Diana had seen Elana's skills with children before, but never one so feral. She couldn't help but wonder how Silver would have fared in Elana's care from infancy.

Elana took a moment to run her hands over her face. She was exhausted, barely sleeping. "Do you need anything from town?" Diana questioned.

Elana shook her head. "We need to get her to the Keep. She needs so much energy. I can't support her alone. She needs her brothers and sisters."

Diana nodded slowly. "No one at the manor has discovered her absence yet, but it's only a matter of time. The Baron is already starting to question Melanda's sudden departure and your disappearance. Can you travel with her? I could rent out a carriage."

Elana considered. "I can try, but I fear I won't last long enough. Or worse, I'll lose the energy to calm her and she'll get scared again. She's a good girl, but she's very dangerous when threatened. She's had to be. It would be better if we could contact Telias and arrange for a seer escort like with her brother."

"I can see if there's a hawker in town who could send a message without drawing attention."

Elana curled her lips. "I'd rather confront the Skaldes directly."

"You can't be serious."

Elana shook her head. "I know it would be dangerous, especially with Silver still here. But I can fantasize."

Diana smiled softly. "You have no idea how many times I've wanted to confront Baron Skalde. He meets me regularly now, trying to learn where you are. He's scared."

"Not scared enough. The Keep won't take kindly to this, and that will unsettle the Ramains court. Being a minor noble won't earn him any favors. I doubt he'll hold a title much longer."

"I pity anyone who earns your wrath."

Elana glanced at Silver. "I'll stay with her. Send a message. Tell Telias we can meet an escort just outside of town. Once we have a response you can tell the Baron we're taking our leave."

Diana nodded. "I'll see you tonight?"

"We'll be here."

"I doubt anyone could move you."

They kissed briefly and Diana left, winding through the forest until she reached the orchard. She avoided the workers, skimming the forest line until she reached the manor. She didn't know much about the town of Rixton, but she hoped she could find what she needed. She didn't know of any town without a hawker, but she needed to be sure her message was sent privately. If the hawker were to read her note and send word back to the Skaldes, they'd be at significantly more risk.

Her thoughts spun as she returned to the manor and her room, finding the supplies to write a message. She'd just found a serviceable quill when there was a light knock at her door. Diana slipped her writing supplies into a drawer and answered. She was surprised to find not a servant, but the Baroness waiting for her.

Isande Skalde looked up at her and her cheeks flushed dark for a moment before fading. The drapes of her long, black skirt shifted as she trembled beneath the mass of the gown. She was all but wringing her hands with worry. "I'm sorry to disturb you,

Min."

Diana shook her head, quickly assessing the situation. "Is there something I can help you with, Baroness?"

"I..." She hesitated, her eyes flicking away from Diana's face, shifting back and forth as she thought. "If you have a moment?"

"Of course." Diana welcomed the baroness into her room and shut the door behind her. The moment they were alone, the Baroness seemed to calm some.

"My husband would not like to find me here."

Diana shook her head. "He won't hear of it from me, Min."

She didn't seem reassured, but through her fear Diana saw determination. "Your companion told me at dinner your first night here about the seers at the Keep. That they're happy. Safe."

"They are. I've been to their abode myself."

"Would you tell me about it?"

It wasn't the question Diana had been expecting. In truth, Diana had only sat outside their doors, but Elana had talked of being among them often. "They live underground for the most part. In stone halls. Their rooms are sparsely decorated but they love music. There are harpists and small fountains, built so the water constantly trickles and swirls. Sometimes they sing. They see more than we do. They like the dark and the quiet so they can more fully exist in their connection with Aggar and each other. They're very kind with each other and very powerful. They keep watch over all of Aggar. Their powers maintain and control the firecaps in the north to keep us safe from their volcanoes. But even with all that power, to sit among them is like the deepest meditation."

The Baroness gazed at the ground as she listened, but a gentle smile slowly formed as she imagined their space. "I like to think of my child there."

Diana took a chance. "It must be very hard to watch your child suffer."

She wiped away a tear. "I never thought I could have children. I wanted one so badly. I didn't care if it wasn't like other children, I just wanted one."

"I know what tradition says about seers outside the Keep," Diana spoke tenderly. "But you shouldn't be ashamed of what you bore. To birth even one seer is a great gift to Aggar. You should be proud."

"Even one." Her words were a whisper, heavy with a lifetime of pain. "It was never my intention to hurt anyone. I was... so afraid. I was weak."

"Min?"

Another knock on the door startled them both, but the Baroness shrank back, her eyes wide with terror. Diana knew the expression and steeled herself for what was to come.

The door opened without Diana answering it and the Baron stepped inside. His eyes instantly shot to his wife, steely and cold. "I had hoped not to find you here."

"The Baroness is here as my guest, Tad," Diana interrupted.

"You will not speak to me so informally." The Baron's voice was poison as he snapped to Diana, all pretense of good will between them gone.

"I'm tired of this, Anton. They can fix this. They can make sure we aren't judged."

"Isande!"

Isande drew a deep breath, straightening her back, and for a moment Diana caught a glimpse of who she could have been if society hadn't worn her self-worth away over her life like water over stone. "Our son is happy. Our daughter could be, too."

The baron lashed out, raising a hand to strike his wife, but Diana caught it, angling herself between the couple. "You will not strike a woman in my presence."

The Baron pulled back sharply, his eyes wild as he was surprised at Diana's strength. He studied her longer and his lips curled. "Amazon."

"If you know my kind, you know I don't stand for abuse. Not of your wife, and not of your children."

"Min?" The baroness whispered.

"We already found the child. She's been taken into our custody and will be transported to the Keep."

The Baroness burst into tears behind her, but Diana's attention was fully fixed on the Baron. "You should have sent her to the Keep the moment you knew what she was."

"She should have died in her cradle," the Baron spat. "No one can fault me for putting her away."

"They can. And they will. Rest assured there will be a full

investigation." Diana reached into the pouch at her waist and withdrew the Order of Blindness amulet. "Of everything you've done."

The Baron flushed. He lurched forward, hid fist raised to strike Diana, but she was faster. She punched him in the face, sending him flying back, crashing into the wall unconscious. The Baroness screamed at the violence, but, she didn't run away as Diana turned to her. "If you feel any sorrow for what you've done, you'll help me get her safely to the Keep. And you'll tell me everything you know about this amulet."

The Baroness nodded sharply. "I promise."

Diana let out in internal sigh of relief. Her own words to Elana about keeping the peace ran through her mind. She wondered what Elana would think when she returned.

The Baroness led Diana to the servant's quarters to the east of the orchard. "Tad Servio is our resident hawker. He's discreet. He can send your message to the Keep."

Diana glanced around the small servant's village. She'd purposefully avoided it while leaving Elana, not wanting to draw attention. There was a large, two-story apartment building, a blacksmith, and a tailor. Craftsmen with small shops and supplies to keep the manor self-sufficient. Near the back of the tiny village was a tower the same height as the trees. A tawny hawk soared overhead and slipped into the roost at the top of the tower, a leather strap tied around its ankle.

"Baroness. Can I help you today?" A young man about Elana's age walked toward them, his arms covered to the elbow with thick leather gloves.

Tad Servio looked like Elana's brother in a way – dark hair, a wiry build, and a pleasant smile.

"Not me, no," the Baroness commented. "But our guest needs to send a message. Tad Servio, this is Min Diana n'Athena."

Tad Servio shook Diana's hand. "My birds are at your command, Min. Where do you need to reach?"

"The Counsel's Keep as quickly as possible."

Tad Servio nodded slowly. "The Keep. That shouldn't be a problem. I'll send the message immediately." He reached out for her letter, but Diana didn't offer it.

"If possible, I'd like to tie the letter myself."

"Of course. If you'll come with me?"

Diana followed him toward his tower, but the Baroness didn't follow. Diana didn't mind the privacy. Tad Servio shut the door as they entered his office.

"There's no need to send your message, Min. The Keep is already on its way."

Diana froze, taken aback by the hawker's sudden change. "Excuse me?"

"I saw you and Min Elana going into the forest with the seer child. I wasn't sure she existed."

Diana studied him and crossed her arms over her chest, suddenly understanding. "You're a Marshal."

"Did you think Tristan wouldn't supply some kind of support?"

"Poor support if you didn't reveal yourself until now."

"You never needed me."

"I don't like Tristan spying on us. If you were already here, why were we sent?"

Tad Servio shrugged. "I didn't come here for you. The Marshals have been keeping an eye on the Skaldes for more than a tenmoon and I expect to stay here for a few more. Tristan isn't pleased with my report on the Baron. I suspect there will be many changes here over the next tenmoon."

"You've been here a tenmoon and you didn't save the child?"

"I hardly had the chance to wander the manor unseen. I'm a hawker, not a Shadow."

Diana pursed her lips. "The Keep is already coming?"

Tad Servio drew a message from his desk drawer. "With a seer and a carriage. They should arrive tomorrow."

Diana took the note and studied it. It seemed like Telias's hand. She thanked every Goddess Elana would have the ability to confirm if the letter was legitimate or not. "If that's the case, thank you."

"Has the Baroness revealed any connection to the Order of Blindness?"

Diana considered. The Baroness didn't know much – she claimed her husband had purchased the amulet from desert tradesmen who said it could bind a seer. Considering Elana and Diana had tracked the Order to the desert not long ago, it seemed a legitimate story. Still, she wasn't sure how much she wanted to reveal whether the information was extensive or not.

"No, she didn't tell me anything incriminating."

He nodded slowly, but Diana knew he didn't believe her. "Well, then perhaps this will help for your next journey." He pulled another message from his breast pocket. It was a slender piece of paper similar to other messages they'd received from Tristan in the past.

She took it. It held the coordinates for a ruined city in the desert. Diana clenched her jaw. She knew the place.

"Tristan tracked an amulet being smuggled into the capitol from that location."

"I suppose he doesn't want to give any more details than that?"

"I would tell you more, but that's all I know myself. Tristan keeps his secrets close to the chest."

Diana slipped both messages into her belt pouch. "I'll see what we decide to do."

Tad Servio shrugged again. "Do what you will. Now you have enough information to make a decision."

Diana appreciated that he didn't ask more questions. "Thank you."

She turned to leave when Tad Servio called out to her. "Min?" Diana glanced over her shoulder. "Tristan didn't write it in his message, but I know he appreciates this. He may not be as personally invested in saving seers as you and Min Elana, but he's sworn to protect the Ramains and all her people. Any corruption you can root out will only make him more of an ally."

"That's an interesting choice of words, Tad."

"It was an intentional choice of words. Go safely, Min."

"Stay safe yourself, Tad."

Diana slipped out the door unsure of how to interpret the encounter. Still, his letters seemed legitimate enough and if the seer arrived the next day she'd have no reason to doubt Tristan's message, especially since it lined up with the Baroness's information that the Baron had purchased the amulet from desert tradesmen.

She needed to consult Elana. They needed to get Silver to safety. Then it seemed they were heading for the desert.

LOSCAN:
BENEATH THE SANDS

Diana knew they were approaching the desert when the smell on the air changed. The weather was getting warmer and the terrain had leveled but it was the smell that always brought Diana home. The north smelled sweet with pine and almost minty when it was cold. She thought of water and cold stones, crackling wood in a fire and the scent of animal pelts used as blankets. But the desert was earthy and spicy, smelling of sage and dust. Her sensory memories brought back scents of horses and rain on warm sand, of sweat and palm.

Diana had spent most of her time on Aggar trading in the deserts and it was as much a part of her as the terrains from her homeworld. Yemaya may have better social politics, but there was a contented laziness about long hot nights in the southern Aggar desert that had stolen her heart.

"Your joy could make me appreciate the desert."

Diana smiled at her lover. There wasn't much she could hide from Elana and her Blue Sight. It could get complicated when Diana was sad or upset, but it made Diana happy to think her joy could be truly contagious for her *soroi*. "There's a beautiful desert on Yemaya. I could get us a house there without much trouble."

"I don't appreciate the desert that much."

Diana laughed. "You never know, you could get used to the heat."

"But not the sweat, massive hair, and exhaustion."

"I suppose we'll just have to compromise, then."

Diana smiled gently, imagining her future home with Elana. She imagined a small house nestled in the hills. A Shae workshop in the yard for Elana and a stable for their horses. She imagined a garden, strung with fairy lights, a fire pit burning merrily in the night as their friends gathered for parties and lazy summer evenings. She imagined Elana in a world where she was appreciated and valued, where her Sight was celebrated and not feared. She imagined Elana happy and safe. She imagined children. She imagined happiness.

Diana glanced at Elana and the younger woman glanced down at her horse, deep in thought. Diana's stomach sank, but she tried not to let Elana's expression affect her. She knew thoughts of leaving Aggar were sensitive for her and she understood. In a short time Elana had lost her grandmother and mentor. They'd spent their days chasing down an expansive cult bent on eradicating Elana and those like her. Diana could understand the pain of considering a new home when the old one was rejecting you.

"I'm fine." Elana didn't need to know Diana's exact thoughts to know what she was thinking.

Diana doubted it, but it wasn't her place to monitor her lover's feelings. "How's your side? Do you want to make camp?"

Elana's hand instinctively went to her side, bandaged from being stabbed in Rixton. The wound had sealed without infection, but she was still tender and at risk of it reopening. Riding for long days didn't help.

"I'll be fine for a few more hours. The days are getting longer."

"We should be able to reach the edge of the desert by the end of the day. The ruins aren't far."

"I don't know what Tristan expects us to find," Elana grumbled. "You said the ruins are abandoned.

"The Royal Marshals don't seem to value explanations," Diana agreed. "But it's been a long time since I visited Loscan. I don't know what to expect. Tristan was right about the Skaldes."

Elana fell quiet at the reminder of their last investigation and the young, feral and abused seer they'd found hidden in the attic. "I'm not convinced he knew anything."

"You think it was coincidence we found Silver?"

"Every town has its secrets and prejudices. The Skaldes could be anyone."

"That's a bit extreme, don't you think?"

"Probably." Elana's voice was hollow and unconvinced.

Diana considered her lover. The longer she had known

Elana, the more Diana had learned how deep the Blue Sight's emotions ran. It seemed obvious a young woman who had been taught to fear her own emotions – particularly her anger and sadness – would have a complex emotional life, but it left Diana out in the cold. She didn't always know what to do or how to help. She didn't know if Elana even wanted her input or suggestions. So she didn't do anything.

"Hopefully Tristan is mistaken and the ruins are fine. You might be out of the desert in a matter of a few peaceful days."

Elana finally laughed sincerely. "One can dream."

"I'm good at dreaming, *Soroi*."

A chill settled over the edge of the desert as Diana swung from her saddle. Her body was heavy, ready to make camp and sleep. Elana hid a wince as she dismounted, her hand tight to her side.

"We should change your bandages," Diana called.

Elana nodded and pulled her bedmat from her gear and laid it on an even patch of ground. She pulled off her shirt and Diana inspected her bandages. They were dry. She removed them, setting them aside. The wound looked better than before.

Diana released a silent breath of relief. "You're getting better. I don't think you even need bandages anymore."

"Good." Elana pulled her shirt back on. "It ached today. I was afraid it had reopened."

Diana squeezed her shoulder. "We can rest tomorrow if you like. Our mission isn't particularly time-sensitive."

Elana considered, but Diana could see her discomfort. "Let me see how I feel in the morning."

"Of course."

Elana glanced at Diana. "And you? You're still well?"

Diana smiled. "I'm fine. I wasn't stabbed."

"Is that the baseline for our wellbeing now?"

Diana laughed and collapsed back, her head resting on Elana's bedmat. "I feel good, truly. A little tired, but nothing a good night's rest won't cure. I'm just happy to be back in the desert."

Elana rested her hand on Diana's stomach, and stared up at the sky. "It is beautiful here, especially at night."

"When the temperature is colder?"

Elana grinned at her knowingly. "It doesn't hurt my appreciation." She shifted and laid with Diana, continuing to stare with her arms tucked under her head. "But temperature aside there's still charm here. The sky seems bigger without trees breaking up the skyline."

Diana followed her lover's gaze. She'd looked to the stars her entire life. Her mother said she was a born n'Athena, destined to strike out on her own off-world. But throughout her life the night sky had lost some of its charm. It was a way to get from place to place, full of space shuttles and ships, planets of multiple races and an empire that moved through them with little thought for anything but self-preservation.

Laying with Elana, their lifestones pulsing together, she could feel some of her lover's appreciation and awe sweeping through her. For the first time in decades, Diana stared in awe at the stars and wondered what it would be like to be among them, this time with Elana at her side.

"I want to be there with you." Diana's voice was soft, almost speaking to herself more than Elana.

"I want to be there, too."

Diana turned to Elana and found her *soroi* already watching her. "Truly?"

Elana kissed her gently, lingering for a moment, her fingers tracing Diana's jaw. "Whatever sadness and loss I feel here, whatever grief I show for the world that birthed me, I know where my future lies. And I'm excited to greet the changes. Be patient with me as I let Aggar go?"

"I waited my entire life for you, *soroi*. I would wait another lifetime for you to be happy."

They kissed again and as they parted Elana stared into her eyes. "There's something else on your mind. Do you want to talk about it?"

Diana felt a chill in her stomach and she instantly knew what Diana was talking about. "It's old memories, nothing between us."

"We rarely have quiet moments like this. Tell me. I don't like feeling anything weighing on your mind."

Diana considered, finding words for her feelings. "I keep thinking about the Baroness. About the way she looked when I knocked her husband aside."

Elana kissed her shoulder. "I still love you for hitting him."

Diana smiled faintly in memory. "Yes. But I was focused on

her. She was so scared of him. He obviously has hit her before."

"I'm afraid that's not terribly uncommon here on Aggar."

Diana nodded. "I know. It's common everywhere."

"Even among the Amazons? There are no men."

"Men aren't the only ones prone to abuse, Elana. Women can be just as spiteful, just as aggressive."

Elana's words were gentle. Diana felt the tender touch of her Sight, trying to comfort Diana. "You've seen it on Yemaya?"

"My aunt. She came to my mother's house with my cousin when I was a child, escaping a bad marriage. She was bruised, but my cousin had been pushed down the stairs. She was older than me, but smaller. I still remember the way she looked in my aunt's arms. Her arm was shattered. It was later amputated."

Elana let out a sharp breath. "Di'Nay, I'm so sorry."

"We had no idea they were suffering, had been suffering for years. I don't know if my aunt would have left if my cousin hadn't been hurt. The thought makes me sick."

"They survived?"

"Yes. Their abuser was banished from the planet. My aunt went to House n'Shae to heal and stayed, eventually learning their ways and serving others. Seeking redemption. My cousin ended up in n'Sappho, a judge."

"So she now protects others before they can get hurt."

"Their lives went on, but... those images, peeking around my mother's leg as she rushed me back to bed, stayed with me. Sometimes when I see someone like the Baroness they return."

Elana watched her a moment in silence, her eyes full of concern and sympathy. "I'm sorry you have that memory, but I'm glad it made you kind."

Diana kissed her. "I'll never hurt you, *Soroi n'ti Mee*. Not even with my words unless it's unintentional."

"I know. I thank the Mother for bringing you to me."

They kissed again and Diana thanked every deity she'd ever heard of for bringing Elana into her life as well.

Diana woke slowly, the sound of shifting and scuffling disturbing her in her dreams. As she woke enough to be aware of her surroundings, she felt her skin prickle with warning. The horses nickered nervously. She could feel Elana still in her arms, but her senses warned of someone else nearby.

She heard the steps growing closer and the shift of her pack being opened. She leapt up and reached into the darkness toward her bag, her fist closing around the back of a wool shirt. The intruder cried out, the voice androgynous and shrill with shock.

"Diana," Elana whispered, placing a hand on Diana's shoulder. Diana calmed at Elana's gentle touch.

"Who are you?" Diana demanded.

The stranger pulled away sharply and spun around. Diana stared. In the light of the moon and stars she saw a young man, in the middle of his adolescence.

"I'm sorry," his words where quick, a plea.

"You were hungry," Elana acknowledged.

He nodded sharply. "No one has passed through this way in a long time."

Elana stood. "We have food to share. You don't have to steal."

The youth watched Elana warily as she moved to her own bags and grabbed a pouch of dried meat. She tossed it to him. He looked down at the bag in concern and sat, resting the bag on the ground as he opened it. Diana watched first in surprise, then as he shifted she could see the truth in the moonlight. The youth's right sleeve on his jacket was tied up close to his shoulder. He was missing his arm.

Elana watched the young man eat, her eyes flicking back and forth between him and Di'Nay. She could feel her Love's surprise at noticing his missing limb and Elana felt a flash of prayer reflect through her thoughts. There was much Di'Nay didn't see. The Mother was often a teacher, and she obviously had a lesson in mind for both Elana and her partner.

"What's your name?" Di'Nay questioned.

The youth glanced up, his eyes flickering anxiety for a moment, but he swallowed the dried meat and spoke. "Gerome, Min."

"What brings you to the desert?" Elana questioned.

"My own business," he evaded. "I apologize for disturbing your camp. I'll go."

Di'Nay waved. "No, please. The night is cold. You're hungry. Stay with us."

He eyed them warily. "You would take in a thief?"

"I would take in a child," Di'Nay admitted.

"I'm not a child."

"A person in need, then," Elana added. "We are supposed to take in the hungry and sick, as the Mother commands."

After a long moment he seemed to calm and Elana relaxed, happy her instincts had paid off. She'd sensed devotion about him and guessed he held the Mother in high regard. Quoting from her edicts, scrawled on many of her temples, eased his mind that he might be around friends.

"I *am* cold," he admitted.

Di'Nay wrapped her blanket around his shoulders. "I'm Di'Nay." Di'Nay introduced herself with the name she used on Aggar when her title didn't matter. "And this is Min Elana."

He acknowledged her with a glance, but continued eating.

"Elana of the Council's Keep," Elana added. Di'Nay turned to her, surprised she would reveal so much about herself, but Gerome froze. His hand shook and he nearly dropped the strip of meet he held.

"A Shadow?"

"A Blue Sight."

He slipped the meat back into the bag and stood. "I think I should go now."

"Have you met a Blue Sight before?" Elana questioned.

"Elana," Di'Nay gasped, unsure of what was happening, but desperate to care for the child.

"I've heard what Blue Sights can do," he answered.

"Can you do those things?"

A dark tension settled around them and Gerome frowned. Elana felt his torrent of emotions quickly coalescing into anger.

"You don't know anything about me, Min," he forced out the words between clenched teeth. He threw the bag to her. "Keep your supplies."

"Do you sense insincerity in me?" Elana asked. He didn't run, but he didn't answer. "You don't have to hide your eyes anymore. You know we recognize each other."

Di'Nay gasped aloud as Gerome's eyes shifted, turning a bright blue that reflected in the moonlight. His eyes were deeper than Elana's, more sapphire than ice. His anger doubled as he dropped his guard. Elana could tell even Di'Nay felt it.

"You'll keep control of yourself around Di'Nay," Elana

warned. "Or were you never taught to guard yourself?"

His frown deepened and Elana struck out with her Sight, connecting gently with him and reigning in his power before it could spill over and knock Di'Nay unconscious. Though her touch wasn't violent, he lurched back as if he'd been struck at the violation of his powers.

"Witch!" he cried out in accusation.

Elana didn't flinch. "You've been alone a long time. Self-hatred won't help you, but training might."

She lightened her touch, trying to send him warmth, comfort, assurance. She didn't intend to hurt him, but there was little more powerful or potentially destructive than a Blue Sight with no training. As her power started to calm him, anger gave way to its true form – fear.

"How can you speak the Mother's words?"

"You don't think you can be true to the Mother and a Blue Sight?"

"Blue Sights are born from the Fates."

Elana let her intense face melt into a look of disapproval. "Don't trust the rantings of country priests," she announced. "The Mother created us all. She created Aggar. And you know as well as I do that none are closer to Aggar than those with the Sight. We aren't opposed to the Mother. We're witnesses to the Mother."

He glanced at the ground. He'd never questioned the teachings he'd heard since childhood, but his desire to believe what Elana said was swaying him. Elana was surprised by the depths of his pain and insecurity. He wanted help, but he had no experience asking for it. She soothed him, trying to assure him through her amarin that he was safe. That she wanted badly to help.

"Where are you going?" His question was soft and unsure.

"We're going to Loscan. Ruins just inside the desert."

His lips quivered and he collapsed back to sitting on the ground. "I am, too."

Elana raised a single brow in true surprise. "Why?"

"My brother... he was taken there. Kidnapped."

"A seer?" Elana questioned.

He closed his eyes. "You can read my mind?"

Elana shook her head. "No. No Blue Sight can read thoughts, only intention and emotion. We're looking for seers, too.

We can go together."

Elana didn't sleep, even though Di'Nay and Gerome eventually did. Her thoughts spun, obsessing in cycles and circles. Another lost brother. Why hadn't he been sent to the Keep or gone there himself? She already knew the answer: he was taught to fear it. How many had been lost to prejudice and fear? How many never got the help they needed? How many Blue Sights had lost control of their abilities and been killed for creating unintentional havoc? How many seers had been abandoned as broken?

She didn't want to dwell on the same fears, but she couldn't get them out of her thoughts. There was nothing to be done. The Council couldn't find everyone with abilities and convince their communities to go against generations of fear and send their children to the Keep for training. Elana wasn't even sure the Keep *should* have that power. But if the Mother was making Di'Nay face her past with her cousin, Gerome was a part of a plan to once again remind Elana that her world didn't accept her. That far too many of her brothers and sisters in the Sight were tormented and ostracized.

Elana wished she knew what the Mother was trying to teach her so she could learn the lesson and never have to face the question again.

Morning came quickly. Diana woke from her restless sleep as the heat of the day made her blankets uncomfortable. She didn't remember any of her dreams but she knew she'd had them. She'd dreamed of her cousin. She'd dreamed of Elana. She dreamed of Loscan. She just didn't have any specific memories of them.

She stood stiffly, stretching her arms over her head and across her chest to trying to work the knots free from her shoulders from a stressful night. Elana stood at the edge of camp, lost in her thoughts. Gerome wandered along the other edge, eating more dried meat and staring out toward the desert. The scent of the spices on the meat seemed to drift on the wind, overwhelming even Diana's beloved scent of the desert. She was hyper-aware of everything about him, but she found it hard to look directly at him.

He was young and fine-boned for a man, making him particularly androgynous. He could almost pass for an Amazon.

Visually he had little in common with her cousin, though they were both more masculine-inclined. Her cousin had been petite and fair, with cropped golden hair and dark green eyes. Gerome was darker, tall and thin. If anything, he could be Elana's son. The thought made Diana shudder.

There were just enough similarities. A way both Gerome and her cousin glanced out of the corner of their eyes, the way they held themselves stiff and on guard even when the moment was calm. He moved awkwardly at times with his one arm and Diana wondered how long ago he'd lost it.

"I can feel you staring," he grunted without looking at her and Diana had to remind herself that he had the Sight.

"You remind me of someone I once knew," Diana answered honestly. "A cousin."

He didn't answer. Diana didn't expect him to. She couldn't understand exactly what he was feeling, but she knew the look on his face. It was the same look Elana carried when she considered her place in Aggar.

"We should reach the ruins by nightfall," Diana called to Elana. "We can get close enough to investigate. If it's safe, we can even camp under its cover."

Elana nodded as she moved to stand beside Diana. She braided her hair back into a thick plait, her long fingers moving nimbly and instinctively. "You think it will be empty?"

"It won't be." Gerome turned to face them. His eyes flashed. "My brother is there."

"You've seen him?" Diana questioned.

"I know it."

Diana and Elana exchanged glances. Elana's expression was clear: he didn't know anything for sure. He was desperate.

"We'll have to be thorough in our investigation," Diana commented. "We'll save your brother."

He stiffened his chin and nodded sharply.

Diana finished securing her supplies to Kaing and patted his neck. He shuffled under her touch, sensing her chaotic emotions. Sometimes his ability to read her made things difficult when she was upset. She patted his nose and shushed him. "You want to see Loscan again?" she questioned, smiling softly at him.

"You've been to the ruins before?"

Diana turned as Gerome stepped behind her. "Years ago. I

used to do a lot of trade in the desert. I found the them accidentally, but started going every year or so. Have you been?"

He shook his head. "I've never been to the desert."

"Where did you come from?"

"Markessa."

"The capitol? It's a long way to travel on foot alone."

"What else could I do?"

Diana nodded slowly. "You're very brave."

"I'm a coward," he answered gruffly. "I can't live without him." He glanced down, hesitating a moment. "You said I remind you of a cousin."

"You do."

"Does he have one arm as well?"

"She does. She lost it as a child in a fall."

He absentmindedly rubbed his shoulder, his eyes flicking back and forth as he thought. Diana noticed he had covered his blue eyes again, shading them in pale gray. "I don't remember losing mine. I was a baby."

Diana was genuinely surprised. He didn't seem as used to the missing limb as she thought he'd be if he'd been hurt as a small child. "I'm sorry."

He shrugged. "They told me it was a carriage crash. My parents died. I was hurt."

"Your brother?"

He didn't answer.

Elana mounted Leggings. "We'll want to leave now if we want to reach the ruins while there's still daylight."

Diana nodded toward Kaing. "You can ride with me if you like, Gerome."

He seemed anxious for a moment, but as she mounted Kaing, he reached up to her and she helped him climb behind her.

The sun was drifting into evening when the expanse of sand and brush gave way to a stony complex. Diana held her breath as they paused at a small oasis barely within visible distance from the ruins, not wanting to come too close if Loscan was inhabited. The oasis was scraggly, the pool at the center shallow. Within a year or two it probably wouldn't exist anymore. Diana knew Loscan once had been built on a sprawling oasis – or perhaps it had once been on the edge of the desert before the sands expanded. She was glad some cover still existed. It had been so long since her last visit, but the memories and emotions the ruins stirred in her were still gripping.

Loscan had to have been some kind of fortress in the distant past, but much of the structure had been lost. The outer walls stood twice as tall as Diana, with the space in the middle spotted with stone foundation remnants where homes once stood and simple post and lintel structures. Only a single building remained relatively intact. She assumed it had once been a church – a small, domed structure that had been build out of rocks obviously quarried elsewhere.

Inside, the walls were decorated with mosaic and primitive art, depicting stories from an afterlife tale lost over centuries, written in a language Diana couldn't decipher. The air was still heavy inside, comforting and warm. Diana knew it was from the way the heat collected in the dome, but it felt transcendent, even holy. Diana used to spend hours there, meditating and wondering what the structure had once been used for and who had worshiped there.

She found it deeply sad and utterly human how much work had been put into the structure, how booming and thriving Loscan must have been once, and now it was lost entirely. Their kings, their leaders, even their gods no longer existed. She wondered what would be left of her in a thousand years.

Elana rode up beside her and glanced out toward the ruins. "The land is too flat for us to get any closer if people are watching for us."

"What do you want to do?"

Elana looked at the sky. "The sun will be setting soon. I could investigate in the shadows."

"If the Order is in Loscan, you won't be able to sense them," Diana warned.

Elana's eyes narrowed, not at Diana but at her own thoughts. "I'm a trained Shadow of the Council's Keep. My Sight isn't my only ability."

Diana nodded. No matter how nervous she was to let Elana advance on the Order alone, she trusted her lover. "I'll stay here with Gerome."

"What?" Gerome tensed. "I want to go."

"It's too dangerous for now. Elana will be able to move

unseen."

He opened his mouth to argue, but closed it, his eyes narrowing into a glare. He exchanged looks with Elana and Diana felt the energy between them. She shifted uncomfortably, wishing she had some way to know what they communicated through their Sight.

"Fine," Gerome finally grunted.

"I won't be long," Elana promised.

"We'll come for you if you're not back by morning."

Elana dismounted Leggings and raced into the distance. Gerome and Diana dismounted and watched until she disappeared.

"She'll be safe?" Gerome questioned.

"Elana is very powerful," Diana confirmed.

"Blue Sight powers."

"Shadow abilities. She trained at the Council's Keep most of her life. I'm sure if you wanted to go you'd be welcomed as well."

"No, I wouldn't. They don't respect the Mother."

"Elana respects the Mother."

"I know about the Keep.

Diana ran her hand over Kaing's sweaty back. She was glad they hadn't traveled far and they had some cover. She removed the bags and saddle from his back and pulled a brush from her bag. She started to groom him, her focus on Gerome even if her eyes and hands were on Kaing. It seemed if the conversation stayed light Gerome was more prone to talk.

"Who told you?"

"The Sisters."

Diana raised a brow. "Sisters?"

"From the Order of the Mother in Markessa. They took me in after the accident."

Diana turned to him. "When were you adopted?"

He frowned and looked away. Diana silently chided herself for showing her eagerness. She returned her attention to Kaing.

After a long moment, Gerome spoke. "Are you two..." his voice trailed and Diana tensed, guessing how her relationship with Elana might be interpreted by a pious young man of Aggar. "Bonded?"

Diana relaxed. She raised her arm, revealing the lifestone embedded in her wrist. "We've traveled a lot together, mostly trying to help people like your brother. Seers and Blue Sights."

"How many children need help?"

"More than you might think. Too many."

Diana finished grooming Kaing and turned to Leggings.

"I think I see something."

Diana paused and moved to stand with Gerome. He pointed into the distance where a shadow approached Loscan. She pulled a spyglass from her bag and drew a sharp breath. A single cart with two riders approached the ruins.

"Who are they?" Gerome questioned as Diana passed him the spyglass. "Only two of them?"

"Perhaps the Order is using the ruins as a cache."

"The cart is open. No one is hiding inside. If there are only two of them, we could take them easily."

"We don't know how many are in the ruins," Diana reminded him. She took back the spyglass and slipped it into her bag. She tried to relax her shoulders, tried not to worry about Elana. "We'll have a better idea of the layout when Elana returns. For now, we should rest and tend to the horses so we can move quickly if we must."

She returned to Leggings as Gerome continued staring out into the desert. She took her time tending the mounts, working until night fell. Gerome ate from the dry food stores, his attention fully on Loscan the entire time. She'd nearly finished brushing her when she realized Gerome was unusually quiet.

She glanced around and her heart sank. "Gerome?" There was no answer. The youth seemed to have disappeared. "Gerome?!"

She spun around, but he was nowhere to be found. How could he possibly have disappeared with so little cover? She looked out to the ruins. He couldn't have gotten too far. She grit her teeth, cursing every instinct that made her take in an unpredictable adolescent in the first place, and ran after him.

Elana crouched along the outer walls of Loscan watching people moving in and out of the central building. The ruins were mostly stony outlines of homes and shops, making it easy to see movement even in the darkness. Over the last hour or so she'd seen a half dozen men – two of which arrived from the north in a cart. She didn't know what she'd expected, but it wasn't so few.

She'd expected a force or nothing at all. From what she could tell, at best the ruins were being used as some kind of remote warehouse. The building was too small to hold much more than she was seeing.

She tried to memorize their patterns to see if any of them were on guard, but they seemed casual and calm, even joking as they unloaded the cart. They didn't expect to be followed, or perhaps they knew they had little of value if they were. Elana couldn't feel them with her Sight. They all had to be wearing amulets from the Order of Blindness. Still, being able to watch them, to evade them, made her feel powerful again.

She knew it was a ridiculous thought, but in the back of her mind she always expected their power – their amulets that left her blind – made her stand out like a beacon. That she'd never be able to hide from them. But she moved around them easily. They were only human.

She settled back against the wall and considered. While the Order had been able to hide seers from her with amulets before, she'd always felt something. She'd sensed a corruption, a darkness in the earth and the living things around the captured seer. There was none of that here. No dark spots. No filth. Just figures moving in the distance her Sight didn't sense.

She couldn't be sure, but she doubted there were any children in Loscan. She frowned. Gerome wouldn't take the news well. He was volatile and proud. He had taken care of himself for long enough he thought he was impenetrable, but he was walking a fine line between functioning and imploding. He was gifted, but untrained. He didn't understand his own abilities and didn't understand what a danger he was to others and himself. Finding out his brother was still missing might be what shattered the last thread of his control. She needed to be sure when she told him about the Order's presence Diana was far enough away she wouldn't be hurt.

She glanced at the sky. The moons were high. There wasn't much more she'd discover without getting closer, and she wanted a plan in place before she advanced. She shifted and eased herself out of the stony crevice she'd perched in. She flipped over the wall and climbed down the broken mortar and stone surface. She moved silently, her feet barely making an imprint in the sand as she traveled.

She was halfway back to the oasis when she felt Di'Nay's panic. She rushed after her, following her Sight and the pull of her lifestone until they met half way between the ruins and the oasis. Di'Nay gasped for breath.

"What happened?" Elana questioned.

"I looked everywhere. Gerome went missing."

"What?"

"He disappeared when I was grooming Kaing and Leggings. He saw the cart moving into the ruins. I think he went after it."

"I didn't see him," Elana assured her. "Maybe he's just scouting?"

"What did you see?"

"There aren't many of them. A half dozen. They aren't on guard at all. They might not even notice him," Elana tried to assure her.

She started to breathe a bit easier. "Do you sense him?"

Elana shook her head. "But he might just be too far. For a landscape that looks so dead, there's a strong web of amarin in the desert. It can be very distracting."

Di'Nay nodded slowly, clenching and unclenching her jaw. Her amarin was a chaotic maelstrom of emotion and fear. "Okay."

"Di'Nay," Elana rested her hand on Di'Nay's shoulder. "He isn't your cousin."

"I know. I just don't want him to get hurt."

Elana nodded slowly, knowing no matter what she said Di'Nay wouldn't be able to dissociate her desire to protect her family from the volatile young Blue Sight. "What if he comes back to the oasis? Should we split up?"

Elana felt a shudder ripple through her entire body and her stomach turned. Di'Nay wrapped an arm around her. "Elana?"

A scream echoed from the distance and both women turned toward it. Gerome. "That explains that," Elana gasped as she fought off the wave of distress Gerome had unleashed on the local amarin and regained her strength.

Di'Nay loosened her grip. "Are you all right?"

Elana nodded. "Let's go."

They raced for the ruins, scaling the outside of the wall. Elana focused on Diana and Gerome, pulling from Di'Nay's amarin to be aware of threats her Sight couldn't detect and waiting with dread for the moment Gerome was cut off from her – bound with an Order of Blindness amulet.

They reached the top of the wall and looked out into the ruins. Darkness had settled, but Elana could use the blazing amarin of the landscape to map out her surroundings. She saw a void where a member of the Order laid unconscious near the southern wall. Elana wondered if the massive shock of energy Gerome emitted in his surprise at being caught was enough to knock out someone wearing an amulet.

"One's down near the southern wall," Elana whispered. "Gerome's amarin is growing fainter."

"They haven't put an amulet on him yet?"

Elana shook her head. She rested her hand on the small crossbow at her waist. "We should advance as far as we can while I can still track him."

Di'Nay nodded sharply. "Follow me."

Di'Nay led Elana further along the wall to a stairwell that led down into the ruins. They moved swiftly, crossing through the tallest remaining ruins, scouting for anyone guarding the central building, but there were none.

As they reached the outer wall of the building, Elana felt Gerome disappear and her heart sank. She touched Di'Nay's hand and she knew what it meant.

The building was small and domed. Elana felt a warmth from it so subtle and gentle she didn't know if she felt it with her hands or her Sight. It had once been a place of peace and meditation, but it had been dampened.

Di'Nay listened at the wall, but neither of them heard anything. How could five members of the Order, supplies, and Gerome be so silent in such a small space? Elana circled around to the entrance and paused. It was empty.

She beckoned to Di'Nay and they both walked into the small structure in surprise. "I don't understand," Di'Nay whispered.

Elana walked slowly through the inner chamber. It was a massive dome with benches lining the center. The dome was painted in faded blues and golds, imagery of the Mother and the Fates were depicted in archaic styles. Elana touched a figure of the Mother set at eye-level, clothed in a blue robe, a golden aura surrounding her like the rays of the sun. She had blue eyes. Elana smiled. At least once on Aggar Blue Sights were valued.

"Where else could they be?" Di'Nay questioned.

Elana followed the artwork, moving from the Mother through a story of her binding of the Fates deep into their Cellar. She hesitated over imagery of the Fates, robed in black, their limbs long and spindly as they were pulled into the darkness. She knelt, following the lines of their limbs to the ground. There was a shallow grove in the floor.

Elana beckoned Di'Nay with her hand, a motion that pled silence as she ran her hands over the stones and her fingers caught on a lip. A cellar.

Di'Nay drew a short sword from her waist and Elana held her crossbow. She opened the trapdoor and peered into the darkness. A carved stone hallway opened under them. Elana listened. She didn't hear anything. She exchanged glances with Di'Nay and they decided as one to descend.

The passage under the church was long and narrow, lined with a handful of torches. The smell of decay and mold filled the air – there had to be water nearby. Elana frowned at the narrowness of the hall with no doors or outlets. It would be easy to get trapped.

"An extension?" Di'Nay whispered, her voice so soft Elana heard it more with her Sight than her ears.

"A Cellar," Elana corrected. "Catacombs. Possibly an aquifer."

Di'Nay drew a deep breath and tightened her grip on her sword. "Great."

Elana touched her hand, knowing her lover's discomfort with closed in spaces. They moved silently down the hall, scanning the walls for any sign of an offshoot or a room. When they reached the end of the hall the passage opened into a larger chamber with more offshoots. Elana could feel the bones of at least a thousand people clustered around her, buried into channels carved into the walls. This place had been used for generations a very long time ago. Despite the smell and heaviness in the air, the feeling wasn't disturbing. The bodies had been laid with care and great ceremony. There was peace in these walls. Evidence of paintings on the walls and names set with the bodies. Elana wished she could have seen it at its height.

Di'Nay held her hand to her ear and Elana listened. Voices echoing down one of the halls. They ran and hid down a dark passage as two men exited a torch-lined hall on the opposite end of the chamber. Elana recognized them as the men who had arrived by cart. They weren't joking and laughing like they'd been before. Their faces were taut and serious, their cheeks dark with fear. Men of Aggar. Both of them visibly wore amulets from the Order of Blindness.

They moved across the room and walked down a separate hall. Di'Nay and Elana held hands, feeling each other's intentions through their lifestones. They raced across the chamber, rushing down the hall the men had come from. The hallway was short, ending in a large, circular room being used for storage.

Elana touched a couple of the crates and her stomach flipped. She knew they were full of amulets even before Di'Nay opened one of the lids. They sorted through the various crates and lists, most standard bills from various merchants for cord, metal, provisions, and medical supplies. Di'Nay paused over a line about children's clothing, but there was no mention of where the supplies were sent.

Elana opened a small crate and hesitated. Vials of dark purple liquid were lined up, padded with silk and fur. The glass and fixtures were fine – definitely a rare or luxury item. She had never seen anything like it, but there was a small card attached to the lid. A recipe. It wasn't familiar to her, but she recognized a few of the ingredients. They were powerful tranquilizers.

"Di'Nay." She held up one of the bottles, her cheeks coloring with a mix of rage and fear. "They have a new toy."

Di'Nay's face was grim as she looked over the recipe card. "I recognize this stamp." She pointed out a mark in the corner of the page. "An alchemist family in Sharapa. I used to trade there."

"A new lead," Elana remarked.

Di'Nay pocketed the recipe and a vile, padding them in her belt pouch with cloth. Elana closed the box and tucked it away where it hopefully wouldn't be discovered until they'd dispatched the cultists in Loscan.

"We need to find him. I can't feel him anymore."

Di'Nay took Elana's hand again. "We'll find him."

Diana stalked through the catacomb hallways, her shoulders tense and every sense hyper-focused. She felt the weight of the earth above her and she fought to breathe evenly. She hated feeling buried. Being surrounded by the dead didn't help, either. She was still shocked to discover the addition to what had once been her secret church – her holy place to gather her thoughts during her travels. If she'd ever made an effort to explore the building she would have found the trapdoor, but she hadn't wanted to disturb the ancient building. It had been enough to just sit and be at peace.

Diana fell into a fighting stance every time she heard a foot fall. Elana had only seen six men moving around Loscan. Diana was sure with surprise on their side they could take on six, but they hadn't been aware of such expansive catacombs then. There could be more. Add Gerome into the mix and she wasn't sure they could defend themselves from more than a handful if they were ambushed.

They reached the main room once more. There was only one path still to explore – the one they'd seen cultists walk down earlier. Di'Nay glanced at Elana. Without her Sight to warn her of oncoming threats, they were relying entirely on Diana's senses and Elana's Shadow abilities. She wasn't sure if they should go together.

Elana raised her crossbow, already loaded with a bolt. Her eyes narrowed as if she could read Diana's thoughts and Diana smiled. Of course they wouldn't split up. Diana led the way, Elana watching their rear as they advanced. The hall turned a corner a few steps down and opened into another large room. The far wall was lined with a shallow pool of water that dipped under the rocky overhang and grew deeper. It seemed Elana was right about an aquifer. It made sense – the people of Loscan would need a consistent source of water.

Deep divots had been carved into the wall opposite the water, spaces set up like individual rooms but without defined walls. Diana peered around the corners, keeping close to the walls as she moved. She instantly spotted one cultist standing in the last divot. There was a sword on his belt and he seemed wary. They had to expect a young Blue Sight like Gerome wouldn't be traveling alone.

Elana raised her crossbow. Diana hesitated a moment, nervous about their surroundings, but their backs were covered and they had space to move. Now was as good a time as any. She nodded and Elana let her arrow fly, piercing the cultist through the neck. He let out a soft, strangled cry and collapsed. They waited a moment longer but no one came after him. Diana breathed a sigh of relief and they raced forward, collecting the body and pulling him into the deepest divot.

They continued forward, moving into a new hallway. The catacombs were getting progressively older as they moved. The artwork from the first main room had devolved to flecks of color and faint lines. Instead of circular slots created in the walls the bodies in this part of the tombs were horizontal, like bunks carved into the walls. The bodies were wrapped in linens, only vaguely human-shaped. Diana thanked her Goddess they didn't seem to have been disturbed.

They turned another corner and Diana hesitated. She could see torches and the shadows of multiple people reflected on the walls.

"No one can track him anymore." A gruff voice echoed, older than Diana.

"*He* found us!" A younger man.

"We weren't hiding. He used his eyes, not his Sight," a third voice, breathy but still masculine.

"We have a glut of seers; Blue Sights are rarer. Samael will want to see him."

Diana made a mental note of their conversation.

Elana crept forward. Even knowing she was there Diana had a hard time focusing on her as she used her Sight and Shadow abilities to blend into the pools of darkness. She moved forward just enough to see the crowd. She aimed. Diana braced herself.

Elana shot and the gruff-voiced man howled. All three rounded the corner, the largest of the three with an arrow in his shoulder. Elana had just enough time to reload and shoot again, finally felling the middle-aged cultist. She rushed back behind Diana, who lashed out at a wiry mad with long silver hair. He blocked three of her attacks, but wasn't as agile as she was and she slit his throat.

"Down!" Elana called and Diana ducked. An arrow whizzed over her head, piercing the youngest cultist in the heart.

Diana scanned the bodies, amazed at how quickly they'd fallen. These weren't guards or warriors. They weren't even berserkers or raiders like she and Elana had faced before. These were couriers. Besides her grief at such wasted lives, she felt a touch of relief knowing they could be dispatched easily.

Elana moved forward, barely glancing at the bodies. She entered the room they had been guarding. Diana froze in the doorway. Gerome was tied to a chair, unconscious. His head was drooped awkwardly, an amulet from the Order of Blindness around his neck. Elana hovered over him, distressed but hesitant to touch him as long as he had an amulet. Diana removed it carefully, throwing it into the corner.

She lifted his head and felt the color drain from her face. His complexion was olive with a sickly yellow undertone. His veins were bright purple, the color thickest at a puncture wound at his neck and rippling out across his face and chest, making a jagged patchwork of geometry just under his skin. His lips were blue. Diana didn't see his chest rise or fall.

Diana's muscles skipped and trembled. Her nerves shot ice cold waves through her bones. Images of her cousin flashed before her eyes, broken in her mother's arms, her face placed over Gerome's like a mask. She hadn't protected him. She'd only known him a day and he was already hurt.

"Is he..." Diana couldn't say the words.

Elana shook her head. "He's not dead. He's asleep. I think this is what the tranquilizer we found does."

"He's not breathing."

"I still feel his life force. It's strong, but I can't wake him."

"There has to be some kind of antidote," Diana remarked. "They can't have something like this here without an antidote."

"I can check the storage room. We didn't look in all the boxes. If there are more recipe cards I should be able to identify it."

Diana nodded and Elana turned to run from the room. A gasp of shock and groan echoed from the hall. Diana ran after Elana, who braced herself against a wall, holding her neck. The last two cultists ran at Diana, but Diana was moving with the ferocity of a terrified lover. They were no more skilled than the others and in a handful of swings they were dead at her feet.

Elana gasped for breath, her hands trembling as they grabbed at her throat. Her skin rippled in color. Her veins were steadily growing darker, the color rising to the surface like strokes from a paintbrush.

"Elana!" Diana cried. Elana clung to her, her eyes rolling into the back of her head.

"I'll only sleep." Her lips barely forming the words before she collapsed, completely unconscious.

Elana stood on the crumbling walls of Loscan, bathed in the light of both moons. The air was cool against her skin, brushing lightly at the hem of her skirt and the curls around her face. She was dressed like she would be back in the Keep – trading riding clothes for a long, pale blue dress. She was barefoot but she didn't feel the cold of the stones, just the grit of sand beneath her toes.

The night was peaceful. The Amarin of the desert sang softly around her. The massive, trailing roots of the cacti and sage brush, spreading deep into the earth to collect every drop of water created a network like threads of a tapestry. There was something divine about it, something removed from the rest of Aggar. Something that made Elana want to stay for a tenmoon or more.

She heard a soft shuffle and turned. Di'Nay climbed up the wall in front of her, settling into a nook in the stones, staring out into the desert. Elana watched her in wonder. She was significantly younger, her frame a bit leaner, her skin smoother, her eyes wider and less experienced. She couldn't have been on Aggar long. She didn't look much different, but she seemed like a different person. She was still older than Elana but Elana couldn't help but see this younger version of her lover as a child.

Elana stepped forward. Di'Nay didn't react, just continued to look out at the open desert. Her Amarin sang. For a moment Elana felt like she had stepped into her body. She could smell the desert as she'd never smelled it before, dusty and warm. She felt a sense of home and knew it wasn't her own.

She sat beside Di'Nay and rested in her presence, Di'Nay's love for the ruins and the world around her wrapped around Elana like a warm blanket on a cold night. But beneath the joy Elana's own heart felt heavy. She reached out, but her fingers passed through Di'Nay's hand. They were close, but so far apart. Di'Nay was so at peace. So happy. Elana couldn't share in her joy, and she couldn't put words to the weight in her stomach.

She closed her eyes and drew a deep breath. As she opened them, she stood on a quiet road in the foothills of the Ramains leading into the desert. The brush rustled softly in the faint breeze. The world seemed to have been filtered through a blue light, subtly shifting all the colors and casting the world in a darker hue more like evening even though the sun was high in the sky.

She turned slowly, trying to find her bearings. She didn't recognize the exact location, but she knew through the foliage and landscape roughly where she had to be. She reached out with her Sight, but she couldn't seem to connect with the amarin around her. She felt it as a presence, but one she was slightly disconnected from. She couldn't communicate with it – she could only feel roughly what it felt like sharing with her.

She moved her hands slowly, flexing and relaxing her fingers. She felt numb, her nerves tingling. She realized suddenly that she was asleep. She was rarely a lucid dreamer and realizing where she was and not waking left her shaken. Was this a vision? What was she supposed to learn?

She felt a sudden pull at her Sight. The feeling of another Blue Sight nearby and a sharp stab of warning. She ran toward the sensation, her feet seeming to float just far enough above the ground that her footfalls felt disconcertingly light. She sped down the road, rounding a small hill and spotted a wrecked carriage in the distance, toppled and mangled nearly beyond recognition. She didn't know what could destroy a vehicle so thoroughly.

She heard the squall of a baby from the wreck and she moved faster. She reached the ruins and dug through the debris. She choked at the smell of death as she made it into the center cabin. A man and woman were already dead, the bones cracked and twisted. They were faceless, more like dolls than people. They were nearly weightless as she pulled them away and laid them beside the wreck.

The infant was beneath them, protected by their bodies. It screamed from a bundle of cream cloth, its skin ebony with panic as Elana pulled him into her arms. She brushed his soft black curls and rocked him as she cooed, trying to calm him.

"Hush, hush, you're safe now," she whispered, stroking one tiny balled fist with her fingers. He grabbed her middle finger, clenching tightly in his desperation to survive. She laid a gentle kiss on his brow. His skin was warm and soft. He smelled of death and sweat, but deep beneath those smells was something sweet and new – the natural aroma of a new life.

He finally calmed as she continued to cradle and bounce him, willing him with Sight and energy to relax, to trust her. He opened his eyes and Elana gasped. His eyes were deep blue, like royal silk or a polished sapphire. If she were anywhere else but a dream she would have sensed it immediately, but the reveal took her by surprise.

She felt a sudden closeness to the child. She thought she could see something of her in his nose and chin, and something even of Di'Nay in his shoulders and the line of his mouth. He was perfect and new. A piece of art created by the Mother. He could be her son. Perhaps he *would* be her son. She wondered what happened to sons on Yemaya. Could Amazons even produce male children? Did they have the genetics?

She knew holding him that she would never live anywhere that would shun such a perfect child.

She took a step back and stumbled over the boy's dead mother. She flopped, her broken body no longer solid, but flopping and malleable like a rag doll. She looked at the faceless woman anew, wondering who she had been, what she meant. Had she been a good mother to her Blue Sight son?

The child shifted and started crying again. She bounced him gently again and kissed his cheek. As she pulled back, his features shifted. Her heart broke and she let out a cry of shock at losing the image of her son, but the pain faded as she realized who the child was. It was Gerome.

She remembered he'd claimed he was orphaned as a child in a carriage accident, but the infant wasn't hurt. His arms were both healthy, reaching out to her and flexing his fingers. He seemed bruised, but his parents had shielded him from real harm.

She studied the child. Was this reality or a manifestation of her mistrust of Gerome's intentions? She couldn't help but think it was a true vision. If she were simply dreaming, she would have full connection with her Sight; her abilities would coincide with and back up her suspicions. But her Sight was limited and she was seeing a new landscape in unbelievable detail, as if she were trespassing in someone else's thoughts and dreams. Could she be connecting with Gerome? Was this the way he'd seen the world as an infant? How he saw his parents?

"What aren't you telling us?" Elana whispered to the babe, petting his fine, feather-soft curls. "Why would you lie about this?"

As if her words triggered a portal to another place and time, the foothills shifted to a rooftop in Markessa. It was deep into the night, thick clouds covering any sign of the moon. The child had disappeared from her arms.

Elana shifted, steadying herself on the sloped surface of the rooftop. If she had any doubt she was experiencing someone else's reality, they were all erased. She may have passed a road in the Ramains foothills, but she had never crept along the rooftops of Markessa.

She felt the familiar pull of a Blue Sight nearby and knew it meant Gerome was near. She crept forward, blending easily with the shadows even in her sleep. In the distance, she saw the silhouette of a young adolescent leaping between roofs, running with a practiced grace. He stopped a rooftop ahead of her and perched like a gargoyle, studying his surroundings.

Elana instantly recognized Gerome. He wasn't much younger than he was when she met him. She studied him. He still had two arms. His clothes were patched and frayed and he clearly hadn't bathed in a while.

He moved, creeping forward to the edge of the roof, his attention locked on the house across the street. He waited until a candle flickered behind a window with a small balcony and a boy a tenmoon or so younger than Gerome stepped outside and waved to Gerome as if he knew he'd be there. Gerome smiled and waved back, but as he shifted he slipped. Within a sickening second – less than a breath – Gerome fell.

He screamed. The sound was twisted and screeching, pained in a way Elana had never heard before. It was amplified by his Sight, sending a wave of agony that nearly knocked Elana backward. She looked down at him, broken and twisted. His arm – the arm that would eventually be amputated – was bent backwards, bone sticking through his flesh as he bled on the cobblestones.

The boy on the balcony screamed his name. Gerome turned his head, looking up at the boy in a mix of anguish and loss.

Elana's body tingled and burned. The edges of her vision started to fade. She was waking up. The world narrowed and faded, the rooftops and child at the balcony disappearing. Soon there was nothing left but Gerome's howls of agony and waves of shock and loss from his Sight creeping under her skin.

Diana held Elana, willing her to wake. Like Gerome, she didn't breathe and her skin was riddled with the branching lines of her veins. But her skin was warm. Beneath the veins there was still color to her cheeks. The lifestone in Diana's wrist pulsed softly, almost lazily. Through the stone, Diana could feel the pulse of her lover's heart. Diana ran Elana's final promise through her mind over and over again. She was only sleeping, no matter what it looked like.

Diana hadn't heard or seen signs of any other cultists but she also hadn't been able to find any antidotes – or at least nothing that was labeled clearly enough for her to give it to Elana or Gerome. She could only wait and hope the drug was like other tranquilizers and would eventually wear off.

She didn't know how many hours passed until the first time Elana moved. It was a small twitch, a movement of her arm. If Diana hadn't been holding her she might not have noticed. Not even an hour later Elana let out a heaving sigh, whatever she was dreaming slowly coming into her reality. She kept breathing. The rich purple of her veins was starting to fade.

At the same time, Gerome shifted, turning over on the floor where Diana had laid him. Had he already taken a breath? Diana hadn't heard it, but she was having trouble focusing on anything but Elana.

Diana turned, loosening her grip on Elana to check on Gerome, but Elana grabbed her arm. Diana paused, her breath caught in her throat and she let out a sob of relief she hadn't known she was holding back.

"Elana? *Soroi*?" She whispered the words gently, lovingly, willing Elana to hear her. Elana's veins continued to fade. Her breath became stronger. As she finally opened her eyes, Diana pulled her closer, kissing her and weeping into her collar.

"I'm fine, Di'Nay, I'm fine." Elana's voice was weak but sure as she ran her fingers through Diana's hair and returned her embrace. "How long have I been asleep?"

"Hours. I don't know how many."

"Not days?"

"No."

"Good." Elana sat up slowly, reaching for Diana to brace herself only once before she found her strength. "Where's Gerome?"

"Still sleeping."

"He must have been given a bigger dose than me." Elana struggled to her feet, but her strength was returning quickly. Her legs steadied. Her skin had returned to normal. Diana wasn't entirely sure if her lover had been given a smaller dose of the tranquilizer or if she was just that strong.

Elana crouched beside Gerome, studying him. Diana stood behind her. He was getting better as well – his veins fading and his breath regular.

"What is it?" Diana questioned, more to herself than to anyone else.

"It's made for seers," Elana answered, her surety taking Diana by surprise. "I had visions under its influence. Strong ones. I don't think the Order knows all its properties."

"So it induces a psychic sleep?"

"In a way. It's not a simple tranquilizer, though it may have been sold that way to the cult. If they're using it in on the seer children in their custody, it will keep them subdued, but it will make them more powerful."

Diana snorted an evil, ironic laugh. "We can pray to the Goddess they're foolish enough to keep the children they kidnap together in one place. With enough time, we may not have to find a way to destroy the Order, the seers will become strong enough together to drop mountains on them."

"Not quite that strong, but it would certainly be a fatal mistake," Elana agreed.

She continued to study Gerome, her face falling as she did. "What is it?" Diana questioned. "Did you have a vision of him?"

Elana nodded slowly. "A few. Among other things."

"Other things?"

Elana paused, considering. "Are there male children on Yemaya?"

Diana was taken aback by the question. Of everything she thought Elana would ask that was the last thing. "No. We can't produce males."

"And in all the time of Amazons traveling different worlds and others from Yemaya entwined in the Empire no one has thought to adopt a male child?"

"What brought this up?"

Elana seemed genuinely upset, the emotion so unexpected and unnerving it left Diana lost for how to predict the best response. Elana looked away, seemingly unwilling to say more, but leaving Diana without any way to inquire carefully about whatever she'd seen.

"I saw him," Elana changed the subject, trying to pull herself back together. "Gerome. I saw him as a child and I saw when he lost his arm."

"In the carriage accident?"

Elana shook her head. "He wasn't hurt as a child. The injury is less than a tenmoon old. And he's not looking for a seer."

"He's still my brother." Gerome's voice rang through the cave, hanging like frost in the air. How much had he heard.

"I don't doubt it," Elana responded, her voice even – she knew he'd been awake. "But I don't know why you lied about so much. You weren't adopted. You weren't injured as a child. Why lie about such simple and unimportant details?"

Gerome sat up, his face full of rage. "You don't know what I've been through."

"No, I don't. But I'd like to understand."

Diana watched with a faint feeling of awe as Elana responded more gently and with more care than she'd ever approached Gerome. Whatever she'd seen in her dreams had changed her.

Elana's response caught Gerome off guard. He locked eyes with Elana a moment, then turned his back to them, holding his arm close to his chest.

"I grew up with Simon in the abbey. I took care of him."

"And you kept taking care of him even when he was adopted," Elana offered.

Gerome nodded his head. "It was a good home."

"What happened?"

"The Sisters were going to send me away to the Keep. I'd hidden my Sight most of my life but I was figured out. They talked about it like the Fates' Cellar but suddenly when I was one of the Blue Sights they were ready to ship me away to the Council. I couldn't leave Simon. What would he do without me? So we came up with a way for him to follow me."

"You made him pretend to be a seer."

Gerome nodded slowly. "I didn't know it would get him kidnapped. What if the Order finds out he's pretending? What will they do with him? He's just a kid."

"Why wouldn't you tell us?" Diana asked gently.

"You're looking for seers. Simon was being taken to Loscan.

I needed help getting inside."

"We would have helped you, seer or not," Elana commented.

"You knew for sure he was coming here?"

"I got close to him once. I heard his captors talking about the ruins."

"But you didn't see them enter?"

Gerome's cheeks darkened. "I followed them into the foothills, but I got sick before we reached the desert. I lost them. The ruins was the only lead I had. Now I don't have anything."

"You have us," Elana remarked. "But we won't get very far on lies. If you want our help still, we have to work together."

Gerome clenched his jaw and glanced away. "It doesn't matter. He's gone. He's lost."

"Perhaps not," Diana offered. She held out a bottle of tranquilizer. "I don't know where Simon or any of the other seers were taken, but I know where this came from. If Simon's captors were headed into the desert, it makes sense to continue on to desert cities where we know the Order has a presence. Where they'd be buying supplies to subdue seers."

"Where?" Gerome questioned, some of his tension falling away to interest.

Diana rolled the bottle in her palm, revealing the stamp of a budding lotus. "This is the symbol for a man named Khasale in Dwaramin. I did a few transport jobs for him."

"You think he's tied to the Order?" Elana questioned.

"I don't pretend to know anything for sure, but I wouldn't think so. Khasale is a businessman. But we might be able to get more solid leads from him."

Elana stood and set her shoulders. "Sounds as good a place to start as any." She glanced at Gerome. "Are you coming with us?"

"Do I have a choice?" he grunted.

"Yes."

They met eyes, first in rebellion, then Gerome softened. "I'll come with you."

Elana reached out to him and pulled him to his feet. "Good. Let's go."

MADRISAH: BROTHERS

T ad Di'Nay!" Tad Khasale pulled Di'Nay into a firm handshake, smiling with genuine affection.

Elana watched Di'Nay and her old business partner from across the desert market. Di'Nay was dressed as a man, her chest bound and her cloak broadened her shoulders. There was something charming about Di'Nay posing as a man, but Elana found herself less and less enchanted by it. Di'Nay didn't like it and Elana despised that the costume was necessary for Di'Nay to earn and keep the respect of her peers.

Elana used her Shadow abilities and Sight to make herself blend with the crowd. She wore a long, dark cloak with a high hood, similar to the robes and hoods of many of the market vendors, shielding her from the desert sun and obscuring her form. The folds covered the lower part of her face, keeping the dust kicked up by passing cart horses out of her mouth as it held the scents of earth and sand constantly near her nose. All that was visible were her arms and eyes, her blue irises turned a dark gray to shield her identity as a Blue Sight. She made herself completely unremarkable, and so held no one's attention.

It had taken days of travel through the desert to reach Dwaramin, a small town centered around a handful of shipping companies and warehouses – the largest of all owned by Khasale. It was the perfect market for the Order of Blindness – small enough not to draw much attention but controlled by merchants with the ability to attain rare goods.

Elana's eyes skimmed the public wares on long wooden tables under colorful canopies, but everything was fairly mundane. Basic travel supplies, clothing, food that would move in bulk were laid out for locals and visitors, with more supplies being packed into crates and loaded onto carts to be sent to other towns.

Elana hadn't expected anything that would interest the Order to be publicly available. The seer tranquilizer Elana and Di'Nay had been able to trace back to Khasale was certainly a special order. Special enough that, despite Di'Nay's charm and history with Khasale, Elana doubted she'd be able to get access to the merchant's client list. The Order would had to have either a lot of money or solid blackmail dedicated to keeping their contacts silent.

Elana frowned. This wasn't the time for diplomacy. Di'Nay was good with people, but she couldn't risk alerting Khasale to her true intentions or even peak his suspicion. It also didn't help that they'd left Gerome at an inn with their horses, leaving Elana constantly on edge that someone from the Order would discover him or he'd get himself into some kind of trouble. He was good at disguising his Blue Sight abilities, and after their talk in Loscan he'd stopped wandering off on his own, but there was so much that could go wrong in a short time. They didn't have a lot of time. Elana had to take action.

Elana moved swiftly through the thin crowd, her eyes moving rapidly to assess her surroundings. The sand was hard-packed from constant travel, but even with her light steps she left little clouds of dust in her wake. She grit her teeth. She'd never liked the desert. She hated the heat, the sand storms, the flatness of the landscape, but it was the lack of shadow and difficulty of moving with any kind of stealth through sand that made it dangerous for her. She was trained to blend with the shadows, to move unseen. It was hard to do under the constant, relentless blaze of the sun.

It wasn't hard to spot Khasale's offices: it was the tallest building in town, three stories with a small warehouse and carts in the back. The building had obviously been added to over time; the levels were uneven and made of clusters of towers, office rooms, and bits of tiled roof over the windows. Elana spotted people moving in and out of most of the rooms, but a small office on the top floor seemed empty.

She waited until the narrow street was momentarily empty and climbed up the first level of the building. She scaled balconies and roof made of clay tile, blending with the shadows and avoiding the people moving through the building. The sounds of the warehouse seemed to cover any sound of her climb and Elana thanked the Mother she was able to find solid grips and remain unnoticed.

She reached the top floor and peered into the window. It was a small office with a couch and bookshelves. The walls were bare and there were no trinkets or personal effects decorating the space, but what was in the room was finely made. A woven, crimson and gold silk rug covered the floor. The couch was soft leather. Paperwork and ledgers were neatly stacked on a polished wooden desk – wood that must have been imported from the north. Elana slipped inside, landing lightly on the carpet, and checked the door. It was locked and she couldn't sense the amarin of anyone else on the third floor.

She turned to the desk. It was immediately clear the office belonged to Khasale. His ledgers and journals were written in a neat hand and detailed. Elana's brows rose at the numbers – Khasale's business was a lot more expansive than she'd assumed. Either the Order was far wealthier than she expected or there was no way Khasale was in their pocket. He simply didn't need their money.

She looked through the books, looking for anything that might link to the Order and carefully replacing each book as she finished. The orders were more the same from the market – travel supplies, food, a few fine items like carpets, jewelry, and figurines. There was some mention of potions and tinctures, but Elana recognized them as basic medications and oils.

She finished flipping through the books on the desk and grunted in annoyance, scanning the room once more. She should have known finding what she needed wouldn't be as easy as entering the building.

She moved to the bookshelves. They were mostly tomes on business, detailed maps and atlases, a few books on languages, and a thick novel on the art of diplomacy. The final bookshelf held an archive of ledgers labeled with dates over the last tenmoon. She grabbed the most recent and flipped through it, finding more the same in terms of goods. Elana didn't doubt Khasale dealt in more rare and fine goods than were detailed in the ledgers she'd gone through.

She replaced the book and scanned the spines again. She

finally settled on one on the bottom shelf labeled in gold instead of black ink. She smiled as she flipped it open. Rare dyes. Gold and precious stone jewelry. Massive silk tapestries. This was where something like the seer tranquilizer would be recorded.

She pulled a stack of books labeled in gold ink and sat at the desk. She flipped through the pages, becoming more and more aware that she might not know how the tranquilizer was recorded. Her smile, however, grew as she found mention of "Seer Narcotic." The recipient was recorded only as "Min." Throughout half a dozen books she found records of the narcotic sold to four different people multiple times and no other item labeled as being for seers.

The records were kept as meticulously as the other ledgers. The orders seemed official and unremarkable. They weren't hidden or marked in any way that would set them apart from other rare items. The more Elana studied, the more she realized Khasale may not know fully who he was dealing with. While it complicated things and left her without a lead to the Order, Elana couldn't help but be relieved. She didn't want Di'Nay's friend to be working for the Order of Blindness.

Elana memorized the names of the people who'd purchased the narcotic and replaced the books. She tensed as she felt someone approaching and heard footsteps. She scanned the books once more, wishing she had more time to study them, and slipped back out the window as Khasale unlocked his door.

"Where were you?" Di'Nay's voice was strained with worry as Elana joined her near the inn on the edge of town, finally removing her hood.

"Exploring. How was your meeting with Tad Khasale?"

Di'Nay sighed. "Not particularly useful." She drew a piece of paper from her pocket. "I have the name and ingredients of the tranquilizer, but not much else." Elana took the paper and studied it. She recognized a handful of ingredients, but most were foreign to her. "It's sold as a narcotic. A hallucinogen. He buys it from a dealer in Karatan."

Elana relaxed. "Does he know what it does?"

"I don't think so. He thinks it's a drug used by religious zealots in the jungle to induce visions. Elana... unless he's a very good liar, I don't think he's knowingly working with the Order. I know Khasale. He doesn't hate seers or Blue Sights and he wouldn't want to be tied up in kidnapping."

Elana folded the paper again and handed it back to her lover. "Let's get inside. I have a few things to show you."

Diana sat cross-legged on her bed, studying the list of names Elana had gathered from Khasale's office. She pursed her lips, using the paper as an excuse to gather her thoughts. Even with Elana returned, sitting across the room from her, Diana's heart sped in her chest. She'd broken into the office of one of the most powerful traders on Aggar. Only Khasale's certainty he was secure in his own outpost – heavily guarded and surrounded by factory workers – and the knowledge that he didn't keep valuables worth stealing in his office made it possible for Elana to move unseen. If she'd been discovered, she'd be killed. There was nothing Diana could have done.

Her pursed lips turned to a frown and she covered her mouth with her hand. She knew Elana would feel her fear, but she didn't care to hide it. She didn't expect Elana to obey her or always tell Diana her plans, but she was becoming more unpredictable. Diana had no idea how to protect her.

"Do you know any of them?" Elana questioned, breaking the tense silence in the room.

"One," Diana admitted, pointing to 'Matthias Arndham.' "Matthias is another trader, a middle man who works in medical supplies out of Salamah."

"Do you think he could be involved with the Order of Blindness?"

"How could you know?" Gerome questioned. His voice was still gruff and moody, annoyed that he'd been left behind.

"I can't. But ordering a tranquilizer for seers makes sense in this small of amounts for a medicine peddler. He's ordered only two vials."

"At least we know who he is. You don't know any of the others?"

Diana shook her head. "These are false names, and not ones I recognize. It's likely they're just false names given by members of the Order directly."

"Wouldn't Tad Khasale know he's being lied to?" Gerome questioned.

"Of course. But many of his clients want to remain

anonymous. If Khasale only thinks this is a narcotics trade, he wouldn't care who was buying as long as he received his pay."

Elana stood, pacing a moment, then sitting beside Diana. "Two of these people have purchased over fifteen vials each. The last order was this week. They or their porters have to be known in town."

"It's possible. I doubt the Order would trust random porters hired by Khasale to handle sensitive goods."

"Then we should investigate. Ask the warehouse workers. The other merchants."

"And if we're discovered asking about false names we have no business knowing?" Diana questioned.

"We'll have to be subtle."

"I can help, I'm not useless," Gerome volunteered. Elana and Diana exchanged looks and Gerome frowned. "You think I haven't had to get information before? I've taken care of myself since I was a child."

"You're *still* a child," Diana remarked.

Elana stood. "I don't doubt your abilities, Gerome. But this could be dangerous."

Gerome's frown deepened. "I know how to hide."

"I believe you." Elana glanced at Diana over her shoulder. "I think you two should go together. Di'Nay can keep you safe."

"And you?" Diana questioned.

"I move better alone."

"Elana –"

"We'll have a better chance at finding what we need if we separate. You need to talk to people. You're persuasive. You can explain having an assistant with you. I don't plan to be noticed by anyone."

"If there's Order presence in town, I don't want any of us to be alone," Diana argued. "You can't sense them with their amulets."

"We won't be gone long, and I'm trying to find the location of the Order's contact, not approach them."

"We can work together."

"Di'Nay." Elana's voice was firm and unshakable. Diana frowned. Why was Elana being so stubborn? "Let's meet back here at dusk."

Before Diana could comment, Elana swept out of the room.

Diana watched her go, feeling a bit abandoned by her lover. Gerome grunted a laugh and sat beside her. "Does she treat everyone like they're inept or is it just us?"

Diana's heart sank. Did Elana really see her that way? Without Sight or Shadow abilities, in a situation like this did Elana see her as a liability? She shook her head slowly, letting the dark thoughts fade. She would find the information they were looking for. She would prove her worth. She would show Elana she didn't need protecting.

She stood and pulled her cloak back around her shoulders. She drew a deep breath and fell back into her masculine stance.

"You hide well."

Diana glanced back at Gerome. She studied his expression, wondering not for the first time what the boy must think of her. He had plenty to say about his thoughts on Blue Sights and religion, but he didn't comment on Diana posing as a man or her close relationship with Elana. "Thank you."

Gerome grinned. "I make you uncomfortable?"

Diana snorted and shook her head. "No. I'm bonded to a Blue Sight. I'm used to my emotions being constantly read."

"I don't mind that you pose as a man."

Diana considered his answer. "I would think with your upbringing you might be uncomfortable with it."

"Do you know anything about the abbeys of the Mother?"

"Not much," Diana admitted.

"Some of the priestesses dress as men from time to time. They say it's easier to move through cities and preach the word of the Mother. To be honest, I first thought you and Elana might be priestesses you're so close."

Diana turned her back to him, examining herself in the mirror. She grinned knowingly, suddenly more interested than ever in Aggar's religious cloisters. "Is that so?"

"But you're just lifebonded. I've heard it makes people close."

Diana nodded. "It does. It binds our lives and souls together. I can even feel Elana's heartbeat in my wrist when we're near."

"No one should be that close to anyone but the Mother."

Diana cocked her head. "Do you plan to dedicate yourself to your Goddess?"

Gerome's smile faded and the spark in his eyes dimmed as he withdrew into himself and his thoughts. It was a look he fell into at least once every time they spoke. When they'd first met, Diana had assumed he was sulking – he could certainly be moody when he wanted to be – but over time she realized it was something else. The habit of a young man who had spent most of his life hiding.

"I used to think so."

"What changed?"

"Simon doesn't want to be a monk."

Diana nodded slowly. "You're very dedicated to him."

The spark returned, flashing hot with anger before quickly dimming. "He's my family."

"He's lucky to have you."

Gerome thought a moment longer then stood. "So I'm going to be what? Your apprentice?"

"It's a believable excuse," Diana agreed as she smoothed her short, golden hair. "Khasale doesn't have any more information for me, but someone in the warehouse might know something useful."

"The Mother help whoever might be hiding Simon," Gerome growled as they headed for the door.

Diana tensed at the sudden venom in his voice and genuinely feared for anyone connected to the seer kidnappings. Between Elana and Gerome, vengeance would be swift and horrible.

Diana stood outside Khasale's warehouse and drew a slow breath. Gerome strolled up behind her, his hands deep in his pockets and his expression sour. His soft, dark hair was ruffled and curling in the heat. Diana was struck once again with how much he resembled Elana.

The longer he traveled with him, the more Diana wondered if her urgent desire to protect him was less about helping a child and had more to do with his physical similarities to the woman she loved and a cousin she hadn't been able to protect long ago. It also helped that Elana seemed connected to him, shifting smoothly between a firm mentor training him in his Blue Sight abilities and a tender caretaker who empathized with his confusion and anger. Diana couldn't help but feel protective of anyone Elana mothered.

In reality, however, she knew so little about him. His brooding and emotional walls kept her at arm's length and he constantly surprised her, making her second guess her assessments of his nature. He'd proven he had no problem lying to her or breaking away from the group for personal gain. But he'd also proven himself useful with time. He was helpful on the road and he'd been quick and charming when questioning the warehouse workers. He was a good liar. The fact left her with even more mixed feelings.

She wondered if she would be so willing to work with him if he had two arms and didn't look like Elana. She couldn't find it in herself to totally distrust him. Her instincts told her to trust him. She wanted to know more about him. She laughed softly under her breath. She was too sentimental. Gerome could thank the Mother he was tailor-made to play on Diana's sympathies.

"That was a waste of time," he hissed. "No one here knows anything."

Diana frowned. She'd known it was a long shot they'd be able to track down any buyer operating under a false name. There was a good chance the names in the ledgers were only used for record keeping and the porters would know the buyers by their real names. But she'd hoped they'd learn something.

"Perhaps we're asking the wrong questions," Diana sighed.

"We don't have time to come up with new answers. This is the only lead we have toward finding Simon."

"We don't know what Elana will find. This isn't a big town. If someone connected with the Order is living here, she'll find it," she tried to assure him. "If they hire their own porters, they may not be connected to the warehouse. We should wait for her to return to decide our next step."

He grit his teeth. "Mother help us."

He walked away, his shoulders hunched, headed back to the inn. Diana drew a deep breath, pushing past her mixed feelings about her young companion, and jogged ahead to join him.

Elana sat in the back of the inn, watching the front door. She sank into the shadows like ink on black paper, nearly invisible in the dense, dimly-it common room. She relished having shadows again, finding freedom in disappearing.

There were three inns in Dwaramin. There was the inn on

the edge of town where she was staying, which seemed to cater mostly to travelers. There was a small, luxurious inn that housed wealthy buyers. Elana sat in the third, a rundown but serviceable structure that seemed popular with porters and temp workers.

She'd watched porters come and go for nearly an hour, studying them each with interest. The check-in process was lax – most of them didn't even sign their names in any kind of record book. Cash earned anonymity, which Elana guessed would be valuable to the Order of Blindness.

For a moment she wished she'd listened to Di'Nay when she wanted the party to stay together. She could use her charm in asking around the inn about the names on her list. But she didn't want any help. She wanted to be alone.

She knew Di'Nay felt the rift that had grown between them and she didn't know where it was coming from. Elana didn't feel like discussing it. In truth, she wasn't entirely sure what she was feeling. She loved Di'Nay. They were bonded. They would always be together – they didn't have a choice. Losing Di'Nay would kill her, both through their bond and her heart. But something was changing. She was pulling away. She knew she was being short, even mean at times. It was becoming more apparent to Elana that she and her Amazon lover were very different.

She didn't want Di'Nay to be upset, but how was Elana supposed to explain to her – an off-worlder, one who could pass as a man in Aggar, one without the Sight – exactly what she was going through? How could Di'Nay possibly understand? It was clear from the way she talked about Yemaya that she hadn't experienced much in the way of fear or hatred. If she was to believe Di'Nay, it was utopian. Perfect. But was it really or was Di'Nay just not the target of anyone's fear?

She closed her eyes, trying to shake away the sudden swell of emotion. She didn't have time for this. She drew a deep, slow breath and felt her dark emotions slip away. For a moment she felt weight in her arms, she could smell the warm, sweet scent of a baby's head. The memory of a child flashed through her mind – dreams of a son.

She clenched her jaw and opened her eyes. She could deal with her feelings later.

She stood as the common room became particularly crowded, using her Sight and Shadow abilities to blend. She would be seen, but she wouldn't be remembered. There was nothing about her to draw anyone's interest. She strolled casually to stairwell up to the rooms, moving slowly and confidently down the hallways. She glanced at each door, feeling the amarin of the people behind each one.

It unnerved her the Order could hide from her, that their amulets could shield their amarin from her Sight, but now it could be a useful tool. If she was the predator and not the prey, she could locate members of the Order by their absence. If she heard someone in a room and couldn't sense them, she would know they had an amulet.

She passed each room, feeling an endless network of life and emotion. She didn't sense any absence. Every sound came with a footprint of amarin until she reached a room on the second floor. The door was unimpressive, a room in the middle of the hallway. She didn't hear or sense anyone in the room, but there was a mark of the Sight in it. It was an overwhelming layer of emotion – grief, fear, pain, hope. It stopped Elana in her tracks, her breath catching in her chest.

Like any Blue Sight, Elana could sense her own kind in close quarters. There was something stronger about a Blue Sight's amarin. Something that was more connected to Aggar. But she'd never sensed the residue of Sight without the Blue Sight nearby. Either the Blue Sight's abilities were incredibly strong, or their emotions were.

The feeling was strong enough to distract Elana from her goal. What was a Blue Sight doing in Dwaramin? Where they still in town?

Elana knocked on the door, and when there was no answer she tried the doorknob. To her surprise, it was unlocked. She slipped inside. The room was clean and tidy with no sign of a guest. The Blue Sight must have recently left.

Elana moved through the room, the feelings of the Blue Sight overwhelming everything else. The emotions were a physical weight against her skin. They warmed the air as it passed her lips. She opened the wardrobe and bedside table. She didn't know what she was looking for, but she could only guess if the Blue Sight's amarin imprint was so strong, something important must have been left behind.

She moved to the desk, opening each drawer. She paused

over the last drawer. A chill froze her blood, bringing a flush of color to her pale skin. An Order of Blindness amulet. What would an amulet from the Order be doing in the room of a Blue Sight? She sat at the desk chair, trying to make sense of the discovery.

If a Blue Sight had been wearing the amulet for a long time, perhaps removing it would create a force of repressed amarin that would linger after the Blue Sight left. But why would a Blue Sight wear an amulet? Had they been forced? Was it voluntary? She couldn't imagine it. Just touching an amulet made Elana sick. What could drive a Blue Sight to live that way? Obviously it had been too much if the amulet had been left behind.

Had a Blue Sight been working for the Order?

She sat for a long time, her thoughts spinning, her stomach turning as she imagined the ramifications of what she was sensing. She didn't realize how long she'd been thinking until she noticed the sun setting outside. Di'Nay would be expecting her back soon.

She stood, glancing around the room once more, and moved to leave. As she took her first step, a knock on the door startled her. She felt the amarin of someone new at the door. She didn't answer, waiting for the visitor to leave. After a moment a letter was slipped under the door and she heard the footfalls of the messenger leaving.

Elana picked up the letter. It was marked as returned – the recipient didn't exist. Elana tucked the letter into her belt pouch and, once she felt the hall was empty, she slipped out and rushed for the exit.

Diana held the letter carefully, looking down at it in shock. Elana stood across the bedroom, her arms crossed over her chest. She looked at the ground. She'd already read the letter.

"She was working with them. She was working with the Order." Elana's voice shook slightly. Her eyes flicked back and forth with her thoughts and her cheeks colored with a mix of emotion.

"How is that even possible?" Diana questioned. "You could barely function when the Order made you wear an amulet."

"I don't know. But I saw the amulet and I felt her presence in the room. She was wearing an amulet long enough to leave an imprint after she left."

The letter was three pages long, written in a careful hand. It was a letter from a Blue Sight woman named Taisa who had been posing as a member of the Order of Blindness out of loyalty to her lover, Nile. She was "Min," buying goods for the Order including the seer narcotic.

The letter was a confession, lyrical and detailed, explaining who Taisa was and her pain at leaving Nile and the Order behind. The amulet was making her sick. She was running away. But the letter had been returned to her room when Nile either refused it or wasn't where Taisa expected him to be. The implications made Diana's stomach turn. Where was Taisa now? She couldn't have gotten far if Elana could still sense her in her old room.

"Why would she do this for so long?" Diana muttered to herself as she read the letter. "Why would she love a man who hated her?"

"Not everyone can admit they have the Sight," Gerome groused.

"That doesn't mean she had to love him," Diana commented. "He would kill her if he knew who she was. It doesn't seem like he coerced or threatened her. They weren't married. She had no reason to stay."

Elana scoffed, her shoulders taut. "Is anyone hungry? I'll get us dinner." Diana's brow furrowed. Had she said something wrong? "Cider? Mead? Stew?"

Diana considered. It was clear Elana was looking for an excuse to take time to herself. "That would be nice."

Elana nodded sharply, relaxing a bit when Diana didn't stop her. She slipped out of the room.

"I don't get it."

"I don't know what's wrong with her," Diana admitted aloud, her voice soft. What was she missing? What was she doing wrong?

"Min Taisa?"

Diana realized her mistake and tried to refocus. "Yes, Min Taisa."

"She put herself in danger. She could have been discovered."

"She was in love," Diana conceded.

"We aren't supposed to love anyone."

Diana turned to him in confusion. "Why not?"

Gerome cocked his head, studying her as if she were

suddenly speaking a different language. "We're dangerous. We could pass it on if we have children. Loving is selfish."

Diana didn't know how to respond. Gerome had been traveling with Elana for nearly a tenday. He'd seen her control over her abilities. She'd nearly convinced him to go to the Keep once Simon was found. How could he talk so casually about celibacy and the Sight like a disease?

"Who told you that?"

Gerome shook his head. "How long have you been here, Min? It's common knowledge."

"Not at the Keep."

"Of course not. The Sight is celebrated there."

Diana couldn't think of anything to say in return, but she suddenly realized why Elana had been so upset. Why Taisa would stay with a member of the Order – not just giving up her power, but forcefully throwing it away. She hated herself. She was afraid of herself. She was indoctrinated. Diana had seen the power of cults and brain washing on other worlds. She didn't understand what could bring a person to that place, and that was why Elana had lost her temper. Diana didn't understand.

Diana scanned the note once more. She had dedicated her life to helping people on other worlds. She was very good at falling into other cultures, melding with them with sensitivity and attention to learning the ways of the people around her. She prided herself on her ability to blend in without sacrificing any of her core beliefs. She understood Aggar and its people, but Elana and Gerome weren't part of Aggar at large. They were the minority. Elana was so powerful, so confident, she hadn't thought much about the common beliefs of Blue Sights who hadn't been raised to see their abilities as a gift. She hadn't done due diligence to understand Elana's world outside of her place in the Keep and Aggar as a planet.

"Are you feeling ill?" Gerome questioned, breaking her reverie.

Diana shook her head and fought to push her emotions from her face. "I'm fine. I think I want to study this letter a bit more. Do you want to help Elana get dinner?"

Gerome raised a single brow, clearly feeling her sudden intense mixed emotions, but thankfully he decided not to question her. "Sure." He slid from the bed and left the room, leaving Diana alone with her thoughts.

Diana sighed and leaned back against the headboard, propping the letter on her raised knees. She had scanned the message, but hadn't yet had the chance to read it closely. Taisa's handwriting was legible but messy. A tear stain blurred one of the words on the second page. Despite the obvious signs of her distress, she was lyrical, writing her tragic story like someone would write a love letter. She hadn't decided to leave the Order because she realized her lover was dangerous. She was leaving because she physically couldn't continue wearing the amulet.

"I don't know what else I can do, Nile. I have nothing left to give. I'm drained. I can't hear my own heartbeat anymore, I can't feel the air in my lungs. This amulet is eating away at me. Only my love sustains me. My love and my will to support your dreams, to see you have all the things you've ever wanted.

I'm going into the wilds. I won't reach out to you again. I know the contents of this letter will disgust you and you won't want to see me again. If I can't support you, I won't be a liability to you. Please know I never meant to deceive you. I never meant to hurt you. I only wanted to be close to you. To be whatever you needed – to fill the holes in your life so you can be complete."

Diana read the words in a mixture of appreciation at the depths of her emotion and the inability to understand her desperate desire to shape her entire being to her lover's will. She had seen women who had their power stripped away through slavery, abuse, and social belief. She had seen women choose submission consciously as a form of power. But she hadn't read such intimate language from a woman who walked away from her own desires without cause. A woman who disregarded the fact that she even had desires outside of pleasing someone else. Taisa didn't want to exist. She wanted to be the perfect tool for her lover to use in creating his perfect life.

The door to her room opened once more and she was surprised to see Elana, not Gerome, returning.

"Gerome's eating in the common room," Elana announced softly. Diana's thoughts about Taisa faded. Finally, a moment alone. Elana nodded to the letter. "Did you find anything new?"

Diana shook her head. "I don't understand her."

"You really don't?"

"No." Diana's word sounded like a confession. "I'm starting

to realize there's a lot I don't understand."

Elana's face softened and she sat beside Diana. "It's very different from your life experience."

"My job is to understand things outside my life experience."

"To a degree," Elana stated. "But we all have blindspots."

Diana reached out and touched her arm, relishing the tenderness between them. "I'm sorry I've been callous."

Elana hesitated, then held Diana's hand on her shoulder. "I don't expect you to understand my Sight. I never have."

"Then what is it? What can I do? I know you're hurting."

Elana finally looked Diana in her eyes. "You never answered me in Loscan. What would happen to my son on Yemaya?"

Diana's brows furrowed. "I don't understand."

"If I had a son, would I be able to raise him on the Amazon homeworld?"

"You can't have a son. You're bonded to me. It's genetically impossible."

"That's not what I'm asking," Elana grunted.

"I don't know what you want me to say," Diana confessed.

Elana looked away and grit her teeth. "Yemaya isn't perfect, Diana."

"Of course it's not."

"You talk about it like it is. You talk about it like it's a bastion of peace and tolerance and hope. But you have your prejudices, too."

"All this over men?"

"No." Elana met her eyes and Diana gasped at the emotion in Elana's Sight. "You've never been feared. Not like I have. Outside of a few sneers about being an off-worlder you can move freely. You can pose as a man if you need to hide. On your own world, you're revered. An Amazon. I'm not."

"You *are*. You're brilliant. Talented. Brave. You'll be loved on Yemaya."

"How can you know that? Would you even see the prejudices of your homeworld if you've never been the target of them? What would happen to my son on Yemaya, Di'Nay?"

The weight of Elana's real concerns hit Diana like a blow to her stomach. Is that what Elana thought of her? Was she right?

"You wouldn't be allowed to raise a son on Yemaya," Diana

admitted.

"Even if he was gentle? Even if he was more feminine than you? More submissive? More harmless? What could one young man do on a planet of women? What threat would he be? Yemaya would take a child from his mother before they'd let a man on their planet? Do you know why?"

Diana's lips formed a tight, straight line. "No," she admitted. "It's just the way things have always been."

Elana leaned back, her face stricken. "That's what I thought. How is Yemaya different from Aggar?" Diana looked away, ashamed for the first time since childhood. Elana took the letter and leaned against the headboard with Diana. "Let's go over this more closely."

Diana leaned her head on Elana's shoulder. Even if the answer was hard, even if it had cut them both, speaking it aloud had mended something. Diana clung to that small bit of comfort as she nodded. "Okay."

Elana adjusted the covering over her face, a location repeating over and over in her mind. Astala. When she'd first read Taisa's note, she'd mistaken it for a town she'd never heard of. Thankfully Di'Nay had recognized it: a family warehouse operating not far from Dwaramin. Taisa had written she was operating out of Astala. It would make sense that she would be in charge of securing supplies from Khasale then transport them to a warehouse operated by the Order for distribution.

Elana crouched low against a sandy dune and watched the warehouse in the distance. It was a single large building surrounded by a cluster of small houses. Close enough to Dwaramin for support and basic necessities, but far enough out to keep its commerce private. Di'Nay said there were quite a few family warehouses and homesteads in the area, that much of the northern desert in the Southern continent was used for storage and commerce. Elana was surprised Astala was so still. She would have expected to see a few carts or at least warehouse workers in the middle of the day, but there was nothing.

She didn't sense any amarin from humans nearby, but she didn't trust her Sight this close to an Order of Blindness compound. She rested back on her heels, letting out a soft breath against the dark cloth of her face covering. Di'Nay and Gerome were camping nearby, ready for her report. With the cover of an uneven landscape dotted with dunes and the excuse of traveling to Dwaramin, Di'Nay could stay closer without being spotted by the warehouse. They were close enough Elana could feel their amarin. They were anxious and curious but overall calm. Elana liked knowing Di'Nay was safe and Gerome was staying put.

She crept close to the ground until she was out of sight of the warehouse then walked slowly back to her party. If the warehouse truly was empty, what did it mean? Had they moved on? Elana knew Taisa had been in the town recently, so she must have sent her letter recently as well. The warehouse should still be in operation. The fact that it wasn't was unsettling.

Di'Nay glanced up as she approached. Elana pulled down the wrap around her mouth and Di'Nay tensed at Elana's frown.

"What did you see?" Di'Nay questioned.

"From what I can tell, the warehouse is empty."

"What?" Gerome took a step forward. "How's that possible?"

Elana shook her head. "I don't know. I didn't see any movement – no carts, no workers. Unless everyone is closed inside and remaining very still, there's no one there."

Di'Nay frowned. "It seems too convenient that Taisa disappeared and her warehouse emptied the same day."

"That's what I'm afraid of," Elana muttered.

"We have to go. We have to investigate before they clear everything out," Gerome insisted.

"You're right. But we should move cautiously. There's still a chance there are members of the Order there."

Gerome grabbed the short sword from his waist that Di'Nay had given him. "We can take care of them."

Di'Nay rested her hand on his arm. "Stealth first," she warned.

Gerome grunted and Elana smiled softly at the wave of adolescent frustration that flared in his amarin. He had no patience for Di'Nay's warnings against violence. "Let's go."

Di'Nay glanced up at Elana and they turned together toward the warehouse. They stayed close to the edge of the canyon, taking cover in the shadows as they circled the warehouse, looking for any other signs of cultists before cautiously moving toward Astala.

Dozens of excuses and escape routes ran through Elana's mind and she could feel the same thoughts rushing through Di'Nay's, but they weren't stopped. They weren't spotted. The warehouse and its grounds were truly empty. Elana shivered. There was nothing. No amarin. No energy. Even the sounds felt muted. She was used to every residence – even abandoned buildings – carrying the imprint of the amarins that had passed through it. It was a noise that had faded into a comforting weight around Elana. The absence of anything felt like a dark hole in the fabric of the planet. The side effect of the Order's amulets.

"This is eerie," Di'Nay whispered as they reached a side door.

Elana peered in the window and, seeing no one, opened the door. The depth of the silence was amplified by the sound of their footsteps echoing through the massive structure as they walked. The space was empty. No barrels or bins, no carts, nothing but a large, clear space. Elana turned in a slow circle, trying to sense anything that might have happened.

"I don't like it here," Gerome muttered, his voice soft and scared for the first time since Elana had met him.

"Because it shouldn't exist," Elana answered. "They must have stored a huge amount of amulets here to destroy the presence of any amarin."

"You don't feel anything?" Di'Nay questioned.

"Nothing. No humans or animals. Just the life in the sands beneath it."

"And even that's muted," Gerome agreed.

Di'Nay clenched her jaw. "At least you don't feel any tragedy."

Elana wanted to draw comfort from Di'Nay's words, but she knew the absence of feeling made it more likely something bad *had* happened. The Order had gone to great lengths to hide the space from any Blue Sights that might pass.

They spread out and studied the warehouse. Elana made note of every crack in the floor and discoloration in the stones.

"Elana." Di'Nay's voice was gruff and serious. The hair on the back of Elana's neck stood on end at the sudden knowledge that she'd found something bad.

Elana crossed the warehouse to stand with her. A rough, dark brown circle stained the stones. Old blood. Elana crouched low to it. She touched it with one finger, sensing the faintest linger of amarin on it. She closed her eyes and focused. It was fresher than it looked. The amarin was far weaker than it should have been, but she could still sense faint flashes of terror and grief. Someone had either died or been very hurt here. She opened her eyes slowly, praying to the Mother it wasn't Taisa.

"It's not very old, just dried. Maybe a day or two?"

"If it's that fresh then it couldn't be enough blood to kill someone," Di'Nay offered.

Elana stood back up. "I hope you're right."

Gerome gasped. Elana turned to him as he spun toward the door. She sensed it a moment before he did – someone was nearby.

Gerome ran for the door.

"Gerome!" Di'Nay hissed, reaching for her weapon.

"Di'Nay," Elana gasped, her voice shaken. "It's a child."

They ran after Gerome, who was already sprinting toward the dune. He stopped in front of the sands as a young child crawled out from under a stack of rocks. He let out a sob of relief and pulled the child into his arms.

"Simon!"

Elana smiled widely as she came to stand beside the boys. Gerome trembled as he held his brother. Simon was barely five tenmoons. He was filthy, his lips dry from being alone in the sun, but he seemed unhurt. Gerome's hand grabbed at his blonde hair as his arm wrapped protectively around Simon's chubby waist.

"You found me!" Simon wept.

Gerome pulled away enough to talk to his brother. "What happened? Did they hurt you?"

Simon's face fell. "I'm fine now. A woman came. She saved me."

"What about the others?" Di'Nay questioned.

Simon looked between his brother and Di'Nay, unsettled by more strangers. "They're safe. They helped me find you," Gerome promised. Simon visibly relaxed.

"Others?"

"Other children?" Elana amended, trying to keep her voice calm and soothing.

"There were no other children. I was alone."

Gerome reclaimed his attention. "They left? You're free?"

"I think so. They... they found the woman. They took her away. I don't know what happened. I hid. I didn't want them to find me."

He started to cry and Gerome held him tight again. "You did the right thing. You're safe now. I'll get you home."

Simon sank into Gerome's hug, losing his strength and bravery in the safety of a savior. "I want to leave. They'll try to find you, Gerome. They'll hurt you."

"They won't," Di'Nay promised. She indicated Elana. "We'll protect both of you."

Simon seemed to draw comfort from Di'Nay's promise. Elana crouched beside the boys to meet Simon's eyes. "Come with us. You look hungry."

Simon nodded and Gerome stood. The boys held hands. Di'Nay leaned into Elana.

"We can't take them back to the inn. The Order may still have a presence in town."

"Then we'll go back into the desert. I'll stay with the boys. You get our things from town."

Di'Nay sighed. "We need some kind of destination."

"We can go to Madrisah," Gerome called to them.

"They abbey?" Di'Nay questioned. "No one is allowed in Madrisah but the sisters."

Gerome shook his head. "They'll take us in. I'm a ward to the Mother. It doesn't matter where I am – the sisters will care for me."

Elana felt Gerome's certainty. Her thoughts rippled back and forth between concern about how she and Gerome would be treated on sacred ground and wondering what it would mean to Gerome about his Sight if she could navigate Madrisah without being condemned as a creature of the Fates.

Elana glanced at Di'Nay. "It's worth a try. Do you know where the abbey is?"

Diana rode ahead, Elana's arms tight around her waist. The abbey was built into a rocky cliffside – a honeycomb of sparse rooms and shrines. The cliff was dotted with circular windows carved into the stone. One of the largest abbeys dedicated to the Mother, and one of the most secretive. Diana didn't know much about it beyond the tidbits she'd learned while traveling past it a handful of times in merchant caravans.

"They say the Mother walked in Madrisah," Gerome told his brother, his voice full of awe and excitement. Diana smiled to herself at his obvious delight. He'd probably wanted to visit the holy site for a long time. "Every priest and priestess of the Mother makes a pilgrimage at some point in their life."

"To do what?" Simon questioned.

"To pray. To meditate. Do you see the windows? Those are all prayer rooms."

"That sounds boring."

"It's beautiful, Simon. You'll see."

Simon yawned and leaned back against his brother. "Okay."

Diana rode toward the cliff, looking for any sign of a door, but there were none, just open passages into the caverns. As they came closer, three older women in plain white linen shirts and pants walked out of the cliffside and waited for them.

"Welcome travelers. What has brought you to the welcoming arms of the Mother?" A woman stepped forward, her gray-streaked dark hair pulled back into a tight knot. Her skin was wrinkled and soft with age but her back was straight and strong. Her voice was deep and clear with an air of authority. Diana didn't doubt she was much stronger than she looked.

"Sister," Gerome called as he dropped down from his horse and knelt before the woman. "My friends and I come seeking aide and sanctuary." He grabbed a pendant from the pouch at his waist and held it out to her.

The woman took the pendant with a careful hand, weighing the chain and amulet in a steady hand. She looked up at Gerome and the party anew. "Child, what's brought you all the way to Madrisah?"

"My brother was kidnapped and tormented. I saved him, but he needs rest. I don't know if we're being followed."

Diana grit her teeth at his honesty. She hadn't expected him to be so blunt right away. The woman, however, barely showed any sign of shock. She turned to the others. "Prepare rooms for them."

"You'll take us in?" Diana questioned.

The priestess smiled for the first time, the expression faint but cheerful. "We protect our own, Min. You are vouched for. We'll give you sanctuary for a time."

Diana felt Elana relax behind her as if letting out a deep, inaudible breath.

"Thank you, Sister." Gerome ran back to Leggings and led her by her reigns closer to Madrisah.

"Come," the sister called. "I'll take you to the stable. You may call me Sister Rose."

Diana marveled at the tight inner workings of Madrisah as Sister Rose, nimble even in her old age, led them to where they'd sleep. The hallways were narrow but smooth, the floors worn away from what she could only assume to be centuries of regular use. Every now and then the narrow passage would open and reveal a massive room, usually a site of prayer or a cathedral, sometimes exquisitely detailed stone statues of the Mother, cradling the world or in silk scarves dancing through time and space.

The walls in these rooms were meticulously painted by hand, some with scenes of the Mother creating the world or battling the fates, others with depictions of her deep in meditation, painted in gold so that she shimmered even in candle light. Many of the smaller rooms were in use, priestesses kneeling before their goddess deep in prayer.

Diana had never seen so many depictions of the Aggar Goddess. She had never taken much time to learn the myths about the Mother beyond what basics she needed to navigate the country, but seeing her so splendidly portrayed made her curious. Madrisah was a treasure trove of religious art. She understood why they were so careful with who they let enter their abbey.

The room provided Diana and Elana was small – barely enough space for two narrow beds – carved into a stone alcove with a wooden door. They were on the ground floor of the complex and Diana assumed it was intentional. She and Elana were barely guests – brought into the holy site on Gerome's word alone. Simon was taken to an infirmary and Gerome refused to leave his side. Diana felt a weight rise from her chest knowing they'd be well cared for. The sisters seemed to have a soft spot for children.

"Feel free to wander, Mins, but we ask that you be respectful of our home. You are free to pray and examine, but interruption of our ceremonies or another's meditation won't be tolerated," Sister Rose explained, her voice never changing pitch but her warning evident.

"We're grateful just to have a safe place to stay and care for Simon, Sister. We won't be any trouble."

She nodded and her smile returned. "If you need anything, ask for me or feel free to ask another sister who isn't in prayer."

Diana nodded. "Thank you."

Sister Rose left, closing their door behind her.

Elana collapsed onto the bed on the floor the moment Sister Rose left. She ran her hands over her face and breathed deeply. Diana sat cross-legged on the floor beside her.

"At least we get the same room. If they held us in more esteem they may have insisted on not making us share."

Elana snorted once in laughter behind her hands. "There are some benefits to us both being women on Aggar."

Diana tenderly stroked her hair, giving her whatever comfort she could. "There are many benefits to us both being women anywhere, Soroi."

Elana finally lowered her hands and smiled, leaning up to kiss Diana's palm. Diana's heart stopped as she savored the touch. There had been so much tension between them she hadn't expected such a loving gesture. "I've grown so used to hiding and expecting hatred on this journey I didn't expect kindness from an abbey."

"Do you think they can tell you have the Sight?"

"No. But part of me expects everyone to know just seeing me."

Diana frowned slightly, her fingers still twining in her lover's thick hair. "Are you still happy you came on this journey?"

"I'm a Shadow of the Keep. I couldn't stay blind to Aggar forever. I was raised by an accepting family and spent most of my life training among my own. I knew when I left the relative safety of the Keep there would be some culture shock. The Mistress always warned me."

Diana remembered their first journey together, traveling through the wilds of the north. Elana had been kidnapped and tortured for her Sight by a madman preparing to attack the Ramains. Elana had known nothing but hatred for her Sight since bonding with Diana. "I'm sorry it was so unsettling."

Elana reached up and held Diana's hand, lowering it to rest their entwined fingers over her heart. "I'm glad you're with me. You keep me rooted, Di'Nay."

Diana hesitated, enjoying the warmth of Elana's body under her fingers. She didn't want the moment to end, but she couldn't stand so many unspoken things between them anymore. "You know I'll always fight for you."

"I know."

"Elana." Elana looked up into her eyes. "Even on Yemaya. Wherever we are, I'll defend you."

Elana's lips pressed together as she understood. Her voice was a whisper as she spoke. "What if it doesn't get any better, Di'Nay? What if I don't fit in your world?"

"Then we'll find somewhere else to go."

Elana's brows rose. "Somewhere else?"

"I want to bring you to my world. I want you to experience the life I had before I left to work with the Terrans. I want you to feel loved and appreciated. But if my people don't welcome you, I don't want anything to do with them. You're my priority. I'll travel to the ends of the universe to find a place we can be together in peace. Us and any children you want."

Elana blinked away tears and kissed her, the touch tender and lingering. "How did I find you?"

Diana smiled and glanced at the ceiling. "The Mother?"

Elana laughed. They kissed again and Elana sighed beneath her. "Something doesn't feel right about touching you here."

Diana smirked. "Defiling holy ground? I never knew you were so devoted to your goddess."

Elana grimaced. "Perhaps we should just sleep?"

Diana slid beside her, wrapping the smaller woman in her arms. "Whatever you want, Elana. Forever."

Diana woke some time later. She wasn't sure exactly how long she'd slept but Elana was dreaming deeply, her body heavy and completely relaxed. Diana smiled at the feel of her lover resting. For all her teasing, she was glad there was some kind of faith in the Mother that still resided in Elana's heart. Perhaps that was why she was able to sleep so well in a house dedicated to the Aggar goddess.

Diana laid beside her for a while, watching her breathe and dream. It had been so long since they'd had a moment like this — peaceful and quiet, just the two of them. For a time, it felt like the tension between them had disappeared and the worries of their travels were locked outside Madrisah's walls.

Diana hoped Elana slept for a day or more. That she took time to recover. Diana wanted desperately to find the missing seer children – to right the wrongs the Order of Blindness was doing all over Aggar – but not at the risk of Elana's sanity or health. They had saved Simon and, in a way, Gerome. For now, that was enough.

After a long time, Diana slid away from Elana, leaving her to her sleep. She quietly left the room, trying to remember the pathway to the stable and their supplies. She didn't expect the sisters to feed them. If she was going to guarantee Elana had something to eat when she woke Diana would have to prepare it herself.

She wandered in the direction that seemed the most familiar and relaxed when she saw the first prayer room she recognized. There were no sisters praying in any of the rooms and Diana guessed night had fallen.

She hesitated as she passed the room with the statue of the Mother dancing. She waited a moment before removing her shoes and stepping into the cavern. The statue was massive, easily five times her height and stretching up to the top of the narrow, cylindrical room. The walls were painted in clusters of gold, the stone and paint mimicking the universe and the night sky. The Mother herself was young, her hair long and wild. She wore silks and carried a scarf, her body twisted and limbs locked in movement.

The only times Diana had seen images of the Mother it was as a woman with child, peaceful and contemplative. This Mother was carefree and untamed – a maiden more than a parent. Like the goddess Persephone celebrated on Yemaya. For a moment, Diana was struck by the idea that a planet that was so patriarchal had a female supreme goddess. Motherhood and femininity should have been held in high regard with such a goddess, but outside the abbeys and monasteries she seemed more a figurehead used in speech than a real deity.

But the ruins in Loscan proved she had once been held in higher regard by the masses. Perhaps a statue like this – a young Mother dancing through the cosmos – was a relic from a time when the Mother was more complex. When women were more treasured. Perhaps early Aggar had more in common with Yemaya than Diana had ever expected.

"Did she speak to you?" Diana spun around in surprise and a young sister laughed behind her hand, her eyes bright and playful. "I didn't mean to scare you."

Diana relaxed and smiled as well. "It's a beautiful representation."

The young woman stepped forward, the hem of her robe brushing the stone floor with every step. "The Mother as a dancer, creating order from the chaos of the universe by turning its madness into music."

"I've never seen her like this."

"We don't put all sides of the Mother up for public consumption. Some things are too sacred. So the dancing Mother only exists outside these halls in the music we play."

Diana considered the statue again. "I like her like this."

"I do, too." She tucked her hands behind her back and regarded the statue with Diana in silence for a long moment. Finally, she spoke. "You're the visitors who brought Gerome back to us."

"Is he well?"

"He and his brother have both suffered a good deal, but they'll recover. Do you need anything? You may be regarded warily by some, but we're very grateful for the sacrifices you made to bring our child back to us. The desert can be a very dangerous place."

"We were happy to help," Diana assured her. "I was trying to find my way back to our supplies. My partner is sleeping and I wanted to be sure she had something to eat when she wakes."

The young woman shook her head. "No need to use your own supplies. We have plenty."

"We don't want to put you out."

The woman raised a hand, silencing Diana's concerns. "The Mother requires us to show hospitality and care with those we take into our halls. As long as you're with us, you and Elana are like Gerome – our children, sworn into our protection. We don't leave our children hungry."

Diana nodded. "We're very grateful."

"Come with me. I'll find you food. And perhaps we can talk more about the forms of the Mother."

Elana shuffled, waking slowly from her deep sleep. She pressed herself up on her arms and glanced around the room. "Di'Nay?" she called softly into the tiny cavern. Her lover was nowhere to be found. She sat up. How long had she been asleep?

She crept out of the room, trying to get some sense of time. She could feel most of the people nearby still sleeping, their amarins gentle and faint. It was peaceful, wrapping Elana in a thin layer of warmth. She passed a prayer room with a window. The sun was about to rise, the night sky a rich dark blue over the desert landscape. People would be waking soon.

She passed prayer rooms and chapels, glancing quickly over each statue and the elaborate paintings on the walls. The work was gorgeous – she had never seen anything like it – but it left her unsettled. She frowned, an uncomfortable ripple like insects running under her skin. Elana had a complex relationship with the Mother. She found some peace in the thought of her presence, but her acolytes made it clear they didn't approve of Blue Sights or seers. While she'd never heard of priests or priestesses of the Mother actively hunting or publicly deriding Blue Sights, she knew the casual fear and hatred in their sermons and sanctuaries only fueled the fires of people like the Order of Blindness.

She wandered without any real direction. Despite her discomfort with the abbey itself, she couldn't deny the peace infused in the amarin of the place. It calmed her heart like a comforting weight across her body and freed her mind to wander down paths she'd been avoiding. The stress between her and Di'Nay, her fears about moving to Yemaya, the pain of understanding how little she was accepted in Aggar, and her dread about what could be happening to the kidnapped seer children flickered slowly through her mind. She thought of Taisa and her heart broke. She prayed to the Mother she was still alive but she had a sinking feeling that no Blue Sight would be able to work with the Order and live.

The problems lingered just long enough to be recognized but not long enough for her to solve. She wasn't used to being so conflicted. Her entire life she'd known what she wanted and she'd worked hard to achieve her goals. Now... now she had no idea what she was supposed to be working toward.

The passage became steeper, the hallway leading her higher up the cliffside. As she reached a new level, she felt

Gerome's presence nearby. She found him in a small prayer room, kneeling before a tiny stone figurine of the Mother placed in an alcove in the wall. He prayed silently. Elana leaned against the doorframe and watched him. He was completely entranced, devoted and at peace. His face was serene and a touch of a smile was on his lips. He was thanking the Mother for bringing his brother back.

Elana had never seen anyone so genuinely taken with religious fervor. His expression and the peace in his amarin was so different from his usual callous attitude it felt like an entirely different person. Elana smiled softly. She liked him like this, thoughtful and focused. Despite her reservations, she understood why he would want to dedicate himself to the Mother.

"It's rude to interrupt," Gerome grunted. His amarin shifted from prayer to annoyance.

"I didn't mean to disturb you. I wasn't going to speak."

"You don't need to. I can feel you."

Elana's smile brightened. "You have such good control for an untrained Blue Sight your age."

Gerome leaned back on his heels and sat against the wall. The serenity that had lit his face turned sour. "Do you need something?"

Elana shook her head. "I don't appreciate your tone. The sisters taught you to respect elders, yes?"

He clenched his jaw, but he didn't argue. Elana sat beside him. "You seemed happy with your prayer."

"There's nothing like conversing with the Mother."

"Does she answer you?"

He chuckled softly to himself, a genuine grin flickering across his lips. "In her own way."

"I see why you want to dedicate yourself to her."

He hesitated. "I don't know what I really want yet."

Elana cocked her head, genuinely interested. "Really?"

"They'll never accept my Sight."

"No, they won't."

He frowned at her forwardness. He hadn't been ready to hear it so bluntly. "I don't want to go to the Keep."

"You don't have to as long as you can control yourself."

"What else could I do?"

"You could return to the capitol with Simon. Find a trade or start a family.”

“I’ll never have a family.”

Elana was startled by his immediate and sharp response. “Why not?”

“What if I... pass it on?”

“It’s not a disease.”

“Isn’t it?”

“I told you not to judge yourself by their religious sermons.”

“I’m not.”

“Then what is it?”

He curled his knees close to his chest and wrapped his one arm around his legs. He struggled to find the words to frame his response. “What if my child is a seer? What if they’re discovered? I’m not strong, and I’ll never be able to fight off a mob. I couldn’t even save Simon and he was pretending! This is a curse.”

Elana darkened slightly in sadness, finally understanding. What could she possibly say to him? What would she say to her own son? There was nothing. She didn’t even know how to navigate the hatred in the world and she’d been trained her entire life to move through the darkness. “There are other ways. Ways to keep your family safe.”

“I’m not sending a child to the Keep.”

“It’s not what you think it is.”

He glowered at Elana and she sighed, clenching her teeth to keep from arguing. “You’re insufferable.”

Gerome laughed, his sudden good nature taking Elana by surprise. “Am I?”

“You know you are.”

“Do you think it comes with the Sight?”

Elana couldn’t help but laugh as well. They leaned back against the wall in silence, the energy between them comfortable yet heavy.

“You’re staying here, aren’t you?” Elana questioned.

He considered his answer a moment. “I don’t know where I’m going. But I’m staying with Simon and Simon can’t go with you.”

Elana nodded slowly to herself. “That’s probably for the best.”

“You almost sound sad. You’ll miss me?”

Elana glanced at him and grinned. "Sometimes I like insufferable."

"I've noticed. Di'Nay is particularly stubborn." Elana raised a brow and he responded with an incredulous glance. "I'm not stupid. Your amarin doesn't keep secrets."

"And you don't find us odd?"

"You'd be surprised what I feel from the Sisters sometimes."

Elana's smile faded into something more tender. "You're a fascinating man, Gerome."

He shrugged off her praise and returned his attention to the statue of the Mother on the far wall. He watched her for a long moment, his expression softening in adoration before he looked away, staring at his knees. Finally, he spoke. "I'm sorry for the time I told you Blue Sights are from the cellar. You helped me find Simon. You saved my life. I think the Mother brought us together and I think she's guiding us both."

"I think so, too."

He looked at her, his gaze serious and focused. For the first time, Elana saw him as more of a man than a youth. "You'll save those children."

"You had a vision?"

"A feeling. I was praying for you."

"Thank you, Gerome."

They stood and clasped arms. "If you and Di'Nay make it back to Markessa we should find each other."

"I'd like that. You'll be at the abbey?"

"Probably. I'll leave a message if I go anywhere else."

Elana rested her hand on his. "Go with the guidance of the Mother, Gerome."

"And you, Elana. Thank you."

Elana pulled him into a hug. He tensed a moment in surprise then hugged her back. "And remember the Keep will always take you in," she whispered.

He pulled back, tossing his head back in a dramatic groan. "You aren't my mother, Blue Sight!"

Elana patted his shoulder, her heart warm at his comment. "You should thank the Mother I'm not!"

"Every day for the rest of my life."

"I'll see you in Markessa."

"I look forward to it."

They looked into each other's blue eyes a moment longer, then Elana turned and left. She felt his amarin calm and the rustle of his pants as he knelt again in prayer.

"You're awake!" Di'Nay waited by the door to their room, plates of breakfast in her hands.

"You spoil me," Elana greeted as she took a plate.

They walked back into their room and Di'Nay closed the door with her foot. "I thought we could better plan the next step of our trip with full stomachs."

"Absolutely." Elana picked at the warm cured meat on her plate as she sat on her bed mat. "Where did you have in mind?"

Di'Nay sat beside her, setting her plate aside to grab Taisa's note and a bottle of the seer narcotic from her pouch. "I only know one trading post in Karatan, but it might allow us to follow the supplier of the tranquilizer. We could stop by Astala again and see if there's anything we missed, then take the caravan's route to the jungle."

"Sounds like a good enough place to start."

"There's... another option."

Elana cocked her head to the side at the hesitance in Diana's voice. "Yes?"

"I found something else in Taisa's note. Or on it." She pulled out the envelope that had held Taisa's letter. She pointed out the seal. "Does this look familiar?"

Elana studied the wax print and let out a slow breath. "Tristan."

"It's similar to his seal, yes."

"You think Taisa has a link to the Marshals?"

"I don't know. Maybe. Or perhaps she has some connection to Tristan's family. But I find it hard to believe a Blue Sight infiltrating the Order wouldn't peak Tristan's interest."

Elana's stomach twisted. "I knew he was a traitor."

"I wouldn't jump to conclusions."

"If she was working with the Marshals, then they abandoned her to the Order!"

Di'Nay touched Elana's knee. "Maybe they were trying to save her. To get her safely out of the Order. Or maybe the seal is a coincidence."

Elana brusquely pushed her plate aside. "I hate being at their mercy."

"We aren't. They're a resource. We don't need them. If Tristan proves treacherous, we'll cut ties."

Elana clenched her teeth. "She shouldn't have been involved with the Order."

"She made a choice. A terrible one, but still a choice."

"I want to go to Karatan."

Di'Nay watched her with concern. "Are you sure?"

"I don't care about helping Tristan and I can't save Taisa. I can save seer children. Stopping this narcotic trade will disrupt the Order's operations and if we're lucky we'll get more leads about where the children are held."

Di'Nay nodded. "Then I'll map out a course. We can leave tomorrow."

"Today," Elana insisted. "I don't want to wait anymore."

"I'll prepare for the journey."

PART TWO

SECRETS OF THE SIGHT

KARATAN: MOTHER'S VISION

The jungle of Karatan was humid and fragrant, a mesh of color Elana had never seen before. The roots and foliage on the forest floor was dense and tangled. Slender tendrils of vining plants hung from the branches of tall, twisting trees. It had rained earlier in the morning and now everything seemed to be sweating, droplets of water rolling down the moss-covered tree trunks and dripping from the vines. Flowers bloomed in a riot of color – crimsons and oranges, golds and even sapphire blue.

Elana felt a part of it. She was stripped down to breeches and a cloth vest, her pale skin damp from the humidity in the air. They'd stabled their horses a few days back at a trading town, the wilds of Karatan too treacherous for them. They only carried what they needed, mostly means to purify water, identify food, and ward off poisonous insects. Thankfully the forest was abundant with water, food that could be scavenged, and broad leaves that made decent temporary shelters.

They had moved between trading towns for a tenday looking for any evidence of the seer narcotic they'd found in Dwaramin. Finally, they'd met a merchant who knew the drug and directed them to a cluster of villages where he made his orders. It was as good a chance as any to locate the supplier for the Order of Blindness, but travel was slow and strenuous.

"My hair is growing again," she grunted, pushing her massive tangle of ebony curls over her shoulder. She'd braided it back with multiple ties as the water in the air made the locks swell and curl.

Di'Nay laughed. She cut a path through the jungle with a sharp machete. She wore the same thin pants and cloth vest, her skin dotted with sweat and rain. Her short blonde hair was stuck to her forehead and nape of her neck.

"When it becomes its own creature can I keep it?"

"I might get jealous."

Di'Nay paused and turned, pulling Elana closer with a teasing smile. "You never need to be jealous." They kissed and Elana breathed the earthy scent of her jungle-tinted lover over her tongue. Perhaps it was the heat or the exotic scents. Maybe it was the patterned and intricate layers of amarin rising from the network of roots that built the jungle. Maybe it was just the delicious way Di'Nay felt with smooth, damp skin wet hair. No matter what it was, it left Elana hungry and passionate.

"I could get used to it here."

"Better than the desert?" Di'Nay questioned. "I thought you hated the heat."

"My skin won't burn here. And you don't have to dress as a man."

Di'Nay's grin grew warmer. "I don't pass as a man now?"

Elana studied her slowly. Despite her ropy muscles and broad frame, there was no denying the swells of her curves barely concealed by her wet clothes and low neckline. "No. Will you wear more vests on Yemaya?"

Di'Nay pulled her tighter and they kissed again. "I don't plan on wearing a stitch for the first year on Yemaya."

Elana relaxed into her embrace. They had traveled for so long through dangerous situations, with companions, or through towns where they had to hide their relationship. It was intoxicating just to be themselves.

"We have to keep going," Elana whispered as Di'Nay's mouth dragged lower over her jaw and neck.

"I am."

Elana smirked. "I mean through the jungle. We have to travel while we can."

Di'Nay eased open the buttons on Elana's vest, freeing the swell of her breasts. "We always travel."

Elana gasped involuntarily at the feather-light brush of Di'Nay's lips across her chest. She patted her shoulder. "The next time we stop."

Di'Nay rose back up, the wickedness across her face making her look a decade younger. "Promise?"

Elana kissed her again and took a few steps forward, not

bothering to button her vest. "When have I lied to you?"

Di'Nay skipped like a child and wrapped her arm around Elana's shoulders as they traveled. "I'll pray for another rain storm."

Elana laughed, wild and free, savoring the way her voice could rise and ring through the trees with abandon.

The moss was soft as a mattress under Elana's back. The broad, waxy leaves Di'Nay had gathered to make a roof bounced and trembled under the weight of the cascading rain.

Di'Nay wrapped an arm around her waist and rested her head against her neck. "I got my wish."

"At nightfall," Elana teased.

"Still."

They kissed and Elana watched her lover. Di'Nay's eyes seemed to shine in the night, but Elana knew it was only the warmth of her amarin filling her Sight. She could feel Di'Nay's heartbeat in the lifestone embedded in her wrist. Was this what it could be like off Aggar? Could they be like this all the time?

She closed her eyes and it seemed for a moment she could hear the breaking of a distant ocean. She'd never seen the ocean, but she could imagine it. She felt the moss under her turn to sand and heard the cry of sea birds. She thought she could feel the humming throb of the song of the seers from the Keep, blanketing the world with their peace. She felt Di'Nay's arms and hands, the weight of her across her body. Her heart swelled at her fantasy. It seemed perfect.

"Elana?" Di'Nay sounded concerned, drawing Elana out of her reverie. "Are you all right?"

"Hmm?"

"You seem a bit... distracted."

"Do I?"

Elana jolted in shock as Di'Nay was suddenly leaning over her, her eyes wide in shock. "Elana?!"

"What?"

"You were unconscious."

"I was?"

Di'Nay pulled her to her feet. "Do you feel sick? Dizzy? Were you bitten by something?"

"I don't think so."

Time seemed to shift again and Elana was laying under a different tree and the rain had stopped. She was dressed again. Di'Nay was tipping a bitter tea in a cup past her lips. Elana coughed and sputtered on the liquid and sat up. She trembled with fear. She had no memories of passing out or feeling ill. She was losing time. What was happening?

"Di'Nay?" Her voice trembled with her fear and Di'Nay pulled her into a tight hug. "I moved you. The tea is an anti-venom. Whatever this is I'll fix it."

Elana clung tighter to her, trying to focus, to sense whatever was happening to her coming again. It wasn't until Di'Nay had been holding her for nearly an hour that she let out a breath she hadn't realized she'd been holding.

"Are you still with me?" Di'Nay whispered. "Tell me you're still with me."

"I'm here."

Di'Nay breathed as well, laying a tender kiss on Elana's shoulder. "There must have been something on the air. Something you're allergic to? I didn't see any bites or marks when I moved you."

"I don't know. I don't remember anything."

Di'Nay leaned back on her knees. "Whatever it is, you've stayed with me longer than before."

Elana rolled her shoulders and brushed her fingers through the brush, trying to feel her body and light her nerves. She needed to remind herself she was awake. "You must be right."

"Are you hungry? Thirsty?"

Elana tried to make sense of her thoughts, but all she knew for certain was she was terrified of losing her mind again. "Hold me?"

Di'Nay was instantly at her side, holding her tight. Elana didn't dare close her eyes, but she drew strength from her lover. Di'Nay had to be right. She was bitten by a bug or had a strange reaction to a new pollen or mold. It had to do with her Sight. It was the only way she could imagine having a reaction that corrupted her sense of time and space.

The night slowly turned to dawn and she didn't lose time again. With dawn's new light she let the last of her fear go. She was safe. Di'Nay had saved her from whatever she'd had a reaction to. She told herself over and over again that she would be fine until she almost believed it.

Diana reached out and helped Elana up a narrow, slipper ledge. Elana's grip was firm, but her eyes were dilated and unfocused.

"The terrain is getting rougher," Diana observed. Elana glanced around, taking too long to answer. Diana tensed, waiting to catch her before she fell unconscious again.

"We must be reaching the mountains."

Diana relaxed as she finally spoke. "We should find the Tysaga River. We should be coming across the riverbed tribes any day now."

"Sounds good." Elana's voice was soft and hesitant, as if she were falling asleep.

"Are you all right, Soroi?"

Elana looked up at her with a blank stare, her face pinched as if she didn't quite hear Diana. "I don't know. I feel... not entirely here. Do you hear singing?"

Diana wrapped an arm around Elana's waist, leading her away from the stony cleft they'd just climbed in case she passed out. "What kind of song?"

"Like the seers. They sing when they're happy."

"I don't hear anything. Could it be coming through your Sight?"

"I never hear the seers unless I'm near their quarters."

"Perhaps it's the amarin of the jungle?"

Elana furrowed her brow, her thoughts almost comically written across her features. "That's not how amarin works."

Diana couldn't help but chuckle. "Forgive me, Soroi n'ti Mee, I don't sense amarin."

Elana rested her head against Di'Nay's shoulder. "Can we rest?"

"We don't know what's wrong with you, Elana. We should find a village. Some place with a healer who knows the dangers of the area better than I do."

"I'm so tired."

Diana gasped and tensed as Elana fell unconscious, her knees buckling and falling out beneath her. Diana caught Elana around the waist and lowered her to the ground. She fought to control her breath, to focus through the panic rising her chest. Last night whenever she passed out her eyes were still open, her face frozen as if she were caught in time. This time her eyes were closed and her face was soft as if she were dreaming. What was happening? How was she supposed to help Elana?

She drew a sharp breath and pulled Elana into her arms, carrying her over her shoulder. Her only option was to find a tribe. They were too far away from any trading post to seek help. The anti-venoms and medical supplies in her bag hadn't done anything to help Elana – she needed a medicine woman or someone who knew what could be happening.

She hiked through the jungle, moving infuriatingly slow between the weight of Elana over her shoulder, their supply bags, and the steadily elevating terrain. Her calves screamed from the effort and she grew nauseous in the heat. She had studied the map they'd purchased at the trading post. It was sparse, but it marked the major rivers and landmarks. She should reach the largest river in Karatan, the Tysaga, soon. Most of the tribes open to trade lived around the river.

She pressed forward, forcing one foot in front of the other, losing the energy to do anything but walk and whisper prayers to any deities that might listen to find help.

She felt her heart pound faster as she heard water flowing near evening. She was so taken with the sound she stumbled, Elana shifting from her shoulder sending them both tumbling to the ground. Diana pushed herself up on her hands, crawling toward Elana sprawled across the ground. Elana sighed and shifted as if deep in sleep. Diana caressed her face. "Elana? Elana wake up." Her eyes fluttered for a moment, opening for a second, but then closed again. "Elana!"

She was unconscious again. Diana, exhausted and terrified, rested her head against Elana's waist, fighting back tears. She had to keep going. She couldn't fall apart now.

She pulled Elana back over her shoulder and continued forward. After half an hour, the trees thinned and opened to a massive river. It seemed to stretch on like an ocean, the trees on the opposite side tiny in the distance. Diana mental went over the map, trying to place where they might be. It had to be a wider expanse of the river, perhaps even a crossing point where a smaller river met the Tysaga.

Elana shifted on her shoulder and Diana tightened her grip. "Elana?"

Before she could answer, there was rustling in the trees and brush. Diana turned as a group of men and women stepped out of the trees. They carried swords and knives, leveling their blades calmly at her. Pale blue tattoos decorated their skin, creating a complex weaving of ruins and symbols. They wore cloth pants, woven shirts, and arm guards. A few of the smaller members sported curved metal hooks on their wrists and ankles – tools for climbing trees.

"You're on our land, Terran," A man with long, dark hair stepped forward. He was slender and tall, his face calm but his eyes wary.

"I'm sorry. I'm looking for a healer," Diana answered slowly, trying to convey calm. "My companion is sick."

"Why would you be traveling this far into the jungle? This isn't your home," the man questioned.

Diana balanced Elana and reached into her pocket for a smooth wooden coin she'd purchased at a jungle trading post. "We were looking to trade. I was told this token would allow safe passage."

The man took the coin, examining it with a curved arched brow. "We're open to trade with outsiders." He handed back the coin. "Surrender your weapons."

Diana didn't think twice. She handed over her machete and Elana's crossbow. "My name is Diana and this is Elana. What's your name, Tad?"

A female scout studied their bags and nodded. Their leader nodded. "I'm Nanowa. Come. I'll take you to a healer."

No one offered to help carry Elana, but Diana wasn't sure she'd have given her up. With renewed hope, Diana felt some of her strength return and she followed them further up the river.

"You'll forgive us for being so careful with strangers. Many kinds of people come through Karatan. Most don't have the best of intentions," Nanowa called back as they traveled.

Diana knew a leading question when she heard one, but she had little energy for playing political games. "We're seeking something very specific. Once we find someone willing to trade for it, we'll leave."

"If you cause no trouble, you won't get any in return."

"I assure you trouble is the last thing we want."

Nanowa led the party to the mouth of the river to a small

village. The homes were mostly wood and moss, built around the trees. Most were on higher ground of propped up by cylindrical pegs to keep the home safe when the river swelled. Gardens dotted every homestead and Diana could see farms in the distance. A small port lined with fishing boats extended into the Tysaga and people traded along the bank for meat and essentials. For its size, Nanowa's tribe seemed to be thriving.

Many in the scouting party dispersed upon reaching town, leaving only Nanowa and three other men. Diana eyed the scouts who seemed bent on protecting Nanowa. Was he some kind of chieftain or was it simply a matter of safety in numbers with strangers?

Nanowa knocked on a door painted pale blue near the center of town. Herbs drying on twine hung from the porch roof like windchimes. A blue hand print marked with symbols had been painted over the door.

"Mahne, we need your aide," Nanowa called.

An elderly woman, her skin tinted darker with age, opened the door. She wiped her hands on a tattered apron as she examined the crowd, her eyes instantly falling on Diana and Elana. She seemed surprised for a moment, but it quickly disappeared, replaced with a firm, no-nonsense expression. "What happened?"

"She keeps falling unconscious. I can't wake her," Diana reported.

Mahne waved them inside and Diana followed. Nanowa took up the rear, closing the door behind them. Diana noticed the three scouts stayed on the porch, waiting.

"Was she bitten by anything? Ate anything she didn't recognize?"

Diana helped ease Elana onto Mahne's table in the middle of the room. She began inspecting her body for marks or discoloration. "I don't think so. We've been careful about what we ate and I couldn't find a bite on her. When she *is* awake, she doesn't feel unusual. If anything, she doesn't notice falling unconscious."

"Does she have allergies?"

Diana was taken aback. She'd never asked. "I don't think so."

Mahne looked up at Nanowa. "Fetch my herbs."

"Yes, Elder."

Diana marveled for a moment at a man with power instantly doing as he was told on Aggar. While respect for the elderly was common in the Ramains, that respect didn't always apply across gender. For a moment, she felt she was with the witches n'Shae on Yemaya again. For all their natural, peaceful, and healing ways, they could be sharp and direct when at their work. Speed and accuracy were more important than manners when saving a life.

Nanowa returned with a satchel. Mahne worked smoothly, barely looking at her hands as she mixed and ground an assembly of elements into a fine powder. She mixed it with water and Diana helped her give it to Elana. After nearly an hour with no change, Mahne crossed her arms over her chest, her brow furrowed.

"Nanowa, leave us alone for a moment?"

"Mahne, they're strangers," he reminded her.

"You have their weapons?"

"Yes."

"Then they are only my patients for now."

Nanowa nodded sharply. "Yes, Elder." He turned to Diana. "I'll be by the docks if you finish before nightfall. We can talk of trade."

"Thank you," Diana commented absently, her attention still on Elana. She clung to every breath and twitch of her muscles. Nanowa left, taking his scouts with him.

Mahne turned to Diana once they were gone, her arms crossed tight over her chest. "Is she a seer?"

Diana nearly choked in surprise. "No, Min."

Mahne gave her an incredulous look, then reached down and opened Elana's eyelid. "As I thought." She started mixing something new from her bag. "You won't want to stay here long."

Diana tensed. "She's no harm to anyone. She can hide her eyes."

"That may be so, but if she was ever found out –"

"We know how to deal with prejudice, Min," Diana interrupted.

Mahne gave her a withering glance at her disrespect. "We do not hate the Mother's Chosen here. Not like the northerners. That doesn't mean there won't be consequences if she's discovered. Blue Sights and Seers are sacred and we deal with out sacred in ways you may not like."

She finished a poultice and attempted to put it over Elana's eyes. Diana stopped her, resting her own hand over Elana's eyes, suddenly concerned. "What's wrong with her?"

Mahne glanced at Diana's exposed wrist, noticing the lifestone in it. She pulled back, her sharpness losing its edge. "I see. You're bonded with her. She's from the Keep? A Shadow?"

"You know of the Keep?"

"We all do, but I grew up in the Ramains. My family returned to Karatan when I was a youth. I understand more than most here, and Mother bless you that I do or I already would have summoned Nanowa."

"What's stopping you?" Diana countered.

"You are not tribe. I don't believe in the practice of kidnapping our sacred." She touched Diana's hand, gently trying to move it away. "Karatan is the center of life on Aggar. There are pollens and serums here that can greatly affect a Blue Sight. She's having a reaction. Her Sight is overwhelmed. I need to draw the allergens from her."

Diana hesitated, but removed her hand. Mahne laid the poultice over Elana's eyes and stepped back. "How long will it take?"

"An hour or two. You said she keeps waking up?"

"Yes. This is the longest she's been unconscious."

"Then her allergy isn't serious. She'll have to apply a poultice every night before sleeping as long as she's in the jungle, but I can give you the ingredients."

"Thank you, Min."

"Elder. Min is a title given by Ramains men who must associate gender with everything."

Diana smiled softly. Mahne reminded her of home. "Elder, then."

"What are you doing in Karatan?"

"We're seeking a serum, a good we've been told can be purchased in the jungle." Diana drew out a small bottle of the seer narcotic.

Mahne's eyes grew wide. "No one would sell this."

"We found it at a market in the desert and again at a trading post just outside Karatan. It seems rare, but it is being peddled."

Mahne shook her head. "This is holy here. You won't find a

merchant willing to trade for it in our village. It may be confiscated if you show it to anyone." She studied the bottle closer and frowned. "This is a novice's work. Cloudy. It won't be any good for visions."

"Visions?"

"What did you think it was used for?"

"It's being used as a tranquilizer to subdue seers."

Mahne's skin grew darker in horror. "Why would you want such a thing?"

"We're trying to keep it from continuing to be sold," Diana answered truthfully. "To cut off its supply."

"If there's illegal trade of our sacred goods being moved out of Karatan and used for ill, the tribes will no doubt want to stop it themselves."

"What if there are forces in other tribes heading up the sales?"

"Then there would be war."

"Is it so serious, Elder?"

"Is the destruction of our most sacred beliefs serious? The desecration of our holy arts? The mistreatment of our most holy children?" She spoke between grit teeth, ever muscle tense and her eyes aflame. "I know how they treat the sacred ones in the north. It's disgusting. The Mother weeps. I'll not have our ways used to further that abuse."

Elana gasped and shifted, moving slowly as if it were difficult. She reached toward her face and Mahne rested a hand on her arm "Relax, child. You're healing." She turned to Diana. "So quickly. She must be very strong." Di'Nay didn't know if it was Elana's strength or her Blue Sight responding to the intensity of Mahne's rage.

"Di'Nay?" Elana called.

Diana gripped her hand, her heart pounding with joy at hearing her voice again. "I'm here, Elana. Rest. It was a reaction to the jungle. You're going to be fine. I found help."

Elana relaxed, but didn't release Diana's hand. Mahne started reorganizing her herb satchel and cleaning her mixing bowls. "Once she's awake, there's a small inn up the road. They'll take your gold."

"Thank you, Elder," Diana remarked. She drew five gold from her pocket and offered them to her. Mahne seemed shocked at the offering, but she accepted it, knowing part was payment for her silence.

Mahne wrote a recipe for the poultice on a piece of paper and tied together a large bundle of the herbs. Diana took them gratefully. "If she has trouble again, come to me. I see to anyone in need, stranger or not."

Diana squeezed Elana's hand and Elana squeezed it in return. "Thank you."

It was nearly nightfall by the time Elana was strong enough to walk on her own. The poultice had left her skin olive-colored and warm, but she was more lucid than she'd been since her first spell. She had enough control over her abilities to shift her eyes from blue to gray before the poultice was removed, despite hearing that Mahne already knew she was a Blue Sight. Elana didn't know how to feel about her abilities being known in such a foreign setting, but Di'Nay seemed unconcerned.

"I can walk on my own," Elana remarked as they traveled away from the inn Mahne had recommended. It seemed the innkeeper had already been informed of their arrival. It felt good to have a sturdy shelter and a bed again.

"You've told me that right before passing out," Di'Nay teased, though there was a serious edge in her voice that betrayed her fear. She hovered like a parent, hyper-focused. She twitched every time Elana hesitated or stumbled over uneven ground.

Di'Nay led her to the village docks where merchants were just beginning to pack away their wares for the night.

"She's awake!" A middle-aged man with his long dark hair braided down his back greeted Di'Nay.

Elana studied him, his amarin a study in compartmentalized emotion. He was cheerful, sincere, and excited to see them, but at the same time he was wary and watched them closely. She knew if they so much as moved with seemingly ill intent his response would be swift.

"And doing well," Di'Nay assured him. "Elana, this is Nanowa. He brought us here."

Elana shook his hand. "Thank you. I owe you a great debt."

Nanowa waved his hand. "We don't abandon guests with good intentions. The Mother demands hospitality to strangers, and I am a very hospitable host."

"You are indeed," Di'Nay agreed. "Are we still able to trade?"

Nanowa's face fell. "I'm afraid most merchants have already closed for the night. You can visit in the morning. Do you know your way around the village yet?"

Di'Nay was less disappointed then Elana had expected. "We've only just come from Mahne's and our lodgings."

"Would you allow me the pleasure of showing you around, then? It will be easier for you to find what you need if you know your surroundings."

Di'Nay glanced at Elana and Elana nodded. "We'd be very grateful, Tad."

Nanowa led them through the main square with the energy of a much younger man. He never stopped smiling. His energy was infectious and inviting and he genuinely took pride in his village. Elana, however, couldn't help but constantly notice the machete at his waist.

"This is where our elders meet for meals and discussion," he announced, resting his hand on a tall wooden post to a long, rectangular building. "We are led by a council, but all are invited to speak, even strangers. If you need anything I can't give, you can petition them."

"Such an open form of government," Di'Nay complimented.

"We won't be staying that long," Elana insisted.

Nanowa shrugged. "There's nothing saying you won't come back eventually."

Elana tightened her jaw. There was nothing malicious in his amarin. What had her so on edge?

"I live here with my family. I'm the head scout and well respected. You are considered my guests. If you have need of anything I can provide, I'll help you obtain it."

"Thank you, Tad," Di'Nay complimented. "Or do you prefer some other honorific?"

"Tad is fine," he stated. "If it's good enough for the men of the north, it's good enough for me."

He continued through the village, pointing out places of interest. The market by the docks specialized in meats and basic goods, but there were others – shops that specialized in fresh produce from the farms, others that cared for animals and sold medicines and poultices, and still more focused on textiles and cloth. She spotted many items for sale that she assumed were made by other tribes, but there were more northern goods sprinkled in as well. It was clear Nanowa's village had grown primarily due to trade. Elana wondered how many northern merchants passed through and if they'd been attracted by Nanowa's somewhat naïve interest in people from the north.

"Here's our temple to the Mother. We've been blessed with the presence of a Sacred One. No doubt she's the reason for our recent good fortune."

Elana froze. She could hear the singing of the seers again, but this time there was no mistaking its source. "You have a seer here?"

Nanowa nodded proudly and raised his arms high to indicate the temple. It was a large stone dome – the only stone building in the village. A permanent shrine to the Mother. It was surrounded by a latticed wooden gate and seemed devoid of windows. The stone temple as well as the gate were adorned with silks and painted runes and symbols. Gifts and wishes written on paper had been laid like offerings around and on the gate.

"A young one! We found her abandoned in the jungle like a gift from the Mother. Her treatment was horrific. She must have blessed us for taking her in. Since her coming, the weather has been good, the crops plentiful, and the catch bounteous."

"You keep her in there?"

Nanowa's smile faltered at Elana's tone. "We keep her as the Mother commands. She is an emissary of our Goddess. She's clothed with the finest silks, fed from our best crops. She has attendants who care for her. She is in constant communion with the Mother. She wants for nothing and in return she blesses us."

"She didn't mean to insult your care," Di'Nay quickly amended. "Things are done differently in the Ramains."

"Ah yes. Mahne has told me. Such vulgarity," he huffed. "We don't treat our Sacred that way."

Elana bit back everything she wanted to say. It wasn't wise to insult their host when there was already such good will between them, but she was steadily becoming less and less willing to watch her brothers and sisters in the Sight suffer because of outside forces. Every seer suffered when alone. She would find some way to reunite this seer child with the others at the Keep.

As if sensing her sudden shift in mood, Di'Nay rested a

hand on Elana's shoulder. "We thank you for the tour, Tad. I'm sure your family needs you and Elana needs rest."

They gripped arms and Nanowa nodded. "It was a pleasure to show you my village. Remember to seek me out if you have any need."

"We will," Di'Nay promised. Nanowa took his leave, jogging back toward his house. Elana's eyes returned to the temple.

"They're keeping her prisoner."

"Mahne told me seers are treated well here, like gods and goddesses on earth," Di'Nay attempted to calm her. "They might not know how they're hurting her. Their intentions are good."

"I don't care about their intentions," Elana commented. "I don't care about anything having to do with them. I care about that child. I care that they must be using the drug to keep her subdued. She could be trapped in her own mind."

"Mahne said the drug we have is clouded. That the real tranquilizer is meant for visions."

"A prison is a prison even if it's wrapped in silk. And drugging is still paralyzing her even if it frees her mind."

"What do you want to do? They'll fight us if we try to take her outright."

Elana considered. "Let's go back to the inn. I need time to think."

Elana didn't sleep even after Di'Nay finally nodded off into dreams. With Elana seemingly healthy again, Di'Nay felt her exhaustion more keenly and Elana prayed she slept long. She knew they would both need their strength soon.

As the two moons of Aggar hung high in the sky, she made up her mind. As a Shadow of the Keep, she was trained to move unseen in the darkness. The trees and rough terrain of the jungle created so many pools of darkness she would be invisible.

She drew on her dark blue cloak, raising the hood high, and crept out of the building. There were a few watches set by the markets, but the deeper parts of the village seemed unguarded. The temple housing the seer was an inky mound against the backdrop of the forest. As she approached, she spotted a glint of light and realized there was a window made of real glass set into the roof of the dome.

For all her anger at anyone keeping a seer separated from

their hive, she was happy to see the temple was so suited for a seer's needs. It wasn't underground, but it was solid and probably let in little sound from the outside world. The light was natural and of Aggar and was probably soothing at night if the seer was at all aware of her surroundings. The nature of the structure might unintentionally have been the only reason the seer was still in such good health.

Elana crept forward, weaving around the homes staying close to the darkest shadows. When she reached the temple, she watched it for a long moment, hidden in the brush across the path from the front door. Nanowa had said the seer had attendants. Elana waited, wondering if they ever left the temple. After an hour, a young woman left, walking slowly back to the village. It was a good enough sign for Elana – one less person to avoid and perhaps only minutes until a new attendant returned.

She slipped out into the open and through the gate. The narrow courtyards created in the spaces between the square gate and rounded dome were full of blooming wildflowers, their fragrance a blend of sweet and earthy scents. For a moment Elana felt lightheaded and closed her eyes, drawing strength. It would make sense a building holding a seer would grow plants that could subdue them, and seers and Blue Sights weren't so different in their abilities.

She slowly opened the front door, feeling with her Sight for any sign of life. The temple was a single massive room. A pool of water lined with tile and stone stood at the center, a fountain in the middle creating the constant, soothing sound of running water. The walls were decorated with images of the universe and the Mother, crystals embedded in the designs seemed to glow like stars in the moonlight streaming through the glass window at the dome's peak. The floors were covered in soft carpets.

Elana felt two more women sleeping along the edges of the dome, shielded by privacy screens. The seer slept on a massive, circular bed at the far end of the dome. The bed was covered in hanging swaths of pure white netting – keeping all dangerous insects at bay while giving the appearance that the seer child was sleeping in a cloud.

Elana removed her shoes, as much out of respect for the grandeur of the place as a way to hide her footprints on the carpets. She tucked her boots inside a potted plant and padded toward the seer, using her Sight to ease the caretakers into a deeper sleep.

The child didn't sense her as she approached. She drew back the curtains around her bed and relaxed for a moment. The child seemed to be in good health – clean, her hair brushed and tied back in a braid. Her skin was rosy. Her cheeks plump. She was young, perhaps four tenmoons. It didn't change Elana's opinion about the danger of her surroundings, but she was relieved to see no signs of abuse.

She sat on the edge of the bed, watching her, trying to make sense of her amarin. She closed her eyes, focusing more intensely. The seer child was obviously drugged, so deep in her dreams and visions Elana couldn't get a firm grasp on her physical feelings. She felt no distress, as if the child's mind was far away, out of her body. The more she tried, however, the louder the singing of the seers from the Keep seemed to grow in her mind.

She frowned. The seers in the Keep were so far away, there was no reason she should be hearing them. Was it the sound of the seers searching for their own? The child wasn't wearing any talisman from the Order of Blindness, she should be visible to the hive. The seers called to their own, and existed in such great numbers at the Keep that distance meant nothing. As a force, they should see her.

Elana tried to think of the last time a seer arrived from Karatan. It was rare. She'd never given much thought to it. Were there less seers in the far south or was it something else?

Elana's stomach tightened as the seer stirred. She was starting to wake, no doubt at the presence of another with the Sight. Elana braced herself for a scream or a cry – the chaos of a seer disconnected from her people – but she was silent. She opened her eyes and turned to look at Elana. Her pupils were wide, so dilated they looked black. She was still under the influence of the narcotic. Elana didn't know if she could even see her. The singing grew louder and a peace so powerful it threatened to put Elana asleep emanated from her.

In an instant Elana realized what was happening. The narcotic, in its purest form, didn't just allow visions. It allowed the seer to reach beyond their limitations, to connect with the network of seers in Aggar. She wasn't in chaos. She wasn't suffering. To her, she was already in the Keep, wrapped in the loving arms of the other seers.

The seers of the keep knew no distance. They didn't tell the Keep of many seers in Karatan because their spirits were already with them.

Elana furrowed her brow, suddenly at a loss for what to do. The seers in the wild jungles of Karatan were safer than the ones in the Ramains. She was cared for. She seemed happy. Was it wise to remove her and force on her a perilous journey just to move her physical form where her mind already was?

She felt someone approach the temple from the outside and slipped away from the seer, hiding in the darkness created by two potted trees. Another young woman removed her shoes and walked behind a privacy screen, laying down to rest like the others. She didn't sense anything amiss in the temple. Elana turned and saw the seer child still watching her, her eyes wide and her head turned to spy her in the shadows. IF she stayed too long, there would be no hiding.

Elana waited until she felt the new woman fall asleep and she slipped back outside, putting her boots on once she was outside the fence. She sat in the darkness for a long moment, thinking. She had never seen anything like this. A way of keeping seers well outside the Keep? She hadn't thought it was possible. The idea unnerved her. There was so much, in the grand scheme of Aggar, that she didn't know.

As the sky grew lighter as dawn approached, she made her way back to the inn, slipping inside her room as she felt the innkeeper rise. Di'Nay had never even felt her leave. She undressed and slipped back into bed, her mind still spinning so fast she couldn't even close her eyes to rest. Were there other ways? Were there other institutions, far from the Keep, that were good for seers and Blue Sights?

The thought was comforting an unsettling all at once. Could she really trust these other ways? Was it terrible of her to doubt a seemingly kind culture just for being different? She liked the thought of more peace outside the Ramains and Southern Desert, but she didn't want to get her hopes up.

The thoughts continued to plague her long after the sun rose and Di'Nay started shifting as she woke. She drew a deep breath and tried to prepare herself for a new day.

Diana knew Elana hadn't slept. She didn't try to hide it. Her eyes were wide open and her breathing even. Diana blinked the sleep from her eyes.

"How are you? Are you feeling all right?" She kissed Elana's shoulder.

Elana nodded. "I'm fine. The poultice seemed to work."

"Just couldn't sleep?"

"I went to the temple to see the seer."

Diana felt a stab of shock. "You went inside?"

"I wasn't discovered."

"Elana! What if you passed out again? What if you were discovered? I couldn't have helped you!" Diana's head spun with everything that could have gone wrong. It stirred every fear she felt when Elana disappeared, taking action without talking with her. "We need to coordinate these plans, Elana. I can be helpful. You stopped me from leaving you to keep you safe when we first traveled together. Why are you doing it to me now?"

Elana sat up, the emotions on her face neither anger nor apology. "I needed to know how she was being treated. I needed to make sure she was safe. I wanted you to be rested in case we had to flee or I had a relapse. I wasn't leaving you behind. I needed to move invisibly."

Diana sighed. "You still need to tell me when you're going away. I can help you. We're a team."

Elana studied her and Diana felt her reading her amarin. Instead of trying to hide, she hoped Elana felt her helplessness, her fear. They were bonded. They were in love. They were also equally stubborn, independent, and used to solving their own problems. They had to learn to communicate better or they wouldn't survive.

"I'm sorry." Elana sounded sincere. "I was trying to take care of you."

"I just want you to stay safe."

Diana watched her, a cascade of emotion crossing her face before she looked away. She was so used to hiding. She'd been raised to keep everything she felt muted and hidden and for good reason – any loss of control or burst of anger could hurt the people around her.

Diana reached out and touched her hand. "I'm not just anyone, Elana."

"I know."

Diana wished once more that she had the Sight. Elana smiled and faced her. "You read me better than anyone else. You don't need the Sight."

Diana narrowed her eyes. "Every now and then I stop believing you can't read minds."

"I don't need to read your mind to recognize that emotion." She shifted, holding Diana's hand back. "I do need you. I need your diplomacy and charisma. I need your strength. I need your loyalty."

"We're a good match," Diana agreed. "I won't fight you or try to control you. I'm not a Ramains husband. I just want to know where you are in case I need to find you or defend you."

Elana hesitated. "I never thought of that."

"That I could protect you?"

She shook her head. "No. That I was thinking of you like a husband."

Diana grinned. "It's a common problem for women who love Amazons. I look masculine. I'm not taken with the darker sides society gives masculinity."

Elana kissed her, taking Diana by surprised. She laughed under Elana's lips. "I said something right, Soroi?"

Elana held her tight. "You did."

Diana kissed her back. "Tell me what you learned last night. Anything I should know?"

Diana listened as Elana explained her adventure the night before.

"How is she connected to the Keep?"

"I'm not sure, but she is. I can only guess the narcotic calms her and frees her conscious enough that she can hear them. Whatever the reason, she's not upset. She feels connected to the others."

"Well that's fantastic, isn't it? She's at peace."

"I don't know. I don't trust it. No one but the Keep takes care of seers."

"We're a long way from the Ramains and the Keep. There could be other sanctuaries for them."

Elana shook her head, deep in thought. "I won't believe anything until I've studied their drug. I need to know if it's dangerous."

"Mahne said no one will sell it to us. Whoever is supplying

the Order is making a knock off without the blessing of a tribe."

"Then we need to get some without buying it."

Diana raised a brow. "You want to steal some?"

"I need enough to study. What we have won't work. I had vivid dreams on the Order's drug. The pure one given to the seer is allowing her soul to leave her body and travel across countries."

"Maybe the purer variety is safer."

"Maybe it's more dangerous. I need to know for sure if we're thinking of leaving a seer child outside of the Keep."

Diana pursed her lips. Elana had a point, but they needed to be careful. "We should try diplomacy first. I don't want to be caught stealing something sacred."

"We could be honest. I could tell them I'm from the Keep."

Diana shook her head. "We can't let them know who you are."

Elana narrowed her eyes. "Why?"

"Mahne was very clear when you were unconscious. You would be in danger if they knew you were a Blue Sight."

"And that doesn't make you concerned for the seer's safety?"

"I *am* concerned. I just want to make sure we don't do anything rash. We're two people in a foreign land. We don't know the terrain. The last thing we need is an angry tribe chasing us down and a reputation for desecrating another people's holy sites."

Elana sighed, the burst of air heavy and aggressive but Diana could see a dozen plans and ideas spinning through her mind. "You're right."

"Let's talk to Nanowa. He seems friendly enough."

Elana shook her head. "He's waiting for us to do something wrong. If we ask about the tranquilizer he'll be suspicious."

"Mahne?"

"You said she wouldn't help us."

Diana held her chin in her hands. "Perhaps I should go to the market and ask a few leading questions. Just because Mahne thinks no one will deal with us doesn't mean there isn't someone open to the idea."

"If it doesn't work I'll return to the temple tonight and try to get a vial."

Diana's stomach clenched at the thought. "I'll get you the tranquilizer."

"We can get it together."

Diana smiled. "Let's go."

The medicinal market was fairly empty when Elana and Diana arrived. They slowly strolled along the short rows of carts and stands. There were drying herbs, tinctures, and oils. They were basic – Diana could identify most of them and Elana could identify the rest.

"It could be that Mahne makes it," Elana muttered as they walked away from a cart selling woven gauze. "These are rudimentary at best."

"She didn't seem like she made it," Diana remarked. "She studied it like a teacher."

"Then perhaps it's made in the temple?"

"It seems more likely," Diana responded. She pursed her lips. "It complicates things."

"I broke in once," Elana reminded her.

"I don't want you to turn into a thief," Diana countered.

"To save a life?"

"You're looking for something specific, Mins?"

Diana turned as a middle-aged woman, her hair tied back in a bun and a worn apron around her waist, walked toward them. "My wares here are rudimentary, but I have more," she paused, considering her words, "...specialized concoctions for sale, as well as the knowledge to make most anything you could be looking for."

Diana cocked her head slightly, the woman's intention clear. Would the seer tranquilizer count as a drug? "Perhaps you can help."

Diana and Elana followed the woman back to her stall. Diana studied her wares more closely. She seemed to sell basic herbs and cold remedies, but she started to notice other paraphernalia – trays designed for powdered drugs and pipes were mixed within her other wares.

"I'm not sure you can help us," Diana stated, casting a lead.

"I assure you, I'm very talented. And discreet."

Diana glanced at Elana. She studied the woman for a long moment, then nodded slightly. She would follow Diana's lead.

"In honesty, Elder, I don't know exactly what I'm looking for. I was sent by a dealer of exotic delights to search for a potion he'd run across during his travels. Perhaps you could identify it for us?" Diana hoped her seeming naivete would protect her if she offended the dealer.

"I'll do my best."

Diana drew out the seer narcotic and pressed the small, glass bottle into the woman's hand. She studied it for a long time and her face fell. Elana tensed. Diana grit her teeth. They'd made a wrong choice."

"Where did you get this again?"

Diana forced a smile. "From a dealer. I apologize for not having more information. He was very vague. Do you recognize it?"

"This is holy, not a drug," the woman argued. "You shouldn't have it, let alone be trying to peddle it."

Diana feigned shock. "I'm sorry, Min, I had no idea."

"Didn't you?"

"You doubt me?"

"Mins!" Diana and Elana turned as Nanowa ran toward them. Diana hid a grimace. "You look well. How goes your trading?"

Diana shook his hand, forcing a smile. "Well, Tad."

"Nanowa, they're attempting to buy Mother's Vision!" The woman pressed the bottle into Nanowa's hand.

Nanowa's expression faded, growing darker. "You come to my village to buy what belongs in a temple?"

"I assure you, we didn't know," Diana countered. "We're middlemen, nothing more."

"Middlemen or mercenaries? No one sells Mother's Vision, but there are plenty who have killed for it."

"We're not mercenaries I assure you," Diana replied. "We didn't even know what this was."

"Forgive me if I don't believe you. Mother's Vision is rare and dear. It's hard for me to believe anyone would carry it without knowing what it is."

"If we've offended you, we can take our leave," Diana offered. "We don't want to overstay our welcome."

"I'm afraid that won't be possible," Nanowa countered. "Either you come with ill intentions or you have a master who does. Either way, I'm afraid I must keep you here until the truth comes to light."

"You're going to imprison us?" Diana questioned, taking a

step back. She was suddenly very aware of her lack of weapons.

Despite Nanowa's calm demeanor, his eyes became increasingly darker. His shoulders squared, his hand went to the hilt of his machete. Diana saw what Elana had seen in him – a cold certainty, a dangerous foe hidden by a friendly face. "Would you rather I send a potential threat back out into the wilds where they can plot a new attack or gather with more Terrans and Desertmen?"

"How are we supposed to defend ourselves? What proof can we offer?"

"Tell me your master and we'll write to him for proof."

"And if we refuse?"

Nanowa drew his sword. "Then I will have no choice but to defend my people."

"Stop." Diana's breath caught in her throat as Elana spoke. "Don't fault Di'Nay. She was lying for a reason."

Nanowa turned to her, but his body and sword continued to face Diana. "Why would she lie, Min?"

Diana closed her eyes as she knew what Elana would do before she did it. Nanowa gasped as Elana revealed her blue eyes. He instantly fell to the ground in a bow, as did the woman in the stall.

"Forgive me! I didn't realize you were one of the Sacred Ones!"

"Di'Nay is my protector," Elana announced. "She was trying to help me."

"Of course, of course. If we had known we would have offered you help sooner," Nanowa promised. "We always take care of our Sacred."

"I'm not yours," Elana countered.

Nanowa looked up at her. "Of course you are. You've come to us. You shouldn't be wandering the world so meanly. You should have a temple. You should be connected to the Mother. It's... blasphemous for you to be among us like a common human. The lack of respect must have deadened your mind. It's divine intervention that you've come to us."

Elana took a step closer to Diana. "If I'm divine, then I'm allowed to make my own choices."

Nanowa stood. "You're mistaken." Diana heard a shift behind her and turned, but she was too late. A sharp blow to the back of her head by the woman in the stall made her ears ring and her mind numb. She tried to reach out for Elana, but another blow sent her sprawling on the ground. She fell unconscious as Elana cried out in shock and Nanowa stepped closer. "Your only choice is to serve the Mother."

Elana stood on a tall, rocky cliff staring down at the ocean waves crashing below her. Sea spray leapt up into the air, its mist reaching Elana's face and clinging to her hair. She smelled salt and brine, the scent clinging to her long wool dress and unbound curls. A wind tugged at her, rippling the hem of her dress and brushing past her cheeks. She could see a storm coming in the distance. The clouds were dark and full. Storms weren't unusual, but this one looked particularly strong.

It was cold, but she didn't want to move. Elana had never seen the ocean before. She'd heard stories and seen drawings, but the mountains and forests had always been her home. She had imagined it, but she hadn't realized how the amarin of Aggar surged through it.

The water itself seemed a living thing – teeming with life, from plankton and microbial life to massive whales and sea serpents. But even more, the water, which didn't carry amarin on the mainland, seemed infused with the soul of the planet herself. It sang in Elana's ears. It seemed to glow with a soft, white light which offset the slate gray of the sky and the stony cliffside.

Why had she never been here? How could she have not felt it always? What was calling her to it now?

She glanced down and saw a small child standing beside her. She was very pale, her hair a platinum blonde, her dress white and soft. She seemed made of clouds or sea foam, her golden eyes watching the horizon. She didn't move or speak. Her face was devoid of expression. Elana could feel her amarin, but it was steady and calm, giving her no clues as to her personality or feelings.

"Elana!"

Elana turned as Di'Nay called to her. When she looked back, the child was gone. "Here!"

Di'Nay jogged toward her, clapping her gloved hands together to ward off the cold. She was dressed simply – pants and a loose shirt, her hair soft and a bit wild from a day's work. "What does the sea say today?”

Elana smiled and stared back out at the horizon. “Nothing for me. But I can't stop listening.”

Di'Nay wrapped her arms around Elana's waist, resting her chin on her shoulder. “Can you stop long enough for dinner? The market closed early for the storm.”

Elana imagined a long night by the fire, the oncoming storm pounding at the windows and roof, the wind swirling around the house, sounding like the eye of a tornado. “I love storms.”

“I know.”

Elana took Di'Nay's hand and they walked together away from the cliffside back toward town. Di'Nay waved at the farmers they passed as they moved their animals in for the night. As one of the masters of the port, Di'Nay worked all day managing trade on and off the island. She knew every merchant, craftsman, and farmer on the island and many of them were regular guests at their dinner table.

Elana, for the most part, was silent. She felt a calm joy at holding Di'Nay's hand in public. She didn't hide her blue eyes and people still waved at her, children still approached her. She was a teacher and no parents complained.

“You ready for the storm?” A farmer in a straw hat herding sheep with a shaggy dog called to Di'Nay. “Looks like it might cause some damage.”

“We'll always rebuild,” Di'Nay responded, unconcerned as always. “Last storm was supposed to last for days and it didn't even hit us.”

“The whims of the Mother,” the farmer agreed. “You two need anything and my wife and I will take you in. Always a warm meal and bed ready for you.”

“Thank you, Tad. And the same to you.”

The farmer tipped his hat and continued herding. Elana squeezed Di'Nay's hand, just happy to exist in that moment. Di'Nay squeezed back and smiled. She knew what Elana was thinking. She always did these days.

The wind started to pick up enough to whip Di'Nay's short hair around her face by the time they reached their house. It was small, but built from sturdy stone and tile. It was made to last, already ancient when they moved in. A single fireplace was enough to warm the structure. It was decorated simply but comfortably.

Di'Nay often returned home with small gifts and luxuries for Elana – feather quilts, silk curtains, fine rugs. They didn't appear particularly wealthy, but they were comfortable and Elana knew how privileged they were to have what they did.

Di'Nay stood by the kitchen window, looking out at Elana's garden. "I hope the rain doesn't drown the new flower beds."

"If it does, we'll rebuild," Elana remarked, mimicking Di'Nay's enthusiasm from before as she set about starting a fire.

Di'Nay laughed. "That we will." She picked at a loaf of bread and moved to join Elana. "Though truth be told I don't think this storm will be the beast everyone fears."

"It won't," Elana commented. "I can feel it on the ocean. It looks more vicious than it is."

"Good. I don't fancy having to make repairs at the harbor again."

A fire crackled along the kindling, licking at the dried wood. Its still-delicate heat licked at Elana's cheeks. She felt the mist from the ocean drying against her skin, leaving behind only the faintest hint of salt.

They sat together for a long moment, letting the stresses of the day slide from their shoulders until there was only the two of them again. Elana dropped back from her knees to sit on the ground, propping herself up with her hands. The fire grew stronger. She watched as Di'Nay's complexion warmed to a rosy red and relished how much her lover adored the warmth.

"This place is perfect for us," Elana observed, not for the first time.

Di'Nay kissed her, taking her time to pull away. "It is."

She stood and finally removed her gloves as their home warmed. "What should we have for dinner?"

The child from the cliff sat at the table, her hands folded in her lap, her eyes watching the loaf of bread and butter that sat in the middle. She didn't move or acknowledge anyone around her. Elana hesitated. She knew she had seen this child before, but she seemed a figment of her Sight – unalarming and unsurprising. She was a spirit haunting the island – or perhaps made of it. She belonged here. This was her home.

Elana tilted her head as she saw a small amulet around the child's neck. She moved for the first, time, drawing a vial from her pocket and drinking it. Her light dimmed. The sight made her head spin and her stomach cramp. What was it? Who was this child? Why did she seem to belong here?

In the blink of an eye she vanished and all thoughts of her went with her.

"There's stew from yesterday," Elana called lazily.

"Is that enough for a cold night? Should we make something else?" Elana leaned back until she laid on the ground. Di'Nay walked to stand over her. Her grin was teasing. "You don't have to make dinner. What would you like?"

Elana wrapped an arm around her leg. "Time with you more than a large meal."

Di'Nay knelt beside her, leaned over her, and kissed her. The embrace was soft, long, and lingering. Elana held her close, her fingers curling through her feather-soft short hair. They both made a point not to let work interfere with time together, but as the days and tendays slipped away Elana found herself sometimes missing the times they would travel together – constantly with each other, no jobs or social politics to get in their way.

"I find myself wishing the storm really would last for days," Di'Nay whispered against her jaw.

The house shuddered as a particularly strong gust of wind battered at the walls and windows. The fire danced from the light gusts whistling through the chimney. "Maybe it will," Elana remarked.

They kissed again and Elana felt her head swimming. She felt she was floating on the water, carried on the waves. Emotions came in rushes that danced under her skin – joy, desire, contentment, peace, happiness, acceptance, love.

"I could stay here forever." Elana's voice seemed to echo in her own mind.

"We will," Di'Nay answered. "I promise."

Diana stood at Elana's bedside, watching her hopelessly. She was unconscious, drugged as thoroughly as the seer child. They laid in bed together, Elana's arms protectively around the child like some sick rendering of a mother and child.

"I wonder what they see when they commune with the Mother?" A young woman – one of the caretakers – stepped up beside Diana and watched Elana and the child lovingly. "It's beautiful they found each other. Truly a gift."

Diana watched the young woman in shock. The cognitive dissonance of the entire village left her speechless. Just days ago she'd been nearly killed by Nanowa and was then attacked and knocked unconscious, waking in the middle of the temple after Elana was already drugged. Now she was greeted as a friend – the protector of the new Sacred One. The village had feasted the night Elana was placed in the temple. Diana was treated like family. All slights seemed to have been forgotten. Diana felt them watching her, ready to attack if she did anything that threatened their Sacred Ones, but they treated her warmly and allowed her to stay by Elana's side.

They really believed. It was the only thing that made any sense to Diana. They thought they were doing the right thing. They thought they were honoring Elana and the Mother but Elana had been right – this *was* a prison. All Diana's training in cultural acceptance and integration into communities very different from those on Yemaya didn't matter anymore. They didn't understand and Diana didn't have the time to try to change them. Lack of interference be damned, Diana would see Elana and perhaps even the seer child set free.

"I have to go into town," Diana muttered. The young caretaker – one of more than a dozen women in the village who took rotating shifts guarding the Sacred Ones, only nodded.

"They'll be watched," she reminded Diana.

"I know," Diana muttered to herself as she walked out of the temple.

Night was coming on once more. It had been nearly a tenday. No matter what she tried, Diana couldn't find a way to steal Elana away. She was constantly watched, constantly drugged into the equivalent of a coma, and the scouts were always aware of Diana's location. She'd never escape on foot in such an unknown territory. She didn't have weapons or even a detailed map.

She needed help. As much as Elana would hate it, she only knew one place to turn.

She walked up to Mahne's house and knocked, forcing herself not to acknowledge the three or four pairs of eyes that watched her. No one would follow her into the village elder's house or listen at Mahne's door.

The elderly woman answered, her face in a permanent frown every time she saw Diana since Elana had been captured.

"I need to speak with you, Elder." Diana spoke softly. "Please."

Mahne considered a moment, then opened the door wider for Diana to step inside. "You put me at risk, Terran," she growled after she shut the door and joined Diana at the center of the room.

"I'm not a Terran," Diana corrected. "And I don't know where else to turn."

"I told you not to let them know who she was."

"I didn't. Elana saved my life."

"And gave up hers in return. I hope you like it here, Min, because you're staying the rest of her life."

"There may be another way. I need to send a message by bird and I've been told you have access to one."

"So you can bring an army from the Keep to our doors?"

"I don't want to fight. I'll avoid it at all costs."

"Who could you message that would bring about a peaceful solution?"

"That's my secret."

"And you want me to risk treason on your word alone?"

Diana crossed her arms over her chest, her face hard and firm. She knew she cut an imposing figure, but Mahne didn't flinch. "I want to avoid bloodshed, but I won't let Nanowa keep Elana. I'll do whatever I must to set her free. I only know of one possible peaceful solution. If you have more, I'm open to hearing them. But without a way to send a message, I only have violence to fall back on."

Mahne considered longer. Her face twisted in disgust and frustration. "You're a terrible protector and she's stubborn as a mule."

"Both are probably right. Can I use your bird?"

Mahne slapped paper and a quill down on her table. Diana let her face soften. "Thank you."

She wrote a brief not explaining her situation and gave the best directions she could to her location. She didn't know how fast it would take a bird to reach Rixton, but it was the closest place she knew for certain a royal Marshal of the Ramains was based. If anyone had the resources to find a peaceful solution to her situation, it was Tristan.

Mahne took her finished message. "I'll see it sent. I won't send it by way of my bird. I don't need this traced back to me so easily. I'm traveling up river to another village tomorrow. One of Nanowa's daughters is ill and requested me to care for her. I'll send the message from there."

"Thank you."

"I hope this works and you both leave my village forever."

"By the Mother's grace we will."

"Perhaps it's unwise to intone the Mother while you plot to kidnap one of her Sacred."

"Then I'll pray to my own Goddesses, Elder."

Mahne huffed and tucked the note under her dress against her skin. "You shouldn't stay long. They'll get suspicious. Take this back to the temple. It's their order."

Mahne handed Diana a basket of dried herbs and flowers ground and compounded into incense. Diana nodded deeply and left Mahne's home, her heart a bit lighter with hope that someone might come to her aide.

Elana sighed gently, her entire body relaxed and light as she laid tangled with Di'Nay in their bed. They had barely moved in an hour, neither asleep but neither with the energy to speak. Their limbs and bodies were so wrapped around each other it was hard in her bliss to tell her body from Di'Nay's. She was warm. At peace. The storm howled around them but its chaos couldn't break through their strong stone walls.

The world had condensed down to nothing but Di'Nay, the softness of their bed, and the sounds of the storm. Nothing else existed. Nothing else mattered. Elana's belief in the Mother was unorthodox at best, but if there was a paradise after death Elana couldn't imagine it was better than this.

"I love that sound," Di'Nay whispered, her voice barely audible as she laid a kiss on Elana's bare shoulder. "That sigh. I know you're happy."

"What if we never got up? What if the sun didn't rise and the storm never ended?"

"It would be enough," Di'Nay responded. "You are always enough."

"I don't want to go."

"Then don't."

"They're coming." A soft voice – a young girl – seemed to whisper in the wind of the storm.

Elana held Di'Nay tighter. "Do you hear that?"

"Hmm?"

"A voice."

Di'Nay laughed, kissing her. "I don't hear anything."

"I do."

A cold crept in, licking first at Elana's feet then spreading up her legs. She felt a warmth over her eyes. The room around her seemed to fade and droop, like paint being washed away. "I don't want to go," she repeated, clutching Di'Nay now so hard the woman looked concerned. "Elana?"

"Please," Elana begged, more a pray than to Di'Nay. "Please don't make me go."

"Elana?!"

Elana woke in darkness. She tensed and her muscles spasmed to sit up but she felt a hand on her chest. It took a moment to realize the darkness was a compress over her eyes.

"Calm down. Calm down. I'm here."

It was Di'Nay, but not the Di'Nay from her dream. The peace was gone, replaced with a seething, cold panic that had obviously lingered for days.

"I didn't expect such a fast recovery."

Elana tensed at the unknown man's voice. Who was with her? Where was she?

"Don't underestimate Mahne," Di'Nay responded.

"Don't underestimate Karatan healing!" Mahne snapped. "You northerners think you're better than us, but your medicine is lifetimes behind."

"I assure you it wasn't my intention to do anything but praise your skills," the man responded.

"Di'Nay," Elana called. Every muscle burned to move. She felt closed in and lost without her vision. Her Sight seemed to be returning slower than her other senses and she couldn't make out the emotional lay of the room.

"Here, Elana."

Elana felt a swell of grief at her voice. Her heart didn't understand that her dream had been a figment of her mind – it was still real. She hadn't wanted to wake up.

"Please take this off me."

"You still have some of the Mother's Vision in you. It must

be drawn out or your recovery will take longer." Mahne's voice was unsympathetic.

"Di'Nay!" Elana called and her voice broke in her desperation.

Without hesitation, Di'Nay lifted the poultice. The light of Mahne's house nearly blinded her, but her eyes quickly adjusted. Her heart sank as real memories returned, painting over the memories of her dream.

Di'Nay leaned over her, concerned but happy at seeing her awake. Elana's eyes flicked around the room, finding a disgruntled-looking Mahne and a Desertman with long, dark hair and tanned skin. A full, neatly-trimmed beard hid what Elana guessed was a bit of a boyish face. He looked out of place in the jungle, the colors and patterns of his clothes brighter and bolder than the clothing worn by the tribe.

"This is Alaykim," Di'Nay introduced. "He came to help us."

Alaykim took a step forward with a kind smile. "Tristan apologizes for his response taking so long, but you're a long way from the Ramains."

Elana tensed. "Tristan?"

Apology was clear across Di'Nay's face. "I had to," she whispered. "I couldn't save you myself."

"And good thing you did. This situation was... politically precarious. Thankfully there were many things we could trade for your return."

Mahne snorted. "With a healthy side of threats."

Alaykim seemed unphased as he looked at the healing woman. "I made no threats. I came bearing gifts. But it should be understood that those under the protection of the Court of the Ramains should be treated with care according to our laws, not foreign policy. Your village will want for nothing for many tenmoons. We just want what's ours back."

Elana tried to sit up and her head spun. Di'Nay caught her before she fell back and eased her back onto the table. "You need to rest until your strength returns."

"I don't want to be here anymore."

Di'Nay glanced at Mahne. The healing woman sighed. "If she's going to panic, you can take her to the inn. But her care will be on your hands."

"Please," Elana begged.

Di'Nay pulled Elana into her arms. "I think it will be best for her to recover alone for a bit."

Elana closed her eyes and drew on what remained of her Sight and her connection to Di'Nay through their lifestones to fill herself with her lover's amarin. She waited as Mahne prepared poultices and gave them to Di'Nay. Di'Nay carried her back to the inn. Alaykim didn't follow.

"There," Di'Nay laid her in bed. Elana finally opened her eyes. Di'Nay knelt beside the bed and brushed the hair from her eyes. "How do you feel?"

"What happened?" Elana countered. "Why are we free?"

"I contacted the Marshals. They arrived and negotiated a trade for you. I know you don't trust them. I know this will probably come with expectations. But I couldn't save you alone."

Elana calculated. "How long have I been asleep?"

"Nearly a month," Di'Nay whispered. "I tried to wake you sooner. And I tried to include the seer child, I really did, but I had to get you –"

Elana shook her head slowly. So much in her dream started to make sense. "She likes it here. She's safe here."

"They took you prisoner."

"And they saved her. She was with the Order and was lost in the jungle."

"How...? Did you dream with her?"

"She spoke to me. I don't know how she got free. She was kidnapped from a village by the sea. I assume the shore near Karatan. She was drugged, too. Perhaps some of the trade we're looking for is near the sea."

"Then we know another place to investigate."

Elana thought of seeing the place in her dream with her own eyes, not living a comfortable life with Di'Nay but investigating hatred and fear. She closed her eyes, holding back tears. "Yes."

"Then perhaps this wasn't a waste of time. When you're better, we'll follow the path from your vision."

Elana tried to shake her dreams away. She tried to come back to reality. She had to be strong, but for now she felt crushed. She grabbed Di'Nay's hand, trying to draw comfort from the strength of it. At least Di'Nay was real. At least Di'Nay was here. "Yes. We'll follow the path."

GOTHIS: ONE CHILD

Elana closed her eyes and turned her face to the wind. She breathed the salty sea air deep into her lungs. It was just as she'd imagined it. The smells, the sounds, even the amarin. She figured it would be. The visions had been borrowed from a seer, someone who was even more connected to the spiritual energy of Aggar than she was. But feeling it was different than dreaming about it. Out there, not far off the coast, was the island from her dreams.

The wooden dock rocked beneath her boots. The bustle of the seaside town and its fish market behind her created a mild swell of noise – unintelligible chatter blending with the ripple of the waves. Gothis was the largest seaside town along the edge of the Karatan rainforest. Di'Nay's map named it as part of another country, Onethis, that stretched further to the south and wrapped up around the rainforest along the coast. The people of Onethis and Karatan didn't seem to get along well, only interacting with each other when necessary to secure trade routes to the sea.

Elana had found it through a series of visions. The travel through the jungle had been slow. They'd had to go a great distance and at the guidance of dreams and whispers from amarin. In the end, Elana had even started taking small doses of the Mother's Vision they still had on hand.

Every time she went back to the same place. Every time it felt like waking up from an awful nightmare. There she lived in joy with Di'Nay in a community that didn't criminalize or worship her – she was just accepted as she was. One of the people.

She never told Di'Nay when she knew for certain the path they were supposed to take. She'd had the map clearly imprinted in her mind a tenday before they reached Gothis. If Di'Nay had known, she wouldn't have let her keep taking the Mother's Vision.

"Looking for someone, Min?"

Elana turned as a fisherman with a speckled gray and white beard approached her.

"A ferryman," she answered. "I'm trying to visit the islands."

He laughed. "You'll have to be more specific than that."

"Horopto, I believe. Something similar." The man's cheeks turned olive in surprise and fear. Elana was shocked at his response. "I may have the name wrong."

"With all respect, Min, it's a rare and likely expensive ferryman who'd be willing to take you to that island."

"What do you mean?"

"They're cursed. Fates worshipers."

Elana cocked her head to the side. "Fates worshipers?"

"Why else would they have so many seers?"

Elana glanced at the ground. That made sense. "Do you know anyone who might take me?"

He regarded her warily, now suspicious. "I don't traffic with anyone who would willingly go there. Sorry."

He walked away with a sharp glare. Elana watched him go. At least in other parts of Aggar she ran into more subtlety in the residents' prejudice.

"I found us a room." Di'Nay walked up behind Elana, clapping her hands together, not yet used to the colder weather by the sea after coming out of the humid jungle. "Did you find a ferryman?"

"Not yet," Elana responded. "But I do know the island supposedly accepts seers and it's feared because of it."

"Seers? Multiple? Did you see that in your visions?"

"No. But I don't usually take facts based in fear and hate seriously."

"Well, either way it sounds like we have the right place. And if they're really as safe as people here fear, they may be able to help us when we don't have time to wait for the Keep."

Elana slipped her hands into the pockets of her breeches and frowned. "Maybe."

"Brothers and Sisters! Don't let them fool you! The witches of Karatan are a threat!"

Elana turned at the bellowing voice. A man surrounded by a cluster of townspeople moved slowly, pausing on a street corner. Elana tensed. She sensed the amarin of the people around him, but he was a black hole in the web of Aggar's spirit energy. He had to be wearing an amulet of the Order of Blindness.

Elana touched Di'Nay's shoulder. "Di'Nay."

"They've never forgotten the great war that gave our city to Onethis. We're a center of trade and commerce, one of the largest ports on the continent. Don't assume we aren't a target! Those seer and Blue Sight demons come from the jungle, hiding among us in the shadows. Unless we root them out we'll hand our city to the savages!"

"They're here in the open?" Elana whispered in shock.

"We have seers in our own city!" Someone yelled in dismissal.

"Controlled!" the street preacher countered. "It's true from time to time some of our own are born with the Karatan curse, but we can manage them. As long as they can be kept safe from the magical interference of the witches, we have nothing to fear. Perhaps even much to learn! Through study, the seers may have handed us a weapon. If we can understand their power, we may be able to use it against them! To defend Gothis and in turn Onethis!"

Elana clenched her fists at her sides and felt her skin grow dark with rage. This again. This rhetoric. This disease in Aggar! The thought of any child in the hands of the Order of Blindness made her sick, but this? Studying? Testing? These were children, not scientific tools!

Di'Nay took her hand, sensing her mood. "We don't have to listen to this," she whispered, pulling Elana down the dock.

"They're listening!" Elana hissed, indicating the crowd.

"They don't matter. If there are seer children in town, we'll find and protect them. They're nothing against us."

Elana looked over her shoulder as she let Di'Nay lead her deeper into the market. She watched the preacher, wanting more than anything to rip the amulet from his chest and show him the real terror of a Blue Sight. If the Order was going to preach and practice hate, she would show them something to truly be afraid of.

The markets of Gothis were tight and twisting but expansive. The smell of the sea and the fish market permeated the city. Its tall stone buildings and narrow roadways made everything appear darker and dirtier than it really was. The town had grown faster than the land allowed. People seemed to live right on top of each other with little space between. Elana wondered if it was just Gothis or if most of Onethis was like this – industrial and dark, productive but full of shadows.

Elana saw tradesmen from Karatan, the Southern Desert, even a few in Ramains garb. There were more she didn't recognize. She knew the great continent on Aggar was vast and varied, but she had never seen so clearly how little she knew about her world and its people.

She found some comfort in the market's diversity. It was clear the xenophobic ranting of the Order wasn't a universal belief – or at least greed won out over hate. It would be stupid for a port city to make enemies of its neighbors, especially one that closed in around them on three sides. Elana wondered how many would die if the Order's message spread. If Karatan banded together and wanted Gothis, they'd have it.

Di'Nay made every attempt to lighten Elana's mood. She smiled and chatted as if they were strolling through the Keep's gardens. She bought foreign sweets and snacks for them to try, knowing Elana's love of adventure and new experiences. Elana forced a smile. She genuinely appreciated Di'Nay's efforts and she knew what her darkness was doing to her partner. Di'Nay had to be more worried about her than Elana sensed to all but pause their mission in a loving attempt to brighten the mood. Still, she couldn't shake the gnawing in her stomach, the mild sense of revulsion she felt from time to time whenever she caught someone watching her.

She knew it wasn't personal – she didn't stand out in this crowd. The occasional onlooker was a merchant looking for potential customers. She felt it with her Sight. She understood it with her mind. But her heart cast everyone as a supporter of the Order of Blindness. Anyone could turn on her. Anyone could hate her. Her ability to pass among them meant nothing. She wasn't like them and their conditional acceptance almost made her feel worse. She was safer, but only because she somehow played into their narrative.

Around noon they walked through an alleyway dedicated to

more exotic trinkets. Di'Nay ran to Elana from down the street with a mischievous smile, her hands tucked behind her back.

"For you." She revealed an abalone barrette, thick enough to pin back Elana's weighty curls. The pattern rippled like water on the sea, holding a thousand different shades of blue and teal. Elana took it with a genuine smile. It reminded her of her dreams, her island, but also her Sight.

"It's one thing you don't have to hide," Di'Nay offered cryptically but Elana knew what she meant. Di'Nay was proving she really saw Elana's mind. If she couldn't walk through a hostile town like Gothis with her real eyes, she could sport her power as an ornament in her hair.

Elana handed the barrette back. "Help me?"

Di'Nay moved behind her and traded the leather cord that pulled Elana's long hair from her face for the clip. She tenderly ran her fingers through Elana's hair under the excuse of smoothing it. "It suits you."

"Thank you."

Elana paused and her smile faded. She turned. A woman at a nearby stall didn't have any amarin. The woman was a native of Karatan, middle-aged and large-boned. Her dark hair was pinned atop her head. She hawked various carvings, poultices, and trinkets, selling them as mystical relics from the jungle. Di'Nay walked around to stand beside Elana and followed her gaze.

"She's wearing an amulet," Elana muttered.

Di'Nay rested a hand on Elana's shoulder. "Wait here."

She moved to the cart as Elana stepped back into the shadows, watching them interact. She felt sick watching Di'Nay charm and flatter the woman, but it was eased a bit by the obvious disdain in Di'Nay's amarin. After only a few moments, Di'Nay returned with a small paper pouch.

"It was disgustingly easy." Di'Nay passed pouch to Elana. It contained a vial of Mother's Vision and a note with an address and time written in a steady hand. "It seems your visions brought us to your island as well as one of the narcotic dealers working with the Order."

Elana's grip on the pouch tightened. How could she betray her people like that?

"The address is where the Order is having its next public meeting. The local leader's courtyard. It seems the Order is an accepted religion around here."

Elana's lips pressed into a straight line, no longer able to feign cheer even for Di'Nay's sake. "Let's go. It starts in an hour."

There was already a small crowd gathered when Diana and Elana arrived. They sat in the grassy courtyard before what had to pass as a manor house in a town like Gothis. The house wasn't as large as the manors in the Ramains, but it was bigger than anything else they'd seen in the city. Its property was sandwiched between a store and a small warehouse, all of which were marked with the same family crest. The sign over the store named it "Dunn and Rafferty's," most likely after the families that at least once had a stake in its success.

A large, grassy yard stood between the warehouse and store, with the manor itself set back so its front corners met the back corners of the store and warehouse. There was so little grass anywhere else in Gothis, with most of the streets cobbled stone. To afford a yard seemed a luxury. The fact that it obviously belonged to a merchant, not a nobleman, was even more dangerous.

Diana was well aware what influence the wealthy could have in a city where everyone seemed to be struggling. Not only was influence a monetized commodity, but the rich could take on a kind of heroic status among merchants. A lifestyle that seemed attainable, but really wasn't. Judging by the age of the family crest on the store, whoever owned the manor now had come from a wealthy family, not built his wealth himself.

Elana stood like a stone statue, her arms crossed over her chest, her eyes locked on the crowd. She didn't move. She barely breathed. Her face was intentionally emotionless but Diana felt every emotion as if she had the Sight. Elana wasn't scared or hurt, she was furious. She was a Goddess of destruction who would see the entire manor burned to the ground if she could. It was the side of Elana Diana found most intriguing and most terrifying. This was the power of the Sight that Elana constantly warned her about. The side of Elana that required intense discipline. The side Elana had spent her entire life training to keep under control.

Diana feared that control was slipping.

"We don't have to be here," Diana told her.

"Most of them don't have amulets."

"That's good, yes?" Diana offered.

"They're being indoctrinated."

They stood in the back as a dozen members of the Order joined the crowd, one standing before them to speak. The message wasn't surprising to Diana. It mirrored the words of the street preacher. The Order was preying on the fears of the common man, aligning their goals with national pride. They were surrounded by the jungle. The people were obviously afraid of being cut off from Onethis despite having access to the entire ocean if an escape was necessary. The Order demonized the people of Karatan and shifted that fear onto the seers and Blue Sights. Within a few minutes poverty, lack of trade, war, and fear of spies and conspiracies had all been linked to seers.

It was a rhetoric Diana had seen before in some parts of the Empire about Amazons. It was a classic yet effective tactic. When troubles were too complicated and messy to be easily removed, focusing everyone on a single target was easy. Many of the people in Gothis wanted someone to blame for their hardships. The Order gave them an easy target.

"This is all nonsense," Diana whispered to Elana. "They don't care about nationalism. They want to kill seers."

"No," Elana responded, her voice almost weak. "They want their power."

Diana glanced at her in confusion. The thought had never entered her mind. "What?"

"Listen to their words when they talk about saving the seers of Gothis. Cure. Study."

"They can't sound like they're turning on their own people," Diana countered. "They have to keep the threat outside Onethis."

"Yes, but it's all code for experimenting. They're not talking about eradication in Onethis, only in other countries. They want to know how our power works. No one takes such extreme lengths to understand power unless they want to know how to wield it."

"Do you think that's why we've found a few seers alive? Why they're being kidnapped instead of killed?"

"I think this goes beyond genocide."

Without another word, Elana turned and walked away. Diana jogged to keep up with her. "Where are you going?"

"This isn't where the elite of the Order meets. If they're all out preaching, they may have offices or meeting rooms left unwatched. I want to know what they're really after, not what propaganda they're peddling."

"I doubt any of their secrets would be totally unguarded, and you can't sense them if anyone's approaching."

"I still have the shadows, my own senses," Elana countered. "And you."

Diana followed Elana toward the warehouse. She peered into one of the windows. It was bustling, workers packing and preparing goods from rows and rows of shelves of supplies. There would be no way to sneak inside unseen in the middle of the day.

Elana frowned and they circled around the building, walking down the narrow alley between the warehouse and the next store. "There." Elana pointed toward a door at the back of the building. Elana peered inside a small window. It was an office, just large enough for a desk and a couple shelves.

"It's probably for the foreman," Diana remarked. "Are the workers inside wearing amulets?

Elana shook her head. "I can feel a lot of them. Too many to guess how many might be wearing amulets. The store may help fund the Order, but I don't think it's totally staffed by it."

"Then the foreman likely isn't trusted to keep the Order's secrets."

"It's worth a look." Elana tried the door. It was locked. She frowned as she pulled a small pouch of lockpicks from a pouch at her waist.

"You pick locks?" Diana questioned in surprise.

"I'm a Shadow. We're trained for many things. Though admittedly I'm not the best at it."

Elana worked the lock as Diana eyed both ends of the long alley on either side of them. It wasn't a very defensible situation, though she would certainly see an attacker coming. If they were found or accosted by anyone with a ranged weapon, they'd surly be shot.

Elana cursed softly to herself as she broke her first pick and drew another. This time she had more luck, the tumbler to the lock clicking and falling into place. Elana placed the locks back in her pouch with a triumphant grin. She opened the door and they both stepped inside.

Diana kept watch at the window, her hand on her knife as Elana skimmed through what paperwork she could find. She searched desk drawers and the shelves, her frown growing deeper as she didn't find anything useful.

"This record shows shipments of amulets and medicines. Likely Mother's Vision."

"Then we know where some of the Order's supplies are coming from," Diana remarked. "No wonder this supplier is so wealthy."

"If we can cut off the supply here we might do real damage to the Order."

"What do you recommend? We can't attack it outright and a fire would put the entire town up in flames."

"I'll think about it."

Diana heard footsteps outside the interior door and tensed, holding her breath until they passed.

"Almost done," Elana assured her. "Ah!"

Diana glanced at Elana. "What?"

"It's a sales plan."

"That's useful?"

Elana held up a piece of paper with a short list of names and a handwritten note. "Noblemen they want to pitch Mother's Vision to. Which means these people are tied to seers and not directly to the Order. One of them is local."

More footsteps outside the door and Diana tensed. "We should go."

"Already have what I need." Elana slipped out the door and Diana followed, hoping the now unlocked door wouldn't cause a terrible amount of alarm.

Elana stood in front of a well-kept townhouse, the home slender and tall between two other residences. She checked the address against a note she'd copied from the foreman's note at Dunn and Rafferty's. Di'Nay had stayed behind, worried that her presence as a foreigner might unnerve the seer's family. Normally Elana wanted Di'Nay at her side in moments that could depend heavily on charisma, but this was Council business – she wasn't afraid.

She walked to the front door and knocked. A young woman about Elana's age opened the door. She was exhausted. Her skin was a pronounced olive shade, the darker yellows and greens in her complexion a clear sign of long-term distress or illness. Her clothes hung just baggy enough on her frame to signify recent dramatic weight loss. Despite the obvious physical signs of distress, however, her amarin was gentle and determined, almost comforting even to someone like Elana. Elana felt the energy of a seer clinging to her. Likely the silence in the house – uncommon in the residence of a seer who isn't connected with their brothers and sisters – was due to this woman's presence.

"Yes?" she questioned cautiously.

"Are you Min Nevin?"

"Yes. Can I help you?"

"I've come representing –"

Her face immediately darkened and her lips pulled taut against her teeth. Elana was shocked by the sudden transformation from sickly waif to predator protecting her cubs. "I'm not interested in anything Rafferty has to say."

Elana shook her head. "No, no. I'm not with them."

"Then who?"

"My name is Elana. I've come from the Council's Keep in the Ramains."

Min Nevin hesitated, her ferocity melting to confusion. "Why would someone from the Council come all the way to Gothis?"

As she spoke, a screeching howl echoed from deep within the house followed by the rushing feet of what Elana assumed to be caregivers. Min Nevin winced and her hand clenched at the door. "I just got her to sleep."

"I came because your daughter is a seer, Min."

Min Nevin tilted her head to rest against the door, both studying Elana and using it for support as her energy wavered. "It seems less likely an ambassador of the Keep all the way in the Ramains would visit me than one of Rafferty's would lie to get me to hand over my child."

"Bring me to the child and I can prove it. I'll calm her without any potion or device."

The child screamed louder and Min Nevin closed her eyes. "My caregivers and I won't leave her side."

Elana used her Sight to comfort the woman, to try to instill if not trust, at least a willingness to give her a chance. "You don't have to, Min. Call a guardsman if you like."

Min Nevin studied her a moment longer, then opened the door wider. "One of Rafferty's or not, if you can calm her, I'll hire you as a nursemaid."

Elana chuckled. "No need."

Min Nevin led Elana up a narrow flight of stairs to the top floor. Three women crowded the child's nursery, offering toys, milk, and soft blankets as the child howled. They separated as Min Nevin entered.

Elana felt some relief at seeing a child's room obviously made with love and care. The walls were painted soft blues in patterns that mimicked the sea. There were toys and knit blankets, a mobile with hand-carved stone animals over a wooden crib. This child had been expected and loved.

Min Nevin leaned over the crib, cooing and bouncing the child and its screams faded from a roar to a squall. The child scrunched its face and clenched its fists, resting on her mother's shoulder for a time, but then wildly attempting to throw her head back. Min Nevin cradled the back of her head to keep her from hurting herself.

Elana reached for the child. "Please."

Min Nevin carefully passed the baby. Its screams faltered as Elana touched her. She felt Elana's Sight and drew some comfort from it. Within a few minutes, the child was asleep in Elana's arms, feeding off the energy of Elana's abilities to connect herself more completely with Aggar and the amarin of the town.

The caregivers and Min Nevin watched her in shock. Elana moved through the room, the child in one arm. She closed the curtains over the windows and blew out the cheerful lantern that cast star shapes on the walls through stamped metal openings. "She's overstimulated. Seer children don't respond well to so much light and color."

"They're gifts from her father," Min Nevin countered.

Elana shook her head, softening her voice. "You misunderstand. This is a beautiful child's room. I can tell you love her very much. But a seer is not like other children."

Min Nevin's shoulders sank and Elana could tell her emotions even without her Sight – she felt helpless. Helpless to connect with her child. Helpless to see her child happy and healthy. There was doubt and shame.

She gestured to the child sleeping in Elana's arms. "Obviously you know what you're talking about."

Elana sighed. She was a good ambassador and a good representative, but it was moments like these she knew Di'Nay would be better. Her voice was soft. "Can we speak privately, Min?"

Min Nevin waved out the nursemaids and Elana relaxed, knowing she was at least somewhat trusted. "You understand you're a good mother, yes?" Elana spoke once they were alone.

Min Nevin started weeping. Elana took a step back in surprise at the sudden outburst, but she collected herself quickly, not wanting to upset her more.

Min Nevin slid to the floor and held her head in her hands. "She won't stop crying. Every time she wakes up she's so upset. I've never seen my baby laugh. I've never had her reach for me or even recognize me when she looks at me."

Elana cautiously sat beside her. "She recognizes you. You got her to sleep before I came here. Did you see her earlier before I took her? You're the only one that stilled any of her distress."

"She still cried."

Elana reached out a tentative hand and touched her shoulder. "Do you know what I am, Min?"

A wave of bitterness spread through her amarin. "I've heard rumors about the Keep, but if they're anything like what Rafferty and his ilk say about seers I probably know nothing."

"I'm a Blue Sight."

Min Nevin glanced up in surprise and Elana let the disguise over her eyes slip away. "I'm not a seer, but I'm more closely connected to them than any other human. She sleeps in my arms now because she can feed off my energy, not because she knows or trusts me. Seers barely exist in our reality. Time means nothing to them. The fact that your child, a seer this young, can even feel your touch means you have a powerful presence in her life. That's no small feat."

Min Nevin's tears started to dry but the look of anguish on her face never lifted. "I always wanted a child. I didn't care that she was a seer. Even before she was born I prayed to the Mother and promised to care for whatever she blessed me with. I want her to be happy, Elana. I don't know how to do that for her."

Elana considered, hoping she found the right words. "Despite what you may have heard, the Keep is a safe place. It's a training ground and sanctuary for people who might not fit anywhere else in Aggar. People with abilities like me. Like your daughter. At the Keep your daughter would live with an expansive network of her own people, cared for where she will always be connected with Aggar. She'll become powerful and strong. She'll be happy. She'll sing. She'll be safe."

Min Nevin's lips trembled as new tears threatened and she sank, resting her face in her hands. "Everyone tells me to send her away."

"But this isn't abandonment. This is where she's meant to be."

"Without me?"

"With you. Don't you see? Once she's part of Aggar, once she's thriving, she'll finally be able to see you. Right now she's reaching out to you so desperately that you can affect her even in the chaos of her mind, but she'll never fully feel your presence here. Once all that chaos is stripped away I doubt her energy will ever leave your side."

They sat in silence for a long moment, Min Nevin considering and Elana giving her the space and silence to do so. Finally, Min Nevin spoke.

"I want to travel with her."

"I'm sure that can be arranged."

"I'm not promising she can stay at the Keep."

"At least go look and find out for yourself that it's what's best for her. See her smile. See her happy."

Min Nevin relaxed and Elana felt her willingness. Tears sprang to Elana's eyes this time at her success. A child saved. A child who hadn't known abuse, who could be happy and healthy. A child torn from the Order's grasp. Elana had finally saved a seer in every way – from death, from kidnapping, from abuse. It was the hope she needed to continue on.

"What do I have to do?"

"We need to send a message. Is there a hawker you trust that could get a message to the Ramains?"

"Yes."

"Good. It will take some time for the letter to be delivered and an escort sent."

"Wait with me? Please? My husband is away at sea. He won't be back for at least four or five tendays."

Elana squeezed her hand. "Of course. I have a companion, also a representative from the Keep. She doesn't have the Sight, but she'll keep us safe."

"I'm sure Rafferty will cause a fuss when he learns my plans. It would be nice to have some protection."

Elana nodded. "That we can both provide. With your blessing, well move in today."

Diana watched as Elana's message to the Council was tied to the leg of a vicious-looking hawk. The creature was small and angular, made for flying long distances. She doubted it would travel all the way to the Ramains. More likely it would stop at a partner outpost in the desert and the message given to a second bird who would fly the rest of the way. Still, as Diana looked into its sharp eyes and sturdy musculature she didn't doubt he could make the journey alone if necessary.

"And you have a second message bound for the Ramains?"

"No, to Seranhold in the desert."

"Seranhold? The embassy? Who do you know there?"

"A friend." Diana carefully evaded all the hawker's questions. It might just be an innocent attempt at getting new gossip, but she couldn't take any chances.

Diana pulled another, thicker message. Her stomach twisted at the sight of it. It was a detail of the events since leaving Karatan, bound for the Royal Marshals in the capitol. The information was the price she'd paid for the Marshals help freeing Elana. A price she paid in secret. Elana wouldn't like knowing Diana was beholden to them in any way. Learning that she was feeding the Marshals information... Diana blinked hard, pushing the thoughts aside. She would deal with it if Elana ever found out. Hopefully she'd be able to save the relationship.

Still, beyond lying to her lover, Diana felt little guilt about the information she gave. She knew how political games were played and she knew that nothing was ever given for free. It didn't make the Marshals corrupt for asking a price. It made them smart. With their power and influence, they might be able to keep the children of Gothis safe. Perhaps they could even close Dunn and Rafferty. There were things Diana knew she and Elana couldn't do alone. She felt more capable with the Marshals at her back.

The hawker tied her second message to a larger bird. Both messages were sealed with wax – if the seal was broken on arrival, it was a clear sign it may have been tampered with. Both were bound for outposts that kept the messages' true destinations secret from any porter involved in the transportation process. Diana wished Aggar had adopted more technologically advanced forms of communication. A single Terran outpost or access to a satellite could see her messages transferred securely and instantly. But she didn't have any access to such tech this far from most Terran bases and any other Amazon contact she might have at the Empire.

She was trained to use the methods and traditions allowed to her by the cultures she settled in, but that didn't make it any less frustrating.

Diana waited at the hawker's until she saw the birds released and successfully make it high into the sky. Diana paid the hawker and bid him hold any messages that arrived for her until she picked them up in person.

The streets of Gothis were busy as usual as she left. Elana was at the Nevins' home helping Min Nevin make her child's room more seer-friendly. Diana could see the toll caring for the child was taking on Elana. She gave so much of herself when caring for children. She'd seen it in Loscan and even, in a way, with Gerome. She didn't know if Elana would last until a Council emissary could arrive.

She walked slowly through the market streets, lost in thought. She wished there was some way she could ease Elana's burdens, but as time went on she felt Elana's pain was farther and farther from her reach. How could she comfort the woman she loved when half of what tormented Elana was so foreign to Diana or outside of her capabilities? How long would her love and support be enough?

She wished, not for the first time, that she'd been able to immediately take Elana off-world. She felt some guilt over the thought, but she was convinced the moment Elana knew what life could be like on Yemaya her doubt would fall away. Aggar might be home for Elana, but home wasn't always the best place to be.

As she reached the Nevin home, she hesitated. A street preacher for the Order was standing at a corner near enough to the Nevin house that Diana was sure he could be heard from inside. She frowned. It seemed unlikely his placement was just a terrible coincidence. Thankfully the crowd he'd gathered was small.

"It's a terrible crime to refuse help when it's offered. Seers are cursed – the threat of Karatan attacking our most vulnerable. Our children. Would you deny medicine to your dying infant?"

"This is enough," Diana called, all her frustration and helplessness boiling to the surface. Her cheeks burned but she kept her voice even, sharp, and assertive. She couldn't stop every person on Aggar who tormented seers, but she could do this.

"All voices are welcome in public in Gothis," the preacher countered. "Perhaps it's different off-world." There was so much disdain in his voice he made "off-world" a slur. Diana clenched her teeth, reconsidering her tactic.

"Voices perhaps. But not threats." Most of the curious who'd gathered to listen dispersed at the tension between them. The preacher grew furious.

"I've threatened no one."

Diana leaned closer, pleased to find she was taller than him. "We both know what you're doing here. Move along. This family is protected."

Instead of anger, he only laughed. "You can't protect someone from the world. Or the divine."

"But I can protect them from you."

"Now who's threatening?"

"I've reached for no weapon, Tad."

"We rule this city, Terran. Every lawmaker. Every merchant with power. You don't need to reach for a weapon. My word will send you to the dungeons of Onethis."

Diana took a risk. "Yet you haven't called a guard." As she'd expected, his eyes suddenly darted nervously. "It seems it's your superiors who wield any power. Superiors who won't risk that power and influence for you."

His glower darkened and for a moment Diana thought he'd throw a punch. "I am one of many. And next time I'll be back in force."

"I'll still be here."

He stalked off and Diana watched him go. She narrowed her eyes. A chill settled in her heart. Perhaps she had been underestimating the Order. Just because they were underground in the Ramains didn't mean they didn't have real power elsewhere. And while the street preacher seemed to be all talk, Diana wouldn't be surprised if he really could gather a force to cause trouble for the Nevin family.

Diana touched the hilt of her short sword, taking comfort in having a way to defend herself and the people she'd promised to protect, and turned back to the house.

Elana cradled the seer child – whose name she'd learned was Arya – as she looked out the nursery window. The houses stacked on top of each other made towers of candle and lantern light that flickered like starlight in the windows. It was a far cry from the city in the day. The darkness hid the grime and rough exteriors, filtering out enough ugliness to give it a strange kind of beauty.

It was so different from what she was used to. The village where she'd spent her childhood had been more open, the streets wider and the homes smaller and better built. Even the capitol seemed spacious compared to the tight corners of Gothis. The wood was different. The angles of the buildings stacked on top of each other were different. Even the scents and amarin were different.

Elana had always wanted to travel. To adventure. She found herself equally fascinated with the new parts of Aggar she was exploring with Di'Nay and terrified by the dangers she'd run into. She'd spent so much of her life fantasizing. She hadn't realized it then. She was logical. She was studious. She was independent and bold. She hadn't realized the other feelings the Mother intended for her to learn. Loss. Fear. Helplessness. Hatred. Fury. They were all a part of her now. She couldn't help but wonder if they'd made her better.

Arya shifted in Elana's arms and tucked her face against the crook of Elana's arm. Elana smiled down at her and shut the curtains to her room, blocking out the moon and candle light. The curtains had once been transparent and flowing, now they were thick and heavy, blocking out all light as Elana had recommended.

She paced the nursery, waiting for Arya to reach her deepest sleep so she could put her back in her crib. The seer took less from her than she'd expected. Despite the screaming, she seemed more comfortable in the human reality than most of her kin. She responded to some touch and efforts at affection from her mother and occasionally a nursemaid. Still, she was hungry after a lifetime of being disconnected from Aggar's amarin.

Every day they waited Elana felt her energy drain a bit more. She would start getting sick soon. Perhaps she'd be on bed rest before the Council could arrange transportation. It scared Di'Nay, but Elana found a strange kind of satisfaction in it. In the grand scheme of things, there was so little she could do to change the world fast enough to save every seer, but she could give until her body broke down. She could suffer pain. She could suffer exhaustion and sickness. She could give until her last breath and perhaps that might be enough.

Arya fell into a sleep so deep Elana felt confident she would rest through the night. She placed the infant back into her cradle and watched her for a moment longer. It was no wonder Min Nevin never gave up hope. When she slept, she looked like any other child. It was a small thing, but the hopeful cling to every little sign that their dreams might be fulfilled. It would be hard for a good mother to watch her child sleep so well and not think that one day the child would live just as well.

When she was sure Arya wouldn't wake, she slipped out of the room, closing the door behind her. Di'Nay and Min Nevin sat at the dinner table, drinking tea in faint lantern light. As she'd thought, Di'Nay and Min Nevin had quickly bonded. Di'Nay couldn't bear to see someone in emotional pain. The nursemaids had already been sent home. The house felt vast and empty despite its compact size.

"Is she asleep?" Di'Nay questioned.

"She should sleep through the night."

Min Nevin held her face in her hands and Di'Nay rested a hand on her shoulder. They didn't speak but the amarin in the room was obvious even without the Sight. The silence felt heavy and somehow deafening. Elana wished she could be more helpful. She wished she had easier answers and solutions. She wished she could give Min Nevin the connection with her child she wanted, or that she could at least impress on her the nuance of her situation. Elana had never seen someone without some form of the Sight earn as much closeness from a seer child as Min Nevin had. It was a miracle. It should have been impossible. But that meant little to a woman who wanted to look into her child's eyes and be recognized.

"You should sleep as well," Di'Nay told Min Nevin. "Both of you should. Tomorrow will be just as long as today. I'll keep watch."

Min Nevin drew a deep, calming breath and nodded. "Thank you."

Di'Nay waved the apology away affectionately. "This is what we do, Min."

As Min Nevin disappeared down the hall, Elana saw Di'Nay's face fall and her brave front disappear. "You should sleep as well," she reminded her lover.

Di'Nay forced a smile. "My strength is most useful keeping the home safe in the night. You have Arya to support and Min Nevin has the weight of her heart."

"You're not useful if you're exhausted when an attack comes." Di'Nay nodded slightly in agreement. "Let me watch a few hours. We can trade. Arya doesn't demand as much as the others have."

"Are you certain, Soroi?"

"Yes. Please."

Di'Nay stood and kissed her briefly before walking down the hall to her room. Once she had disappeared into the darkness, Elana moved from the dining room to the parlor. She looked out the windows again, watching the streets in front of the house. Ever since Di'Nay's run in with the Order's street preacher there had been a crowd gathered every day. They were mostly loud and obnoxious, but there was an implied threat in their presence and their refusal to leave. Every day more and more of the crowd wore Order amulets. Some days Elana couldn't even feel their size they were mostly invisible to her Sight.

Thankfully there seemed to be rules about loitering at night that even the Order didn't attempt to break. Harassment would begin again at dawn, but so far the nights had been peaceful.

She sat in the parlor's window seat and leaned back against the wall, losing herself in the candlelight once more and wondering how much longer it would take to get Arya and her mother out of Gothis. Inevitably, her thoughts drifted even further, fixating on her dreams of Horopto. Caring for the Nevin family had given her some respite from her obsession, but in the quiet moments – when she was lazily cradling Arya or up late in a quiet house, she still lost herself.

It was too sweet a dream. She wished she'd never had it, but now that she had she couldn't let it go. She'd considered sneaking away some of the Mother's Vision Di'Nay had purchased from the market, but she knew it would be unwise. She needed to be conscious and aware. There was no reason for her to dream. Di'Nay would be suspicious, and Elana still didn't know how to explain herself.

She was fantasizing about being somewhere else. She was hungry for a world that didn't exist. Hungry enough to drug herself. How would Di'Nay take that? How could she understand Elana wasn't running away from her, but to a world where they could be together even more fully? Would she be offended? Would she ever leave Elana alone with Mother's Vision again?

The thought shocked her out of her reverie. Was her reasoning for not talking to her lover so selfish? Was worrying about offending Di'Nay really as important as maintaining her supply of a vision drug? What was she becoming?

She sat up straighter as she heard a creak and patter, like soft steps, downstairs. She reached out with her Sight but saw nothing. It wasn't as comforting as it should have been.

She crept toward the stairs, keeping close to the walls and sinking into the shadows. The Order might be able to hide from her Sight, but she could hide as well. She rounded the landing by the front door to face the stairs down into the basement. She saw movement in the darkness large enough to be a man. She grabbed the hilt of her knife, not yet drawing it for fear the glint from the blade would betray her.

She reached the bottom of the stairs unseen. Two men dressed in dark clothes, scarves around their mouths, fumbled in the darkness. They weren't trained thieves or assassins, it was clear in their movements. They were sent by the Order or inspired by the preaching of the Order. Likely they were just local residents.

"You should leave."

One man shouted in surprise at Elana's voice coming from the shadows. He stumbled back, knocking over an empty water barrel. The sound woke Di'Nay. Elana took comfort at feeling her amarin spark to life out of her sleep.

"This house is protected," Elana hissed.

The frightened man turned to leave but his fellow grabbed his arm and looked blindly around the darkness.

"You can't scare us, demon!"

Elana chuckled. It wasn't the first time she'd been accused of being a denizen of the Cellar, but this was the first time she found some amusement from it. Stalking through the darkness, threatening grown men stumbling through the shadows she could navigate without struggle... maybe tonight she was a demon. At the very least she felt some power being in control of two people who could hide from her Sight.

"Get out."

Elana lashed out, stabbing the braver man in the leg, then withdrawing. He howled in pain and released his more frightened counterpart, who immediately took off and slid out the small cellar window high on the wall onto the street.

The braver man swung wildly and Elana crouched, ducking out of his way and creeping around him. Instead of stabbing again, she grabbed the clasp of his amulet chain and, despite the sickness she always felt touching something associated with the Order's amulets, she was able to undo it and throw it across the room.

The man's fear was almost tangible. It had a musk that wafted over her nose and tongue that she knew must be carried on his amarin but felt like it was real. Despite his appearance, he was trembling with fear. It was the down side of belonging to a cult that called her kind demons and lethal threats to Aggar – when most in the Order were alone with her, she had the upper hand.

"Get out." Elana filled the threat with all her Sight, bearing down on him like the demon he feared her to be. She filled his body with the pain of his stab wound, she amplified every horrible thing he'd heard about seers in his mind. He was a quivering mess in an instant, barely able to move, totally unable to form words.

He fled like an animal and Elana raised her chin as she watched him go. *Run. Run like a coward. Run like prey. If you're going to hate me, I'll give you something to hate.*

"Elana?"

Elana turned as Di'Nay stood in the doorway. She was crouched on the stairs, pale and shaken. She hadn't been Elana's target but undoubtedly some of her power had overcome her. Elana pulled her rage back inside herself, trying to use her Sight to comfort her lover. "I'm sorry."

She took a step forward and Di'Nay reflexively reared back.

The instinctive movement stung Elana to her core. Di'Nay recovered. The fear fell from her eyes. But for a moment she had been scared. She had looked at Elana like a monster. Elana took a step back into the shadows and Di'Nay's face fell as she realized what she'd done.

"Elana, I didn't mean... I was just surprised..."

Elana swept past her, running up the stairs into Di'Nay's room. She couldn't shake the look in Di'Nay's eyes. She couldn't push the fear away. She was spinning out of control. She couldn't focus, and that was dangerous with the power she'd recently allowed herself to set on someone else.

She needed to get away. She needed to escape. She told herself it was to stop her power from getting out of control but she was a terrible liar, even to herself. She knew it was stupid. She knew it was selfish. But for a dangerous moment she didn't care. She wanted to be somewhere else.

She took a drink from the bottle of Mother's Vision in Di'Nay's bags. She felt a moment of shame and self-loathing before collapsing back onto Di'Nay's bed completely unconscious.

Diana sat at Elana's side, watching her as she dreamed. Arya was resting in the crook of her arm, able to draw on her energy even in her drugged state. Diana brushed the locks around Elana's face. The curls were already neatly tucked away from her face, but Diana couldn't help herself. She felt helpless. She had to do something.

She hadn't expected Elana to drug herself. She'd known Elana was in a dark place, but this seemed so out of the blue and out of character. She hadn't expected Elana was using the Mother's Vision for escapism. She still didn't understand it. How could Elana have fallen so far without Diana noticing?

She'd been unconscious for the better part of the day. Diana had told Min Nevin that Elana was exhausted and so far Diana thought Min Nevin believed her. Arya was still soothed. The Order hadn't moved against them since Elana's attack the night before. For now, they were all right, but Diana didn't know how long it would last. If the Order decided to retaliate, Diana would be an ally down and now had one other person to protect. She didn't know when Elana would wake or what her state of mind would be.

It was a precarious situation Diana wasn't sure she could juggle and without Elana she felt... alone. Isolated. How had they grown so far apart? How had she been so blind?

"I miss you," Diana whispered and kissed Elana's brow. "I've missed you for a while."

As if responding to her voice, Elana shifted, turning away from her embrace. Diana's breath caught in her throat. It wasn't the first time she'd moved under the influence of Mother's Vision, but she couldn't help hoping she'd wake every time she did. Arya grunted in frustration at Elana's movement, but quickly settled again.

Diana leaned over Elana and stroked her cheek. "Come back to me, Elana. Please. Come back." Elana shifted again and Diana felt a swell of hope. She kissed her, hoping the touch combined with the need in her amarin would be enough to find Elana in the depths of her visions.

"Di'Nay?"

"I'm here," Diana beckoned as Elana spoke. Her eyes were still closed and her voice seemed faint and far away.

"I don't want to leave."

Diana hesitated. Did she mean she didn't want to leave reality or she didn't want to leave her dreams? She took Elana's hand and held tightly.

"I need you," Diana pled. "Please."

Elana's eyes fluttered open and Diana let out a sharp breath of relief. "Di'Nay?"

"I'm here."

Elana glanced around the room in confusion and Diana's heart sank at the look of loss in her eyes. "Oh."

"Elana?"

Elana squeezed her hand back. "What's happened? How long have I been away?"

"A few hours," Diana answered. "Elana, I'm so sorry. I didn't mean to hurt you."

Elana's lips pressed into a tight line and she shook her head. "Don't. Please. You didn't do anything wrong."

Diana's eyes flicked across her face trying to interpret what Elana was feeling. She felt so lost and incapable at understanding or helping the woman she loved. "Then why did you run away?" Elana turned away, her eyes falling on Arya. "Elana, you need to talk to me."

Elana huffed, but she considered. After a time, she looked again at Diana. "I've been escaping to my visions. They're the same every time I sleep. Every time I take Mother's Vision. You and I living on Horopto. We work. We exist. We're accepted. That's all. We're happy. And I can't let it go. I can't stop thinking about it. I don't want to leave it. It breaks my heart every time I wake up."

Diana felt some relief knowing she was in Elana's dreams, but the way she talked about her visions... there was darkness in her voice. Addiction. It wasn't safe. "But it's not reality."

"But it could be."

Diana cocked her head to the side. "Is it a vision of the future?"

Elana shook her head. "I think it's a vision of the way our life could be if things changed. If we'd never been sent on our mission. If we could be selfish. I shouldn't want it, Di'Nay. I should find joy in what we're doing but I can't. I hate it. I hate every bit of this mission. I just want a moment of peace. I want to be with you without fear or desperation. I want to get away from all this hate and just... live."

"Maybe it could be our future. Or something like it. Your visions brought us to Gothis and eventually to Horopto for a reason. We're saving Arya. We'll go to Horopto."

"I don't know if I can step on that island. I don't want to spoil it. I can't stand the thought of going there as a warrior instead of an immigrant. What if it's not like my dreams? What if it's just like everywhere else?"

"We still have each other, Elana," Diana reminded her. "We're still together. Isn't that what you find most comforting in your visions?"

Elana thought. "No. Not just that. It's the island itself. It's the amarin. It's the peace. I don't have to hide there. *We* don't have to hide."

"It's a *dream*," Diana stressed again. "Elana, I'm sorry, but it's a dream. I'm real. I'm here. I need you with me."

Elana closed her eyes, summoning her strength. "It was terrible of me to run away like that."

Diana wrapped her arms around Elana's shoulders and laid beside her, resting her head on Elana's shoulder. "We've all run away from something before. I don't know what you're going through, but I know your strength. If it made you want to disappear, it must be awful."

"I'm so tired, Di'Nay. I'm so tired of traveling all of Aggar and just seeing more and more pain. I know people fear the Keep, but it seems knowing its near is at least a deterrent to hurting the people the Keep serves. But out here... the Keep is nothing but a story. A nightmare.

"I can feel their intention and emotion. I feel the fear people feel when they listen to the Order – even the ones who don't ascribe to them. I feel how people react when they know who I am. I can't avoid it."

Diana listened intently. She had always known the Sight was powerful, but she hadn't thought of all the ways it could wear Elana down. She always seemed so strong. But perhaps assuming that strength would always win out is what got them both where they were.

"We're chasing the Order. The places we go aren't representative of all of Aggar."

"But they are. Even if they don't have a system that hurries the process of abusing seers, they still fear us. I can't walk down any street in Onethis with my eyes showing and expect safety. I can't even expect to be seen as human. Even you in the basement…" Elana clenched her own teeth to stop speaking and Diana's stomach dropped.

"No, let's talk about this. Even I in the basement?"

"You were scared of me," Elana whispered. "And I *was* something to be afraid of. But I would never have hurt you."

"You're powerful, Elana. Like a goddess. But I wasn't scared of your abilities. I was surprised by you. You hide your emotions so well that it's shocking when you show something so intense. I was scared because I didn't know what to expect. I didn't know you had that rage inside you. But I'm glad I know now. You should be able to feel whatever you're feeling without being afraid."

Elana shook her head, her eyes closed. Diana kissed her, trying to shake her out of her dark thoughts. "It's not safe for me to do that. I overstepped my bounds."

"It's all right to be angry. Anger is human. The anger of the oppressed leads to change."

"Not just anger. Any emotion. Anything that overwhelming. I could hurt you. I could –"

"Stop worrying about me. I love you. You can surprise me, frustrate me, even scare me and I'll still love you. We're bound together."

"But how long will you be happy with me? I don't want you by my side just because our lifestones require it."

"My happiness isn't dependent on whether we never fight or upset each other. Please. Trust me to love you as you are. Trust me to tell you outright if you cross a line. And tell me if I cross any of yours. We can't keep running instead of talking."

Elana drew another deep breath and blinked away the tears that had formed in her eyes. "Okay."

Elana walked with Di'Nay down the street from the hawker's, a message from the Council's caravan held tight in her hand. Their caravan had reached the edge of the desert and were entering Karatan. Elana wasn't totally sure how long it would take them to reach Gothis – her and Di'Nay's path through the jungle hadn't been particularly straight and rarely included maintained trading roads – but she assumed it wouldn't be long before they arrived.

She was relieved at the thought. She was exhausted, mentally and physically. Arya's needs were becoming more demanding as she grew used to connecting with Aggar. She was fighting to cut ties with her dreams of Horopto and the future there with Di'Nay that would never be reality. She felt numb. She ignored her Sight more and more, unable to cope with all the feelings of the people around her along with her own.

But she still had Di'Nay. She seemed to draw strength from Elana's attempts at being open and she had thrown herself into caring for Elana as much as she could. She kept Elana to a sleep schedule. She made sure she was eating. Di'Nay even forced her to take short walks every day, either to the hawker's or just to wander up and down the street.

While she felt a bit like a child, Elana appreciated someone else taking over her health. If she'd been left to her own devices she had no doubt she would have stopped eating and sleeping and the fresh air, even in very short spurts, really did help clear her mind. She even thought it was good for Min Nevin – even if Arya cried, it gave her short moments alone with her child again. Enough time to see for herself that she could comfort Arya in the minutes she was away from Elana's Sight.

The streets of Gothis seemed a bit emptier than she was used to, but she didn't miss the bustle. The less she had to be around people the better. She knew once she got back to Min Nevin's, Di'Nay would meet her at the door, she'd ask how she was doing. Her face would be full of love and hope. Elana always felt guilty for admitting she didn't feel any different. It was better than feeling worse, but still. She hated meeting Di'Nay's optimism with reality.

More than once Di'Nay had suggested they take a break after the Nevins were safely with the caravan. Elana didn't like the thought of pausing. They had so much to do. They needed to stall the shipments at Dunn and Rafferty. They needed to find the missing seer children. They needed to move on to Horopto, though Elana wasn't sure how safe the journey would be. The tasks felt impossible. Elana wasn't usually one to give up hope, but holding on was getting harder every day.

She hesitated as she reached the end of the street. A crowd was running further ahead, their amarins a mix of fear and curiosity. Elana could smell a faint whiff of smoke on the air. A fire in Gothis?

Her cheeks colored with fear and she took off running. She pushed her way through the crowd and froze with fear. The Nevin house was engulfed in flames, the fire licking at and spreading to the neighbors as firemen and volunteers rushed hoses that pumped water from the sea to the building. Gothis was so cramped it had to have a powerful firefighting brigade. The fire was being extinguished but the Nevin house was destroyed.

"Di'Nay!" Elana screamed, pushing through the crowd in desperation. She held the lifestone in his wrist, trusting with everything she had left that it would tell her if Di'Nay was hurt or dead. "Di'Nay!"

"Elana!"

Elana collapsed into Di'Nay's arms as her lover found her, holding her tight. Di'Nay smelled of fire and soot. Her clothes were singed and her skin dusted with ash. "It was the order. A bomb in the basement," Di'Nay whispered, her words sharp and furious. "I never suspected it."

Elana pulled back, looking intently into Di'Nay's eyes. "Arya? Min Nevin?"

Di'Nay's features fell and Elana felt her knees buckle. "I was in the kitchen when it happened. I tried to find them. The blast made it impossible to go upstairs without the floor giving way. I tried, Elana, I really did."

Elana stopped hearing her voice. Whether it was Aggar herself reaching through Elana's Sight to save her mind or her own depression finally claiming her, Elana lost sensation of everything.

"One child," she whispered, unsure if it was even audible. "I can't even save one child from pain."

She had no memory of Di'Nay picking her up, carrying her to the inn they'd stayed in before. She didn't remember how Di'Nay bartered for a room or being laid in bed. She was caught somewhere between her visions and reality, everything a haze and an inaudible blur.

She knew she had to be somewhat aware. She had knowledge that days passed. She knew Di'Nay was near. She knew when she was moved from the inn onto a boat. It was night. The sailors wore masks to keep their identities hidden. She knew the rocking of the sea and the ship. She smelled the salt of the sea.

She knew the moment Di'Nay carried her onto Horopto. She started to return the moment she was on the island. She knew when Di'Nay cried over her, willing her to wake. She felt it, but something in her Sight clung so hard to her own destroyed amarin and wouldn't allow her to wake. Truthfully, she didn't want to wake.

She could still feel Arya in her arms. She could still feel the warmth in Min Nevin's smile and the need in her amarin to care for her child. The first seer child Elana had met who might have been spared the abuse and pain of the others like her. She should have been safe. She should have been happy.

If Elana couldn't stop her death, what was the point of ever waking again?

HOROPTO: OUTSIDE OF TIME

Elana sat in the tall grass, watching the ocean crash against the broken stones of the cliff far below. The briny air slipped past her lips and nose and filled her until it was a part of her and her tongue was coated with salt.

She closed her eyes and watched the world through her Sight. The amarin of the ocean was exactly how she knew it would be. It had been loud at the docks in Gothis, but here, surrounded by it on all sides, the amarin sang like the seers in the Keep. She felt an array of life, aware of creatures as small as plankton living in vast clusters of life and as large as whales and sea serpents resting on the ocean floor.

She had never heard of sea snakes before, not like she was feeling now. She had never heard of creatures with the Sight before. They were powerful and still, sleeping as if they'd never wake. Only their amarin feeding into the song of the ocean proved they were still alive. She wondered if they'd wake one day. She wondered if they'd be peaceful or fierce. The thought of creatures connected to her Sight with the power of nature at their beck and call filled her with a mix of terror and joy.

Perhaps that's how the world would end. Perhaps the suffering of those with the Sight would accumulate and wake these creatures of the deep.

The wind tugged at her hair, tightly curled and swollen from the humid ocean air. It brushed against the quilt wrapped tight around her shoulders. Di'Nay had found it for her in the Horopto marketplace, spun with blue threads and pieced together with heavy, textured fabric. Di'Nay had hoped the weight would soothe her and the textures would wake her senses. In a way, it did. Elana felt Di'Nay's intention in it. But even her love barely reached her.

They had been on Horopto for a tenday. Elana had barely been conscious when she'd arrived on the island. Her grief had become so great her Sight had consumed her to keep her alive. Di'Nay had brought her to the island out of desperation, hoping the place she'd dreamt of for so long held something that would bring Elana back. Elana could walk around on her own. She was aware. But she was numb. Her Sight had consumed her, stranding her partially outside the reality where everyone else existed. She didn't talk. She didn't respond. She couldn't seem to remember how.

She wondered briefly if this was a taste of how seers felt. Disconnected from everyone else. Unable to interact in any meaningful way. But she did see what was around her. She saw what she did to Di'Nay. She saw the look on her lover's face when she waited for a response – for any response – and Elana no longer knew how to give it.

"Elana?"

Di'Nay approached and sat beside her. Elana's eyes stayed locked on the sea.

"You keep coming here. Was this in your dream?"

Di'Nay didn't really expect a response, but she hoped. After a moment of waiting, she touched Elana's arm. "It's getting dark. We should go back."

She stood and pulled gently on Elana's arm. Elana didn't fight her. She stood and they walked back together, arm in arm. Elana's eyes scanned the landscape. It was just how she'd seen it in her dreams. The soft dirt paths. The farms. The shepherd and his dog tucking his sheep in for the night, nodding to Di'Nay with his hand on his hat.

There were no inns on Horopto, but Di'Nay had found a small cottage for rent. It wasn't the cottage from her dream, but it was similar. Stone with wooden beams, built to withstand storms. There was already a fire dancing in the fireplace when they returned and a stew boiling on the fire. Di'Nay led Elana inside and sat her at the dining room table while she finished dinner.

"It seems you were right about the islanders' views of the Sight." Di'Nay chatted without expecting a response. She'd taken to speaking aloud all day in the hopes something she said would pull Elana from her mind. "Most have noticed your eyes. Beyond a few questions, they don't seem to care."

Di'Nay put a bowl of stew in front of Elana. Elana ate silently, going about the motions as if it were as natural as breathing or blinking.

Di'Nay sat across from her. "They're very isolated. Many have lived here for generations. Everyone knows when a seer is born. I've never seen a people so unaffected by the Sight. It's... a bit inspiring after what we've seen, to be honest."

Di'Nay reached out and brushed Elana's hair back over her shoulder. "They're very curious about you. They think you're sick or perhaps a seer. They'll be genuinely happy when you're better."

Elana finished her meal and set the bowl aside. Di'Nay watched her, her grief flickering behind her eyes. She was trying to appear strong. She was clinging to every sign of Elana coming back. She'd openly wept the first morning she woke to find Elana not catatonic in bed, but wandering the small cottage garden. But she hadn't changed much since then, and Elana knew she was starting to doubt.

She stared at the table, feeling Di'Nay's amarin, and tried to remember what to do. Every time she felt she was coming close, reality seemed to shift and she wasn't entirely sure what was real and what was a dream anymore. She wanted to give Di'Nay what she needed. She wanted to be what she'd been before. But her Sight was stopping her for a reason. She remembered her grief and rage. They must have become so strong it would be dangerous for her to feel them again.

Elana glanced up, finding the strength to look into Di'Nay's eyes for the first time since she'd fallen unconscious. She hoped Di'Nay saw her attempts. She hoped Di'Nay really sat in front of her and she wasn't just dreaming.

Di'Nay's eyes filled with tears as they connected, but Elana looked away before she saw anything else. She heard Di'Nay take a deep breath, steadying herself, then she took both their bowls to the sink. "We should get to bed early. They were talking about a rainstorm coming in after nightfall."

Di'Nay led Elana to their bedroom and helped her out of her dress. She tucked Elana in like a child before preparing for bed as well. Elana watched her dress for bed and wash her face. She wondered why she never grew tired of watching her. She wondered if Di'Nay would eventually grow tired of caring for her.

Di'Nay glanced over her shoulder at her and smiled. "What are you thinking about?"

She shimmered and stuttered, flickering in and out of existence. Elana blinked, trying to clear her vision, but Di'Nay disappeared entirely. Suddenly, a young girl with white hair, pale skin, and a white dress stood in the middle of the room. Elana remembered her. She was the seer child kept in a temple in Karatan. The seer who had first given Elana visions of Horopto. She watched Elana, her eyes sad and pleading.

Elana reached one hand out to her. Why was she sad? What did she need? She flickered and suddenly it was Di'Nay again, holding Elana's outstretched hand. Her smile had disappeared and her face had fallen with grief.

"Come on, Love. Let's sleep." She blew out the lantern that lit the room, plunging them into darkness. She climbed into bed beside Elana and Elana moved to rest her head on Di'Nay's shoulder. Di'Nay responded, holding her close as she did every night. Her hands trembled, but she clenched them once and they stilled. She kissed Elana on the brow – she couldn't bring herself to kiss Elana's mouth anymore.

"I love you, Elana," she whispered.

Elana held onto the promise in her words. A promise that Di'Nay wouldn't leave. A promise that she'd help Elana get better. A promise that she would never give up hope. Elana wanted so badly to return that promise, but she couldn't even find the strength to look Di'Nay in the eyes again. Instead she rested against Di'Nay's heart, each pound setting the world awash in new colors and twinkling lights, and hoped Di'Nay could somehow feel her love as well.

Diana sat at the dinner table in silence, her chin resting in her hands. Her exhaustion rested heavily on her shoulders. It was still dark outside. She hadn't been able to sleep since coming to Horopto. There was something about resting next to Elana that left her uneasy. Sometimes, like at dinner, she knew Elana saw her. She interacted with her or responded to her voice. But other times, she knew Elana was seeing something she didn't or knew Elana had no idea Diana was even in the room with her.

How aware was Elana? Did she really see her most of the

time? Feel her? Know she was there at all? It felt somehow... nonconsensual. And once she was awake, her mind twisted and turned until sleep was impossible. So she slept in spurts, resting as long as Elana leaned on her, obviously connecting with her, but woke the moment she turned away. The moment Diana felt like a stranger in her own bed.

She took a sip of her tea, listening to the wind and gentle rain outside. She used to sit up late and listen to storms as a child. She had never been afraid of them – she'd reveled in them. Now they were soothing, the chaos outside mirroring the chaos in her mind.

She didn't know how long Elana would be lost. If she would ever come back. Diana had set aside nearly all the funds she had left from the Keep to rent the house. If they stayed much longer, she would have to start working at the docks to pay for their quarters. It would be worth it. Elana was more awake here than she'd been in Gothis and the people didn't intrude in their lives, even knowing Elana's nature. But this was still new to Diana. Of every future she'd imagined for herself and Elana caring for a mute lover with little sense of the world around her wasn't one of them.

She had to bring her back. She'd brought her back from her visions in the jungle. She would bring her back now. She just needed to know what was going on. Was it a natural reaction to grief for a Blue Sight? Was Elana running away with her Sight in the same way she'd run away with the Mother's Vision? Had Diana chosen poorly bringing her to Horopto? Was the island of her dreams really helping her or was it just blurring her lines between reality and her dreams?

Or was it something else? A side effect to the drugs that was just waiting for a large enough emotional response to activate? She needed to find out. The island was welcoming to seers and Blue Sights. There had to be a medic who had experience with their needs. Or perhaps she could go to Karatan in search of a medicine woman with experience working with Mother's Vision? Elana had proven she could care for herself for short periods of time. She could...

Diana shook her head and ran her fingers over her face. She didn't want to leave Elana. She wanted to think her love alone could bring Elana back to her, but that was proving less and less likely. Did that say something about their relationship? Was Elana running away from her on purpose? She didn't have any answers and she might not ever get them.

She finished her tea and took it to the sink to wash. She couldn't let herself get lost in grief or questions that didn't serve any purpose. If she was going to survive, she needed to assume Elana could be brought back. She had to assume it had nothing to do with their relationship and everything to do with Elana's horror at finding out Arya and Min Nevin's fate or the effects of the drugs she'd been using to escape.

She had to make the world right so when Elana came back she wouldn't be upset about their time on the island. She needed to keep trying to bring her back with her love. If the Mother was real at all, if there was justice in Aggar or the Sight was a power and not a curse, then it had to understand Elana was more useful awake than wherever she was now. Diana had to believe. She had to plan. And she had to save Elana.

She leaned over the sink and watched the sun rise outside the window. The rain still fell and the heavy dark clouds blocked the sun, but the landscape steadily grew lighter. Diana had to admit the landscape was beautiful. Rolling green hills and the wide expanse of ocean beyond. It felt so separate from the rest of Aggar. A bit of paradise. Diana wondered what kept it that way, how the people seemed so different than anyone else.

If Elana was well and there weren't any missing children, it was a place she could see them settling down. She would love to see Elana as she'd been before, focused and joyous, standing on the cliffs of Horopto. The beauty of the vision only made Elana's current condition more terrible.

Diana glanced into their bedroom. Elana was still in a deep sleep, breathing peacefully. Diana's heart ached at how normal she looked. It made the cabin suffocating. She stoked the fire once more to ensure the house stayed warm and pulled on her cloak before walking out into the light rain.

The scent of wet dust lingered over the trail into town. Diana didn't know how many would be awake yet in town. The farmers would undoubtedly already be up waking their animals, but the market seemed a bit slower than in other towns. Diana suspected it didn't get much trade and the population was small enough demand for anything but the essentials was fairly low. She didn't mind. She wasn't particularly anxious to be around other people, but she didn't want to be alone with her thoughts.

As she'd thought, the market was mostly empty. A few people milled about, waving tiredly to each other before going about their business. Diana kept her hood up and they mostly ignored her. She reached the small port and wandered along the shore, watching the fishermen setting out to shore. It was peaceful. It felt like another reality.

She strolled further down the docks and hesitated at a small shop already lit and open. She saw painted canvases on the walls – a museum or art shop. Diana cocked her head. She hadn't seen anything quite like this in all her travels on Aggar.

She stepped inside the shop. The paintings were surprisingly abstract for a world as primitive as Aggar. The color scheme was decidedly lyrical abstractionism, though with subjects more grounded in reality. Forests. Grassy plains. The sea. They were dreamlike, colorful in a way that almost reminded Diana of home. Yemaya's color scheme was slightly different from Aggar, and seeing more lavenders and blues blended into the greens and browns of Aggar captured Diana's imagination.

"Good morning."

Diana turned as a young woman stepped out of a back room, drying her hands on a cloth. She wore an apron splattered with paint. Her blonde hair was bound up on her head. She was as pale as Elana, seemingly out of place so far south.

"Good morning," Diana returned, extending her hand. "Min...?"

"Dhalin. Maria Dhalin."

"Your work is beautiful, Min," Diana complimented. "So different."

"A little strange, yes. But I like it."

"Perhaps strange here," Diana agreed.

"Is there work like it in the empire?"

"I don't know much about Empire work, but this would be appreciated on my homeworld. Probably on the mainland here as well."

She stood beside Diana, examining the painting of a forest landscape. The trees were highlighted in lavenders and aqua, the shapes hazy as if seen in a vision. "I've sold a few off the island, but most sell to the locals. They seem to like them."

"You have a gift. They could hang in a gallery in Markessa."

Maria smiled softly to herself. "That's very kind of you. And perhaps you're right. But Horopto is small and is known for very little outside of the rumors in Gothis. I like that my work is special. That it can be a kind of gem just for the people here."

Diana reconsidered the work. "I like that."

"I've heard you're taking care of a sick woman."

"Yes."

"A Blue Sight?"

Diana studied Maria, waiting for judgment or prejudice but there was no hate in her voice. "Would she like one of these?"

Diana's brows rose. "I don't know have much money and we may not be staying long."

Maria shrugged. "Then return it before you go."

"Why?"

Maria removed the painting of the forest from the wall. "You're in a rental cottage. You should have a few beautiful things during your time here."

Diana held the painting carefully. It meant something to her to imagine a piece this beautiful – a piece that was rare and unknown to the rest of the world – in Elana's space as she recovered.

"Thank you. I think she'll love it."

"I hope so. Perhaps you'll bring her for a visit sometime?"

"I will. It was nice to meet you, Min."

Maria smiled again and disappeared back into her workroom. Diana watched her go, still stunned by her generosity. She liked the thought of bringing something beautiful home for Elana. Perhaps it would give her some kind of peace.

Elana sat in the middle of the parlor staring up at the painting Di'Nay had brought her. It hung on the wall over the fireplace mantle. Elana hadn't been able to take her eyes off it since Diana had brought it to her. It seemed to exist exactly on the edge of her visions and reality. It was beautiful. It was complex. She couldn't imagine anyone without the Sight being able to create it.

But even more than that, it was the small, illuminated figure of the seer girl in Karatan wandering beneath the trees that capture Elana's attention. She moved, as if exploring the dreamlike landscape. Elana knew she couldn't really be there, at least not in any way Di'Nay could see, but the child seemed happy there. A heaven designed specifically for her.

Elana leaned back across the floor, propping her head up on her arms. Di'Nay was spending the day in Gothis getting supplies, visiting the hawker, and running other errands. She trusted Elana to stay in the cottage or the nearby grassy plains. Elana didn't have any real desire to wander away, but the painting held her transfixed and somehow focused her all at once. Eventually the seer child sat beneath a massive pine and looked back at Elana, holding her gaze. She wanted something.

Who was the artist? Elana had to meet her. To see her other work.

As the sun rose high into the sky, she stood and wrapped a cloak around her shoulders. She walked out onto the dirt road. Her bare feet were cold on the wet ground but she didn't mind. She liked feeling connected to the earth. She felt eyes following her as she made her way into town, but she kept her head down and her hood pulled up.

She remembered Diana talking about the gallery by the docks. She made her way through the town with little difficulty. There was a small market, mostly run by the wives and children of the local farmers and fishermen. There were a few homes and buildings mostly inhabited by dock workers, an island council, fishermen, and a few farm hands.

Horopto was surprisingly self-sufficient. Elana didn't see anyone from off the island in the docks, but she knew they had to come through from time to time. She wondered if it was their reputation or if they chose to disconnect from the outside world. She wouldn't blame them for hiding. They had a small piece of paradise. What did they need the rest of Aggar for?

She reached the docks and paused a moment as the movement of the floating walkway set off her Sight. She blinked hard, trying to focus as colors shifted and the amarin of the sea became thunderous. She saw the seer of Karatan in the distance, standing in front of a shop window.

As Elana's grasp on reality began to return, she walked carefully across the docks to the shop where she'd seen the seer. She looked into the gallery's windows in awe. Whitewashed walls held carefully mounted paintings on stretched canvas. The sunlight streaming through the windows and strategically placed lanterns, lit even in the day, caught light on the artist's work, show the array of color and life.

They were mostly landscapes, many of them from around Horopto, but they were abstract, colorful, peaceful. They held intent that went beyond capturing realism or a true moment in time. These were dreamscapes and fantasies.

And every one of them held a rendition of the seer of Karatan. She wandered the meadows and swam in the sea. She dove with the whales, her white hair floating like a cloud around her face and ivory skin in stark contrast with the deep blues of the massive creature and the water. She climbed trees. She basked in the sun. They were all her worlds.

Elana stepped inside and studied each one. She saw the seer moving, sometimes just bobbing a foot as she rested, other times dancing wild. Elana had never seen such an innocent, childish expression of joy anywhere, let alone in a seer.

"I'm glad you like them."

Elana spun around in shock, grabbing her chest as her heart threatened to pound right out of it. She let out a deep breath as she crossed realities once more, her mind detaching from the seer she was certain wasn't visible outside of the Sight to a woman she knew was standing in front of her.

She was taller than Elana and more curvaceous, but she was slender and pale for this part of the world. Elana wondered if she'd been sick, but she sensed a good deal of stress, anxiety, and grief in her that didn't make it to her smiling face. She was very good at hiding.

She extended a hand. "I'm Min Dhalin. Or Maria if you like. You must be Elana."

Elana shook her hand. Maria lingered over the gesture, but didn't wait for a response as if she knew she it wouldn't be given. She turned to her painting.

"I've never met a Blue Sight, but I assume you're like a seer?" Elana cocked her head, curious about this woman who stood out even more than Diana did in her mind's eye. Her breath caught in her throat as she realized it before Maria said it – the pale of her skin, the ashy tone to her hair. "My sister was a seer."

The seer child in the painting clapped with joy. It was a jungle landscape with flowers blooming in riots of colors and tangling vines wrapping around tree trunks. The seer child had one of the flowers in her hair. Elana wondered when Maria had seen the jungle.

"What happened to her?" Elana's voice sounded foreign even to her own ears. Her throat was raspy and faint with disuse. Her jaw ached from the movement. How had she found her voice again?

Maria looked at her in shock, but covered the emotion. "She disappeared. I took her to a healer on the mainland. There was a raid. I looked everywhere for her." She turned back to the painting and her amarin became labored at the memories but once again they didn't reach her composed face. How many years had she spent trying to hide her emotions from her seer sister? "I used to paint these for her alone. I would do them over and over again until they had a design that made her happy. She didn't talk. She didn't calm easily. But she liked these. I don't know how to do much else but keep making them now that she's gone. I was happy I could send one home to you. I hope it gave you peace."

The child danced and twirled on a vine and Elana was reminded how happy her amarin had been when they'd shared visions together in the jungle. It made sense that she'd return here now that her spirit was calmed by the network of the other seers. Why she would choose to spend her time in the landscapes her sister had made for her instead of wanting to hide in the embrace of the Keep.

"What was her name?" The question was entirely selfish of Elana. It was clear the child didn't identify with a name, or else she would have communicated it to her. But it was important to Elana. It was important to humanize the child who had been leading her all this time.

"Camilla." A moment of silence passed. "I didn't know seers could talk," Maria admitted. "Shows how much I know about the world."

"I'm not a seer," Elana countered. "Blue Sights are very different."

Maria smiled sadly to herself. "I see. Well, I'm glad you like my work anyway. The people in town seem to appreciate it as well, but for different reasons. Maybe the same things calm us as humans regardless of our abilities."

The seer child in the painting urged Elana, showing frustration and impatience for the first time.

"I've met your sister," Elana admitted.

Maria turned to her in shock. "In a vision?"

"No. In life. She's in Karatan, being cared for. Being treated like a goddess. They're doing well by her. She's at peace."

"It's a pretty thought," Maria whispered.

"It's the truth. With her body at peace, her soul wanders. She's on this island. She's in every one of your paintings. She's with you."

Tears formed in Maria's eyes. "I feel her sometimes when I paint. I work and work and try to capture everything she was but every time I get it right, the second I see her she disappears. I can't look at the painting again."

"She loved them. She loves you. She... sent me to you. She wanted you to know she was well. That when you feel her near she really is. She felt guilty for all the things you went through raising her. For the chaos in her mind that wouldn't let her show you how much she loved you. But she can show you now."

"If your eyes weren't blue I'd accuse you of spinning stories to make me feel better."

"This isn't a story. She wants you to remember the day you took her to the meadow when the blue flowers were blooming. How you tied them into a crown and sang to her and for a moment she was at peace. She smiled the first and only smile she could give to you before she was taken away. Lately all she can do is smile."

Maria covered her face with her hands to hide her tears. Her shoulders didn't shake. She didn't make a sound. She wept in silence like Camilla remembered she would do every time life was overwhelming. She didn't want to upset her sister and she didn't want to upset Elana now. Perhaps that was why Camilla had chosen Elana; Her sister wouldn't believe the stories from anyone else. Maria had to see some of her sister in the messenger.

"She'll be your muse if you like. The guardian angel of Horopto. She has power now she couldn't manifest through her physical body. You gave her everything. You kept her alive. She would like to return the favor if it's something you want."

"I need to be alone." Maria spoke through her hands, her voice heavy with her tears.

Elana nodded. Her message had been delivered. "Of course."

She walked out of the gallery and no longer felt the presence of the seer. She was now with her sister, her voice heard.

There was nothing more for Elana to do but get well.

The burned ruins of the Nevin house had been cleared away, but a dark scar still marked the earth and scorched the cobblestones of the Gothis street. The neighbors' homes, once connected in a long row, were being repaired from where the fire had spread. It had been a miracle the fire hadn't gotten out of control. In a town as packed as Gothis, a fire could level everything.

Diana stood on the sidewalk and stared. Things had been going so well. They'd lived with Min Nevin long enough for the Council's caravan to reach the jungle. Diana had kept everyone safe. But she'd been distracted. Too distracted to see Elana's failing health. Too distracted to tell when the Order had planted a bomb in the Nevin house basement. If she had just...

Diana shook her head and pushed the thoughts aside. There was no use in shame or guilt. No good would come from it, only more distraction. She needed to be focused. There was so much to do and without Elana to help Diana feared she wouldn't be able to get it all finished.

She had already been to the hawker to get the message from the Council caravan that they would reach Gothis before dusk. Diana had told them of the tragedy days ago, but they insisted on meeting with Diana to discuss bringing Elana home. They had come all this way. They had lost so many seers. No doubt the Council would deem the mission too dangerous for a single bonded pair to investigate, especially with Elana in her current state.

Still, Diana wasn't sure moving Elana again was the best idea. She was getting better. It was slow and might not be permanent, but she was better. She'd been dreaming of Horopto for a reason. Diana wasn't sure she could heal anywhere else. Still, it was worth talking about. The Council representatives had come too far to be ignored.

Until their arrival, there was plenty to do. While they had enough food on the island, there were little things they could use that weren't as readily available. Some of Elana's favorite foods, especially the fruits imported into Gothis, would be a welcome addition to their pantry. Diana wondered briefly if she should invest in apple trees. She didn't know how long she and Elana would be on the island, but surely the people of Horopto would appreciate them even after they were gone?

She let her thoughts linger over farming and landscaping to avoid her other thoughts. Her worries about Elana. A possible fight with the Council if they determined Elana should return even if Diana decided it would be unwise. There was also the constant presence of the Order of Blindness in Gothis.

It seemed the street preacher she'd fought with before the bomb was right about the Order's legal connections. The fire had been blamed on fallen candles, despite the obvious explosion. The Order was blameless. They were preaching on street corners and continuing to bring the people of Gothis into their cult as if they hadn't proven they were capable of murder and terrorism.

And then there was Dunn and Rafferty. The shipping company was the largest in Gothis, selling general goods to the public cheaper than the merchants could afford to counter and offering exotic luxuries gathered through their worldwide connections.

Diana hadn't heard of them before arriving in Onethis, so she guessed their trade was far more prevalent in the south than the north, but she knew their tendrils reached at least through the desert. They were one of, if not the only, supplier of Mother's Vision to the rest of the international chapters of the Order of Blindness. The serum that paralyzed and tranquilized seers to make them easier to transport and hide.

It would be a major blow to the Order to stop the shipments. It would make it harder to kidnap and store the seers. They would need to be more selective about their kidnappings and would probably need to keep them together in remote strongholds or risk people hearing a screaming child seer. Diana smiled at the thought of the seer children being kept together, creating their own network of amarin, and freeing themselves. It would serve the Order right.

But short of sabotaging a single shipment, there was little Diana could do to a massive operation like Dunn and Rafferty, especially in the town they practically owned. Something as dramatic as a fire had a high risk of costing innocent life and would only delay shipments, not stop them. She needed to be more subtle, and she needed more political and monetary power than she had.

It's why she had also sent for the Marshals. She hated

involving them so soon after she'd called on them to help free Elana from Karatan. She also didn't know if the secret force from the Ramains would hold much power over a shipping giant who rarely dealt with the Ramains. But they were the best political card she had and their leader, Tristan, had made it clear his first priority was supporting her and Elana. Whatever price they eventually asked for their help, Diana would be sure to pay it.

Diana turned to head toward the market when she felt a tug at her belt. She turned, expecting a pickpocket, but it was a young woman reaching out of nearby alleyway.

"Marisol?" Diana questioned in shock and relief. She pulled one of Min Nevin's nursemaids into a tight hug. "I didn't know if you'd made it out of the fire!"

Marisol shushed her, her eyes urgent and her body tense. Her dark hair was braided back, the locks rough as if they hadn't been brushed in some time. She was dirty, her clothes tattered. Diana was unsure if it was some kind of disguise or if she was living in squalor. "Please be quiet. I need your help."

"What's going on?"

Marisol tugged on her arm. "Follow me."

Diana let the younger woman lead her through town, keeping mostly to alleyways and attempting to remain unseen. Diana kept her hand on the hilt of her knife. She was overjoyed to see a friend had survived the fire, but she didn't trust anyone in Gothis not to be somehow connected with the Order.

Diana became more hesitant as they left the borders of the town and reached the coast, following a thin, sandy stretch of beach north of the town. Marisol started to relax the further they got from Gothis.

"What's going on?"

Diana heard a distant wail and her heart stopped. "Arya?"

Marisol led her to a nearby grotto. The small cave opening led to a wide, circular cavern with layers of rock like wide shelves reaching up the walls that would allow someone to stay clear of any incoming water at high tide. A small wooden crib sat on one of the shelves. Arya's wails filled the cavern, rebounding off the walls. Marisol climbed up to her and pulled a bottle from her belt pouch. Arya drank hungrily.

"How?" Diana was at a loss for words.

"I was able to get out of the house. Min Nevin was trapped

in Arya's room. She couldn't get out, but she dropped Arya from her room into my arms. I hid. I didn't know what else to do. I didn't know if anyone else survived." Marisol's voice cracked and trembled as she spoke. "I was in the city to get formula when I saw you. I've only been there a handful of times for food and once to send a message to Tad Nevin."

Diana climbed up beside her and pulled both the nursemaid and Arya into a tight hug. She couldn't believe the child lived. It was a miracle. It would be a miracle to Elana, too.

"I'm so happy you're both safe."

"I can't go back home. The Order is looking for any survivors still. They never found Arya's body so they doubt her death. If they found me..." She trembled at the thought. "I don't know where else to go. Where did you and Elana go?"

"We're on Horopto," Diana explained. Marisol paled and Diana smiled. "It's not what they say. Just an island. No curses that I can tell."

"Are they seer worshipers like the stories say? Could you take Arya with you? Would she be safe?"

Diana shook her head, her smile growing wider. "The representatives from the Council are still coming. They could take you and Arya. You could start fresh somewhere new if you like. Arya will be taken care of."

Marisol's shoulders sank. She started to cry and Diana held the young woman tighter. "I thought they would have left already or would have been turned away."

"You found me just in time," Diana assured her, happy that her broken promise to protect Arya and the members of the Niven household could be redeemed, if only in a small way. "We'll get you both to safety. I promise."

Elana sat at the window seat waiting for Di'Nay to return. Ever since she'd spoken to Maria and delivered her sister's message, she'd felt a weight lift from her soul. It wasn't the cause of her stupor, but the pressure of it had halted her healing. Perhaps once Camilla realized Elana could help her, she'd intentionally sabotaged Elana's return to reality. But whatever the reason, she felt herself starting to wake up.

It was like a numb limb starting to regain feeling. Elana's entire body, her every sense, seemed to prickle and sting but the pain brought sensation and with sensation came focus. Awareness. She had found her voice again. She'd hummed and sang softly to herself the rest of the day to keep from losing it once more.

Night fell and Elana started to prepare a meal. She couldn't remember little things like how to crack an egg, but somehow more complex things returned. She made bread. She warmed the stew from the night before. She started a fire. They were things she'd done thousands of times before. Things that were a part of who she was. She smiled to herself. She had missed being in her own skin, even if she wasn't entirely returned yet.

It was nearly midnight when Di'Nay returned. She was joyous. Her amarin practically glowed. Elana turned and stared at her in awe, the warmth of her soul a physical presence. She seemed like a goddess come to earth, bathed in golden light.

Di'Nay paused in the doorway and smiled at Elana's immediate response to her arrival. "Hello to you, too," she greeted. She glanced at the fire and the stove. "You cooked?"

"You had a good day?" Elana forced the words, her throat somehow still unused to speaking despite the conversation she'd had in town.

Di'Nay didn't respond. Instead, she ran at Elana, pulling her into her arms and crying against her shoulder in joy. "You spoke! Elana!"

She pulled back to hold Elana's face in her hands and stare in awe into her eyes. The affection was intense, almost too much for Elana to bear. Like looking directly into the sun. But Elana withstood it for Di'Nay.

"A lot has happened today," Elana whispered, finding it easier to speak softly.

Di'Nay wrapped herself around Elana again, almost childlike in her need to hold onto Elana. Elana held her in return, kissed her brow and her hair, letting her cry and rejoice. She had been through so much. She'd lost so much hope. Elana felt her stronger than she had since falling apart. Without the distraction of the seer child, Elana only had Di'Nay to focus on.

"What happened? What brought you back? Was it the painting? Was it gradual? Did you... did you feel me in Gothis?"

Elana cocked her head trying to make sense of the question. "Feel you?"

"Elana," Di'Nay sat up and held Elana's hands in her own.

"I found Marisol. She's been hiding since the fire. She had Arya."

Elana's brow furrowed and she closed her eyes in confusion. She had to be hearing things. She needed to focus. It had to be a dream. But it didn't feel like a dream.

"She had Arya?"

"Yes. She's alive, Elana. She didn't die. I delivered her to the Counsel's caravan just a few hours ago."

"But Min Nevin…"

"She got Arya to Marisol. She sacrificed herself for her child. And tonight she was delivered to the Keep like Min Nevin wanted. I thought perhaps you felt it, that it was why you started waking up. We didn't fail. Arya is safe."

Elana felt tears in her eyes. First Camilla, now Arya. She hadn't been a failure. This mission wasn't worthless. Two children were safe. Children who had known little to no hurt or abuse. Counting Silver and even Gerome and his brother, Elana realized every child that had somehow been in their care had been delivered to safety. Perhaps there was still a chance. Perhaps there was still some good to be done.

She opened her eyes, unable to find the words to express what she felt. Instead she just kissed Di'Nay. The embrace focused her, drawing her scattered thoughts and Sight to a single moment in time, a single sensation of her mouth and Di'Nay's. Di'Nay responded tentatively at first, unsure, but gradually spurred on by Elana's confident and conscious touch.

"Are you back? Are you really here with me?" Di'Nay questioned.

"I'm here with you," Elana assured her. "Help me find my way back for good."

Di'Nay laid her back against the window seat, her mouth and hands becoming more insistent even as they stayed careful and aware of any sign of Elana slipping away or protesting. Elana reveled in the touch, her own amarin singing in time with the sea. It was her dream, only amplified because it was real. Di'Nay. The cottage. The island. The sea. It was paradise, but she was alive. Her heart beat and her blood pounded. She breathed and tasted her lover on her tongue and in her mouth. She was coming home, and this time she had no desire to leave again.

Diana sat in The Wharf, the small tavern on Horopto. She was hidden amongst a rowdy crowd of fishermen and farmers unwinding after a long day at work. No one paid attention to her, and they paid even less attention to Elana in the back of the room, hidden in a dark cloak and shadows as she watched. Diana was still unsure how much she liked Elana coming with her back to Gothis, but Elana had insisted and Diana couldn't deny her anything.

It had been another tenday. The council caravan had come with more gold – a request the seers must have insisted upon since Di'Nay hadn't thought to ask in any of her letters before the caravan left. The money had been enough to pay for the cottage on Horopto for another couple tendays in case it was needed as well as resupply them for the next leg of their travels, wherever that might be.

Elana had returned in leaps and bounds after the discovery that Arya and Marisol were alive and well. Every now and then Diana would still see her drift off or lose herself in her thoughts, but she wasn't entirely convinced it was more than Elana usually allowed herself to drift away. She was present. She was focused. She was the Elana Diana remembered and perhaps a bit more. Still, Diana doubted she would ever relax again when it came to Elana's health. A relapse was never out of the question.

Diana eyed the door, waiting for someone to meet her eyes. A representative from the Marshals had arrived, probably once again from the embassy in the desert. Elana was surprised at their speed, but she had stopped questioning the Marshals' resources long ago. She would never know the full extent of them and as long as they continued being able to help, she didn't need to know.

Elana, however, was less sure. She had thankfully agreed that the Marshals were their best weapon in taking on Dunn and Rafferty, but she doubted their intentions more than Diana did, and Diana wasn't particularly trusting herself.

Elana lifted her brows as a middle-aged desertman step into the bar. He seemed out of place – his skin darker than the average resident of Gothis, his head shaved, his clothes fine and his black goatee carefully maintained. There was no reason a man like that would come to a bar like The Wharf unless he was looking for someone.

Diana raised a single hand to him, eyeing him carefully. He seemed relieved to see her and made his way through the crowd to sit at her table. He handed her a marked gold coin, the emblem stamped with the house crest of the leader of the Marshals, Tristan. Diana would have bet money he worked as a merchant, which made sense. Tristan would want to hand a mission like this to someone who knew shipping and trade. "Min n'Athena, I presume?"

"Yes." Diana shook his hand. "You?"

"Tad Salazar. I work out of the Ramains embassy in the Southern Desert."

Diana felt a moment of relief – the Marshal who had helped her in Karatan came from the same embassy. "I hope your journey went well."

"Took me a good deal of time to figure out how to get to this island," he grunted, obviously unamused.

"I'm afraid this is the only safe place to talk. Gothis has a lot of prying ears," Diana remarked. She didn't add that Elana refused to let him near their cottage.

"I think I may have perked a few of those ears asking about Horopto. You didn't tell me the island this feared by the locals."

Diana studied him. She'd spoken with a lot of Tristan's associates among the Marshals, but Tad Salazar was the first who had such a sharp attitude. "I'm glad you were able to make it," Diana commented, skating around his complaints. "How much do you know about our situation?"

"A fair amount, between the briefing when I accepted this case and information from a few of my contacts. I warn you that trying to stop any sales at Dunn and Rafferty isn't going to be a trivial task, even if it is just a designer drug."

"Dunn and Rafferty is providing a seer tranquilizer to the Order. It's allowing them to keep kidnapping children. We need to stop their entire business."

Tad Salazar chuckled. "Stop all of Dunn and Rafferty?"

"It would be best. They're owned by the Order and actively supply them with goods."

"They're also one of the biggest exporters to Onethis, Karatan, and parts of the desert."

"They're kidnapping children," Diana reiterated, shocked at his nonchalant attitude.

"And putting them out of business would result in hundreds, perhaps thousands, of lost jobs."

"Jobs that are supporting a cult of child kidnappers and

seer torturers. Tristan deemed the Order a major threat to the Ramains."

"The Order, yes. But Dunn and Rafferty – regardless of their origins – do barely any business with the Ramains. The company isn't a threat. I'll help you cut off their supply of the narcotic, but that's it."

Diana felt Elana's eyes burning against the back of her head, unamused. Diana clenched her teeth. She hadn't realized this would be a negotiation. The Marshals had always helped her with whatever she needed.

Diana had dealt with a lot of merchants, negotiating deals and prices with more than a little skill. She recognized his posture and the gleam in his eye. He was haggling. Perhaps he even did significant business with Dunn and Rafferty – something Diana assumed Tristan would have seen as a benefit when he assigned Tad Salazar to this mission. But it was clear his allegiances laid less to the Marshals than his pocketbook.

"The cult killed our friend in Gothis. They think they killed more. A baby and her mother," Diana stated, hoping to express the severity of the issue. Min Salazar didn't seem phased.

"I'm sorry for your friend, but you need to see this from my perspective. You're working to save the lives of a handful of seers. I'm saving the livelihoods of ten times as many people at least. What about their children?"

"If we don't stop them now, they're going to keep feeding the threats in the Ramains."

"Not if I stop the drug."

Diana clenched her teeth. It was clear she wasn't getting anywhere with him and she had nothing to bargain with. At best, she could write Tristan. "Fine. What do you need from me?"

"I need to know the name, properties, and look of the drug. I'll handle negotiations from there."

Diana pulled a small bottle of Mother's Vision she'd purchased from Gothis. "It's called Mother's Vision. It comes from the jungle, but it's supplied to the Gothis merchants through Karatan immigrants. It puts seers into temporary comas, induces visions, and has general tranquilizing effects."

Tad Salazar slipped the bottle into a pocket in his robe. "Excellent. I'll be back in half a tenday with a progress report."

"That's all you need?"

Tad Salazar smirked and the hair on the back of Diana's neck stood on end in frustration. "I can handle this. It was good to meet you, Min."

They shook hands again and Tad Salazar disappeared from the tavern as quickly as he'd arrived. Diana watched the door almost in shock. Elana moved to sit beside her.

"That's not what I expected," Diana muttered.

"That's exactly what I expected," Elana growled. "The only thing more powerful than hate is greed."

"He had a point about jobs."

"The market will recover. The seer community could be eradicated due to the Order."

"I'll write Tristan. He should at least know what his representative is up to."

Elana shrugged. "You expect more out of him?"

Diana chose her words carefully. "He's always been there for us. It's more likely there's a bad egg among Tristan's ranks than the entire organization is corrupt."

"They have a massive amount of secret information. They're spies and informants. Tad Salazar isn't just annoying with access to that information – he's dangerous. That makes the Marshals a potential liability no matter what Tristan's intentions."

"Even more reason to write Tristan."

"Do what you like, but I'm going to figure out our next move."

Diana touched Elana's knee under the table, not wanting to fight or disconnect from Elana so soon after getting her back. "I'd like your ideas about what to do. I don't like him. I don't like trusting Tristan. I'm just trying to make the best use of our resources."

Elana shoulders sank and she laid her hand atop Diana's, squeezing once affectionately. "I know. I'm sorry for being sharp." Elana stood. "Let's go home."

"Home?"

"Home for now."

Diana smiled. "I like thinking of it as home, at least for a while."

Elana grinned in return. "I do, too."

Diana stood and they left the tavern together, stepping out into the chilled night. A thin layer of fog had settled over the island, shrouding it in a sense of stillness and mystery. Diana and Elana held hands the moment they were outside the borders of the main town, strolling casually back to the cottage.

"We should go to Gothis tomorrow. Make sure he does what he says," Elana suggested.

Diana didn't feel like arguing. "We can see what the morning brings. I don't want you overexerting yourself."

Elana turned, ready to fight, but she stopped herself. "Thank you for worrying about me."

Diana was shocked at her softness. "I don't want to lose you again."

"I know." Elana kissed her cheek. "I'm going to try to have a vision. I need guidance about where we go next."

"Elana!" Diana gasped.

"Not with Mother's Vision. Just a dream, I promise."

"What if you relapse?"

"I won't."

"Elana –"

Elana stopped and turned to face Diana. She looked hauntingly beautiful in the foggy light of evening. The night painted her skin dark blue and her eyes seemed to glow like gemstones. "This is what I do, Diana. The way I can help. I don't want to run away anymore. I'm here with you. But we're out of leads."

Diana drew a sharp breath past her lips. As unsettling as it was, Elana was right. They took risks. They put their lives on the line. It was part of the mission. She would have to trust Elana would always come back to her.

"All right."

Elana kissed her. "Thank you."

Diana nodded slowly. Elana took her hand again and they continued their journey home in silence.

The cliffs of Horopto were a completely different experience for Elana with her wits about her. She smiled against the breeze and closed her eyes, listening to the music of the sea like before, but this time it was quieter, soothing, whispering of depths and mysteries that made Aggar's amarin more complex, not overwhelming. She felt present, the prickle of the tall grass around her brushing at her sides, hands, and bare feet. The breeze lifting and playing with her hair, skating along her nape and brushing her cheeks. Even the crash of the waves against the rocks far below seemed more playful than before.

She wondered how many other places and experiences were dramatically different through a seer's eyes. As a Blue Sight, was she blind to certain realities or was her relationship with Aggar just different? Seers were unbelievably powerful, and in groups they were even able to change the landscape of Aggar. As a Blue Sight, her role was to observe, not to interfere. Perhaps Aggar was more at peace with her than someone with the ability to take control. Or perhaps there were always layers to amarin she would never sense without a deeper connection to the spiritual plane.

Either way, she found she didn't care. Her time just dipping her toes into the reality of being a seer was more than enough for her. She liked being able to immediately tell reality from spirit and existing in a plane where her thoughts and emotions couldn't completely change her surroundings. The experience had, however, given her a new sympathy for seers, particularly the children. No wonder they screamed and wept. It had to be so confusing, so chaotic. And even Elana had to admit the moments of peace – the moments where it was quiet, warm, and safe and she could free her mind – were incredible.

She'd never been able to leave her body or take control of her surroundings the same way Camilla could, but she could see the network that connected everyone, now just see it, but exist in it. What she had to sense as a Blue Sight was just another sense – immediately known and part of her reality. She had slipped in and out of visions, every emotion and touch made a piece of artwork out of her world. It was magical. She could only imagine what it was like for a real seer, or a seer in the company of others. No wonder the seers in the Keep sang with so much joy. They were more connected and more lovingly aware of each other than other humans would ever be.

The wind rustled more insistently against her right cheek and she turned her head to block the sudden sting. She smiled as she suddenly saw Camilla standing to her left in her mind's eye. She seemed so happy – smiling and laughing, her amarin totally at peace.

"There are other ways to get my attention," Elana whispered and the child clapped her hands as if to say she knew, but moving the wind was more fun. "You seem happy."

Camilla beamed and for a moment she seemed to carry a golden aura, as if she emitted sunshine. Maria must have believed Elana. Or perhaps knowing her sister was near allowed Camilla to better interact with her. Either way, Camilla wouldn't be so happy if Maria wasn't coming around.

"Have you come to say goodbye?"

Camilla shook her head and suddenly Elana felt more. She saw Arya cradled in the grass as if it were a bed. She laughed and reached out to Elana. Her senses were still weak and her mind that of a child, but her message was clear – she was safe. She was with the two seers who had made the journey in the Keep's caravan to save her. She was finally happy. Elana wondered how much she would grow to remember the mother who had died for her.

Behind her, Elana felt a third presence. Silver stood in the tall grass, wearing a white dress like Arya, but her long white hair blew in the wind and her jaw was clenched. She held her baby brother in her arms, the first seer Elana and Diana had saved from the Order. She was strong and present. She reminded Elana of an Amazon. She had known real pain, but was now getting stronger for it. She seemed to have a watchful presence over the younger souls, despite the fact that Camilla and Arya could never have met her in person.

Elana wondered at it, but even before she could speak, Silver responded. She was the oldest of the children Elana had freed. Within the community of seers, they were a tribe unto themselves. Elana's children. The survivors of the Order and their hatred. Silver was sure others would soon join them.

Elana wondered at the feeling of Silver in her mind. She had to be at the Keep – there was no other way her presence would be so strong. Was this what Diana regularly felt like when Elana responded to her feelings before she spoke? It made Elana smile.

"You were always so strong, Silver."

Silver lifted her chin and Elana saw a touch of Di'Nay in her. Just as she'd once dreamt of her son in her arms, she now saw Silver as a daughter.

Elana closed her eyes to better see them, standing out like lights in her mind. They all watched the sea for a moment, basking in its power and energy. When their silence started to carry a feeling of expectation, Elana spoke.

"I'm trying to figure out where Di'Nay and I go next. Where we'll do the most good. Should we be staying to tie up loose ends or are there others that need our help more? I know you're searching for others. What advice can you give?"

Silver walked up to her and crouched behind her. She set had brother on the ground and he toddled off into the grass, sitting in wonder beside Arya. He laughed aloud and Elana's heart trembled at the sound of such a happy baby, not yet able to form words but able to exclaim in joy at what he found wonderful.

Silver smiled at him, her eyes those of a parent, then she turned back to Elana. She raised her hands and covered Elana's eyes from behind. Elana couldn't see her but she felt the heat of her, felt the strength of her hands as if they were physically pressed against her cheeks.

She was instantly caught up in a vision. She saw a forest of long, slender green reeds rising taller than she was. She heard a woman breathing heavily as she ran, saw the reeds sway and rustle. She was suddenly in the woman's body. She looked down at her running feet. They had been cut in her haste, little flecks of blood rising around the straps of sandals. She looked over her shoulder. Elana didn't see anything, but she felt the woman's terror.

Little bits of information came from the woman's mind she temporarily inhabited. Bamboo. Darkness. Marshals. The Order. Nile.

Elana gasped as Silver pulled away and the vision disappeared. She opened her eyes, grounding herself and trying to make sense of what she'd seen. "Taisa? She's alive?"

Silver clapped her on the back in congratulations, more like a sister than a child. Elana couldn't help the burst of laughter that escaped her lips. Silver saw herself as Elana's caretaker now.

"Are we Blue Sights so hard to herd in the right direction?"

Silver only grinned at her, then stood.

"I don't know what bamboo is," Elana admitted.

Camilla drew a map against the rock, somehow forming the sea spray into a design that didn't blow away. It was a map of Aggar. She circled a place further south than Onethis and to the east – a landmass separated from the main continent. An island large enough to be its own country. Elana and Di'Nay would have to travel by boat.

Beneath the map were written the words "Mountain" and "Jidoin." If Taisa was there, she had to have been taken there on purpose. Had she fled on her own? Or had the Marshals planned her escape?

"It's as good a place to start as any," Elana admitted. "Thank you."

They all smiled at her and Elana felt their thanks. She realized, in that moment, just how much she had done. How much she'd saved. They were happy and strong, no matter where they started. Even Silver, despite the horrors she'd lived with, seemed to be somewhat better for it. At least more capable.

She didn't know how long they'd guide her, or even how long they could. She seemed to be traveling further and further from home with every new mission. But she was more determined now than ever to see more among their ranks. To return any abused or stolen seer child home to this beautiful space. She would save them. She *could* save them. And for a moment, that knowledge was enough.

JIDOIN FOREST: MONSTER

Elana stood on the edge of the fishing boat, staring out at the distant stretch of land. Mount Yul rose high into the sky surrounded by a wide expanse of an emerald green bamboo forest.

"Are you sure you want to do this?" one of the fishermen questioned. "That forest is not good."

He spoke the Ramains dialect in stilted sentences, but he was fluent enough to take the job. The fact had surprised Elana, since they were so far south from the Ramains. She'd always been good at languages, but the nature language in Cheongu seemed to have a different root than the language in the Ramains. She'd picked up bits and pieces, but finding someone who could passably speak her own language had been a gift.

"Yes. Thank you for your help getting this far," Elana responded. He seemed unsure and nervous, but he nodded and went to prepare the rowboat.

"Min... You're not going there to leave, are you?"

Elana shook her head, reading his real question in his amarin. "We aren't suicidal. We're looking for something."

"Nothing there but the Fates."

The Fates were everywhere according to many urban legends Elana had heard in her journeys. Every time the people didn't understand a place it was a doorway to the Cellar. "We'll be swift and quiet."

"Mother willing," he intoned.

The fisherman and his two employees wore cloth masks over their faces, either to retain their anonymity from passing ships or to ward of some kind of disease or curse Elana didn't know. They hadn't been on Cheongu long – just long enough to figure out their destination and hire a ship. It had taken a good deal of gold. No one in Cheongu wanted to go near Jidoin. Even now Elana and Di'Nay would have to travel alone the rest of the way.

It had taken far longer than Elana expected to reach the island nation of Cheongu in search of the missing Blue Sight, Taisa. Elana had never learned about it in her studies, and her visions guiding her hadn't included the name of the nation. She'd been led to search for Jidoin. Only the map she'd seen in her dreams had helped her get to Cheongu.

Elana and Di'Nay had traveled by boat, horse, and foot, backtracking multiple times and getting false leads from ferrymen. It wasn't until they'd traveled further south that the name Jidoin was recognized. It was a bamboo forest on the north side of Cheongu. A forest that was said to be home to the Fates and their creatures.

"Are you ready?" Di'Nay questioned as she walked up behind Elana, studying their path into the forest.

"It's odd seeing it outside of my dreams. Taisa is always afraid, but with my own eyes it seems beautiful."

"That's unsettling."

"Yes. Taisa has the Sight. She wouldn't be afraid of nothing."

"We'll have to talk to her about it when we find her."

Di'Nay placed a reassuring hand on Elana's shoulder, squeezing once, then went to help the fishermen load their supplies into the boat. Elana climbed aboard when it was ready to be lowered, steadying herself in the tiny vessel swung on the ropes of a pulley system. Di'Nay tipped them for their help, hoping with enough gold their voyage would be kept a secret.

The fishing boat didn't wait for them to reach land to leave. They sped away after only a moment of watching to be sure the rowboat moved safely. Whatever happened from then on was up to Di'Nay and Elana alone.

Elana steadied the small rowboat as Di'Nay climbed out onto the beach. The narrow stretch of sand was completely buried during high tide, but was the only way to reach the steep path up into the bamboo forest. Elana and Di'Nay had waited in their small rowboat for hours until the beach was revealed.

"This is ridiculous," Di'Nay grunted as she pulled the boat to shore and stored the oars under the bench seats. Elana pulled her backpack onto her back and handed Di'Nay her bag.

"It makes sense to disappear to somewhere hard to get to." Elana and Di'Nay lifted the boat onto her shoulders and started their climb up the hill.

"Still."

Elana smiled. "At least we got to land."

"Finally."

Their hike was slow and arduous, taking a physical toll on both women despite their levels of fitness.

"I'm starting to see why the locals think this forest is cursed," Di'Nay paused to catch her breath and dug her heels into the sand to keep from falling back. Elana drew a deep breath, grateful for the break.

"Not cursed. Forbidden," Elana reminded her.

"Why is everywhere we go cursed or forbidden?"

"The last one turned out all right for us."

Di'Nay glanced over her shoulder at Elana. Sweat gleamed on her brow and her cheeks were rosy from the climb. "True." She readjusted the boat and continued forward. "Any chance this one will go as well?"

Elana's voice was weak and breathy. Her sides ached as she tried to speak. "Let's hope so."

They reached the top of the hill and set the boat down. Elana let out a sharp huff and held her side. She looked down the sharp hillside to the ocean, then back up to the canopy. The wind rustled through the tall bamboo trunks behind her, creating a tone that reminded her of wind chimes. Elana had never seen anything like it outside of her dreams. The bamboo with their long, smooth emerald trunks and wispy leaves seemed impossible. They swayed, far more flexible than trees, and grew in surprisingly sharp lines like poles stuck directly into the shallow, grassy underbrush. No raised roots. No wild, twisting branches. The forest seemed almost man-made.

Elana trusted her visions, but if she ever doubted, it was moments like this that reassured her. She could have never imagined this on her own.

"The greens here are so different from the greens back home," Elana observed.

Di'Nay laughed, regaining her energy. "An interesting thing to notice."

"Have you seen anything like this before?"

Di'Nay nodded. "Back home. One of the Shae centers I studied at was in a forest like this. If anything, I'm surprised we have such similar flora."

Elana was mildly jealous of Di'Nay's travels, but it was quickly wiped away by her joy at seeing something so new for the first time.

"Now that we're here, where do we go next?" Di'Nay questioned.

"This is as far as my visions took me," Elana admitted. "We should probably pause for the night and I'll try to gain more guidance."

Di'Nay sighed appreciatively. "I was hoping you'd say that."

"Tired?"

"Are you saying you're not?"

"Not at all. It will be easy to dream today."

Di'Nay scanned the forest. "Not easy to build a shelter with so little to work with."

"There's no rain coming and the weather is warm enough. I'd settle for a flat place to lay our bedmats."

Di'Nay wandered forward a few paces, testing the ground with her feet. "Here?"

Elana laughed. "So lazy, Love."

"I don't want to carry the boat anymore."

Elana grabbed the bedmats from their supplies. "Neither do I."

Elana napped for the rest of the day, fading in and out of consciousness as Di'Nay rested, scouted, and prepared a meal. Visions never came. She had never been able to call them to her, but since her visit from the seers she'd saved with their message about finding Taisa she'd dreamt of Jidoin every night. It seemed now that they were there, she had to make her own decisions.

As night fell, the forest became significantly more eerie. With their long, skinny and branchless trunks, the bamboo made cross patterns of shadows that felt strangely like prison bars. Unlike in a forest, where there were many places to hide, the forest was both covered and incredibly open. She seemed to see things out of the corners of her eyes often. She understood why so many would assume it was full of spirits.

"Are you too well rested to sleep through the night?" Di'Nay questioned.

"No. I couldn't seem to rest long."

"It is a bit unsettling here."

They peered into the darkness and everything felt unusually silent. They'd seen fewer animals than Elana had expected – mostly birds and the occasional insect. Night felt more unnerving silent than full of the chaos of nighttime creature noises.

When they laid down to sleep together, Elana and Di'Nay held each other tightly. Elana wished she hadn't been so quick to accept a place to sleep with so little scouting. Perhaps if they'd tried a bit harder they could have found a more sheltered location. She found she couldn't sleep.

As the Mother moon was high in the sky, Elana heard a massive shift in the bamboo, as if a massive wind had hit them. She sat up, startled. Di'Nay woke from her sudden movement. "What is it?" she muttered tiredly.

"The wind," Elana whispered, still unsure. Then, she felt something warm on the back of her neck. It was Sight, not real, but it twisted her stomach with anxiety. It felt like the cold breath of a predator. "Something's near."

"What? An animal? Taisa?"

"No."

Elana felt it closer and stood, looking around.

"Elana?" Di'Nay stood as well, now nervous.

"We should go."

"The boat?"

"Leave it. We know where to find it. We need more shelter."

They grabbed their bags and Di'Nay lit one of her flashlights, bought off a small Terran trading post along the way. Elana didn't need her light. She saw well enough in the dark with her Sight. Too well, sometimes, for her to feel safe.

"What kind of shelter are we looking for?" Di'Nay questioned.

"Just something better protected."

"What do you feel?"

As Di'Nay spoke Elana felt suddenly consumed by the heat

on the back of her neck. They'd been spotted.

"Run!" she shouted and they took off.

A creature made of mist and shadow took form behind them. It was massive – well over three times Di'Nay's height – and broad. Elana didn't have time to examine it, but she had definitely seen four thick legs, a whip-like tail, and horns. Its body was incorporeal, passing through the trees like smoke. It snorted and growled, its feet pounded at the ground as if it had hooves and the earth quaked with its every step. Based on Di'Nay's sudden cry of surprise and horror, Elana knew it wasn't just a creature of the Sight.

They fled like mice before a cat, weaving and dodging in the hopes of finding some way to shake their attacker. The creature didn't stalk or pounce, it only raced, running at them like a bull. Elana didn't feel much from its amarin, only a need to run.

"Here!" she called, grabbing Di'Nay's hand and leaping off a small ledge that had been hidden by the grass. They dropped to the ground and pressed up against the wall of the ledge, hiding in its slight overhang.

The creature, surprisingly, didn't stop. It continued running into the distance, blowing the bamboo around it as he went.

Elana coughed and gasped as she tried to regain her breath and still her pounding heart.

"What was that?" Di'Nay whispered.

Elana leaned back and closed her eyes. The heat on the back of her neck still lingered, but the creature was obviously getting farther away. "A creature of the Cellar?"

Dawn came and the forest seemed to finally still. Diana loosened her grip on Elana. The forest had stopped quaking at the creature's rampage. It had been running all night. They'd been able to tell its path by how violent the earthquakes became. The bamboo rarely fell, even when it was near, but they bent and swayed dangerously. Thankfully, their small alcove had seemed to protect them from the beast and the quakes.

"I think it's gone," Elana announced. "I don't feel it anymore."

"Do you think it will come back?" Diana questioned.

"I don't know. I didn't expect there to be an actual

creature.”

“Have you ever seen anything like that?”

“Never.” Diana leaned back against the ledge that had protected them and closed her eyes. She was exhausted. Elana stood and walked out into the forest, scanning the trees for any sign of life. “I don’t think it was looking for us.”

Diana opened her eyes. “What do you think it was looking for? It materialized right behind us.”

“I don’t know. But it never went after us once we escaped its path. It seemed… mindless. I don’t think it could stop running. Maybe we were just unlucky in terms of where it appears.”

“Whatever it was, we should try to avoid it in the future.”

Elana seemed distracted, but she eventually turned back to Diana. “Agreed.” She sat beside Diana again. Diana loved the weight of her head on her shoulder as Elana leaned against her. “You should get some sleep.”

“We should find shelter to get us through tonight,” Diana countered. “Perhaps if we head toward the mountain we can find a cave or a bigger outcropping. Once we’re set up well, I can sleep.”

“And if we don’t find anything and we spend tonight awake as well?”

Diana smiled, though she dreaded the thought. “Then you’ll have to carry my exhausted body tomorrow.”

“I’ve done it before.”

Diana chuckled. “That you have, Love.”

They pulled themselves out of the alcove and into the new dawn light. Diana didn’t know what she’d expected, but she hadn’t expected the forest to look exactly as it had the day before. No snapped bamboo, no damage, not even missing grass. What kind of creature could do all this?

“It’s like it never even existed,” Elana observed. “If you hadn’t been here, I would have thought it only existed in the Sight or I’d had a vision.”

“I definitely saw it,” Diana confirmed, shuddering at the memory. “I thought things like that only existed in stories.”

“I’ve never heard stories like that.”

“The Ramains is significantly different from Cheongu.”

“I never realized how much I didn’t know.”

“I felt the same way the first time I went off-world.”

“I like it.”

Diana smiled, reminded once more how much of a kindred soul she'd been lucky enough to find in Elana. "I do, too."

They continued their hike through the forest, heading toward the mountain. Every sound made Diana's heart pound. Did the creature only come out at night, or would it attack again? Were there others like it? What made Taisa stay here?

By midday they reached the base of Mount Yul. Diana looked up through the breaks in the forest at the mountainside towering high overhead.

"Hopefully a thunderbird won't burst out of the mountain tonight," Diana teased, though the humor was laced with a strain of truth.

"Perhaps it would fight off the bull?"

"We can only hope."

Elana paused. "It's disconcerting how little noise there is in the forest."

"I'd think most animals wouldn't settle here."

"Still. Doesn't it feel like everything's a bit muted? Even the rustle in the bamboo."

Diana paused to listen. Elana was right. The noises were all a bit softer, lacking depth and tone. It was like they were far away or played through a speaker. The moment she realized it, she couldn't stop hearing it. It left her unsettled. "What do you think it is? Is there something off in the forest's amarin?"

"Not that I can tell." She hesitated. "Wait."

Diana glanced at her, her muscles tensing as she prepared to fight or flee. "Do you sense something? Another creature?"

"Not a creature."

Diana heard the sharp click of a crossbow and grabbed Elana, pulling her back as an arrow plunged into a bamboo stalk behind her. Diana instantly grabbed the short sword at her hip and Elana grabbed her bow. There was a flicker of movement and Diana took off after the shooter, catching up quickly and pinning the archer to the ground.

Diana relaxed her grip when she saw it was a young woman. She grabbed the crossbow and threw it to the side. "Taisa, I presume?"

The woman paused her fighting and stared up at Diana in surprise. She was smaller than Diana had expected, shorter and more slender than Elana. Her auburn hair was pulled back in a long braid. Her shirt and pants were worn and big on her, indicating new weight loss. Her blue eyes were darker than Elana's, standing out sharply against her olive skin.

"How do you know my name?" she demanded. She looked between Elana and Diana. "Are you Marshals?"

Diana exchanged glances with Elana and released Taisa completely.

"We're not Marshals," Elana stated as she reached down and helped Taisa stand. They locked eyes and Taisa backed away in shock.

"Blue Sight!"

Elana sighed in frustration. "Like you."

Taisa looked between them again, more tense and suspicious than ever. "You travel with a Terran."

"I'm not a Terran," Diana argued.

"I know an off-worlder when I see one!" Taisa spat.

"Not all off-worlders are Terrans," Elana remarked, trying to defend Diana. "We've been looking for you. We need to talk."

Diana sensed what Taisa was going to do before it happened. She lurched forward to stop her, but Taisa was faster and more agile than she'd expected. Within seconds she'd grabbed her crossbow and fled into the forest. Diana and Elana chased after her for a while, but she quickly disappeared into the thicker foliage along the mountain. She had obviously been here a while – long enough to smoothly know her way around the wilds.

"That wasn't what I expected," Elana muttered as they stopped.

"She seems to harbor a lot of hatred, even of her own kind."

"That seems to be a theme among Blue Sights raised outside of the Keep," Elana agreed.

"I wonder how much of her beliefs are her own and how much is from her time with the Order."

"I'd never considered she ever believed the lies they spread," Elana admitted.

"Community and brainwashing can be powerful. We don't know much about her. She might not be willing to talk to us."

Elana squared her shoulders. "She doesn't have a choice." She adjusted her backpack and continued walking deeper into the woods.

Elana stared up at the sky as dusk fell over the mountain. The mountain, while sporting thicker underbrush and more recognizable foliage, seemed even more open than the forest. The bamboo didn't seem to grow as well on the rockier surface. If they were attacked again, there weren't many places they could avoid the bull.

"How does she survive?" Di'Nay asked herself as she scanned the mountainside.

"Taisa?"

"She has to have some way to avoid the beast. We saw her running up the mountain. There must be something we're missing."

"Maybe the beast still forms near the beach. It may not even climb the mountain."

"Hopefully."

They continued hiking. Elana could feel Di'Nay's energy steadily waning as her own head started to swim. They had to focus. The mountain grew steeper as night fell and Elana reached out through the network of amarin in the undergrowth, looking for signs of divots, alcoves, or any rocky outcropping that could provide some kind of shelter.

The hair on the back of her neck rose as she felt the ground tremble. She turned and looked down at the forest below. Near the beach the bamboo rustled and waved, marking where the bull had appeared. It instantly started running, leaving the bamboo trembling and swaying in its wake. The burning on the back of her neck returned and she knew the bull could sense her again.

"It's back," she announced.

The earthquakes grew stronger as the bull sped straight for them. They ran, searching desperately while being careful not to lose their footing on the rockier ground. It seemed from the size of the creature that it wouldn't be able to climb the more narrow trails they'd been following, but Elana had no doubt a creature made of mist would be able to go wherever it pleased regardless of terrain.

As the trail they were following fell away, ending at a sheer cliff, the bull appeared behind them. It moved effortlessly, its misty legs pounding at the earth as if the terrain were as smooth as in the forest.

"Here!" Di'Nay shouted as she dropped over the edge of the

cliff.

"Di'Nay!" Elana screamed in shock, but as she reached the edge she saw a ledge not far below.

She slid down the cliff, falling into Di'Nay's arms as the bull rushed off the cliff after her, running for a time in the air before dissipating into nothingness. Di'Nay set Elana back down. Di'Nay was trembling, fighting her most primal fears being on such a high ledge. Elana held her hand as she looked around, trying to find a way back up the cliff. To her surprise, instead of a trail she found an opening in the side of the cliff on a separate outcropping. A narrow ledge about the width of Elana's feet bridged the two ledges.

"Di'Nay."

Di'Nay looked and let out a breath of relief. Elana continued holding her hand as they slowly traveled toward the cave. As they reached the second outcropping, the ground started to tremble again. The bull had reappeared.

"We should be safe here," Elana tried to reassure her lover. They turned into the cavern. It was deeper than she'd thought. The opening was the door to a pathway leading deeper into the stone. Elana stepped inside and gasped.

"Elana?" Di'Nay held her shoulder tighter, afraid of what her gasp meant.

Elana rushed down the pathway to the larger cavern that opened at the end. It was warm, a fire burning in the center of the circular room. Taisa sat against the wall, wincing as she unsuccessfully tried to bind a broken leg with small bamboo stalks and rope.

They met eyes again and Taisa glowered. "How did you find this place?"

Elana felt Di'Nay relax as she saw what had shocked Elana so much.

"We were running from the bull," Elana announced. She indicated Taisa's broken leg with her eyes. "I assume you were doing the same."

Taisa's lips pulled back in a snarl. "Get out."

"If you don't bind your leg, it could heal crooked," Di'Nay warned. "If you don't get an infection that takes you first. We can help you."

"You've hunted me down in the most remote part of Aggar.

You expect me to believe you want to help me?"

Elana crouched in front of Taisa, trying to meet her eyes but the Blue Sight pointedly looked away from her. "You know my intentions," Elana announced.

"I don't know anything."

"You have the Sight, same as me."

She huffed and Elana felt swells of self-hatred, denial, and misery. She had felt some of it before when they'd met earlier in the day, but here it was so strong she could almost touch it. "Get out," Taisa repeated.

"You'd rather die here of a fever or cripple yourself for life than admit you can feel I mean you no harm?"

Taisa only huffed and continued staring at the wall.

"No matter what you want, we aren't leaving until morning at least," Di'Nay announced as she sat on the ground. She pulled dried meat from her pack and started to eat. Taisa tensed and Elana felt a new emotion. Hunger.

Elana reached into her bag and drew out a piece of tack bread. She offered it to Taisa. "There are no animals here. At least not enough to hunt. You must be hungry."

Taisa continued to ignore her, but Elana set the bread and some meat on her lap and walked away to sit with Di'Nay. As they shared a meal, mostly ignoring Taisa, Elana was pleased to see after about an hour Taisa discretely ate what she'd left her.

"You should sleep," Elana told Di'Nay. She glanced at Taisa. "We'll be safe here."

"What about you?"

"I'll sleep in a shift after you. I want to make sure she's safe."

Di'Nay nodded and leaned back against the wall, falling asleep nearly instantly. Elana watched her for a moment, smiling softly as her lover finally got much-needed rest. She then settled back and watched Taisa, hoping the silence would become too heavy and uncomfortable for her to stay silent.

She was more willful than Elana had suspected. She felt Taisa was in pain, she was hungry, she was uncomfortable at Elana watching her, but she barely moved for hours. She had existed off fury and pride for so long it seemed nothing for her to outlast Elana's exhaustion. Just when Elana was about to give up and sleep, Taisa tried to move and cried out in sudden pain. She grabbed at her leg, tears falling down her cheeks as she fought the urge to cry.

"Let me help you," Elana pled. "This is ridiculous."

Taisa didn't respond, and for a moment she thought Taisa would continue to fight her, but eventually she sat up taller and looked at Elana. She removed her hands from her leg in silent acceptance and Elana rushed to her side.

Elana quickly assessed her injury – thankful the break seemed to be clean and hadn't broken the skin – and bound it back together with the stalks and rope Taisa had gathered. Taisa clenched her jaw through the entire process, refusing to scream or cry. Her skin flushed with pain, but it was the only outward sign of the agony she was in.

"There," Elana announced as she finished tying the rope and pulled away. "You need to keep weight off it for three tendays at least."

"Impossible here," she argued. "I'd starve."

"Di'Nay and I can help you." She glared and Elana shot back an equally fierce glance. "Or you could die. There's pride, and then there's stupidity."

Taisa huffed, but she seemed to acquiesce. After another moment of silence, she seemed to relax. "Why do you travel with her?"

"Di'Nay?"

"The Terran."

"She's not a Terran."

"She's not from Aggar. Those imperialist dogs are taking our land."

"Not everyone who comes to Aggar from another world is an ally to the Terrans." Elana rolled up her sleeve, revealing the lifestone embedded in her wrist. "We're bonded."

Instead of tensing in disgust at proof Elana came from the Keep, Taisa seemed curious. "What is it?"

"A lifestone. You've never seen one?"

"Not in someone's arm."

"Where do you come from?" Taisa fell silent again. "Taisa. Please. If I wanted to hurt you, I would have already. If you don't want to trust your Sight, talk to me. I'll answer anything you ask."

She considered and Elana fought a smile when she felt the last of her stubbornness slide. "Why did you come here?"

"We need your help. Di'Nay and I are looking for seer children. Children kidnapped by the Order of Blindness."

Taisa looked like she was going to be ill. "I'm not with the Order anymore."

"I know. But you were. You hid who you were and you followed them for a long time. I thought you died in Dwaramin, but obviously you didn't."

"You were in Dwaramin?"

"Looking for the seers, yes. I discovered you accidentally."

"How? I covered all my tracks."

"You can't cover your amarin. When you took your amulet off the power of your Sight left a mark on your room. You'd bound yourself for so long. It must have been torture."

Tears came to her eyes again, but she grit her teeth and pushed all feeling away. "I survived."

"You did. I don't know how. But there was a child at the Order's keep near Dwaramin. A seer who said a woman hid him in the desert."

"He wasn't a seer," Taisa argued. "He was pretending."

"Is that why you saved him? He wasn't a real seer?"

Taisa's gaze grew fiery. "I didn't know about the children. Any of them. I wasn't going to let him get hurt."

Elana calmed at her announcement. "We found him and got him to safety because of your sacrifice."

Her chin trembled for the first time, the thought of saving Simon more powerful than the pain she'd endured in silence. "I'm glad he's all right."

"We found blood in the warehouse. It was yours."

She ran her hand through her hair instinctively, the hand trembling at the memory. "I was supposed to disappear. I wasn't supposed to go back. But I couldn't leave Simon after I knew he was being kept there. The Order doesn't like defiance."

"But they didn't kill you?"

"They tried."

"What happened?"

She considered. "How do you know so much about me? You can't see details with the Sight."

Elana reached into her backpack and drew out a faded letter she'd been carrying with her since Dwaramin. "This was delivered when I was in your room."

Taisa took it slowly, her breath caught in her throat. "My letter. I thought... I thought he had received it..."

"I'm sorry for the invasion of your privacy, but we had to know more about the Order."

Taisa held the letter closer to her heart, lost in memory and grief. "He saved me. They had me in a cage and he saved me. But he couldn't look at me after he learned what I was."

"Why would you follow him? Why the Order?"

"You don't understand."

"I understand love. But this..."

"It wasn't just about love. I was trying to save him from them. They'd infected his mind. They took him away from me. He'd only listen if I was one of them."

Elana hadn't considered that option. Her letter seemed so blindly passionate. Perhaps she'd been saying what he wanted to hear. The woman before her was hardly the submissive, desperate woman in the note. "I can't imagine what you went through."

"They made sense at first. We both went to hear them speak. Nile was angry about the Terrans invading our planet like we were nothing. I... I hoped they had a way to cure me. But then things got worse. They were violent, targeting more people from Aggar than Terrans and Blue Sights. There's a lot more going on in the Order than they pretend."

"Like what?"

She fell silent once more, this time not from anger, but fear. "I don't want to talk about it."

Elana didn't push her. "You asked if we were with the Marshals. How do you know them?"

"I assume if you know who they are, you've run into them as well. The Marshals saved me. They brought me here. They bring me supplies occasionally."

"Why would they do that? The Marshals don't do anything for free."

Taisa snorted. "Free. No, they don't. I earned my freedom. I reported on the Order for a tenmoon. I risked my life over and over sending reports, maps, and technology. And what do they do in return? Strand me on an island that's the night time hunting ground for some infernal pet of the Fates!"

Elana scowled. "Sounds like them."

"I'm not convinced they're any better than the Order,"

Taisa growled. "Disloyal, persuasive bastards."

Elana felt a new bond with her fellow Blue Sight at their shared distrust of the Ramains' secret service. "Do you want to leave? Di'Nay and I could help you."

"Where else would I go? The Order is everywhere. They don't come to Cheongu because they're poor and don't care about seers. The minute I set foot on the mainland, they could find me."

"You could go to the Keep in the Ramains."

"No." She said the word and her intentions were clear and final. "I'd rather be consumed by the bull."

Elana let it go. There was still time to plan. "What do you know of the creature?"

"It comes out every night, always hunting. It can sense me. It spends hours running over the cliff, trying to get to me, but it can't pause or exist disconnected from the ground. This cave keeps me safe, but I don't know any other way to ward it off."

Elana sighed. "You were lucky to find this place."

"I'm sure I found it the same way you did. Fleeing. Falling. It's a miracle I'm still alive."

"You seem very strong."

"Perhaps."

"Not perhaps. I've worn an amulet of the Order of Blindness. I nearly went mad."

Taisa looked away. Her voice was soft. "I'm not sure I didn't."

Elana reached out to touch her good knee, trying to give some kind of comfort. She was pleased that Taisa didn't flinch. "We should all sleep. You need to heal and Di'Nay and I are exhausted."

Taisa nodded sharply. "You're right."

Elana laid down beside Di'Nay and felt Taisa fell asleep as her own mind started to wander into dreams. She smiled softly as peace replaced the uncomfortable silence in the room. It wasn't perfect, but her new relationship with Taisa was a start.

Diana pulled herself over the ledge of the cliff and took a moment to appreciate being on more solid ground again. The ledges had been wide for a cliff, but Diana thanked the Goddess that their cavern wasn't far from the top of the cliff and she'd been able to climb it in the light of day.

Elana was staying with Taisa, watching over her as she healed. It was up to Diana to find food – with some instruction from Taisa – but there was more on Diana's mind. There had to be something to the creature's appearance. A piece of tech, some kind of summoning... she had no idea what it could be, but she refused to believe it really was some kind of demon. The Terrans didn't seem to be a strong presence in the more southern parts of Aggar, but they did exist on the planet. If the bull was some kind of elaborate hologram, she wanted to know.

She stood, adjusting her backpack on her back. She'd written down the description of various edible plants Taisa had given her. Diana didn't know how Taisa would be able to survive much longer with such limited food sources and no way to tend a garden or farm. Even if she had the seeds and tools she needed, the bull's nightly rampages would make any plot hard to care for if it survived the creature's hooves at all.

Over night Elana and Taisa had become closer. Diana could tell from the way Elana spoke to her that she was trying to get Taisa to come with them back to the Keep. Diana wasn't sure what the best course of action would be, but Taisa's options would certainly open up if Diana could figure out the origin of the bull and how to stop it.

Diana hiked through down the mountain back into the deeper parts of the forest. She timed her traveling, making sure she'd have plenty of time to return before dark. Along the way, she collected herbs, root vegetables, and even found a berry patch in the undergrowth of Mount Yul. With the bull scaring away most animals, the food-producing plants remained fairly undisturbed. While it wouldn't be filling and would certainly be lacking in certain nutrients, there would be enough to eat for a couple days.

Once Diana reached the forest, she followed the base of the mountain. Most of Jidoin was flat and visible through the spaces left by the slender bamboo stalks. If there was some kind of machine creating the bull, it was far more likely to be in the mountain. But if that was the case, why would the bull keep appearing by the beach? It didn't make sense.

As midday turned to evening and Diana was preparing to turn back, she turned down a mountain path she'd never taken but she assumed would lead her in the general direction of Taisa's cave. Less than a mile up the path, she paused. The ground felt different and the light seemed to catch and reflect off white stones beneath the brush. Diana bent and stared in awe. There were pockets of lifestones – clusters of it – growing in the mountainside. Diana ran her hand over the opalescent veins and they warmed in response. The lifestone in her wrist warmed until it was almost too hot. Diana drew her hand away and smiled. Could Elana feel it, even a few hours away?

She stood as she made a mental note of the lifestones' location. She would want to come explore again tomorrow. She continued down the path, following the veins like a trail. There were multiple deposits, some larger than others, but the veining was consistent. She hadn't seen so much raw lifestone since her journey through the Wildlings' caves in the Ramains.

Diana wondered at the nature of the stones. They were obviously connected to amarin, to Aggar. They worked in an almost magical way. How did they function? Were they powered by their carriers or Aggar itself? Would the raw lifestone in the cliffs be more connected to Elana's Sight than the stones Diana and Elana carried in their wrists?

The thoughts fluttered in and out of her mind as she traveled, keeping an eye on the deposits as well as watching out for more food. The journey was slow and as she reached the edge of the cliff, she found herself significantly higher up the mountain than she assumed. She clenched her jaw as she searched for a way down. Night was falling. With the backtracking she'd have to do, it would be night before she reached the cave.

She walked faster, looking for a route further down the mountain. By the time night truly fell and she felt the first quake of the bull she was still high above the path to the cavern. She stopped running and instead looked desperately for some kind of cover. She scrambled up the path, small stones skittering past her feet as the bull grew closer. To Diana's shock, however, it didn't come after her. Instead, it sped down the path toward the cave, running off the cliff and disappearing as it had done the night before.

Diana paused, watching as it reappeared by the beach again and resumed its cycle. She leaned back against the mountain and watched it repeat the same process. Why was it still targeting a cavern it couldn't reach? Was it because there were two people in the cave, and therefore drew more of its attention? Or perhaps it was something else?

She started moving between the bull's cycles, pausing as it drew near and then running as it repeated its run. It never came after her. It didn't even seem to notice her presence. As she reached the proper path, she hid, waiting for one more run before continuing to the cave. This time, however, the bull tossed its head as if confused and slowed its run without stopping. Diana felt a jolt of fear. Was she too close? Would it find her this time?

The creature continued its run, seemingly unable to stop as Elana had surmised, but this time it turned its massive head and looked at Diana. She felt as if she'd turned to stone. She had never taken time to look at it closely.

It was indeed a bull, pulling its mist into a tighter shape as they locked eyes and it raced past. It had nine tails, each one a slender whipcord that flowed behind it like a cat-of-nine-tails. Its horns seemed lighter than the rest of its inky black body, like polished flint. What grabbed and held her attention, however, were its eyes. It had lifestones for eyes.

It continued its run, falling off the cliff. Diana had no doubt it would chase her on its next cycle, so she took off at a sprint. She felt the earth rumble and roll as the creature sped after her, trying to overtake her, but as it reached Mount Yul Diana was already sliding over the edge of the cliff and racing into the cavern.

Elana grabbed her in a tight hug, obviously terrified when she hadn't returned after dark. In the safety of the cave and in Elana's embrace Diana felt the full weight of what she'd seen. The fury in the creature's lifestone eyes had been like burning embers. There had been some degree of intelligence in its gaze along with a fair amount of primal instinct. It had looked so solid, so real. It wasn't a hologram. It was a creature. It was real. A creature made of pure darkness and stone. She had seen many new creatures and plants on Aggar, but she hadn't imagined the existence of monsters. The bull was something out of story and myth. It shouldn't exist.

"What happened?" Elana questioned.

"I need to sit for a moment," Diana whispered as she slid off her backpack, tossing it to the ground and sitting. She tried to will her body to stop shaking and she winced at the sound of the bull leaping off the edge of the cliff once more.

Elana crouched beside her, more concerned than she'd

been when Diana first returned. "Di'Nay, what did you see?"

"I saw the creature. We met eyes. Elana, it has lifestone eyes. It's a creature of Aggar."

Elana's voice was a soft whisper as she fell back to sit beside Diana. "It has the Sight."

Elana handed Di'Nay her waterskin, watching her hopefully as her color started to return. She was shaken, pale. The bull had a huge impact on her.

"I've heard of creatures like that," Taisa offered. Elana turned to her. "Creatures with the Sight."

"What have you heard?"

Taisa dug through Di'Nay's bag, fishing out berries and fruits. "Just legends. Creatures created by the Mother and the Fates in the beginning. Elementals. I never believed in them."

"I felt sea serpents with the sight at the bottom of the ocean near Horopto," Elana announced.

"Sea serpents?" Di'Nay gasped.

"Sleeping deeply. Practically stone."

Di'Nay didn't seem comforted by Elana's assertion.

"There are supposed to be others, too. Fire creatures, wind creatures, earth creatures."

"Do you think the bull is one of these legendary creatures?" Di'Nay asked.

"What else could it be?"

Elana leaned back against the wall, propping her arms on her knees as she considered. Lifestone eyes. She'd never heard of such a thing, but it would certainly imply the creature was more connected to the Sight and Aggar than she'd expected. But it obviously didn't sense the peaceful side of amarin. It was all rage.

"Perhaps it woke because of Taisa and I?" Elana suggested. "Maybe it can sense our Sight."

"It preferred to go after you over me, even knowing you were unreachable," Di'Nay agreed.

Di'Nay and Taisa talked, trying to make sense of the creature's nature. Elana barely listened, lost in her own thoughts. Creatures with the Sight. The thought still caught at her mind and refused to let go. The bull, like the sea serpents, were mysteries she'd never even considered. She always felt like an outsider among the people of Aggar despite knowing logically that she was more connected to the planet than anyone without the Sight. The thought that there were animals – and perhaps plants – that also existed in the Sight reaffirmed her beliefs that people like her – seers and Blue Sights – were created by the Mother herself.

Perhaps the first people on Aggar were all Blue Sights. Perhaps, once, every living creature had some attachment to the Sight. Perhaps creatures like the bull were remnants of older races just like Elana was.

Despite its rage and destruction, Elana felt a sudden affinity for the creature. It had to continue existing. Still, she refused to sacrifice anyone she loved to it. Perhaps it would even calm once she and Taisa were gone. If it hadn't met any others with the Sight, it made sense that its primal mind would interpret everything new as a potential threat.

"We should get off the island. All of us."

Taisa and Di'Nay turned to her in surprise at her sudden interruption.

"I can't go anywhere else," Taisa remarked. "Even if I wanted to I can't run."

"We can travel in spurts. Find cover along the way. Di'Nay and I have a boat."

"And even if we survive getting to the coast, where do you expect me to go?"

"Stay with us. We'll figure it out," Elana offered.

"If the Order finds me, they'll kill me."

"We'll protect you," Di'Nay promised, trying to back Elana's decision.

"I'm not going to the Keep!"

"You don't have to," Elana insisted. "But if you stay here you'll die. You'd already be dead if we hadn't found you. You can't live on berries and roots alone, and the moment you get hurt away from shelter the bull will catch you."

"You don't know that."

Elana caught her eyes, her insistence filling the amarin between them. "I do know that."

Taisa snarled and turned away, ignoring Elana's Sight. "What could I even do? I'd slow you down."

"You could lead us to the Order. You could tell us where other seer children might be kept."

"That would be suicide."

"Staying *here* is suicide. With us, you can at least save a few of the lives you put in danger."

Taisa fell silent at Elana's words. Elana genuinely didn't know what her response would be. Would she cling to the Order's ideals and the fears she'd been raised with? Would she refuse?

"I'll think about it."

Elana relaxed a bit. It was probably the best she could expect.

"Please do. Think of saving dozens of children. Think of taking down the Order so you don't have to be afraid anymore. Think of being free."

Elana knew her words stung, and she meant them to. At the end of the day, Taisa had helped the Order, even if it was just for a short time. Her self-hatred had been inflicted on others like her. Children who couldn't defend themselves. She wished they could work together, that Taisa would prove she'd really changed her ways. But if Taisa refused to come, Elana wouldn't lose sleep over leaving her.

The bull thundered over them again and Elana frowned at the noise and constant earthquakes. She turned her attention from Taisa to Di'Nay. She touched her lover's shoulder. "We should sleep. We may have a long day ahead of us."

Di'Nay nodded and they laid down beside each other. Elana felt Taisa's mind spinning and she appreciated that the Blue Sight was giving Elana's offer real thought. She doubted Taisa would get much sleep.

That night Elana dreamt of the bull, its eyes sparkling white with veins of fiery color. She dreamt the lifestone in her wrist connected them. She dreamt of running with it, feeling its fear and rage, felt the primal power of racing at full speed. She and Taisa had upended so much coming to Jidoin. The locals were right. The forest should be protected and left empty.

When Elana woke in the morning, she knew she'd been right about her impressions of the beast. She wondered what it would be like to find the beast at enough of a rest that they could connect through the Sight. Was it ancient or some young, wild offspring of creatures that had lived in Jidoin for ages? What was it thinking and feeling when it wasn't driven mad by others with the Sight?

Elana pondered it as she made breakfast, using the fire to

roast vegetables Di'Nay had found the day before. Di'Nay was already out scavenging for more food. Taisa sat in silence the entire time, just watching. As Elana served her a skewer with the cooked roots, she finally spoke.

"Do you really think I could do some good?"

Elana felt a sense of triumph, but she tried not to let it show. "Di'Nay and I have been traveling on visions and word of the Marshals alone. We don't have any ties to the Order and therefore have little idea where their strongholds, warehouses, and most powerful cells are. We don't even know what their strategies are in different regions. Even if your knowledge is limited, you know more than we do. You could guide us."

"And you'd protect me."

"With our lives." Elana hesitated. "You may not like the Keep. I don't know what stories they tell about it this far south. Even if you held a good opinion of it, it's unlikely you'd be able to reach us. You don't have to find sanctuary there. But we have resources, too. If you're going to trust your safety and identity to anyone, trust the others like you. We wouldn't have abandoned you in a place like this."

Elana saw a seething fury beneath Taisa's skin, a reaction from a lifetime of hating everything to do with the Keep. It was the same emotions she'd seen in Gerome, but even more so. Still, she didn't speak. She didn't refuse Elana outright.

"I'll think about the Keep. I've been fooled many times about what to believe. I don't trust anyone not to do it again. But you're right about the Order. It needs to be wiped from Aggar, and if anything I know will bring them down, I'm willing to go with you."

Elana nodded sharply in approval. She would come a long way. "Good. Now we just have to figure out how to get you to the beach."

"I know a few different places to hide. We wouldn't have to get to the beach in a single day. But each leg would still be risky, especially as we get closer to where the bull appears."

Elana sat back against the wall, considering. "We can wait a while, let you heal more. Perhaps I can even find something to make a poultice for you to help you heal faster."

"You said this would take multiple tendays to heal."

"Yes, to heal completely. But you'll be able to put some

weight on the leg in shorter time. It will be easier than if Di'Nay has to carry you the entire way."

"But our escape depends on reaching your boat. What if it's crushed or harmed while we wait? We don't have time to repair it. There's nowhere safe to hide on the beach."

Elana hadn't thought of the boat. She pressed her lips into a tight line. It did complicate things.

"Let's talk to Di'Nay when she gets back. We'll get off this mountain, Taisa. All of us. I promise."

Diana eased Taisa up over the edge of the cliff, Elana supporting her from below. Taisa bit back her cries of pain as she used even her broken limb to push herself up over the edge. Elana followed more quickly with their supplies. She'd be carrying both bags as Diana carried Taisa.

New dawn light lit their way. They'd started out the moment the bull had disappeared. Elana had fashioned a thick stalk of bamboo into a crutch for Taisa in case of an emergency, but for the most part they'd travel with her slung over Diana's arm. She was even lighter than Diana had expected, being both small of stature naturally as well as probably undernourished. Still, it would be a difficult journey onward.

"The first place to hide is at the base of the mountain a few hours into the forest. There's a small pocket there covered by bamboo that fell during a storm. The bamboo is hardy, even after it's been cut. We'll have to do without a fire and the bull may run over top of us, but there's enough depth beneath the bamboo roof that we'll be safe. The bull is dangerous, but it isn't heavy. It can't stomp us out."

Diana held onto her words – just a few miles from the base of the mountain. With healthy legs and a good pace, they could make the journey back to the beach in a couple days. With Taisa, however, and the placement of her refuges Diana didn't know how long it would take.

Still, they had agreed the danger of losing the boat was too great to risk. The forest was vast and none of them knew much about it outside of a few days journey in any direction. If the bull had access to the entire region, losing the boat would be a death sentence.

"Rowing won't be pleasant, but we'll be able to reach the

first village in Cheongu in four days," Elana stated. "From there we can hire a ferry or fishing boat to a larger coastal town. We can get Taisa better splinted, restock supplies, and get a boat to the mainland."

"We might want to stay a while. Let Taisa do most of her recovering under the care of an actual healer. You said the Order isn't in Cheongu?" Diana asked Taisa.

"No. The Order has nothing to gain here. Cheongu is poor and suspicious of strangers. It would take a good deal of work to get a foothold here. They'd rather focus on cities and large centers of trade."

"Good," Diana announced. "At least the Marshals seemed to pick a good region, even if the forest was a terrible idea."

"Not knowing the nature of Jidoin was unacceptable," Elana argued. "The locals even warned us. You'd think the Marshals would at least investigate before leaving an informant here."

Diana chuckled at Elana's sharp response. "I wasn't defending them, just trying to look for the positive."

Elana fought back her frustration and calmed. "Sorry. I just don't understand how they could be so incompetent sometimes."

"It's because I wasn't useful to them anymore," Taisa spat. "At the end of the day, despite what they said, I had become useless and I was cast aside."

What cheerfulness Diana had tried to cultivate disappeared at Taisa's bitterness. Even Diana could tell it came from a place that had little to do with the Marshals. No wonder it was hard for her to trust Elana and Diana – had anyone ever been trustworthy in her entire life?

The sun was just setting as they reached Taisa's hiding place. Diana eased Taisa inside with a rush of gratitude and prayer to the Goddess for the small miracle of keeping them safe for another day. Diana's body ached as she slid under a patch of strong, fallen bamboo arranged into a flat roof over a deep pocket in the earth. It was deep enough that if the creature ran overhead, the bamboo could sway and tremble without hurting them, but it wasn't deep enough for anyone to stand upright.

Diana wasn't concerned with standing. Her strength was gone. Her body screamed. She secretly hoped Elana would insist they spend a day resting before continuing, but she would make whatever plan everyone agreed on work. Goddess knew she couldn't wait to be out of the forest.

Elana checked Taisa's leg, readjusting her splint and using her Sight to soothe Taisa's amarin. It wasn't enough to heal anything, but it reduced swelling and pain enough that Taisa could rest. Diana wished there was some way to make them all sleep as the bull started its run. It went mad the moment it felt them all near, speeding over the bamboo above them in a seemingly endless cycle.

It seemed Taisa was right about its weight. The bamboo above them bent and rustled at the pounding of its hooves, but they didn't splinter or crack. Diana thanked the Goddess it was made of smoke and mist.

After a while the trembling and rush of hooves became almost hypnotic. Elana drifted into a shallow sleep, resting for a time before a particularly violent run would temporarily wake her. Taisa slept more peacefully. Diana wondered at how quickly they grew used to such a strange setting. If they stayed for years, would the bull became like the wind and the rain?

Still, a few hours before dawn, they all found themselves awake at the same time, watching each other with exhausted eyes.

"This will only get worse the closer we get to the beach," Taisa reminded them, her voice heavy and breathy, more talking to herself than anything else.

"All the more reason to get to the boat as quickly as possible," Elana responded.

Taisa ran her hands over her face, trying to wipe away her sleep. "Once we resupply in Cheongu we should go to Onethis."

Diana listened more closely. Taisa had been tight-lipped about where they should go next.

"Why Onethis?" Elana questioned.

"The Order started there. They're strongest there. Their goal was always to reach the Keep, but their strongholds are mostly in the south. If there are children being kept alive, they might be there."

Diana and Elana exchanged glances. "Where in Onethis?"

"The swamps near Saranthis. They're hard to navigate, but I know they have camps there. The government largely turns a blind eye to what happens in the swamps. They can act openly. It's as good a place to start as any."

"Where are their other strongholds?" Diana questioned. "Private ones that might hold children?"

Taisa seemed hesitant to answer, but she finally spoke. "Their centers in Onethis are public for the most part. They preach. They have seats on the Onethis council. Outside of the swamps, any secret meeting places in Onethis have to be mobile. There are strongholds in the desert. Probably a few in the Ramains. They have little hold in Karatan."

"Then that's where we'll go."

Diana studied Taisa, wondering at the sudden revelation. She had said in the cave she didn't know about kidnapped children, and Diana had little reason to question it. Still, if she'd been to two of these secret camps, and if there were children there now... The thought unsettled Diana. Diana knew there was more to Taisa than she let on, but how much?

Elana could smell the sea. The realization gave her extra strength to continue. Her arms ached and her knees felt weak. The sun was already starting to sink beneath the horizon and Elana knew their escape would be close. She questioned every decision they'd made, every time they could have rested longer to be stronger in the end or every time they had stayed too long in a hiding place. Still, she knew no matter what they'd done it would always have been close. It was always in the Mother's hands.

"How are you?" Elana asked Di'Nay. She was sweating and rosy, her eyes fiery as she forced focus.

"I'll last."

Elana watched her a moment longer, terrified in her exhaustion Di'Nay would trip or hurt herself as well.

"It's coming," Taisa called out, her voice filled with terror.

Minutes later the earth trembled for the first time and Elana found new strength. She burst into a sprint, glancing over her shoulder from time to time to make sure she could still see Di'Nay. She heard the growl and snort of the bull not far behind, sensing them immediately.

The earthquake became more violent as Elana saw the sea for the first time. She saw the boat in the distance, still seemingly whole. She turned to see Di'Nay, using the last of her strength, the bull visible far behind her.

Elana reached the boat first and grabbed it in a burst of adrenaline. She slid down the steep path, barely keeping her footing as she moved. She tripped halfway down and felt her ankle twist and her arms bruise as she slid into the sand water, now at high tide.

The water was cold enough to bring her violently back to focus, allowing her to right the boat as Di'Nay and Taisa reached the top of the path and pull herself inside. Instead of trying to run, Di'Nay and Taisa sat and slid as if on a violent slide, skidding into the water as the bull reached the top of the path and suddenly came to a stop.

Di'Nay climbed into the boat and helped Taisa inside. Elana, however, was completely focused on the bull. For the first time since they'd arrived, it had was still. Elana could see its details more fully, just as Di'Nay had described them. She could see the details of its hide, its hooves, its horns. Its tails stood up behind it almost like peacock feathers, the ends bent slightly, the tufts of hair swaying gently in a wind that didn't reach Elana.

It seemed suddenly proud, no longer in a rage. It seemed all they had to do was leave the forest. Elana looked at its lifestone eyes, not raw stone like in the mountains, but polished and delicately carved like pupils and irises.

It looked at her and for a moment they connected. Elana felt the weight of his age. She felt his territorial nature – the forest was his. He would never leave its borders, but he would defend it from invaders. He didn't see her as weaker or even recognize her as different. They were created from the same cloth. They both were creatures of the Sight. He was an elemental of smoke – the remnant of the fire beast he'd once been when Mount Yul had been an active volcano. Elana was an elemental of the earth, one of the many creatures that had been given dominion over the land.

She and Taisa were invaders. They were trying to take his place, something he wouldn't allow. When they didn't make a move to return to shore, the bull snorted loudly, setting a puff of smoke into the air, and he disappeared.

Elana still felt his presence. His understanding of her stayed with her, made her reevaluate herself once more. If this ancient creature saw her and her kind as equals, what did that mean about her origins?

"We should sleep here," Taisa gasped as she laid back

against the boat, all strength gone as her adrenaline fled.

Di'Nay was already mostly asleep. Elana's leg throbbed but she knew it wasn't broken. It would heal with time. It wasn't cold enough for them to be wary of hypothermia in their wet clothes. For now, they were safe. The bull wouldn't come after them on the sea.

Elana stripped off the bags she'd been carrying, resting them on her lap, and leaned back against Di'Nay. Everyone pressed close together in the smaller space, but instead of being uncomfortable, Elana found the physicality was comforting.

"Sleep as long as you like," she whispered, though Taisa was already asleep.

Elana stayed awake for a time, still feeling the bull's presence watching her. When she finally drifted off to sleep, she continued dreaming of the bull, the serpents, and a woman who looked like her – a woman who had lived long ago. The first Blue Sight. The woman who had been equal to the other behemoths. The woman whose power flooded Elana's body.

And then Elana dreamed of unleashing that power on the Order of Blindness.

CHEONGU: FESTIVAL OF LOST SOULS

Elana pulled herself onto the dock, gasping as her legs finally had a chance to stretch after days in a small rowboat. She longed for a bath, a bed, a warm meal. They finally seemed within her reach.

She heard the stomping of multiple boots running toward her. Two fishermen helped her stand. They spoke in native Cheongu. Elana had learned bits of it from the fishermen who had taken her and Di'Nay to Jidoin, but in her exhausted state she couldn't find the focus to attempt to understand.

"Do you speak my language?" she asked in her native dialect.

"Are you hurt?" one of the men asked. His speech was halting and broken, but Elana could understand. "Did your ship sink?"

"Yes," Elana lied, grateful to find her strength once more and even more grateful that someone spoke her language. "My friend needs a healer."

She indicated Taisa, still in her make-shift splint. The fishermen helped Di'Nay and Taisa out of the boat. Di'Nay lifted Taisa into her arms.

"Elana," Elana introduced herself, placing her hand on her chest.

The fisherman who spoke her language touched his own chest. "Tae." He touched the other's. "Jeon."

"Thank you for your help, Tae," Elana stated.

Tae gestured for them to follow him and they started walking down the dock Elana was amazed at their instant willingness to help strangers practically washed up on their shore.

They were about Elana's age, their long black hair braided down their backs. They seemed to be brothers, resembling each other with their darker skin, sharp chins, and narrow eyes. Tae continually glanced back at them, beckoning and encouraging them.

The fishing village was small, nestled against a series of hills and copses of fruit trees that would eventually turn into the bamboo forest of Jidoin. Elana spotted a market, dozens of homes built from dried bamboo and thatch, and what looked like a school.

Tae and Jeon brought them to a large building on the other end of the docks. When they opened the door, Elana was relieved to see rows of beds and a couple women wearing aprons. It was a kind of hospital, probably built to treat the fishermens' injuries.

Tae spoke with the women in his own language, indicating Taisa. One of the women waved Di'Nay forward, pointing to one of the beds.

"She says to lay your friend there," Tae translated. Di'Nay did as she was told. Taisa looked around the room nervously, but Di'Nay stayed at her side.

"Do you have an inn where we can stay?" Elana asked Tae.

He glanced back at Taisa. "I should stay and translate. Most here won't understand you." He spoke to Jeon, telling him to take Elana to an inn and help her secure a room. Jeon seemed eager to help, but it was clear he didn't understand a word Elana said.

Elana turned to Di'Nay. "I'll stay with her," Di'Nay stated, nodding to Taisa.

"I'll come back soon," Elana promised.

Jeon led her back into the village, past the market deeper into the copses of trees. Elana was surprised to see the village was far larger than it looked, opening into orchards and an expansive village square, where lanterns were being hung from the trees and banners erected for what had to be some kind of festival or party.

The inn was on the western side of the square, large enough to make Elana wonder how many people visited the village. Jeon easily secured her a place to stay and Elana was thankful the innkeeper accepted her gold.

Elana felt lost, not understanding what anyone said. She tried to pay attention and absorb some of what was being said, but their language clearly wasn't related in any way to her language, and they seemed to have a different accent than the Cheongu fishermen she'd interacted with before. She was good with languages. She knew it would come in time, but for now, she was at everyone's mercy.

Jeon showed her to her room – a large room with smooth wood floors and bed mats rolled in the corner. He tapped the symbol on the door that had to be the room number, raising his brows and asking, Elana assumed, if Elana would be able to remember it on her own. She nodded.

"Thank you," she stated with gratitude, hoping he would understand from her inflection.

He smiled, the expression more endearing than she'd expected, and offered her a short bow before pointing out the window toward the docks. Elana nodded, guessing again at what he meant. She'd taken him from his work long enough and stolen his brother for at least a few hours. She could find her way back to the hospital, he should return to his work.

He bowed again and left, running back toward the sea.

Elana watched him go, wondering once more at his unquestioning kindness. Was it just a part of the culture, or was it something else? Most cultures were at least wary of strangers.

Elana took another look at the symbol to her room, committing it to memory, and left. She walked slowly, studying everything as she went. She garnered a few different glances and whispers, but no one seemed startled. Everyone seemed busy preparing for the festival, hanging decorations and the merchants bringing out special products. There were costumes and brightly-colored masks, toys for children and paper lanterns. One stall sold only colored paper. Elana paused to look at it in surprise. She'd never seen dyed paper before. The merchant wrote on a piece of pale green paper with golden ink, the language expressed in pictographs instead of letters.

Elana watched his calligraphy, marveling at the artistry of it. He looked up at her with a smile and gestured to his wares. He didn't seem to be selling anything.

"I'm sorry, I don't understand," she answered on the off-chance he spoke her language. He picked up a piece of pink paper and pressed it into Elana's hand. She tried to offer him gold and he shook his head, pushing her hand away.

"He won't take your gold, Visitor."

Elana turned as an elderly woman walked up to her. The

skin on her face was loose and wrinkled, her hair white streaked with gray. She was stooped with great age and her bony fingers wrapped around the head of a cane as she walked. She wore a scarlet robe over white pants and a shirt. Elana was shocked she spoke her language so clearly.

"What is it?"

"It's wishing paper. During the festival of Lost Souls, it's customary to write your wishes and hang them from bamboo. You're a visitor to our town. All visitors are welcome during the festival. Not many will take your money. It would be impolite."

Elana put her gold back in the pouch at her waist and held the paper closer. The merchant smiled and bowed quickly to her, as if she was giving him a gift instead.

"Do you get visitors often?"

"No," the elderly woman explained. "Mostly just during the festival. Lost souls are drawn to us. It's the Mother's will."

Elana raised her brows in surprise at the response. "I'm sorry. This is very new to me."

The woman laughed. "Of course. You're a lost soul. Don't worry, dear. We'll take care of you."

She turned and waved Elana on. "Come with me, Visitor."

Elana followed her to a copse of trees north of the market. They came to a temple hidden in the trees. It was unlike anything Elana had seen before. The building wasn't thatched like the houses, but carved from wood. The roof rose in multiple peaks, stylized with curved corners making it look almost like waves on the sea. There was a small porch, where a young woman wearing the same red robe and white underclothes swept. Elana's eyes, however, were caught by a brass carving of a bull with nine tails crouched as if changing direction while charging. The tufts at the end of each tail were flames and flames rose from his ankles and swept around his neck like a mane.

It was the bull from Jidoin, still a beast of fire as it had been in its prime. She turned to the woman and she watched Elana's reaction, her gaze knowing and almost smug. "My name is Jisoo. I'm the high priestess of the Jidoin shrine. If you need anything, my sisters and I can help you."

"Thank you," Elana responded, her eyes wandering back to the bull.

"Now you should return to your friends. The hospital will

help you recover."

Elana heard the dismissal in her voice and bowed as she'd seen the others do. "I'm sure I'll be back."

Jisoo bowed as well, lower and slower than Elana had. "We'll be waiting."

She stayed in her low bow as Elana walked away, her amarin calm but knowing, almost motherly. She felt Jisoo's eyes following her until she was out of sight, and Elana found it oddly comforting, even though the action should have left her suspicious. She should be anxious to leave. She should be concerned she was drawing so much attention, but all she could think about was when she'd return to the shrine.

Diana sat at Taisa's bedside, watching as the Cheongu healers cared for her leg. The healers had tried to give Diana her own bed, but she'd declined. She could sleep when they went to the inn. For now, it was enough to have fresh water, food, and the ability to walk around and stretch her legs. Every muscle was still tense and sore, but she knew in a couple days she'd feel as good as new.

After applying a layer of mud and loose poultices to Taisa's leg, the healing women applied a real splint and bandages to Taisa's leg. Diana was relieved to see she hadn't developed an infection or other complication.

One of the women approached Diana, gesturing to Diana's legs. Diana tried to make sense of what she was saying. She regretted sending Tae back to the dock to help his brother once Taisa was cared for.

"My leg isn't broken," she guessed, but the woman shook her head. Without waiting for another answer, she knelt and pulled Diana's right boot off. With hands like iron she started to massage Diana's calf, twisting and pulling the muscles as if she were trying to remove them entirely.

Diana gasped at the pain, but she forced herself not to move away. She'd had painful massages before, and perhaps it was just what she needed to regain her strength after so long cramped in the boat. Still, she was shocked and impressed at the strength in the small, slender woman.

Taisa laughed at Diana's obvious surprise. "I didn't realize a Terran could yelp so loudly."

"I'm not a Terran," Diana repeated as she drew a deep

breath to remain relaxed through the pain.

"What's the difference? Off world is off world."

Diana glanced at her sharply, wondering if her ignorance was genuine and could be changed, or if she was speaking out of hate. For the sake of their relationship as traveling companions, she hoped it was the former. Diana could work with ignorance. She had no desire to waste energy trying to cure xenophobia.

With Tae gone and none of the healers seeming to understand a word she said, Diana decided to take a risk. "I'm an Amazon."

"A what?" She asked with little interest.

Diana was tongue-tied. Of all the responses she expected, that wasn't one of them. Had Taisa really never heard of Amazons? She'd been ready for hatred or disgust, but not indifference. There was something refreshing about getting to describe herself without battling preconceived notions about who she was.

"A people from the planet Yemaya. We're peaceful. We're not part of the Terrans' war."

"Then why are you on our planet?"

"I came her as a liaison between the people of Aggar and the Terrans. I'm trying to make sure the Terrans act as ethically as possible. To make sure your voices are heard."

She huffed as she focused on eating the rice she'd been handed by one of the healers. "Good job."

Diana tried to ignore the sarcasm in her voice, but she couldn't act like Taisa was wrong. While Diana was proud of her work, and the work of the other Amazons on Aggar, none of them had expected the Terran presence to grow so large and widespread.

The healing woman moved to Diana's other leg and she relaxed in her moment of relief. Her right leg was hot and sore from the treatment, but Diana felt her tendons loosen and as she moved her foot in wide circles she was impressed at the range of motion.

"It seems a futile job sometimes."

Taisa cocked a brow at her, impressed that Diana hadn't risen to her bait. "Well, I suppose the Terrans are the least of my worries now."

"At least we don't have to worry about the Order here," Diana answered.

Taisa's face fell and her teasing energy seemed to evaporate. "I'll always worry."

Diana flinched as the massage began on her left leg, but her focus was still on Taisa. Diana understood her fear. They would never really know if the Order was near, and as long as Taisa was recognizable to them, she was a liability in public. Diana wondered how she would live her life after this. Would she every be able to feel safe? To relax and pursue a family or career?

"We'll figure something out," Diana promised. "You're protected now."

Taisa gave a tense smile but Diana could see in her eyes that she didn't find any comfort in Diana's promise.

The healing woman lightly slapped Diana's knee as she finished and stood, looking expectedly down at Diana.

"Thank you," Diana answered, smiling in a way she hoped was reassuring and shared her gratitude. It seemed good enough for the healer as she walked to the back of the room to wash her hands.

Diana slipped her boots back on as Elana returned, her face still and her eyes thoughtful. "Did everything go well?"

Elana nodded. "We have a room at an inn nearby."

"Would you stay with Taisa for a little while? I want to visit the market."

"Of course." Elana answered, still lost in her own thoughts. "They're very welcoming to strangers." The healers walked to her and sat her down, fussing over her like they had Diana with food and water.

Diana grinned. "Good luck."

Elana flashed her a smile, reassuring Diana that whatever had her caught up in her own thoughts wasn't unpleasant.

Diana turned to Taisa. "I'll be back soon."

She yawned, trying to play unconcerned again. "I'll probably be asleep."

"That wouldn't hurt," Diana responded.

She slipped out the door and walked to the market, grateful for the flexibility returned to her legs. She was surprised to see the people of the town preparing for a festival. She admired the painted silk banners and elegant paper lanterns being hung from the trees.

Diana drew looks wherever she went. She wondered if it

was because she was new or obviously from another planet. She didn't see the animosity that would follow her in other cities, however. They seemed curious, not upset. She was beckoned by multiple vendors as she entered the market. She wandered to a clothier, who excitedly ran showed her his wares.

They didn't speak the same language, but they were both merchants and seemed to connect on a level that had little to do with the words spoken aloud. She eventually picked out a dark gray cloak with a tall hood that could be drawn low over the wearer's brow and a lacy black cloth mask that covered half the wearer's face in a curve like a crescent moon.

The masks seemed to be a part of the festival, variations on material and design at multiple carts. A few of the people decorating for the festival also wore them. Diana pulled gold from her pouch, ready to haggle, but the man shook his head and waved his hands. Diana hesitated. He couldn't possibly be giving her such fine things.

She tried to hand him more gold, but he gave her a slight push back, waving his hands again and smiling. "Gift. Gift." The word was so heavily accented Diana barely caught it.

"A gift?" she answered, wondering if she'd heard correctly.

"Gift," he repeated, the word clearer as he mimicked her. "Festival."

Diana hesitantly slipped the money back into her pouch and nodded. "Thank you."

She walked away slowly, waiting to be called back or accused of stealing at any minute, but the merchants only smiled and let her leave. It was unnerving, too welcoming for a town that could obviously use more wealth. She contented herself with the thought that gifts might be a common part of their festival.

She returned to the hospital to see Elana in bed half asleep. Taisa's was sitting up, deep in thought. Diana walked to her side and presented the cloak and mask. "We'll come up with a better solution in the future, but for now I hope these give you some kind of peace."

She took them slowly, examining the weight of the soft woven cloak and intricate design of the mask. When she spoke, her voice was heavy with unshed tears and relief. "Thank you."

"There's a festival being set up in town. The masks seem to be popular. You won't draw attention."

"It's beautiful," she complimented as she slipped it over her face. It obscured enough of her features to render her unrecognizable. "It might draw attention in the city, but no one will know it's me."

Diana chuckled. "I'm glad you like it. Now do you think you can get some rest? It seems Elana has decided we don't need to go to the inn yet."

Taisa glanced at Elana and smiled, half of her lips blocked by her new mask, cutting the expression oddly. "I think I can sleep now."

Diana patted her shoulder and yawned. With Elana already going to sleep, there was no reason to fight it anymore. "Good." She climbed into her bed and pulled a heavy white quilt over her tired body.

"Tomorrow will be a new day." Taisa's voice held a touch of hope.

Diana closed her eyes and held onto her words. Tomorrow would indeed be a new day. She could only pray it was a good one.

The Festival of Lost Souls started every night at dusk. The town square and markets were lit with lanterns and candles, creating pools of light in the silk banners as if the stars had fallen from the sky to settle in the trees. The town was a lot bigger than Elana had expected once everyone had returned from their farms and the sea. Children ran through the streets, playing with toys, wearing new clothes with ribbon in their hair. Some wore small masks, their designs more playful and boldly colorful than most of the adult masks.

The costuming seemed to come from a theme or story Elana had never heard. There were many masks, but while some wore dark cloaks, others wore gold silver in shimmering materials that seemed to mimic the sun and stars. Others still were dressed as if they were characters from a play – bold sailors in crimson sashes and satin shirts, dancers wearing a bold rainbow of sashes and layered skirts. Many, men and women, wore ribbons and elaborate clips in their hair. It was obvious this was a tradition they waited every year for.

Elana wandered the market. Watching the festivities with a smile. After everything she'd been through since the Mistress's death, it was nice to be around so much joy. The amarin of the people of Cheongu was like fireworks in her heart and stomach. They glittered and sparkled. Some even seemed to glow in her Sight. She hadn't thought any group so large could be so pure.

Di'Nay ran to Elana from the town square with a bright smile. Elana rarely saw her lover so radiant. Her skin was flushed with joy, her golden hair tousled from dancing and celebrating. Her loose shirt was partially untied, laying haphazardly across her chest like a child at play. She wore a strip of gold ribbon wrapped around her throat and tied around each wrist, set off by the cream sleeves of her top.

For a moment Elana was speechless. She was the goddess of the sun. Divine.

"I got you something," Di'Nay announced, extending her hands, her palms cupped together.

Elana opened Di'Nay's hands, revealing two crystal-encrusted hair clips and a silver ribbon. Elana gasped at their beauty, surprised at something so fine. Di'Nay smiled wider.

"You like them?"

"I love them."

Di'Nay moved around her, undid her hair, then rebraided it with the ribbon twining around the plaits. She then secured the clips, using them to secure the stray hairs that often escaped her braid to fall in her eyes.

"Like stars in the sky," Di'Nay complimented as she stood before Di'Nay to study her work. "Beautiful."

Elana knew she wasn't talking about her hair and she wished she could kiss her without drawing attention. She wished they could dance like the husbands and wives in the town square. She wished they could share a bed without scaring Taisa. But that wasn't the world they lived in.

Instead she took Di'Nay's hand, squeezing it gently, her touch lingering. "How's Taisa?"

"As good as she can be with her crutch. She isn't dancing much, but the locals are lavishing her with care. Jeon and Tae haven't left her side."

Elana smiled. "At least she'll always have a translator."

"It is helpful," Di'Nay agreed. They walked through the market to the square. Taisa sat at one of the outdoor tables, Tae at her side. They laughed together as if sharing a joke. Tae was dressed in white and black with a red sash about his waist like a dancer. He wore a mask around his eyes. Taisa wore her mask and cloak, hiding nearly all her distinguishing features.

"She seems more outgoing with a disguise," Elana observed.

"It's nice to see her have hope."

"Di'Nay!" Taisa called, waving her over. "Come dance with Tae!"

Elana and Di'Nay exchanged glances. "Better go. You'll break his heart," Elana teased.

"He calls me auntie."

"What a strange way to show attraction."

Di'Nay was suddenly nervous. "Do you sense that in him?"

Elana laughed even louder. "No. Go dance with him. He's all joy tonight, and so are you."

Di'Nay squeezed her hand again then she and Tae raced each other to the dance floor. The dance was raucous and wild, spinning and twirling to pounding drum beats and harps. Elana watched Di'Nay for a while, marveling at the vibrant woman she was going to spend the rest of her life with.

After a couple songs, however, her attention was caught by Jisoo wandering the opposite side of the square. She wore no mask, but a crimson cloak pinned to her gray hair with black crystalline pins. She wore the robes that marked her as a priestess and handed toys and treats to passing children.

Elana made her way toward her, still taken with their conversation from earlier. Jisoo walked slowly through the crowd and finally paused behind a group of children sitting and watching a puppet show. Elana walked up beside her and Jisoo held a finger to her lips as she nodded to the stage. Elana turned her attention to the show and tensed in sudden surprise.

A puppet of a massive bull raced across the stage, tossing his fiery mane and whipping his many tails. The children gasped and pointed at the bull. Elana felt a mixture of fear and admiration in their voices. Elana didn't know the language well enough to follow the story, but she recognized some of the imagery. She recognized the Mother, this one wrapped in vibrant greens that reminded Elana of the bamboo in Jidoin. Her stomach was swollen under her robe, great with child, and her hair now black and drawn up in a tight knot. The hem of her robe was dusted with stars and a golden crown shaped like rays of the sun adorned her brow.

Elana also recognized the Fates, here represented by three figures clad in black robes. One trailed dark silver stars under his feet while holding a crescent moon. One wore a sash of fiery crimson. The last was shrouded in a haze of mist and shadow, represented by intricate fishing net.

Elana recognized the door to the cellar, constructed like the door to a real cellar – wood and black hinges marked with moon, flame, and shadow symbols. The bull raced between the Mother and the Fates as the background changed. Plants grew under his feet. The black curtain background changed to green bamboo. Puppets of children rose in clusters to cheer the bull.

"In everything there must be balance. The Mother and the Fates. The sun and the moon. One without the other is impossible." Jisoo's voice was calm and certain. "The bull of Jidoin is balance. He is to be feared and respected. He grants our wishes and kills all who enter his forest. All creatures like him were created to bring balance to Aggar."

"You worship the Fates," Elana observed without looking at her, though Jisoo's words hung heavily in her heart. The bull and those like him. Blue Sights.

Jisoo chuckled, the sound dry and cracked. "I worship no one and nothing. I respect the balance of nature. We all do. I pray to the Mother and I summon the knowledge of the Fates. There's wisdom in pain and hardship as well as light and peace. One can't be allowed to overtake the other."

Elana had never considered the mythology of the Mother that way. The Fates had always been something to fear – demons of destruction and chaos. But Jisoo made sense. Where would Elana be without chaos?

"Why is this called the Festival of Lost Souls if it's about the balance between the Mother and the Fates?"

"Because for these few nights balance is restored. Lost souls have no balance. Those who need us most will find their way to our shores and we'll do our best to help them on their journey. It's our duty."

"That's why you're all so kind to us."

"You came in pain. You had suffered. You were lost. We'll heal you."

Elana glanced at Jisoo out of the side of her eyes. "What if we had come in good spirits?”

Jisoo grinned. “No strangers reach our shores who have an abundance of the Mother’s blessing. I can pray they find balance, but it’s not our place to dole out the will of the Fates rashly.”

Elana relaxed and Jisoo touched her hand. Her fingers felt like silk. “Come, write a wish. This is the night it may come true.”

Jisoo led Elana away from the puppets to a large table covered in colored paper and ink. People surrounded it, writing wishes on their squares and hanging them on potted stalks of bamboo. Elana pulled the folded piece of pink paper the merchant had given her the day before and took a quill with golden ink. She paused, trying to decide what she wanted. There were so many wishes – so many things she could ask of the Mother.

But Jisoo’s message of balance echoed in the back of her mind. She couldn’t bring herself to ask anything of the Fates, but she realized, as she thought of the Cellar, what she might want from the darker dimensions of Aggar. What she might want for her Sighted kin.

She wrote a simple wish: she wanted the bull of Jidoin to live in peace. She remembered his rage and fear and she wished he would never experience it again. He was already a creature of chaos. If there was really to be balance, he deserved mercy.

Jisoo helped her cut a hole in the paper and tie a ribbon in a loop, making a hanging ornament. She added her wish to a cluster of bamboo, the stalk more paper than plant. A young man dressed in a crimson sash – a sash Elana now realized signified one of the Fates – approached Jisoo with a smile. They spoke quickly in their own language and Jisoo rested her hand over Elana’s plant. She seemed to be blessing it, but her voice held little ceremony. As she lifted her hand, the man took an oil lantern and lit the bamboo on fire.

“Now the wishes will travel to Jidoin.”

Elana watched the glowing bits of paper rising from the flames and she felt at peace. While she knew it was nothing but a tradition with a nice thought, she liked to imagine her wish reaching the bull, making him feel less alone. Helping him find balance.

Diana spun away from the town square, laughing and gasping from dancing. It had been so long since she’d been surrounded by so much merriment. It reminded her of the season festivals back home on Yemaya. It didn't matter that she didn't speak the language – they all knew what laughing, cheering, and beckoning hands meant. Tae clapped and laughed with joy before being scooped up by a new partner.

Diana leaned back against a post holding a silk banner and watched the dancers a moment longer. The moons were high in the sky, blending with the lantern light to make every ribbon, shimmer of metallic paint, and polished mask glitter. She looked for Elana, but she seemed to have disappeared. Diana hoped she'd found something amusing. She imagined sneaking away with her into the dark of the orchards, but she imagined many of the youth in town would be looking for dark corners to romance tonight.

I she searched for her lover, she spotted a stand further down the square where a woman was painting streaks of hair dye into another woman's hair. Hair dyeing wasn't uncommon on Yemaya, but Diana hadn't seen it in Aggar.

She walked over to the booth and watched as the dye – a dark blue that blended subtly into the woman's dark – was painted with a brush. It was just enough that in the noonday sunlight her black hair would have a blue sheen. There were hair clippings on the ground and a pair of sharp scissors on a nearby table, proving the woman cut hair as well.

She raced across the square to Taisa. She laughed at Diana's excitement.

"Having fun?" Taisa asked.

"I have an idea about disguising you."

She raised a brow and Diana helped her stand. She moved slowly with her crutch, but she was so happy to be able to move on her own again that Diana didn't mind. The dancers moved out of their way as they approached, letting Taisa move freely.

Taisa's eyes grew wide as she saw the hair stylist, suddenly understanding. "You don't have to if you don't want to," Diana commented.

She shook her head. "No. I like the idea."

Diana smiled. It was hard to believe it wasn't even a tenday ago that Taisa had tried to shoot Elana at their first meeting.

Diana searched the dancing and beckoned to Tae, who came running. "How long does the dye last?"

Tae glanced at the stylist. "It's permanent."

"Good. Taisa would like to have her hair done."

Tae glanced between Diana and Taisa, who was already lowering her cloak and undoing her braid of auburn hair, letting it fall long and loose down her back. "Oh really? She has beautiful hair!"

"She'd like a change."

He seemed confused, but he talked with the stylist after she finished with her client. After a moment, she smiled and beckoned Taisa forward.

"What do you want?" Tae asked.

"I want hair like Diana's."

Diana was shocked at the request. Her hair had grown out some with time, but it was still definitely a man's cut. Tae was just as surprised. He pointed to Diana. "You said like her hair?"

"Yes."

Tae and the stylist exchanged confused glances, but they didn't argue with her. The woman grabbed her scissors and brushed out Taisa's hair. She froze after the first cut, waiting for Taisa to reject, but when she just sat still, the woman continued.

She was clearly an artist, making every cut quickly but carefully. Her eyes were bright with the intensity of her focus. She collected the longest locks in a basket. It took some time, but at the end of it her hair was cropped, the top longer than the back, still framing her face in an oddly feminine way despite the length. Diana smiled. It was a very Amazon style.

Taisa ran her fingers through her new hair and smiled softly to herself. She looked up at Diana. "How do I look?"

"Different."

"Perfect."

Tae and the stylist spoke again as the stylist studied her work. She seemed pleased. She presented Taisa with a mirror. Taisa seemed to glow as she studied her reflection.

"You wanted to color it, too?" Tae questioned.

"Black. I want it black." She spoke with more confidence, like a woman who was making decisions about her life for the first time.

Tae relayed the request and the stylist sighed, disapproving but dedicated to her work. Tae stood with Diana as the stylist mixed and blended her dyes and potions.

"Black is so common," Tae muttered.

"Not as common where she's from," Diana answered, not wanting to admit looking more common might be Taisa's point.

Taisa sat still as the stylist painted the dye into her hair. As Taisa sat waiting for the color to set, she wiped tears from her eyes. Tae moved to stop the stylist, but Diana touched his arm. "She's fine."

Taisa looked at him and smiled. He calmed.

"She seems very sure of herself."

"I think she is," Diana answered.

"At least you don't seem to want to change."

Diana laughed at Tae's sullen attitude. "I'm honestly surprised anyone here likes the way I look, being an off-worlder."

"They love Terrans here." Tae's answer was given simply, an unsurprising fact.

Diana's brows rose in shock. "Love?"

"The Terrans don't bother us here. They've never seen a military camp or been raided. So to most in Cheongu, Terrans are fascinating strangers. I hear it's even fashionable in the capitol to dress in silver and white like Terran flight suits."

"You talk like you've met a few Terrans."

Tae crossed his arms over his chest with a sigh. "I went to study in Onethis when I was younger. Jeon still makes fun of me for it. It hasn't done much for us here and it made me a worse fisherman. But one of my projects took me to Karatan. I had to work with a Terran camp for half a tenmoon. They aren't all the people in the capital expect them to be."

"That explains why you speak the Ramains language so well."

"I speak a few languages. I know I'm not the best, but I'm glad I was able to help you."

"A Terran?"

Tae smiled. "You're not a Terran, even if you're from the Empire."

Diana grinned in return. Finally, someone who didn't make assumptions.

After nearly an hour of waiting, the stylist rinsed the extra dye from her hair and padded her hair dry with a towel. Taisa's now-raven hair hung damp around her eyes, laying long against the angles of her brows and cheeks. She pushed it back until it was slicked away from her face. The moment was like watching her step out from under a veil. She was a different woman. She seemed calmer, more assured. Diana wasn't sure what she'd let go in changing her physical appearance, but she could feel it was a big part of who she had once been.

"She doesn't look bad."

Diana smirked at Tae's change of heart. "No, she doesn't."

The stylist brushed any remaining hair from Taisa's shoulders and gave her one more inspection before squeezing her shoulder and speaking to Tae.

"She was honored to work on you."

Taisa bowed to the woman in gratitude. "Tell her thank you for me?"

The woman and Tae spoke again. "She wants to know if she can keep the hair she cut. She thinks it will bring her business good luck."

Taisa's brows furrowed at the thought. "Good luck?"

"You're the guest. You're fortunate." Tae stumbled over the words and muttered to himself, trying to find better words to answer her question but it only made him flustered.

Taisa stopped him. "Tell her I'd be honored."

He breathed a sigh of relief and translated for the stylist. The woman smiled wider than ever, bobbing a bow to Taisa and gathering the basked of hair into her arms. Taisa secured her cloak back around her neck and pulled herself to her feet with her crutch. She paused as her eyes caught on another booth in the distance.

"I want to go there next."

Diana turned and saw a cluster of merchants and their customers, the merchants using ink and needles to hand-draw tattoos.

"You want a tattoo?" Diana questioned.

"I want to be different."

"Are you sure? They're very permanent."

Taisa turned to Diana and her glance was so certain and incredulous at being questioned it took Diana aback. She felt a small swell of pride at witnessing what felt like Taisa's rebirth. How long had Taisa thought of this?

"A lot of my choices have had permanent consequences," Taisa answered, cutting off all opportunity for argument.

"You're right." Diana turned to the tattoo merchants. "Let's go."

Elana sat along the edge of orchard, half hidden in shadows as she watched the festival start to wind down. Many wouldn't leave until dawn, but small children were falling asleep in their parents' arms and those who weren't used to staying up late were nodding off. They started to file away in small groups and the revelers that remained grew rowdier and more drunken.

Still, the spirit seemed to be in good fun. Elana didn't sense any danger outside of a few mild personal feuds that became stronger when drinking was involved. Elana didn't see Di'Nay, but she could feel her. She was happy. She was focused. Part of Elana wanted to join her, but the other part enjoyed just feeling her.

Elana curled her knees to her chest and became a rock on the forest floor, an object hidden through her shadow abilities that didn't affect the world around her, only experienced it. She closed her eyes and used her Sight to more fully immerse herself in the beauty of the night.

Over time her thoughts began to wander, to return to the ideas Jisoo had set in the back of her mind. She had always been certain of her world. She had trusted the interpretations and societal norms she'd been raised with. Blue Sights were powerful, but dangerous. Through strict control and learning she could turn her unstable nature into an asset to the world. It had given her purpose and meaning, but on second thought, she wondered if it was much different from the shame other Blue Sights had been raised with.

She had been given a purpose for her powers and a way to make use of them, but her nature was still a source of shame. They were a part of herself she was supposed to overcome. A part that was dangerous. Even with the Mistress's lessons about her power and special abilities, she'd internalized so much shame and guilt about every loss of control it had nearly driven a wedge between her and Di'Nay. It had kept her compliant and still. If she hadn't traveled, she would never have considered that the way she was raised might not be the whole truth.

There were more creatures like her than she'd ever imagined. She'd seen amazing powers from the seers and more than enough evidence to consider that the Sight and seer abilities were linked. Perhaps they had even been one and the same long ago.

Now Jisoo talked of balance and being chosen. She talked about Elana's skills like they were important and necessary, but also a part of the natural cycle of Aggar. She was different, but not an outsider.

She didn't know what to make of her new thoughts. Why were they affecting her so much? Why did she believe what she did? Why hadn't she considered other truths before?

She wanted to learn more from Jisoo, to study her beliefs like she'd studied at the Keep. She wanted to study every region's thoughts and theories on the Sight. Perhaps then she'd get closer to the actual truth.

After an hour or so sitting along the outskirts of the festival, she stood and walked slowly through the trees. The orchards were full of lovers, but they were easy to avoid. She knew the general direction she wanted to go, but had little urgency. Away from the lights of the festival, all she had to guide her was the moonlight and her Sight. She continued to ponder, weighing her old beliefs against what she'd experienced on her journey.

Deep in the forest, when she was as far from another human as she could be, she felt new presences around her, following her. With her Sight she thought she could see Silver flitting between the trees. Camilla laughed as she swung between branches. The smaller children weren't with them.

Elana smiled at feeling them near, like guardians sent by the Mother. She didn't believe in destiny, but their presences had been such a guiding force she felt like she was going in the right direction when they were with her. She reached Jisoo's shrine and the seers flickered away, following their own astral paths.

Elana approached the front gates and stepped inside, startling one of the priestesses inside. The woman screamed and jumped up from where she'd been sitting on the shrine's porch. Elana didn't know why she hadn't sensed her at first. Her amarin must have been at peace.

"Oh, I'm sorry," Elana apologized as the woman held her hand to her chest, trying to calm her breathing. She wore the same scarlet robe as Jisoo, her black hair tied back in a sleek knot, but she was a good deal younger. Perhaps Di'Nay's age. "I didn't realize anyone was here in the dark.

"No, I apologize," she responded. "I was meditating and

should have lit a lantern."

"Do you expect many visitors during the festival?"

The woman smiled, lowering her hand as she finally grew calm. "Isn't that the point of the festival? What brings you to the Shrine of the Bull, visitor?"

"I... I'm not sure. I just wanted to be here again."

"Ahh. I see. Come sit with me."

Elana walked up the porch steps and saw a soft, woven black rug on the ground where the woman had been meditating she sat cross-legged on one end and Elana mimicked her, sitting across from her.

"I'm Hana," she introduced.

"Elana."

"You're from the Ramains?"

"I'm surprised you speak my language so well," Elana stated.

"Our shrine mother wants us to be able to speak to anyone who visits our village. I took to her language lessons better than the others."

"I was always good with languages, too."

Hana smiled softly. "Perhaps we were meant to meet. What brings you here tonight? I thought you'd be enjoying the festival."

"I just wanted time to think."

"And you came here?" Hana's voice was both understanding and knowing. There was no point in hiding from her.

"I've been talking with Jisoo about your belief system. I was curious about it."

"It seems the balance you seek wasn't to be found at the party," Hana observed. "Or perhaps you're already balanced."

"I'm far from balanced," Elana remarked.

"All creatures with the Sight are balanced." Elana tensed. She had never shown her eyes since leaving Jidoin. "You're surprised we could tell? We keep the Shrine of the Bull. It's our duty to know when the spirits of Jidoin need our help."

"I'm not from Jidoin," Elana whispered, wondering if they had some kind of access to the Sight as well. She didn't sense any seers in the shrine or any other Blue Sights. How could Hana possibly know? Who else knew?

"Perhaps not your body. But you're still a creature of the

Mother's Sight. An agent of balance. You wouldn't have come here during our festival if you weren't. You're a lost soul, Elana. It is our divine duty here to help you find yourself."

Elana stared at her hands, her mind spinning in an attempt to understand what was happening. She searched desperately for some kind of threat, for darkness, but she didn't feel anything. Perhaps it was time she stopped trying to make sense of everything right away. "My companions and I are going to be here for a time. They have to heal. I'd like to learn more about your beliefs."

"You want to train with us?"

"For a time, if you'll have me."

Hana reached out and took Elana's hand between both of hers. Elana felt a sudden happiness in her amarin. "We would be honored to have you. The world needs more great agents of balance."

Elana felt her cheeks darken in a flush at the thought. She had never been looked at with such sincere awe and acceptance, especially not when discussing her Sight.

"Thank you, Hana."

Diana walked along the coast, scanning the harbor for Tae. It was just past dawn, the sky painted orange and violet as the sun rose over the horizon. Taisa was waiting back at the inn and Elana was undoubtedly at the shrine. They had been in the village for nearly over a tenday since the festival. Taisa was healing quickly, walking without her crutch again. Diana doubted she could run yet, but she was getting closer. Elana had visited the Shrine of the Bull every day for most of the day, meditating and studying with Jisoo and the other priestesses.

Diana was curious about what her lover was learning, but whenever Elana tried to explain it she got frustrated trying to put her epiphanies into words. It seemed personal, like she was making more discoveries about herself than anything else. Diana liked the change in her. She seemed to be calmer, more self-assured. A lot of her confusion and anger that had marked a good portion of their journey was turning to something more peaceful.

But their time in Cheongu was over. They needed to head toward Onethis and continue their search for where the Order was keeping kidnapped seer children. Diana didn't much care for the thought. Her friends were thriving in Cheongu and she feared what tangling with the Order again could do to them. But they were already well behind schedule. Children could be suffering. The Order was still at large. The mission had to come before comfort.

Diana had no doubt she'd be able to charter Tae to take the three of them to the coast in his fishing boat, but the journey wasn't the only thing on her mind. When Elana was held prisoner in Karatan, Diana had made a deal with the Ramains Marshals to keep them up to date with regular reports of their journey in exchange for freeing Elana. She hadn't sent any messages since they'd reached Cheongu. Tristan would be expecting to hear from her soon, but Diana was unsure how much she wanted to reveal about her current situation.

The Marshals had hidden Taisa in Jidoin. She'd spied for them in the Order of Blindness and, when her position was compromised, the Marshals seemed to have helped her. But Diana wasn't sure if she'd been moved to Jidoin for protection or to get rid of her now that she was no longer useful. Was it safe to tell the Marshals Taisa had joined their party? Were the Marshals safe at all?

The docks were bustling with fishermen and dockworkers preparing the boats to ship out for the day. Soon most of the fishing boats would be out at sea. Diana spotted Tae, Jeon, and their captain Jimin at their fishing boat. It was simple – a sailboat large enough for ten at most with a single sail and just enough supplies to take in a day's worth of fish. It wasn't the best boat in the harbor, but it wasn't the worst. Still, Diana often thought the three men could barely be bringing in enough to scrape by.

Tae spotted her coming and waved her forward with a smile.

"Everything well?" he questioned as he loaded fishing nets onto the boat.

"Very well," she remarked. "We're about ready to continue on our journey."

Tae's smile faded a bit. "So soon?"

"We have a lot to do and Taisa is getting better so quickly she may be fully recovered by the time we reach Onethis."

"You're traveling to the mainland instead of the capitol?"

"You seem to have plenty of supplies here for us to restock. There's no need to delay."

Jeon approached his brother, speaking in his own language. He was concerned but Tae soothed him.

"He's sad to hear you're leaving," Tae translated. "We all will be."

"Leaving doesn't necessarily mean forever," Diana remarked. "I think Elana would want to visit again someday to continue her studies."

"No one comes back to Cheongu once they can leave," Tae argued, casting his attention to his nets. "We'll take you to Onethis."

"We can pay," Diana assured him. "More than enough to cover what you would have caught during the voyage."

He started to brush her offer aside, but he paused, glancing back at Jeon. "Thank you. Sometimes it's hard to make ends meet."

Diana reached out and they clasped arms, an acknowledgment of their sadness to leave each other, but the understanding that they both had responsibilities that couldn't be overlooked. "I knew you were putting yourself out helping us so much."

Tae shook his head and waved his hand dismissively, always polite. "I helped you because my education is rarely useful around here. It was good to be of use again. Also, the shrine maidens have assured me my family will have good luck for helping."

"Mother willing."

"Yes. Mother willing, we'll all be guided and kept safe."

They released arms. "I'll come see you tonight after you've sold your catch to discuss details."

"That should be fine. I'll talk to Jeon and Jimin."

"Thank you."

Tae returned to his work and soon they were pulling away from the docks. Diana watched them go, thankful for such good friends willing to help.

"You think they have any idea who they're helping?"

Diana tensed, startled by the new voice speaking her language. "Excuse me?" She turned and spotted a man moving to stand beside her. He was from Cheongu, but she'd never seen him in the village before. He was middle-aged, his long black hair tied back in a single braid. His robe was finely woven – too fine for most in the small fishing village.

"I'm sorry to startle you. It's Diana n'Athena, yes?" He

reached out for Diana's hand, but Diana was hesitant to take it. He smiled and the expression felt condescending. "Tristan told me about you."

Diana tried not to let her shock reach her face. "Tristan sent you to find me?"

"No, though I expected to find you and I admit I've been watching you for a few days. Tristan wrote, concerned he hasn't heard from you for a while."

"We've been healing," Diana stated. It wasn't a total lie. "There hasn't been much to report."

"A bit of advice – never guess what Tristan will find useful. Keep writing to him, even if you think your report will be useless."

Diana didn't care for being lectured by a stranger, especially a man who had apparently been stalking her for a few days. "If you aren't here for me, why are you here?"

"We have an agent in hiding in Jidoin. I've been sent to ensure she's kept safe until we can be sure she's no longer being pursued. Have you met her?"

There it was. Diana couldn't begin to guess from the man what his intentions were asking about Taisa. If he'd only been on the island a short time, he might not have recognized her yet. If he had, however, and Diana lied she would at best lose an ally in Tristan.

"I met her briefly," Diana lied. "In the forest, right?"

"Yes. Though she seems to have gone missing."

"She had a lot of underground shelters. Perhaps she's just keeping to herself."

"Perhaps."

There was suspicion hidden behind his smiling eyes and seemingly casual demeanor. If Diana hadn't been certain they needed to leave before, she was now. "I hope you like it here. Elana and I are leaving soon," Diana informed him, hoping the information was enough to look like she was cooperating. "I'll write a letter to Tristan once we reach the mainland."

"I would recommend it. Tristan is a very powerful friend, but he can also be a powerful enemy if he feels he's being taken," the man warned.

"It's a good thing I'm providing him a service, then," Diana remarked.

"Very good."

"If you'll excuse me, I should return to the inn before Elana gets back."

"Of course. I'm not here to stop you," he commented. "Good luck on your journey."

"Good luck to you as well."

Diana walked away, feeling the Marshal watching her. He might not be in Cheongu to directly stop Elana and Diana, but Diana had no doubt he would continue watching her. She had to be careful. Taisa had to be even more careful. And they needed to leave in the morning.

Elana stood on the bow of the fishing boat, looking out at the open expanse of water ahead. She didn't think she could ever get tired of the sea. As tall as the sky felt over her head, the sea felt infinitely deeper. So much life. So much primal amarin. Tae said the journey would take five days if the weather stayed clear. For the first time Elana hoped for minor setbacks.

"I like you like this."

Elana smiled as Di'Nay walked up beside her. She didn't look at Elana, but Elana felt mental energy of her full focus. Being constantly surrounded by strangers meant not touching and hiding their real feelings for each other. All they had were these little moments standing together, feeding their intentions and love into small touches, meaningful glances, and private jokes and messages. It wasn't what Elana would want out of her life, but it could be exciting for a time.

"Like what?"

"At peace."

Di'Nay stood behind her and massaged her shoulders. Elana bowed forward at the sweet pain of the tension at the base of her neck spreading a web of electric shocks through her body. Di'Nay's hands lingered in her hair and over her skin, taking a moment to touch her, skating the line between intimate and innocent they had to walk in public.

Her fingers lingered over healing, raised lines at the nape of Elana's neck. She parted Elana's hair and lightly drew her thumb over a small, pale blue tattoo. It was the raised tails of the bull, winding together into a small circle that resembled waves on the sea. It was the symbol of the shrine. Elana could tell Di'Nay recognized it. "When did you get this?"

"A few days after the festival," Elana stated. "The message of the shrine… lingered with me."

Di'Nay slid away from her to lean forward on the ship's railing. "I'm glad you found something to connect with."

Elana reached over the railing and let her fingers catch the droplets of the water spraying up past the bow. "Can we live by the sea on Yemaya?"

"We can live anywhere you want. On any planet."

Elana considered Di'Nay's answer. She felt the honesty of it the release of both of their expectations for the future. There were so many unknowns. Her meditation at the Shrine of the Bull had given her some focus. She was a bringer of balance, and the Sisters in Cheongu lived to give balance to those chosen by the Mother and the Fates. But she had given up trying to predict anything. As long as they had each other it didn't matter where they ended up.

"I dream of a place like Horopto. A place where the mountains are lavender and the grass grows to my knees. I dream of days spent teaching and healing with quiet evenings listening to the rain and the waves. I want to know what the amarin of Yemaya looks like. I want to know how the trees sing."

Di'Nay covered her face with her hands, holding back tears at sharing dreams that had somehow become painful with time. Elana felt swells of emotion and worry about both of them. Elana knew she was thinking the same questions that had haunted her since they were bonded and Elana had agreed to leave Aggar – would Elana be happy on Yemaya? Would she grow resentful to Di'Nay for taking her off-world? Would the differences in their ages and life experiences eventually turn into a rift? Was it healthy to dream so dearly of a peaceful future?

Elana didn't have any answers for her lover. She feared some of the same things and many more. But there was nothing else to be done, only hope. She touched Di'nay's back and waited for her to gather her strength again. After a long moment, she stood straight once more, pushing away from the boat railing but not hard enough Elana had to lower her hand, which slid to wrap around her waist. Beyond some color in her cheeks there was no outward sign of her emotional distress.

"You shouldn't hold me," Di'Nay muttered.

"The people of Cheongu are much more casual with touch," Elana reminded her.

"Not Taisa."

"She'll be fine."

"She has the Sight."

"And she ignores it. At best she could tell that we have an affection for each other."

Di'Nay relaxed reluctantly, but it didn't take long before she was drawing strength and shelter from Elana's touch.

"I came to see if you wanted anything to eat. Jeon made a good catch today and we'll have fresh fish soon."

"That sounds nice."

The sound of laughter rang from the other end of the boat. Elana and Di'Nay turned to see Tae and Taisa perched by the stern. Tae spoke slowly in Cheongu and Taisa tried to copy him. Based on his childish glee and Jeon's shocked reaction, he had taught her something that wasn't particularly polite. Elana had learned enough of the Cheongu language to recognize a few insults directed at Jeon.

Taisa colored beneath the pale blue lines of her new facial tattoos, the color rising around the primitive markings, making them stand out even more. Di'Nay said she had designed each marking and it showed. She looked totally different from the woman in Jidoin, but she seemed much more comfortable in her own skin.

"He told me to say it!" she protested.

Despite not understanding Taisa, Jeon smacked his brother over the back of his head, but Tae only laughed harder. Taisa's blush turned to a warm smile.

"We have to watch those two," Di'Nay warned, only half teasing.

"They're both lonely. I like seeing them getting along," Elana remarked, silently enjoying the motherly protectiveness in her partner.

"They aren't just getting along."

"That bothers you?"

"They're impressionable and prone to unhealthy attachments."

"That won't matter in a few days," Elana commented. "Maybe Taisa will go back to Cheongu when this is over. Or Tae will join her in Onethis. Traveling would suit them both."

"Are you being a romantic?"

Elana shrugged. "She deserves some happiness. They both do."

Di'Nay only grunted in response and Elana laughed as she tightened her grip on Di'Nay's waist. "Will you be this watchful over your own daughters?"

"Undoubtedly. It's a universal fact that young people are trouble."

"Taisa is about my age."

"And you're trouble."

Elana grinned at her wolfishly. "Then it's good I'll be there to thwart you. Young people deserve to be a bit wild."

Di'Nay's eyes softened and Elana felt her desire to kiss her like a weight against her skin. "Don't think I'm so easy to thwart."

"I know exactly how to handle you."

Di'Nay let out a labored, frustrated breath, her eyes flicking to their companions. "Trouble."

"Me or them?"

"The world."

Elana squeezed Di'Nay's side as she withdrew her arm. "Let's get something to eat."

"I would give up food for a week for an hour alone with you," she muttered, making Elana laugh loud enough to draw attention.

Tae beckoned them to the other end of the boat. "Come! The food is almost ready!"

"Come on Soroi," Elana commented, leading Di'Nay forward. "We have plenty of time to be morose and even more time to be alone in the future. For now, we have to heal and prepare for Onethis."

Taisa and Tae burst into peals of laughter again, this time wrapping their arms around each other like children. Di'Nay tensed and Elana let out an exaggerated sigh as they walked forward to join their friends, relishing a moment of peace in their long journey. They both knew it wouldn't last long.

PART THREE

A NEW ERA

ONETHIS: BURIED IN THE MUD

The swamps of Onethis seemed both massive and intimate all at once. The navigable stretches of water seemed to twist and flow in a narrow channel like a river, but the marshes and water flora left enough of the land visible it seemed to stretch forever in every direction. The heavy scents of mold and mud lingered in the air. The heat and humidity made the air thick like a wet mist.

Elana fussed with her hair as it swelled and tangled, becoming almost impossible to braid. She silently cursed herself for letting it hang down for so long, but Di'Nay liked it and there were so few things she could do to acknowledge her lover while they were surrounded by people who didn't know about their relationship.

"It really has a mind of its own, doesn't it?" Di'Nay teased as she walked up behind Elana and took over braiding.

"It's going to grow larger than I am someday."

Di'Nay finished the braid and wrapped it in a thick strip of leather from their supply bags to make it particularly secure. "There."

Elana ran her hand over the leather wrapping, happy to have her hair off her cheeks. "Thank you."

She turned to face Di'Nay. Her Amazon wore a sleeveless vest and breeches. She wore a thick leather cuff bracelet to hide the lifestone embedded in her wrist that connected her to Elana. Her pale skin was dotted with sweat and her short blonde hair was heavy along her brow. Her skin was flushed from the heat. Elana felt a knot of desire tighten in her stomach. It had been so long since they'd touched, since they'd been free to be themselves.

Sometimes Elana thought she'd go insane.

Di'Nay noticed the heat in Elana's eyes and returned it, their energy so warm and hungry it almost felt like they were touching.

"We should reach Saranthis within the hour."

Elana shook herself out of her reverie as Tae approached. His shoulder-length ebony hair was tied back in a short ponytail. The men on the boat had removed their shirts long ago, though it didn't seem to ward them from the humidity. Elana still wished she had the same freedom. Even a cotton tunic and breeches felt like a thick blanket against her skin.

"Good. Jimin isn't having any trouble with the swamp?" Elana questioned.

Tae shrugged. "Jimin's a good captain. He'll handle whatever comes our way." Tae's voice was stronger than ever, his confidence speaking the language of the Ramains growing every day. Elana wondered how much his practice had come from his long talks with Taisa during their journey from Cheongu to the Onethis coast.

"Did I hear we're only an hour away?" Taisa approached, already wearing her long cloak despite the heat. Elana saw the tell-tale swell of a crossbow on her back and a quiver of arrows strapped to her thigh.

Her fear and insecurity about being recognized by agents of the Order of Blindness had prompted her to do everything in her power to disguise her identity. In Cheongu she'd dyed her hair from auburn to black and cut it short like a shaggy men's hairstyle. She'd also marked her face with simple pale blue tattoos – dots around her eyes, lines along her cheekbones, and small, symbolic designs etched into her hairline that had private meaning to her.

The changes gave her a mysterious kind of beauty that made her unrecognizable from the woman she'd been when Elana first met her. She'd had a sweet, innocent kind of charm before – nothing that made her particularly exceptional. Now she looked like a young, wild rendition of the Mother.

While Elana was sure some of her changes had been inspired by a genuine desire to reclaim her identity, Elana could feel the anxiety rising beneath her that made risking dehydration and heat stroke more ideal than being seen as the same Taisa that had been a double agent for the Ramains Marshals in the Order of

Blindness.

"Yes. Though we should be entering more populated waters much sooner," Tae responded. "We'll dock in the harbor and restock. You're welcome to stay for a while."

"We'll want to get out of the city as quickly as possible. It's sure to be crawling with the Order," Di'Nay reminded them. Elana felt Tae and Taisa's moods fall.

"Of course," Tae agreed. "That makes sense." He shifted uncomfortably, then glanced to his brother on the other end of the ship. "I should go help him."

"Tae –" Taisa tried to call to him, but he ignored her. She bit back whatever she'd wanted to say and drew a deep breath, settling herself in the present.

"We can go back someday," Elana offered, trying to ease her pain at separating from someone she'd formed a genuine connection with.

"If we survive." There was so much finality in her voice. Her pain spread through Elana like an ache in her bones. Taisa wasn't particularly powerful in the Sight, but her emotions could still seep into the people around her when left unchecked. She clenched her jaw and shook aside her emotions. "We'll need a small rowboat. I can take you to one of the Order outposts, but it's hard to reach and impossible to navigate with a large boat or on foot."

"Tae offered to get us one," Elana commented. "I gave him the gold to secure it and supplies. It shouldn't take long."

"Good." Taisa pulled her hood up over her head, the long hood hiding most of her face in shadow. She retreated to the starboard side of the boat and cast her focus on the swamp.

"They're so sad," Elana muttered.

"We knew this would happen," Di'Nay reminded her.

"That doesn't make it less tragic."

Di'Nay held her hand. "Maybe it will end up for the best."

"Maybe."

Jeon called in the Cheongu language to his brother, and Tae translated: "Merchant vessel ahead."

"We should take cover," Taisa responded, heading toward the supplies piled near the mainsail and sat among the crates. They would draw little attention, covered by the railing.

Di'Nay and Elana joined her. Hiding from passing ships,

Elana felt the joy they'd found in Cheongu slipping away. They were back in the line of fire. Back to skirting danger. She could only hope their determination would bring their journey to a quick and successful end.

It took Tae and Jeon longer than Elana had expected to find them a boat. As they sat hidden among supplies in the swamp heat, Elana found herself growing drowsy. She leaned against Di'Nay's shoulder and her eyes fluttered closed. Soon she slipped into dreams.

Elana sat on a crimson mat in the courtyard of the Shrine of the Bull in Cheongu. The sisters around her prayed and hummed low in their throats, focusing and meditating on their duties. Their invocations were said to soothe the Bull of Jidoin – an ancient creature of the Sight who had been created by the Mother and the Fates together. A creature meant to bring balance to the world. He was a creature of fire. Elana and the original Blue Sights were his cousins – creatures made of the same earth as the rest of the humans, but blessed with the same gifts and powers to create equilibrium.

Elana didn't pray. She let the soft sounds of the priestesses soothe her soul as she let her mind wander. She felt a flicker of flame against her cheeks despite there being no fire nearby. It was the light of the bull, calm and noble. He was at peace in a way she'd never seen him in Jidoin. His flaming mane and tails flickered slowly like a campfire in a gentle breeze.

The sisters sang louder and Elana felt herself communing with the beast. There were disturbances on Aggar. There was a threat to the servants of balance. The bull didn't know what it was, but Elana did – the Order of Blindness. They had kidnapped seer children and murdered Blue Sights. They were growing strong in the far south and their tendrils had made it all the way to the Keep. If their wild zealots, without any strong leadership or ties to the original Order in Onethis, could nearly destroy the Council's Keep, Elana was afraid of what they'd be able to do at full force.

They had to be stopped to restore calm on Aggar and only the human Blue Sights had the ability to act. Elana squared her shoulders and felt her tattoo – the mark of the Shrine of the Bull on her nape – burn her responsibility into her skin.

She had once been afraid of the Order, but not anymore.

She was tasked with destroying them wherever possible. Elana had never been particularly religious, but she knew the Bull was real. She felt him as she might a dear cousin. He was asking for help, and she would come through.

If the Order wasn't tracking them already, they undoubtedly would be by the time they were done in Onethis. Elana had a lot of plans for the Order of Blindness, and none of it was easily forgettable.

The swamp was thick and muddy, the oars of the long rowboat Tae had been able to secure for them seemed to fight with every row. Diana's arms ached from the exertion even with Elana's help. She'd become a bit complacent with her fitness in Cheongu and it was catching up with her.

Away from the larger towns the swamp seemed a living creature. The flora was tall and stringy, the trees growing directly out of the water and their branches reaching out like arms trying to catch them. Their leaves were hanging and limp like wet hair or some kind of vining moss. The stumps of old and fallen trees mingled with the living, their broken and jagged tops like mountains in this forest of water.

It smelled just as Diana imagined it would. Mold. Decay. Mud. It smelled and felt as wet as the air, bathing them all without a single drop of rain. Diana had heard Cleis – her sister in arms on Aggar – had once been stationed on planet that was largely swamp. Diana thanked the Goddess she hadn't been with her.

"We want to stay close to this line of trees," Taisa directed, hunching low over the prow of the boat. "It winds to the east in a sharp arc. There will be a bit of land there. We can hide the boat and sneak up on the outpost on foot."

"When were you last here?" Elana questioned.

"A tenmoon ago, perhaps a bit more. I've spent the better part of my time in the desert."

"You think this cell of the Order is still active?"

"We'll find out."

"Do you feel something off?" Diana questioned, her voice gruff from the exertion of rowing.

"It's hard to feel anything specific here. There's so much life. I didn't realize a swamp would be so active."

Diana glanced around, the thought of the trees and

creatures hidden in the watery shadows of exposed roots and decaying stumps being alive and attentive wasn't a pleasant one. At least the landscape would provide plenty of cover if need-be.

"You shouldn't try to use the Sight. It will only distract you here," Taisa advised. "It's not like you can sense members of the Order anyway."

"I can't make myself stop Seeing," Elana remarked.

"You can learn."

Elana frowned. Diana had never heard someone be as dismissive of the Sight as Taisa. Even Gerome, who had hated his abilities, still saw them as a part of himself. Either Taisa wasn't very gifted with the Blue Sight or she had some special ability Elana didn't share.

Diana did as Taisa advised and kept as close to the edge of the tree line as she dared. Every now and then she saw the glowing golden eyes of swamp creatures in the darkness and tensed. She wished she knew more about the native fauna of the region so she could guess at what they were. For all she knew the eyes belonged to a breed of friendly toads, but without any frame of reference her imagination grew wild and unsettling.

Elana felt her caution and smiled, resting a hand on her knee. The touch centered Diana, wiping away her worries and replacing them with thoughts of her lover. She longed for the days they trekked alone in Karatan. A good portion of training to be an Amazon was learning how to fit in with local culture. Diana had known that meant often hiding her attractions, sparring with her personal ethics, and pretending to be something she wasn't. It had been easy until she met Elana.

Diana had been in love before and she'd lusted even more. She was no stranger to the heady addiction of affection and romance. But she'd never had a partner like Elana. A woman who held her own, who could keep pace with Diana in life. She was the first woman who had made Diana pause and reconsider her goals and work in life. She was an Amazon – an adventurer born to leave Yemaya and grapple with politics, new worlds, and cultural differences in an attempt to make and keep peace in the universe. Now Elana had her dreaming of a home by the sea with children and uneventful long nights in her lover's arms.

She wanted to know more about every bit of Elana – her body, her mind, her soul. She couldn't do that with Taisa or thoughts of the Order getting between them. She was dedicated to making Aggar safer, to not just saving seer children but ending the processes that allowed them to be kidnapped in the first place. She knew she was doing the right thing, that it was selfish to linger over thoughts of being somewhere else.

It was common for new lovers to become obsessed with each other, but they'd had so little time when they were both at peace, healthy, and had the time to indulge in just being in love. It seemed to get harder every day to pretend they were just companions, just friends. She wanted to be openly in love. She wanted days, weeks, months without chaos or danger. Elana's touch was a promise of better days to come, but it always left an ache in the pit of Diana's stomach.

"Up here," Taisa called, her voice soft.

As she'd described, the tree line curved suddenly to the east, revealing a slender rivulet crossing an island of dry land. The land was narrow, the mud thick on either side. If the land didn't widen before they reached the outpost, it would be hard to hide without jumping into the water.

"The outpost is about an hour ahead, depending on how stable the ground is," Taisa explained as Diana drew the boat as close to land as she could, and then jumped out to pull it more ashore.

The water was only up to her calves but her feet instantly sank to the ankle in the wet soil. Diana realized what Taisa meant about ground stability. Even when she pulled the boat to the dryer sections of land the earth felt somewhat spongy and soft. It would be easy to get stuck or lost in such an environment. She tried not to think about how they would navigate such a place once it got dark.

Once Elana and Taisa were on land, they pulled the boat into a section of the ground partly shielded by hanging, slender tree branches with willow-like leaves. They trekked slowly along the strip of land. Diana was pleased to see it steadily grew wider into a small island. They would need to be sure they weren't followed as they left, but they'd have decent coverage in their approach.

Nearly an hour into their hike, Taisa crouched lower and indicated a small building in the distance. It was made of wood and thatch, standing on wooden legs to protect the base in case of a flood. It wasn't dissimilar to the homes Diana had seen in Karatan.

She was surprised it was so small. The Order wouldn't be able to house many people there. The thought made Diana breath a soft sigh of relief. Even if they had to fight, they would probably be all right.

They waited a while, watching the building. After a few minutes, they saw the shadow of someone pacing inside. There were no sounds of talking or signs that the man in the building had a companion. Once they were sure there weren't many people inside, Elana crept forward, staying low to the ground. Diana watched her for a moment, marveling at her Shadow abilities as she blended with shadow. Diana knew where she was – she didn't disappear entirely – but her eyes had a hard time focusing on her and if she didn't know she was there, they probably would have slid over her entirely.

She got close enough to the building to see inside the windows. She waved Taisa and Diana forward and, as they started moving toward her, she stood and sent a crossbow bolt flying through the window. The gurgled cry of surprise inside the building signaled that Elana had hit her target. Diana was taken aback at the swiftness of her action.

"There's no one else inside," Elana said aloud. She walked to the building boldly, scanning the forest for anyone else who might be lingering around outside.

"We'll have to get rid of the body," Taisa grunted as they entered. "They regularly rotate the people stationed here. If he's alone, a companion should be arriving soon."

The building was small – only a couple rooms. It appeared to be some kind of office, with a desk and cabinets. The smaller room in the back was a makeshift bedroom.

"I thought there'd be more here," Diana admitted. She frowned at the dead man in the middle of the room. He had been shot through the throat, his eyes bulging and his blood staining the ground.

"It isn't particularly important to the Order," Taisa admitted as she started digging through the cabinets. "But they store a lot of information here. They send out assignments, they might even have maps of other outpost locations."

Elana crouched beside the body. She shifted the collar of his shirt to reveal and Order of Blindness amulet and glanced up at Diana. "Help me?" Diana grabbed his legs and Elana his arms.

They carried him out of the building and Elana nodded to the water.

"Do you think he'll be discovered?" Diana questioned.

"Not until long after we're gone."

"We need to keep one step ahead of them or they might relocate any seers they might have in the forest."

"Put him down."

They lowered him to the ground and Elana cut his shirt away and then into strips. She used them to lash a large rock to his body. "This should buy us enough time. If we're between rotations they might assume he's late before they'll suspect he's dead."

They threw him as far out into the swamp as they could and Diana was grateful to see he didn't float back to the top. Taisa was scrubbing the last of the blood out of the floor when they returned. Thankfully, Elana hadn't seemed to cut his arteries. Taisa covered the spot with a small rug in case the mild discoloration was noticed.

"I found a map," Taisa remarked, laying a large piece of parchment on the table. It illustrated a good portion of the swamp with various outposts marked in black ink.

"Any record of seers?"

"No," Taisa commented, "but there's some record of what a few of the outposts are for. We can mark them off as not holding prisoners. It's a good enough start."

Elana scanned the shelves, double checking Taisa's findings. Diana searched the rest of the outpost, being careful not to leave signs of her presence. When she returned, Elana was folding the map and tucking it into the pouch at her waist. "Taisa's right, but now we have new leads." She pulled a box from a cabinet and shut it with her foot.

"What's that?" Diana questioned.

"Amulets." She opened the box, dumped the amulets onto the bloody rag Taisa had used to clean up after their kill, and replaced the box. She tied the rag off like a bag and threw it out the window into the swamp. Diana felt a small burst of pride at the confidence in her lover, this time not tainted with rage or sadness. Elana was decisive, strong. She had a mission, and she was going to see it through.

The swamp became even more lively after dark. Elana could feel the nocturnal creatures stirring in the water and moving through the trees. She didn't feel the presence of anything particularly dangerous – a few water predators hunting along the edge of her Sight, but uninterested in their boat. It was mostly birds, bats, insects, and amphibians. The croaks and chirps of some of the smaller creatures combined with the rushes shifting in the light breeze, making a soft melody Elana found entrancing.

Elana couldn't sleep. Her thoughts were on the map she'd studied to the point of memorizing it – on which of the outposts could hold kidnapped seer children. She imagined them in a place like this, so full of life and a chaos of amarin energy. They had to be kept heavily sedated – the amarin would drive them mad and more than two or three seers held together would be able to overpower most guards. If a cluster of seers were being held anywhere in the swamp, they would be bound, drugged, and forced to wear Order of Blindness amulets.

Elana imagined even two of the seers waking enough to bind together. She imagined the young seers creating a small hive of their own. She imagined finding the ashes. She smiled. The Order was hateful and extremely skilled at hiding from the Keep, but they were nothing compared to a group of seers. But the Order couldn't have operated this long without knowing how to keep the seers bound. If they made careless mistakes, they wouldn't exist anymore.

Taisa rustled in her sleep and Elana felt the whisper of her nightmares. Their boat was long – big enough they could escape with a half dozen seer children without risk of tipping the boat, but it became much smaller with all three women lying flat in an attempt to sleep. Taisa's occasional thrash knocked against Elana's feet and legs.

Elana wondered not for the first time how strong a Blue Sight Taisa really was. Her abilities seemed stunted. She didn't seem to grasp shifts in amarin that should be obvious. As far as Elana knew, Taisa hadn't guessed that Elana and Di'Nay were more than bondmates. At first Elana had thought it was due to a lifetime of intense repression – maybe she had even been born with less ability than most. But now Elana wondered if it was something else.

Perhaps so long with the Order – so long wearing one of their amulets that bound her Sight – had done irreparable harm.

Or perhaps over time her abilities would return. Elana hoped the work she'd done in Cheongu to reclaim herself and distance herself from the Order would lead to some kind of acceptance if her abilities reasserted themselves.

Taisa woke with a gasp, a shot of frightened amarin filling the air. Elana raised her brows in surprise. Taisa held her chest for a moment, taking slow breaths with closed eyes. Elana wondered how many times she'd had to soothe herself from what seemed to be violent nightmares.

"I'm sorry," she whispered, knowing Elana was awake without looking at her.

"Are you all right?" Elana questioned.

Taisa nodded slowly and ran her hands through her cropped hair. "I was dreaming about the children."

"The seers?"

Taisa nodded. "My overactive imagination."

"It could have been a vision."

Taisa tensed. "I don't get visions."

"Are you sure? What did you see?"

"Elana. Please."

Elana was quiet for a moment, but dared one last comment. "You worked so hard in Cheongu to reclaim yourself. The Sight is part of who you are. It makes you powerful."

Taisa was still, pondering Elana's words. Elana felt her amarin slowly disappear as she pulled it tight into herself. Within a minute or two she might as well have been wearing an amulet – Elana couldn't feel anything from her.

It was a protective gesture, but it was all Elana needed to feel to know the root of Taisa's skills. It was difficult for any Blue Sight to keep full control over their abilities, even ones who were trained at the Keep. To be able to completely withdraw all amarin markers from other Blue Sights was a wonder. It was clear Taisa *had* been trained, just by survival instincts and the cruel teachings of the Order of Blindness instead of the Keep.

"The Sight is dangerous, Elana. It ruined my life." Taisa's voice was soft and calm, matter of fact.

"It is dangerous. For them. Hate is born of fear. If the Order is attempting to purge the Sight from Aggar it's because they're terrified of it."

"I'm terrified of it."

"You have to learn to wield it responsibly. You already have amazing control, you just have to trust yourself with it."

"That's easy to say as an expert."

Elana laughed so loudly she was afraid she'd wake Di'Nay. "I'm scared of my Sight all the time."

Taisa turned to face her, some of her control over her own amarin fading. She was shocked at Elana's announcement. "I've never seen you out of control before."

"I knew how to find you in Jidoin because of visions I had when I broke under the weight of my Sight. I couldn't talk. I couldn't tell reality from spirit. I nearly lost myself for the rest of my life."

Taisa's eyes widened. "What could do that?"

"I was afraid. I lost sight of who I was. It isn't easy for me to have the Sight, Taisa. But I wouldn't give it up for anything. It's who I am. It's who you are, too. And it will help you find those children if you let it."

Another long silence, then: "Do you really think my dream was a vision?"

"I don't know. What did you see?"

I saw five children, blindfolded, bound, and wearing amulets. They looked dead but I could see them breathing. There were members of the Order standing around them. They had knives and crossbows. One was a Terran."

Elana raised her brows in surprise. "And the location?"

"Wood paneled walls. Shuttered windows. I think the roof was thatched."

"It sounds like the outpost."

"It looked like the outpost," she whispered.

"Sounds like it may have been a vision to me."

It was clear in her body language Taisa thought it was real, too. She just didn't want to think about it. "I didn't see much else. I just sat with the children. They were laying on the floor, dirty and lifeless."

"They were drugged. The Order has access to a Karatan vision drug that keeps seers sedated. Thankfully, it isn't unpleasant for the children."

"One was waking up."

"Really?"

"I saw his foot move."

"What happened?"

"It woke me up."

Elana's mouth formed a hard, straight line. "We need to get to him before the Order silences him again."

"Why do they keep them, Elana? Why steal them? They don't keep Blue Sights. They talk about cleansing Aggar, not holding hostages. They're not demanding ransoms. What are they gaining from this?"

"Seers are more powerful in numbers than any other force on Aggar. It would make sense the Order would be most afraid of them."

"Then why keep them alive?"

The comment hit Elana hard. She pushed aside thoughts of the children executed on the floor of the Order's outpost. "There must be something they still want to know about them. I don't know."

Taisa frowned. "If I dream about anything more specific, I'll tell you."

"Thank you." Elana was already lost in Taisa's question. She knew the Order was a larger force to be reckoned with than she had evidence of. She still had no idea how their amulets could block the wearer's amarin or how the Order had discovered them. They were politically and technologically savvy in a way that didn't match with their origins. It was clear there was a separation between the members of the Order that believed in some divine duty to cleanse Aggar and a smaller, more secretive sect that was more concerned with information, kidnapping seers, and anti-blue sight technology. They were the ones to fear, to destroy.

What really was the Order's end game with the seers?

Following clues Taisa saw in her dreams, they were able to pare down their options on the map even further. She had clearly dreamt of a larger outpost, and in the four days they'd already traveled deeper into the swamp she'd seen signs of another nearby building, had heard multiple boats come and go, and had heard complaints from Order members that the outpost was far from larger, more navigable waterways.

It had narrowed their targets down to one outpost. Taisa was nervous it would be the wrong one – that she was only dreaming, not having visions – but Elana trusted her and that was good enough for Diana when it came to understanding the Sight.

The members of the Order in Taisa's dream had been right to complain about this particular outpost. While the swamp was massive and had no set rivers or streams, there were larger swaths of water that were easier to travel unimpeded. To get to Taisa's outpost, they had to leave those waterways behind and depend on smaller channels. More than once they had to carry the boat over muddy tracts of land to stay on course. The swamp seemed to be constantly changing due to the accumulation of mud, tree growth, and changing water lines. The map showed distance, but wasn't useful for much beyond that.

"This better be the place," Taisa huffed as they lowered the boat back into the water off a particularly sharp and wet mud island. "If all this is for the wrong outpost I'll tear my hair out."

"It will be the place," Elana promised.

Diana dug her heels into the soft soil, trying desperately not to fall. Luckily, they were all able to climb into the boat relatively dry.

The bottom of the boat was filthy from their muddy boots and there wasn't much they could do to clean it. Diana's face was pinched in disgust as she took the oars once more, double checked the map and her compass, and continued on.

"You look miserable, Diana," Taisa observed.

"I'm trying to imagine a warm bath and clean boots," Diana commented.

"And a bed," Elana sighed.

"And warm food," Taisa agreed.

"For us and the children." Elana's voice was both sobering and hopeful. Diana thought of them – not only in this bog, but bound and held prisoner, locked inside themselves with amulets and drugs. They had to be so scared.

Diana shifted her expression from disgust to stillness, trying to hold onto what mattered. She could deal with mud and the smell of decay, and the heat for those children. It would only be a little while longer.

By midday on their fifth day since leaving the first outpost, their target came into sight. Diana had planned to spot it, then backtrack just enough to hide their boat like before, but this time she hesitated. She could see thick plumes of smoke in the distance and smelled ash. Both Elana and Taisa tensed, Elana gripping her oars so tightly she stopped rowing.

"We need to go to the outpost," Elana remarked.

"Not hide the boat?"

"I don't feel anything."

"You wouldn't, not with everyone wearing amulets," Diana reminded her.

"No. I mean from the trees. There's been a fire. A big one."

Elana and Diana rowed together, leading the boat directly to the small dock of the outpost. There were no other boats in the water. The remains of what looked like three outposts and many trees in the surrounding area had been reduced to ash. Judging by the smoke and the heat, the fire had died very recently. Diana couldn't imagine a fire burning this intensely in such a wet environment.

The smell of fire hung heavy in the air but Diana could smell the rotting whiff of burned flesh under the stronger scents. People had died here.

Elana and Taisa climbed out of the boat as Diana secured it, circling the ashes in shock. Diana finished securing the boat and turned to join Elana, but paused. She'd seen a flash of white out of the corner of her eye. She turned to the water and felt her muscles tense and her breath catch in her throat. A small child's shoe floated half-submerged in the water.

Diana skirted the shoreline and grabbed the shoe. It was made for a young child, a little larger than Diana's palm. It was soft leather – it had once been very fine before it had been stained in mud and soot.

"Di'Nay?" Elana called.

Diana turned and held out the shoe. Elana took it in trembling hands and slid into the water. By the time the water was up to her thighs she had fished out a boot for an older child, a doll, and a night shirt.

"Elana!" Taisa called. She lifted a sword. "I've found human remains."

Elana climbed out of the swamp. Water flooded off her pants, boots, and cloak but she didn't seem to notice. She followed Diana to Taisa and they studied piles of ash with bits of bone.

"These aren't the children." Elana breathed a sigh of relief.

"The fire must have been incredibly hot. Bodies don't burn like this fast." Diana studied the charred trees. "It must have been an explosion. The fire would have spread if it got this hot naturally."

"The children did it," Elana stated. "They must have. They woke up and banded together to escape."

"That's a leap," Diana cautioned.

"How else do you explain it? Only Terrans have this kind of technology and what Terran base would be targeting an outpost in a swamp?"

"It could have been the Order," Diana guessed.

"These are adult bodies. These were the Order."

"They were young. They can't survive on their own." Taisa's voice trembled. "The oldest couldn't have been more than six tenmoons!"

"As a unit, they're stronger than most children," Elana remarked. "I have to believe they're alive. I can't think of them in this ash."

Diana rested her hand on Elana's shoulder and Elana drew a deep, calming breath. "You're right," Diana commented. "We have to assume they're alive. Where do you think they'd go?"

"They'd try to find shelter, darkness, and quiet," Elana stated. "I don't know what they'd consider a safe place around here."

"I can try to dream again." Elana and Diana turned to Taisa. She seemed more sure than she'd ever been about her abilities. "I got us this far."

"I can try to help," Elana offered.

Taisa hesitated, but she nodded. "We can find them."

"We can," Elana agreed. "With your help."

Diana looked between them. "We should go down river in case members of the Order come to investigate this attack. Then we can find a place to make some kind of camp. I'll keep you safe while you meditate. Maybe even find some food."

"Thank you," Elana stated. She clutched the seer childrens' things tightly and together they returned to the boat.

Taisa stifled her cry as she woke in terror, coming out of her nightmares with a violent start. The glanced in embarrassment at Elana, a hand over her heart as she tried to calm down.

"I'm sorry," she whispered.

"Did you see anything?" Elana asked.

They had found a small patch of dry ground to sleep on for the night, but Elana found she couldn't rest. Taisa's dreams were vivid and violent to her Sight, like someone screaming in her ear. Taisa's Sight was returning in leaps and bounds.

Taisa held her head in her hands. "I can't remember. Everything's a blur."

"Try to remember."

"I do try," Taisa growled. "The moment I wake up it becomes a jumble."

Elana let out a soft sigh, her thoughts spinning. She had to find a way to make sense of Taisa's visions. For some reason, the seers were only reaching out to Taisa – Elana hadn't had a single vision dream about the children or the Order and Taisa hadn't slept without some kind of message or image about where they needed to go next.

Elana tried not to be jealous or frustrated, but at the end of the day she couldn't help but think that they'd be moving much faster if she had the visions. She had the training to remember and interpret her dreams. She had the focus and skill. Taisa was much more unpredictable.

"Perhaps I can help you remember," Elana offered.

"What do you mean?"

"We form a bond. Communicate through the Sight. If you let me in, I can coax your memories back to the surface."

"You want to go inside my mind?"

Di'Nay sat up from where she'd been sleeping. She'd been awakened by Taisa's gasp, but hadn't wanted to interrupt Elana and Taisa's conversation. Elana smiled softly. As polite as the gesture had been, even a weak Blue Sight could sense when someone was awake.

"It isn't dangerous," Elana assured them both. "It's meditative."

Taisa regarded Elana cautiously and Elana knew what she was thinking. She didn't trust anyone or anything that sought to control her mind. Elana didn't blame her, but unfortunately they had few options left.

"I'm not sure."

"Every night we waste time the seer children are in more peril," Elana pressed. "For their sake, we have to do anything we can to get to them quickly."

The argument dropped some of Taisa's defenses. Elana felt her relax and Taisa cast her a meaningful glance that said she felt Elana take notice of her amarin. "You promise it's safe?"

"Very. Trust me."

"I don't trust anyone who asks for my blind obedience. But I hate the thought of those children trapped in this swamp."

"Perhaps then I can prove my trustworthiness," Elana offered. "Come sit across from me."

Elana sat up straighter and crossed her legs over each other as she had while meditating in Cheongu. Taisa joined her, sitting face-to-face, their knees touching. Taisa was buzzing with Blue Sight energy, throwing Elana off guard. She could understand why Taisa couldn't interpret her dreams.

"You need to calm your mind," Elana instructed.

"My mind is never calm," Taisa argued.

"Try." Taisa closed her eyes and drew deep, regular breaths. Elana could sense the chaos in her mind and used some of her own Sight to calm her. Within a few minutes Taisa was far from perfectly at peace, but she was close enough.

"I want you to focus on your dream. Remember to keep yourself emotionally detached. These visions aren't personal to you. They aren't a threat. They're information. The secret to controlling the Sight is controlling yourself. Push anything but logic away."

Taisa steeled herself and Elana felt a hint of practiced detachment. She hadn't been formally trained, but she knew how to survive with the Sight. With gentle guidance from Elana and a concerted effort to remain calm, Taisa started to slip back into her darker memories, sorting out what she'd seen in her dreams.

"I saw footprints in the mud. Small ones," Taisa whispered. "They're shallow."

"Children?" Elana pressed.

"Yes. I... I think if the older ones were carrying the smaller children there'd be enough prints for all of them."

"You think they all survived?"

Taisa nodded, her eyes still closed. Elana felt a gentle touch of relief at the thought. Taisa's nightmares had seemed so severe she'd started to fear the worst."

"Did you see them?" Elana questioned.

Di'Nay watched them both intently, her presence protective

and strong. It gave Elana the strength she needed to support Taisa.

Taisa's brow furrowed and sharp lines formed in the corners of her lips as her memories became more distressing. Elana fed her healing and soothing energy but it barely helped.

"Yes," Taisa gasped. "They're hazy, but I saw them. They're traveling at night in a cluster. They seem to know where they're going."

"Can you tell where they are?"

"No. I just see them surrounded by the swamp." Her face started to soften as the memories became more natural to her. "The baby cries at dawn, but the others shush her. They're strong together."

Elana smiled softly. As she suspected. "They'll form a hive."

"They aren't alone. I see others, white lights like ghosts. A girl with silver hair."

Di'Nay and Elana exchanged startled glances. "An adolescent?"

"I think so."

"Silver," Di'Nay whispered.

"Her presence, yes," Elana agreed. "It's a good sign."

"I smell fire."

"Around the children?"

"On the children. It's subtle, maybe in their clothes."

"That confirms our suspicion that they started the fire," Di'Nay commented.

"Taisa, think hard. Can you sense anything that would guide us to them? A bend in the river? A change in the density of the trees?"

Taisa started to sweat more than normal. Her cheeks colored, making her pale blue tattoos stand out more brilliantly against her skin.

"They've been on land for a long time, so it's somewhere with a long spit of soil."

"That's good. What else?"

Taisa's amarin started to stutter and tremble like the air crackling before a lightning storm. Elana tensed, trying to understand the sudden change and calm her friend.

"I think... I think I feel where they're going."

"Where?" Di'Nay questioned.

"An abandoned outpost. It..." she gasped for breath and

Elana reached out, setting a hand on her knee. "I see it. It's empty and the roof is patchy. The wood is soft, but stable. It can't be far."

She clenched her jaw and Elana leaned forward, squeezing Taisa's shoulders. "Taisa, you can come back. Breathe with me."

Elana expected her to argue, but to her surprise Taisa immediately obeyed. She forced a shallow breath past her grit teeth, following Elana's lead. Elana breathed progressively slower, extending the inhales and exhales until she felt Taisa's shoulders relax.

"Come back," Elana stated, her voice firm and confident. After a few minutes, Taisa opened her eyes, fully present once more. Elana smiled brightly. "You did very well."

Taisa smiled as well and Elana faltered. As Taisa's expression shifted and her peace swelled, Elana felt something through their shared connection. Something she hadn't expected. A new root for Taisa's energy and probably the reason her skills were growing.

Very faintly, like a whisper in the gale of Taisa's amarin, Elana could hear another voice.

Taisa was pregnant.

"Taisa," Elana whispered in shock and Taisa's expression fell.

"What?"

Elana debated whether to tell her. She obviously didn't know yet. The child couldn't be very far along – new enough it was obvious who the father was. In the end, Elana decided it would be unethical to keep the secret. Taisa deserved to know before she rushed into further danger.

"Taisa... do you feel any different? Anything in your amarin?"

Taisa's gaze fell and Elana knew she had, but had been writing it off. She was good at ignoring the instincts of her Sight. "It's true?"

Elana nodded. "You're pregnant."

"What?" Di'Nay gasped.

"When did you start to sense it?" Elana asked.

"A few days ago. I thought I was just rattled by the dreams."

"Tae?" Elana glanced at Di'Nay. Her lover's amarin was a bit smug.

Taisa shifted uncomfortably and looked away. She was

cloaked in darkness, drawing her amarin tight into herself. "I don't want to talk about this."

Elana stopped herself from pressing for more answers. They needed a plan. What would they do with a pregnant traveling companion? The child was already messing with Taisa's Sight — how far would that interference go? How would they tell Tae? *Would* Taisa tell Tae?

Elana wanted a plan of action, but it was clear this wasn't the time. Taisa was far beyond logical thought and Elana knew it was best to let her have her space. She released Taisa's shoulders and sat back. "Of course. Take your time."

Taisa stood. "I'm going for a walk."

"Don't wander far," Di'Nay called, protective and worried about leaving an emotionally unstable Taisa alone.

"I'll stay in your line of sight," Taisa muttered and continued down the spit of land as far from Elana and Di'Nay as she could go without disappearing or wading into the water. She sat and held her head in her hands, deep in thought.

Di'Nay crouched down beside Elana. "I knew this would happen," Di'Nay muttered, not out of anger but sadness. "They were both so lonely."

"Maybe it's a blessing? Tae's a good man. If she wants his help, he'll give it. Maybe they'll even be happy together."

"It isn't going to help her fight the Order, though," Di'Nay remarked. "And that's Taisa's whole purpose right now. We have to watch her. I don't know what she'll do."

Elana nodded slowly. "I don't either," Elana admitted. Dozens of thoughts and possible futures raced through her mind, set against her instincts about Taisa's child... and whether that child would have the Sight. "She has a lot of choices to make."

Diana felt Taisa's tension rising as they sped through the water, closing in on the location she'd seen in her dreams. Diana was getting used to rowing — she could feel herself getting stronger every day and her skill at navigating the swamp was becoming more instinctive. The way had been fairly clear all day and they skimmed over the water with ease.

The calm journey left her plenty of time to consider their situation. Taisa's dreams had returned after her meditation with Elana, but the knowledge of her pregnancy had pulled her deeper into herself. She barely initiated a conversation anymore, answering only when spoken to. She was quiet, thoughtful. Diana watched her for signs of where she was emotionally but Taisa was a master of hiding her emotion. Her face was stone. Her eyes were blank. Diana didn't know if she intended to see the pregnancy through or not. She couldn't even tell if she was suicidal or considering running away to keep her child safe.

Not even Elana could tell what Taisa was feeling. What Taisa lacked in sensing abilities with her Sight she seemed to make up for in cloaking ability. Diana thanked the Goddess she was a good observer. She would make sure Taisa didn't do anything rash.

As they drew closer to the abandoned outpost, Diana also trusted her senses as she scanned the landscape. Despite their fairly safe journey so far, the swamp could be treacherous. There was also the possibility they'd be attacked by seer children defending themselves, or perhaps even members of the Order of Blindness who were tracking the children. If there were any members of the Order near, Elana and Taisa wouldn't be able to sense them.

A small bird burst from a nearby bush, catching Diana's attention. It was faun brown with a long beak, probably for getting bugs out of the knots of the spindly trees. Diana had seen them hopping around their campsites whenever they found a bit of land big enough and dry enough to sleep out of the boat. Sometimes, in the early morning, they cooed and sang. Diana had come to love them – one of the only sweet and gentle things in the swamp. She wondered if the birds were comforting the seer children as well.

"I can sense them," Taisa called.

"I do, too," Elana agreed, her voice full of joy. "Just ahead."

Diana started to row faster, then hesitated. Something felt off.

"Di'Nay?" Elana called back over her shoulder as Diana hesitated in her rowing.

Diana's eyes flicked across the landscape, searching the shadows for signs of camouflage. A movement out of the corner of her right eye caught her attention and she rowed hard to the opposite shore with a sharp motion. "Down!" she screamed. Taisa and Elana ducked as crossbow bolts flew through the air, one striking their boat, two more hitting the wake in the water Diana left behind their boat.

"The Order!" Elana called and Diana instantly knew her companions' Sight would be useless.

They reached land and slid out of the boat, ducking into the foliage. Elana and Taisa exchanged crossbow bolts with the men across the water, but all fire was dodged. Eventually, they stopped shooting, electing to save their arrows. Their cover was thick enough and their reflexes fast enough that they avoided enemy fire. Then, for a moment, the firing stopped.

Elana shot again as six men leapt into the water and started to cross. They held blades above the water as they walked. They were dressed in dark clothing, painted in mud and grass to better hide. Diana drew her short sword, taking in her opponents, their weapons, and constantly looking for more hiding in the shadows.

The men moved with significantly more skill than most of the members of the Order they'd encountered before. They were either better trained or hired mercenaries. Diana figured the later, as their camouflage suggested they didn't know how seers sensed people around them. The thought didn't sit well with the Amazon. They were a strong team, but going two to one with trained killers was a risk.

Elana shot more bolts and the men dodged. She finally landed an arrow in one man's shoulder as they reached the shore. He grunted in pain and was distracted just long enough for her to shoot again, pegging him between the eyes. He dropped and the others barely took notice.

Taisa and Diana waited for the men to come closer, their blades drawn and ready. As the mercenaries drew within arm's length they clashed. Diana moved gracefully, her skills better than her enemies but barely. While she preferred a longer blade, she was grateful to have speed on her side. The land was narrow and Diana needed mobility to avoid falling into the water.

She stabbed one opponent in the stomach and used the force of the blow to push him back into the swamp. The dark water was soon stained in swirls of his blood. Taisa thrust and parried two attackers, her teeth grit in an animalistic growl as she fought with the ferocity of a beast. Diana was nearly distracted by her – she had never seen Taisa fight with a blade, let alone with so much anger.

Elana shot, dispatching one of Taisa's attackers before returning to her own battles. Diana went for the man who looked like the leader of the group and his first blow nearly knocked her to her knees. He was a lot stronger than he looked and nearly a head taller than Diana, who was far from short herself. They exchanged blows, every one of his strikes shaking Diana to the bone but she was able to deflect his killing strikes.

Diana hissed as she blocked his blade, but the force of his thrust allowed the edge of his sword to bite into her waist. The injury was shallow, but her shirt was quickly wet with blood. Elana shot at the man, but he twisted away, parrying Diana's blow at the same time. Diana's blood raced behind her ears as she heard Taisa grunt in pain, accompanied by the heavy thud of a landed blow. They were being overtaken.

"The amulets!" she heard Elana shouting, her voice desperate.

Diana took immediate action, not trying to interpret Elana's message, only to act. She swiped at the mercenary's neck. He blocked her attempt to behead him, but Elana reached her true goal – slicing through the cord at his neck holding his amulet from the Order of Blindness. It fell to the ground with a soft, metallic click.

The instant it hit the ground, the man doubled over in pain, grabbing at his head. Blood ran in rivulets from his nose and he grabbed his scalp, his nails biting into his skin until he bled. He screamed, the sound primal. Haunting. Diana had never heard a man scream like that before. A moment later, he fell to the ground dead. Diana thought she could see a small curl of steam escape his ear.

She heard the heavy thuds of more bodies and spun around to find her friends, but they were all unharmed. All six of the mercenaries lay in pools of their own blood, three of the six due to their amulets being removed.

Diana turned to her lover in shock and horror. "Elana?"

"It wasn't me," Elana rebutted. She nodded to a nearby bush. Two adolescent women – twins – stepped forward. They held hands, standing side by side. They wore matching tan dresses, the cloth worn and littered with holes. They were barefoot, covered to the knees in mud. They were small for their age, wearing their dark hair in matching long braids. Neither of them looked directly at Diana or her friends. Diana knew instantly they were seers.

"Thank you," Elana called to them.

They didn't answer, but their energy was disturbingly pleased and gentle for young women who had just seemingly burned the brains out of three men.

They turned and walked further down the narrow bit of land. "Do we follow them?" Diana questioned.

"Yes," Taisa answered as she cleaned her blade on one mercenary's shirt and walked after the seer sisters. "They'll take us to the others."

Diana glanced at Elana, who seemed less sure. "We've followed her this far," Elana reminded Diana.

Diana nodded. "Too far to give up now."

Together, Elana and Diana followed Taisa deeper into the swamp.

Four seer children had gathered in a cluster in the darkness created by two willow trees whose branches intersected, creating a curtain of leaves and ivy-like branches. They were filthy, covered in mud and half-dressed, but they seemed calm. They sat together, holding each other. Three had their eyes closed. The oldest watched the younger ones with rapt attention. Only she seemed to notice Elana, Taisa, and Diana enter their clearing with the twins.

Elana moved quickly to their sides, checking them for injuries. The younger seemed distressed by the intrusion, but the eldest helped Elana, keeping a firm grip on her charges but showing they were safe.

"We kept them healthy," she insisted.

Elana smiled. "You speak?"

"I'm weaker than they are."

"What's your name?"

"Janis."

"You may feel weaker than them, Janis, but your awareness kept them alive."

Diana watched the exchange, the knot in her stomach and heart quickly loosening, seeing them safe and at peace. If they had been even an hour later, it wouldn't have been so peaceful.

Janis blushed deep olive. She nodded to the twins. "They saved us. They woke up together."

Diana eyed the twins. They were slender and small, obviously older than their size indicated, but not by much. Perhaps 13 years old. While all the other seers bore marks of soot or burned edges on their clothes, they were free of any signs of fire. Perhaps being together from birth made it easier for them to remain calm and develop their abilities. They had created their own seer cell since infancy. It was a miracle they'd been able to free themselves.

Taisa watched as well, her arms crossed tight over her chest.

"You did it," Diana whispered to Taisa. "You brought us here."

She had meant to comfort Taisa, but it didn't seem to break through her new barriers. Her face didn't move. Diana thought, however, she saw her eyes soften.

"I'm glad they're all right. We need to get them out of the swamp."

"We're safe here," Janis insisted.

"We stopped a group of Order mercenaries on our way to you. They could come back."

The girl's face dropped. The two children, feeling her fear, started to fuss. The twins automatically comforted them.

"Where will you take us?"

Elana hesitated. "Somewhere safe."

Diana cocked her head to the side. She hadn't expected the question to be a hard one for Elana.

"They won't travel well. They're tired. They'll be loud."

Elana turned over her shoulder, looking at Diana. Diana spoke. "We can get you out of the swamps. We'll find a place to hide near Saranthis and secure better long-term transportation."

"The Order controls the harbor. You can't trust anyone," Janis insisted.

"We have a boat we can trust." Diana glanced at Taisa as she spoke. Taisa glanced away. "Tae didn't go far. He thought we might need help."

Diana could tell that wasn't the whole reason he would delay leaving, but she didn't press it. "Can you reach him?"

She tensed. "You can meet him in Saranthis. He told me where he'd be every three days for the next couple tendays. At most you'd have to wait a couple days to see him."

Diana noted her lack of interest in contacting her lover and sighed. "We'll get to Saranthis, find a secure place for you all to take shelter, then I'll go into the city. Once safe passage is secured, I'll come back for you."

Elana nodded slowly, trying to assess the situation, but

Diana knew it was their best course of action. "We'll travel at dusk."

Janis clutched the smallest seer closer but nodded. "We're at your mercy."

Night fell and the seers calmed with the growing darkness and cooler weather. Janis sat with them as always, even as they drifted to sleep. Elana handed her a portion of dried meat and she took it without a word, her eyes never leaving her charges. She was being lulled to rest by the younger ones, their bond tight enough it kept their cycles in sync.

Elana wondered how hard it must have been for her to fight that pull of rest and calm to stay alert while the others dreamed. They were lucky Janis was weaker than the others, able to navigate the swamps and predators that could have killed them. They were lucky the twins had been kept together – their connection increasing their power.

At the Keep, Janis would act as an intermediary between the seers and the Council. She'd be treasured, immediately taking an important seat at the Council table. But Elana wasn't sure she wanted to bring them back to the Keep. The journey would be arduous and very dangerous. If Di'Nay could secure Tae's boat, perhaps the best course of action would be to take them to Cheongu. Jisoo's temple wasn't equipped yet to care for a large cell of seers, but the modifications wouldn't be hard. The seers would be treated well, be at peace.

Elana sighed and shook her head. She would need to consider more.

"How are you doing?" Taisa questioned as Elana returned to her side, far enough from the seers they didn't risk waking the children with their presence.

Elana regarded her slowly. It had been a while since Taisa had reached out to anyone. "I'll be better when I know they're safe." Taisa nodded and stared off into the distance, her body tight as if she was fighting the urge to speak. "How are *you* doing?"

Taisa seemed to collapse inward, her shoulders hunching forward in a subconscious attempt to protect her heart. She ran her hand through her short locks. "I don't want to see him right now," she admitted.

"You aren't going to tell him?"

"What am I supposed to say?"

Elana considered her response, choosing her words carefully. "What are you thinking of doing, Taisa? If you plan to keep the child, he deserves to know about it."

Taisa held her face in her hands. "I don't know. How am I supposed to be a mother?"

"Perhaps Tae wants to be a father. If you don't want to care for the child..."

"No, I don't mean that. I mean, how am I supposed to be a mother to a Blue Sight?"

The response stunned Elana into silence. She had been so concerned about Taisa killing herself or abandoning the child she hadn't thought the root of Taisa's fears was what kind of abilities her child might have.

"I can't even take care of myself, Elana," she insisted. "What if the baby is stronger than me? I can't teach it anything. I can't even show my face in public long enough to give a child a home. A family."

"You're so sure your child will have the Sight?"

"These new visions aren't mine. I've never had anything like this before. If I'm suddenly stronger in the Sight it's because the child is."

Elana pressed her lips into a tight line. She had theorized as much, but hadn't known for sure.

Taisa's hands clenched into fists. "And what would Tae think? I haven't even told him *I'm* a Blue Sight."

"You haven't? After how they received me?"

"I can't trust anyone. Not for long."

"Taisa... Tae's a good man. I know you felt it, too. And in his culture, having a Blue Sight child would be an honor. Your child would be raised to love their abilities, in a village with a school that would teach it to live in peace. Cheongu isn't like Saranthis or the Ramains. You don't have to hide. I'm not going to tell you what to do with your life or your child, but I will say if you have any real interest in Tae as a husband or companion, you might be happy."

Taisa fell still, her mind spinning. "I'll think about talking to him."

"It's your decision. Di'Nay and I will help you any way you need."

She nodded slowly and raised her chin off her arms. "You two are very close."

Elana tensed, unsure of where Taisa was going. "We're bonded," Elana reminded her.

"I mean emotionally."

"Yes."

"Emotionally close with an Amazon." Taisa turned, leaning her head on her raised knees and studied Elana more closely. "It's forbidden, you know."

"We don't intend to stay on Aggar long."

"That would probably be best."

Elana's face tightened into a look of warning and Taisa raised a hand in retreat. "I'm not speaking for myself. I have no room to judge anyone anymore. I just mean you already have the Sight to make you outcast on Aggar. But a female lover?"

"I won't compromise who I am for Aggar," Elana stated, her voice sharp and final.

"I wish I was that strong."

"You could be."

Taisa looked back out to the swamps once more. "Maybe."

A soft cry from one of the young seer children echoed in the night air, quickly muffled by one of the older seers. "We all need to be stronger, at least until they're safe. Until we see the Order wiped off the face of the planet."

Taisa's blank expression turned hot with rage, her eyes seeming to flash for a moment before dying down. "That we can agree on."

RETURN TO MADRISAH

The seer children felt like buzzing bees, their amarin on edge and sparking with shocks of anxiety and frustration. Elana held the youngest child in her arms as the twins stood on either side of her, watching the child intently. His face was pale and he cried like an infant as his stomach grumbled not with hunger, but nausea.

Elana was sure it was some kind of mild flu or cold. The toddler wasn't feverish to the touch, rather cold and a bit clammy. He still had the strength to draw a full breath to cry and his voice didn't sound hoarse or constricted. Still, the others felt his sickness and it disrupted their bond. Elana knew the stronger seers in the Keep often shared illnesses even if they weren't in physical contact with the ill party. If they didn't find a way to soothe the child's stomach soon, they might have more sick children to care for.

"How is he?" Janis questioned as she approached Elana. She didn't seem as disrupted by the child's illness and Elana was once again thankful one of the seer children was weak enough in her abilities that she was more in the physical world than the world of Amarin. Despite Janis's obvious frustrations at being less connected than the others, it was likely her clarity of mind that kept the party alive before Elana, Di'Nay, and Taisa could reach them.

"He'll be fine. Just needs to get out of the swamps and into a warm bed with real food. The climate is too much for him.

"He was from Gothis," Janis informed her. "It's not as warm there as Karatan or the Saranthis."

"I've been to Gothis," Elana remarked with a frown. "The Order seems to have a very strong hold there."

"They have a strong hold everywhere."

"Not where I'm from," Elana commented. "Though not for a lack of trying."

Janis sighed. "They're going to kill us all."

"No, they won't. You saw what the twins did to your camp."

"Then the seers will kill us all."

Elana paused. "Are you scared of them?"

"I think they'd do anything to defend their own. Even if that meant wiping everyone else off the planet."

Elana considered her comment. She knew how powerful the seers were. In the Keep, their combined powers kept the continents stable in the more volcanic regions. They certainly had the power to cause great destruction if they wanted to, but they had always been so peaceful. She didn't see it in them to be that destructive unless directly attacked as a group, and even then, they wouldn't attack the planet as a whole.

At least she thought they wouldn't.

"They wouldn't hurt you," Elana reminded her. "You have seer abilities yourself."

"I would rather die than be the last one walking in both worlds. I'm not afraid of being hurt. I'm afraid of being alone."

Elana wiped tears from the cheeks of the child she held. "I was told I had the ability to be a seer once."

"You? A Blue Sight?"

"If I had allowed myself to fall into those abilities, to take a different path, I wouldn't be unlike you. A seer who walked both worlds. I think they are more aware of Aggar than you give them credit for, but know that if your fears have any truth in them, you won't be the only one like you left. There are more of us than you know."

Janis paused and thought over what Elana had said. Her brow creased and she placed a hand on one of the twins' shoulders instinctively. The younger girl leaned on her hand and wiped away a tear of her own. All the seers often comforted, embraced, and reacted to each other without words, knowing instinctively what everyone else most needed. Elana wondered what it would be like to live in even a small community that was so in-tune and free of fear of each other's abilities.

"They're still talking." Di'Nay approached the small camp. She sat beside Elana and wiped a line of sweat from her brow. Elana loved the way her cheeks turned rosy red in the heat instead of olive and tan like a native of Aggar. There was something endearing about it. Like little red flowers blossoming across her otherwise masculine lover's skin.

Has she told him yet?" Elana questioned.

"Not that I know of. Tae seems like a sensitive man. He knows something's wrong."

"She should tell him," Elana sighed.

"In her time," Di'Nay agreed.

One of the seer children, a young boy only half way to adolescence, his cheeks and limbs still plump with baby fat, toddled to Di'Nay and sat in her lap. He had become very fond of her energy, insisting on napping beside her. Normally, a seer child would fuss in Di'Nay's embrace, but being near such a tight group of seers kept him happy and at peace.

Di'Nay smiled down at him and allowed him to claim one of her arms as a makeshift pillow. Di'Nay watched him for a long moment, her eyes soft and her amarin quietly yearning. It was no secret Di'Nay wanted children and Elana delighted in the thought of building a family with her someday.

"They seem sweeter than other children sometimes."

"When they're at peace, they are," Elana remarked. "Though I think he's less tired and more concerned for his little brother."

Di'Nay ruffled her companion's soft chestnut hair. "Then I'm glad I give him some peace."

"We need to get them all out of the swamps," Elana stated.

"We can give them a moment more." Di'Nay glanced out toward the water where the top of Tae's sail could be seen.

Tae and his brother, Jeon, had brought their fishing boat back to Saranthis, braving the small bit of swamp between the town and their camp to pick everyone up. The boat had taken minor damage in a surprisingly shallow area of the swamp and they had worked hard to make repairs. The palpable tension between Taisa and Tae, however, was causing a rift. Taisa didn't know how to talk to her lover, and Tae – who had no idea she was pregnant – only sensed her sudden coldness.

Elana didn't like to see them fight. She had clear ideas about what she thought Taisa should do, but it wasn't her place to insist or make decisions. At the end of the day, it was Taisa's choice. Elana just wished she'd make one.

"North."

Di'Nay and Elana looked down in surprise at the child in Di'Nay's arms. He seemed asleep, but he had clearly spoken. It was the first time Elana had heard any clear words from him. His voice was small, high-pitched and weak. "North," he repeated.

"North?" Di'Nay questioned.

"Blindness in the north. Darkness in the north."

They waited for him to say more, but he only let out a soft sigh and turned slightly, falling deeper into his dreams.

"What did that mean?" Di'Nay questioned.

"I think he was prophesying. Or Seeing."

"Blindness in the north. Does he mean the Ramains? Is the Order growing in the Ramains?"

Elana frowned. "We should keep an eye on him."

Taisa hiked back toward them, her irritation and frustration clear on her face. "We'll be ready to launch soon. The children can board."

"Good." Elana stood, holding the child in the crook of one arm as she beckoned to Janis, who roused her fellow seers. Together they moved to the ship. Elana smiled as she imagined a clean bed, a warm meal, and significantly less mud in her future.

Diana helped Jeon scan the hull of the boat for any other signs of damage as well as scan the area for fallen tools. Everyone else was already aboard – Elana had eased most of the seer children to sleep, Tae and Taisa were ignoring each other. Jeon and Diana didn't speak enough of the same language to communicate beyond pointing and noise, but it was clear they shared a similar goal in avoiding the tension on the boat. Jeon was frustrated with his brother and Diana couldn't help but feel the same about Taisa. No matter how much they understood the situation, it felt like needlessly complicating the situation that no one was communicating well.

Jeon sighed as they made a final round and stared up at the deck of the boat. His black hair, caught back in a short ponytail, was limp from the heat but his skin hadn't turned olive or dark – he was more used to the heat than Elana or Diana. Diana watched him for a moment and thought of Elana's concerns not long ago about having a son. The thought of parenting a boy hadn't been on her mind growing up – men weren't allowed on Aggar – but meeting Gerome in the desert and now these good men from Cheongu had made her consider a future where it would be possible. If she had a son like Jeon, she would be proud.

Jeon glanced at her and indicated toward the ship with his head. It was time to go. She nodded in return and walked toward the gangplank but froze before stepping onto the wooden board. Rustling in the bushes. The swamps were full of creatures – water reptiles, birds, insects – but something felt off.

Jeon turned as well. They exchanged a look that clearly said he felt it, too. He drew a long knife from his belt, the blade serrated for gutting and cleaning large fish. Diana drew her short sword as well.

"Di'Nay?" Elana called nervously.

"A moment," Diana called back. "Stay on the ship."

Jeon and Diana stalked carefully forward, scanning the brush and trees for signs of human life. Jeon gasped and spun as a crossbow bolt barely missed his chest. Diana's eyes snapped to where the bolt had been fired and she dodged a second bolt from her right. Her eyes started to adjust and she saw them – dressed to blend with the shadows of the low-hanging leaves. More mercenaries.

Diana pointed them out but Jeon was already charging, dodging arrows with surprising dexterity. Three more mercenaries came at Diana, holding blades instead of bows. Diana backed up a pace, assessing their landscape for any small advantage, and met their blows with her own parries and dodges.

One of Diana's attackers on her left went down with a crossbow bolt shot from the ship. Taisa stood at the rail, guarding the boat and the seer children as Tae raced down the gangplank, a spear in hand. He joined the fray, and the two of them were able to finish the two mercenaries off fairly quickly.

Jeon stalked through the trees, attacking the men with crossbows like a panther. Diana caught glimpses of him and watched in awe as he managed to catch many of the men by surprise. Tae and Diana joined him, taking blessedly minimal damage as they killed the rest of the mercenaries – eight in total.

Tae and Diana let out sharp, controlled gasps as they tried to calm. They had scratches and bruises from the brush and their combatants. Tae had a shallow cut on his arm from where he had barely dodged a crossbow. Jeon cleaned his bloody knife on the shirt of one of their attackers. He didn't breathe as hard as his brother.

"Is he trained?" Diana questioned.

"He served many years in the military," Tae acknowledged.

"Cheongu fights?"

"Not other nations. But there are bandit cells in the forests."

Diana looked Jeon over again. That explained his adeptness at moving through trees. She wondered if he was a fisherman now because he didn't want to fight anymore, or if it was out of duty to his brother.

"Can you thank him for me?" Diana questioned. "We couldn't have done it without him."

Tae spoke to his brother in their native language and Jeon nodded sharply to her. His eyes seemed darker, almost clouded. His face was taut and still. For all his silliness and joy on the ship clearly hid something more painful.

Jeon nudged one of the men with his foot and spoke to his brother.

"He said they weren't well trained," Tae observed. "They aren't soldiers."

"We ran into more like them when we found the children. That band was a little more skilled, but I think they're volunteers."

Jeon knelt beside one of them and patted at his clothes. He removed the crossbow from his dead hands, collected his bolts, and discovered a dagger at his back. "He wants to search them for resources," Tae observed, his lips tight and his eyes never leaving his brother. He was worried.

"It's a good idea," Diana remarked carefully. "We can always use the bolts. Taisa and Elana both shoot."

"I'll finish the men near the trees. You search the ones by the water."

Diana nodded sharply and raced away from the brothers and knelt beside the men with swords. Their blades were simple and worse quality than her own – not worth carrying around. She was able to find some gold, a compass, more useless knives on them. She pocketed the gold and compass.

"I found something!" Tae called. Diana ran back to her friend. He held piece of paper and his hand rested on an insignia sewn into one of the men's shirts, hidden by a jacket. "I know this sign.”

“Where from?” Diana questioned.

“Gothis. They were a band of mercenaries formed from ex border patrol agents who worked in Karatan. Rumor had it they were discharged for causing unnecessary trouble with the natives. I saw them in the dock bars a lot. Thought they were just drunks who wanted to feel important after losing their jobs.”

“What would the Order hire them for?”

“They’ll work cheap. They know how to move in areas with thick undergrowth and heat. Plus no one would believe them if they said they were hired to track down seers.”

“Risky, sending a group so ill prepared.”

“The Order must not have expected you to be so good at fighting. Or they didn’t know you were here and were sending in expendable men to try to subdue violent seers.”

“What’s that,” Diana questioned, pointing at the paper. He handed it to her.

“Orders, I think. Possibly the names of the children?”

Diana scanned the short list. She spotted Janis’s name, but the list was too long to just be the children they’d found in the swamps. Her eyes stopped at another name she recognized. Gerome. How did they know about him?

“I think they’re finally tracking Elana and me,” Diana muttered. “Or at least our movements. We need to get back to the desert. We have a friend in trouble.”

Jeon joined them, his hands full of arrows and his pouch carrying more gold. Tae glanced between Jeon and Diana and sighed. “Let’s get the children to safety and then we’ll find a way to get you to your friend.

Elana smiled as she entered the Temple of the Bull once more. Jisoo greeted her with a short bow and a wide smile. The elderly woman had quickly become family to Elana – like an aunt to her grandmother who had been Mistress of the Keep when Elana grew up.

The temple was calming for Elana. With its hardwood floors polished to a gleam, its red silk curtains, plush mats for kneeling in meditation, and incense that smelled like bamboo and rain it made her think of the forest where she’d met the supernatural bull that protected the forest of Jidoin – the temple’s namesake. Being in the bull’s lair hadn’t been pleasant, but Elana had grown to appreciate his presence and power. He was a creature of Aggar, a protector created by the planet herself. Much like Elana was. All things lived in balance.

Elana mindlessly touched the small tattoo on the back of her neck she'd taken after her studies with Jisoo. The elderly teacher smiled wider at the motion. "Lost in thought already, I see?"

Elana shook her head, trying to focus on the present. "I need your help, Jisoo," she began. "Have you felt it?"

"I've heard rumors. Did you really come with seers?"

"Your information network travels fast."

"Everyone loves to gossip."

"You're the only one I trust to care for them."

"They have a home here. We're dedicated to the chosen of Aggar. But I fear our accommodations won't be what they need."

"I can help you with the specifications. One of them walks between the unseen world of a seer and our reality. She can help as well."

"A dual soul? How rare and wonderful!"

"She would appreciate hearing that."

Elana stepped outside and waved the children, guarded by Janis, inside. They moved slowly, wary of strangers, but Elana felt their amarins settle as they stepped into the building. The elements that made the space powerful for meditation were exactly what seers found soothing. With a few adjustments, the temple would be a very comfortable space for them. A Keep in the south.

"This is Janis. She's the one I was telling you about," Elana introduced. "Janis, this is Jisoo. She's the mother of this temple."

Janis took her hand warily, but seemed to draw comfort from the soft silk of Jisoo's hands and her smile which set her wrinkles rippling back like water. "Elana tells me you walk between worlds. That's very special."

"I'm weak," Janis clarified.

"Far from it. You all look like you could use baths and food. I'll gather resources." Jisoo turned and three temple maidens rushed out of the back cloisters to her side. Jisoo glanced back at Janis. "Will they be comfortable with baths? I don't want to scare them."

"Give us a couple tubs and we can care for ourselves."

Jisoo nodded to her acolytes and they rushed to do as they

were told. "And food?"

"Anything warm will do."

"So simple to care for."

"We care well for ourselves."

Jisoo turned to Elana. "This will be easier than I thought!"

Elana laughed and after a moment, Janis did, too.

"Child, I've been led to believe you and the others may have been stolen from your families. Do you need to reach out to them? Let them know you're safe?" Jisoo questioned. "We have the ability to send messages."

Janis's face fell. "Most of us weren't kidnapped. We were handed over. We aren't missed."

Jisoo's eyes flashed with anger and for a moment she was younger, fierier, a true devotee to the fire bull she cared for. "The arrogant often don't see what's right under their noses. You're always welcome here, for as long as you want to stay."

Janis snuck a look to Elana and Elana nodded. "They're good, Janis. I promise. The whole town is... a pocket of joy. They understand you here. Or at least they respect you."

"And we'll never hold you. If you all wish to leave, you're free to," Jisoo insisted.

"We like to settle," Janis remarked hesitantly. "Where we feel safe."

"Well then, let's hope we can provide some of that safety you desire. Come with me. I'll show you where you can stay for now. This village treasures the nature of balance and respect for Aggar's chosen. We don't have much, but there are many good craftsmen who would be honored to help build the perfect home for you and your siblings. Just tell us what you desire."

"That's very generous," Janis remarked. Her voice trailed as she was distracted, drawn as if in a trance to the other seer children.

They were sitting around the incense bowl at the front of the room. Their souls sang. The sound, heard through the power of Elana's Sight, made her breath catch in her throat. She missed the sound of the seers singing through the amarin of the Keep. The sound was pure happiness, pure connection. Janis was right to be concerned – at a young age she'd now become the primary keeper of her new family. But the rest of the seers had already marked the temple their new home.

The feeling, which drew Janis in until she nearly disappeared into the world of amarin that only seers could truly traverse, made her spirit glow. She smiled – the expression soft and sweet. A tear came to her eye. She blinked hard, fighting the pull of her siblings, and nodded to Jisoo. "I think we'll be happy here."

"You're children of the Temple of the Bull now. Happiness is your right. You have had so much sadness. Balance demands you experience the other."

Jisoo and Janis walked toward the back rooms together and Elana watched them go. There had been so few times since beginning her journey that she knew she'd done the right thing. Answers were gray. People where gray.

But here she felt a stir of destiny and the unmistakable sense of joy in both her heart and her feelings about the future. Something important had happened today. Perhaps even more important than the rest of her mission. And it was beautifully, unmistakably good.

She ducked back out of the building and returned to the harbor. Diana was helping Jeon, Tae, and their fellow fisherman Jimin assess the boat once more. Tae and Jeon had agreed to sail them to the desert, but the voyage was long for a small boat. It would save them many tendays – crucial time if there were other assassins assigned by the Order to hunt down Gerome – but it could be a strenuous trip.

"How is it?" Elana asked Di'Nay as she joined her on the dock.

Di'Nay rubbed her hands with a cloth. Her arms were bare as she worked and Elana smiled as she watched the muscles in her upper arms – more defined from rowing for days – shift as she moved. All other wonderful traits aside, Di'Nay was a beautiful creature of strength.

"Well, I think," she stated. "The boat weathered the return better than the arrival into the swamp. Jimin is going to join another party while they're gone to make up some of their fishing loses. We're going to need to pay them more gold."

"I assumed so. It's not a problem. I'm sure the Keep will want to privately offer a rather large donation to the village for taking in so many seers."

Di'Nay smiled. "That's a good thought."

"Will they linger in the desert or return?"

Di'Nay's smile wavered. "Tae wants to come with us."

Elana hesitated. "With Taisa's blessing?"

"She's very against it."

Elana sighed. Taisa was a good warrior and a sister in fury and arms, but she was still very young and her temper could make travel unbearable. "Has she talked to him yet?"

"No. He just knows something is wrong. He won't leave until he knows she's safe."

"He loves her."

"Poor soul."

Elana glanced out to the ship where Tae and Jeon worked, their brotherly comradery clear. "Do you think he'll be an asset to us?"

"Jeon is better in a fight, but he's insistent on returning to Jimin. No amount of gold will put fish on their friends' tables. The village is too small to lose a food supplier."

"It makes sense."

"Tae's work with languages could be useful. And he's a strong opponent in a fight. We could use another warrior. We could do a lot worse."

Elana nodded slowly. "I'll talk to Taisa."

"Careful," Di'Nay remarked with a grin. "I hear Blue Sights are hard to manage."

Elana shot her a cocky grin, letting a moment of teasing that melded into desire pass between them before turning toward the inn where they had stayed before.

Taisa sat in the back of the inn's common room, nursing her drink as she glared into the distance. Her amarin was an aura of dark fire that seemed to burn cold. She was immediately aware of Elana's presence, but didn't look at her as she sat beside her.

"It's cider," she remarked as Elana glanced at her cup.

"I didn't say anything."

Taisa finally met her eyes and for a moment the illusion she'd created over her irises lifted and her eyes flashed blue. She didn't need to say any more. "You want to talk about Tae."

"I want to talk about how we're going to get back to the desert in a timely manner."

"Transporting us isn't the same as accompanying us on foot."

"Are you really against the idea?" Taisa wavered and it was all Elana needed. "We don't know what we'll be facing once we get to the desert. Tae was helpful in the swamps. We could use another fighter, and one that has experience traveling and working hard isn't easy to pass up. But I want you to make the decision. His presence will become a hindrance if it distracts or upsets you."

Taisa looked deep into her mug for a long time. Her emotions reflected across her face as minute shifts in her muscles, switching from frustration to sadness to confusion and finally to hope. "I'm not ready to tell him yet."

"You don't have to say anything."

"Di'Nay wants me to."

"Di'Nay doesn't always get what she wants."

Taisa gripped her mug harder and drew a long breath. "If he'll be helpful, I would be stupid to reject his help."

Elana clapped her on the shoulder and smiled. "I'll tell them. We'll leave as soon as the ship is ready."

The dry heat of the desert was more bearable than the humidity of Saranthis, but Diana still found it hard to adjust from the cool ocean breezes. The desert stretched around the party, nothing but sand visible in any direction. They rode horses they'd secured at port after Jeon had left to sail back to Cheongu. It felt good to be in a familiar setting again. Diana had chosen a life of travel and adventure, but there was joy in returning after a long time away.

She glanced over her shoulder at her small party. Elana examined their map carefully, tracking their position with an expert eye. Tae and Taisa rode near each other without speaking. Tae wore a dark head scarf that wrapped all the way around his face, revealing only his eyes. His weapon, a slender and strong spear, was strapped to his back.

Diana figured the heat and sand of the Southern Desert wasn't anything Tae had encountered before, but he did everything without a single complaint. He was quick to help, avoided Taisa's sharp temper while staying close to her side, and kept up well enough. Diana's respect for the man grew every day.

"We should reach Madrisah before nightfall," Elana announced.

Muscles Diana hadn't realized she'd been holding tight relaxed. Their journey had been so smooth – smooth enough she was worried what might lay ahead. If she believed in cosmic balance, they were due a lot of trouble. But perhaps she was just being too pessimistic.

"Let's hope Gerome hasn't returned to the city," Diana remarked.

"He seemed very happy in Madrisah. If luck is on our side, he either stayed all this time or returned after bringing his brother back home."

"Luck has been with us this far," Diana agreed. "It can last a little longer."

Elana's prediction was right, and as the sun started to sink beneath the horizon the rocky cliffside of Madrisah rose before them. The pitted texture of windows carved into the rocks made the abbey look like a beehive, one of the great wonders Diana had seen on Aggar.

"You've returned." Sister Rose, the elderly head priestess of Madrisah, greeted as she stepped out into the sand.

"We're looking for Gerome, Min," Elana called as she rode forward. "Is he still here?"

"Brother Gerome has decided to stay with us until winter, yes. Is something wrong?"

Diana let out a sharp breath of relief, but at the same time she felt her muscles tighten again. Things were going too well. She clenched her teeth and forced herself to be grateful instead of cautious. "Can we speak with him?" Diana questioned.

"Of course." Sister Rose waved to her attendants and they rushed forward to take the horses. Diana, Elana, Taisa, and Tae followed Sister Rose into the stony cloisters of Madrisah up a narrow hallway carved into the cliff. She took them to a group prayer room, the walls covered in detailed paintings of the starry night sky. "I'll fetch him for you. He may be in meditation."

"Thank you, Sister," Diana responded.

She rushed away, her eyes narrowed as she sensed the tension in her visitors. "She seemed like she was expecting trouble," Taisa observed.

"She did," Elana agreed softly. "I wonder what's happened since we were away."

They didn't wait long before Sister Rose and Gerome joined them. Diana couldn't help but smile at the sight of the young man.

"You've gotten older," Diana observed.

"Young people do that," Gerome remarked with a grin.

"So fast?"

"Unfortunately." Diana smiled wider. He seemed much happier than when she'd last seen him. "I assume you didn't just come for a visit? Are you on your way back to the Ramains?" He looked over Taisa and Tae. "You've gathered friends."

Elana's eyes darted between Gerome and Sister Rose and Gerome stood straighter, his intention clear – Sister Rose was welcome to hear anything about him. "We have reason to believe you're in danger. We came to help you."

Gerome's smile faded. "In danger from who? Simon's safe back in the capitol. No one but the Sisters know where I am."

"You were on a list of names targeted by the Order."

Gerome's cheeks colored in shock and fright. "The Order doesn't know who I am."

"They do now."

"Because I traveled with you?" There was no anger in his voice, but his tone stung.

"Probably," Diana stated softly. "Which is why we came to protect you."

Sister Rose took a step forward. "Madrisah is very strong. Brother Gerome is safe behind our walls."

"I'm sure he's well protected, Sister, but the people after him are very cunning," Elana warned.

"What do you want me to do? Where is safer than here?"

"Anywhere else," Taisa remarked and everyone turned to her. "Anywhere you've never been before. The Order will learn about you. They'll learn everywhere you go, everywhere you call home. You're a Blue Sight with one arm. You don't hide well."

Gerome regarded her with the same sharp indignance he had given Diana when they'd first met. "I'm not going to throw my life away for them."

"You don't have a choice."

"Of course I do."

"Stop it, both of you," Elana's voice was sharp.

The tension between Gerome and Taisa was palpable and Diana wondered what had passed unspoken between them to escalate their feud so quickly.

"We're not saying you have to change anything. We wanted to see you safe and warn you," Diana stated, trying to reestablish peace.

"Thank you," Gerome replied, his comment genuine but his eyes still sharp. "Will you be staying long?"

Diana glanced at Elana. "For a while, if it's all right. We need to do some regrouping now that we know you're safe."

"We're always happy to offer safety and shelter to the weary," Sister Rose replied. She rested one hand on Gerome's shoulder and he relaxed. "I'll have rooms made up for you."

"Thank you, Sister," Diana sighed. "I'm sure a bit of rest will help everyone."

"We couldn't have asked for a better outcome," Elana replied as she knelt and prepared a bed mat.

Diana watched her, grateful for a moment alone. Gerome had seen that they got a room together, stating that they were long-time companions. It was a kindness Diana wouldn't forget. It had been so long since she'd been alone with her lover. Just the quiet, the ability to stand in the same room with Elana without being constantly aware that they were being watched, was a gift. She felt like she was taking her first breath in years.

"Does that unnerve you?"

Elana smiled at her and Diana's heart stopped. "Don't question miracles."

Diana found herself transfixed by Elana's beauty. By the thought that she was her's. It was sudden and sentimental, but she had spent so long hiding her relationship it was like seeing Elana for the first time. "I wouldn't dream of it."

Elana stood, knowing Diana's thoughts without the need for her Sight. She stepped into Diana's arms and they kissed, Diana's hands grasping the smaller woman desperately, savoring the moment as if she'd never have to release Elana again.

"I missed you," she whispered into Elana's hair, her voice so soft it was almost inaudible.

"In an abbey?" Elana teased as she had the first night they spent in Madrisah. "Some would consider our embrace in this place a blasphemy."

Diana watched her, relishing the way her eyes flashed, her hair curled against her cheeks and jaw, the weight of her in her hands and against her body. To Diana, there had never been a more perfect woman. "Soroi n'ti Mee... touching you is the most sacred prayer I can offer."

They kissed again and Diana felt every thought slip away... every thought but the heat of her lover, the ecstasy of their touch, and the pounding of their synchronized hearts thrumming deep within the lifestone at her wrist.

Diana woke slowly, Elana still draped across her. She took a moment to run her fingers through Elana's hair, to watch her lover at peace. She was sleeping deeply, her face completely still and her breathing soft and deep. It was the most perfect moment Diana could imagine.

The peace was disrupted by the growling of her stomach and a cramp in her leg. Elana was tangled around her, pinning one of Diana's legs between her own. The position, held for hours as they slept, had left her stiff and sore.

Diana grunted softly. It was little moments like this that reminded her of her age. Elana scoffed at Diana's jokes about getting old, and Diana knew she didn't mind the age difference, but she couldn't stand the thought of Elana waking from a night of passion to a lover with stiff joints.

She carefully extricated herself from Elana and made sure her love was comfortable before she dressed and stepped out into the hallway. She knew it was still deep into the night – it didn't take long to find an empty prayer room large enough to stretch.

She winced as she sat, straightened one leg, and leaned over it, grabbing her foot and trying to bring her chest to the ground. Everything ached. She may have gotten stronger, but she hadn't kept up with her flexibility.

"Interesting routine."

Diana leapt to her feet, her heart pounding at the sudden voice in the darkness. "Hello?"

Two men walked into the room, their arms crossed. Diana had never seen them before, but they weren't dressed like priests. "Don't be afraid. We won't hurt you," one of the men offered. He was about Diana's age, his dark hair short and framing a chiseled face. He was dressed in garb common in the Ramains, but Diana had trouble placing his exact ethnicity.

"Who are you?"

"Guests of Madrisah," the second man offered. He was younger, but not by much. His blonde hair fell down his back in a long ponytail.

Despite their obvious genetic differences, their features were similar enough they could be brothers.

"And messengers from Tristan."

"Marshals," Diana stated, her heart pounding hard enough she heard her blood behind her ears. "How did you know we were here?"

"We didn't. We came to watch Gerome. Your arrival was luck."

"The Mother smiling on us, per se," the blonde man commented with a chuckle, raising one hand to the small stone carving of the mother at the head of the prayer room.

"Tristan was concerned when we stopped hearing from you," the dark-haired man let his arms fall to his sides, but the tension in his frame betrayed the motion as anything but an act of peace.

"We didn't have access to a messenger for some time."

"Then you have reports we can deliver?"

"We're heading back to the Ramains soon. We can meet Tristan in person."

"He'll want to hear from you sooner than you can ride on horseback."

"We can wait for you to finish them," the blonde man offered. The two had shifted into a clear charade – one of them aggressive, the other forgiving. Diana wasn't fooled by their act, but she was grateful that they didn't seem ready for violence.

"I'll get them to you tomorrow."

"Very good, Min," the blonde man responded. "We know you're not one to break a deal."

"Has Tristan said yet what he's using my reports for? Has he made any headway in stopping the Order in the Ramains?"

"We don't ask Tristan his plans. It would be useless," the dark-haired man countered. "You shouldn't ask, either."

The blonde man laid a hand on the other's shoulder. "The Sisters have been kind enough to grant us shelter. They can lead you to us when you're ready."

"We'll check on you this time tomorrow if we haven't seen you," the dark-haired man remarked with more than a bit of threat in his voice. The implication was clear – they would be watched from now on. "You must be relieved to be back in a nation where you can easily find a hawker to send a message."

"Come, we don't want to take up more of her time," the blonde man stated. "We await your visit."

They left and Diana clenched her fists in rage. She didn't like being intimidated. She liked being followed even less. Whatever happened, she would see Tristan again. She would know what he was doing with her reports. What she had helped him accomplish.

A sharp knock on the door woke Elana from her slumber. She blinked hard, coming back to reality slowly. She must have been sleeping deeply. She smiled as memory returned and she wasn't surprised she had rested so well.

The knocking continued and she shifted. She noticed Di'Nay was missing and wondered briefly what it was about Madrisah that made her lover disappear in the night.

"A moment," Elana called as she gathered her clothes and made herself decent. She opened the door. "Gerome?"

"I hope I'm not interrupting," he stated.

Elana shook her head. "No. What is it?"

"I was wondering if we could talk? I... I figured since Di'Nay is already up you would be as well."

Elana turned to let him into her room. "You've seen Di'Nay?"

"She's in the library." He entered and glanced at the messy bedmats and blankets. "I did wake you."

Elana wondered what Di'Nay was doing in the library as she absentmindedly waved Gerome's concern away. "I could have slept for days. I needed to be awakened."

"It is getting late," he remarked, more than a bit of teasing in his voice. "I never mistook you for lazy."

She shot him a good-natured glare and he smiled. The expression put Elana's mind at ease. He wouldn't be so calm if there was something wrong. "What did you want to talk about?"

"I've been... dreaming since you left."

"Visions?"

He thought of his answer for a moment, then slowly nodded. "Sometimes."

"You're embracing your Sight more."

His smile disappeared. "It isn't my Sight, Elana. It's the

Mother."

Elana hesitated, regarding him slowly. "A gift from the Mother she's shared by way of your Sight."

"No. I mean I've been dreaming of the Mother. She's been telling me things. Prophecying. It's why I returned to Madrisah. They think I've been touched with the gift of prophecy."

"You are. You're a Blue Sight."

"It's different."

Elana frowned. She thought he was getting better at making peace with his Sight, but his religious leanings were strong. If he wanted to frame his abilities as something else, she wouldn't question it. Anything was better than his self-hatred. "What has the Mother been saying?"

"She's been warning me about the Order. They're planning something new. I know about their hold over the far southern nations, but they're growing in the north, too. Not as a religion, but as an army."

Elana mulled over his statements, trying to make sense of them. "Someone would notice an army in the Ramains. They're very protective of their power."

"But they're still doing it. They're farther along than any of us could have guessed. And there's more. Something... darker."

"What?"

"I don't know. The Mother wouldn't say. But I felt it. It felt like... a hot knife in my brain, right between my eyes. People are suffering."

Elana leaned back against the wall, her arms crossed tight over her chest as she thought.

"I know you're not religious –" Gerome began, but Elana cut him off with a shake of her head.

"I don't doubt your belief, Gerome. I'm just trying to understand what to do with the information."

"You believe me?"

"I have visions, too."

"They're different."

Elana sighed and closed her eyes. In her mind's eye, she could see Jisoo's face. It suddenly struck her how similar she was to Sister Rose and she couldn't help but smile. "Maybe they are. What do I know?"

Gerome watched her for a while then spoke. "You've

changed.”

“I've learned a lot since we last saw each other,” she revealed. “A new way of looking at the world.”

“You've learned more but say you don't know anything?”

“The more I learn, the more I realize how little I know. Have you ever studied Cheongu?”

“Cheongu?” his brows furrowed in confusion.

“It's a small island nation far to the south. I'd never heard of it before either. Which is probably best. They have an interesting way of worshipping the Mother. Of understanding the Sight.”

“They made you believe?”

“I like the way they see the world. I hope they're right.”

“I'll have to learn more about them.”

“You should.” Elana dropped her arms to her sides. “It's nice to see you again, Gerome. I'm glad you're doing well.”

“I am. I... I'm finally able to let go a little. Let go of Simon. My past. The Sisters have been so kind to me here. I feel like I belong.”

“We can't ask for more than that.”

“Even if it's religious?”

“What put it in your mind I hate religion?” she teased.

“They don't like Blue Sights.”

“It doesn't endear me to them, but you never know what minds you can change. As long as you find peace within yourself and spend your life doing good, I'm content.”

“I do a lot of good,” he assured her. “And I intend to keep helping people for the rest of my life. If the Order doesn't stop me first.”

Elana felt her stomach clench at the thought and she frowned sadly. She already hated the Order. The thought that they would seek to snuff out a light like Gerome's – to put an end to someone who could do so much good for the people of Aggar – only fueled her fire.

“I'll worry about the Order. Your place is as a priest to the Mother. Let me be vengeance.”

“Vengeance doesn't lead to anything good,” Gerome warned.

“Justice, then.”

He started to say something, but stopped and just smiled. “I can get behind justice. Wipe them off the planet.”

"Such harsh words for a Brother."

"I'm in training."

The shared a smile – a moment between peers – right before someone outside started screaming.

The cry turned into a chorus, many voices shouting in terror. Elana and Gerome raced out into the hall, running to the nearest room with a window. Elana froze in horror. A militia – probably 50 men – were charging toward Madrisah. Arrows were fired at the women working at the stables or walking outside. They ran for the doors, pausing to carry any of their fellows shot by the raider's arrows.

"The Order," Gerome whispered in shock and Elana knew he was right. While they looked like any other band of thieves, she couldn't sense their amarin. Neither of them had felt them coming They had to be wearing amulets.

The rumble of doors being closed behind the fleeing sisters echoed through the narrow halls. "Will the doors hold?" Elana questioned.

Gerome was dark with fear. "We should get weapons."

Diana raced from the library at the first sounds of screaming. The library was tucked deep underground where the manuscripts would be better preserved. The sound was disturbing; echoing and bouncing off cavern walls. It felt wrong in such a peaceful place.

The sisters ran with her, some splitting off to hide or protect the younger trainees while others gathered weapons. Diana grabbed her sword, grateful that she'd thought to bring it with her to the library. With Marshals around and the lingering fear of attack from the Order, she hadn't wanted to leave it behind even in the religious cloisters.

"What's going on?" she called to a sister as she ran in the opposite direction."

"Raiders!"

Diana tensed. Were raiders a constant threat in such a fortress of an abbey? Sister Rose had seemed so sure of their defenses.

She finally reached a level with windows and looked out into the courtyard. A band of men on horseback had charged, ramming at the massive wooden doors and defending themselves from the arrows shot from higher windows. They were wearing more sophisticated armor than Diana would have expected from desertmen.

Diana watched in horror as one of the raiders shot into a window and a sister fell with an awful scream, landing dead in the chaos of horses and attackers.

Diana ran to higher levels, searching the prayer rooms whose windows had become wide embrasures for archers. She let out a sharp breath as she spotted Elana and Taisa kneeling in the same room, taking careful aim.

"Elana!" Diana called.

Elana glanced back at her, a moment of relief passing between them. "It's the Order!" Elana called.

Diana's brow furrowed. "The Order?"

"They're wearing amulets."

"They don't fight like this. Assassins and mercenaries, maybe, but a band of raiders?"

"They're changing tactics," Elana grunted.

A fresh swell of shouting rose from the lower hallways and Diana peered out the window. The raiders battering at the door had cracked the defenses. Diana touched Elana's shoulder then sprinted out of the room, racing toward the door where a dozen sisters with swords and short-range weapons fought to keep it closed. The support beam was giving way, splintering more and more with each pound of the ram.

"Di'Nay!" Gerome called to her. His back was pressed against the door, a sword in one hand. Tae helped him hold the door closed.

Diana joined them leaning against the doors as she scanned the room, looking for some kind of strategy.

"We can't hold this long," Diana hissed.

"The halls are narrow. We'll always have the high ground if they get through," Gerome rationalized.

"They have armor. They have armor and better weapons. They'll run us through like butter if we're forced into a line only two to three wide," Diana warned.

"These aren't normal raiders," a sister growled as she a pound from the ram made her lose her footing. She threw herself back at the door with a feral snarl. "These are mercenaries."

Gerome colored and glanced away. Diana watched him with sympathy. He must already know who they were.

The battering paused and a howl of pain rose from just outside the door. Diana gasped at the sudden smell of roasting flesh and gore. The feral sister grinned. "They boiled the oil."

Diana knew a moment when she saw it. "Our archers have killed at least half of them. The oil at least seriously injured more. They're vulnerable for a moment. We need to meet them in force."

"They have horses! Armor!" one sister gasped in fear.

"Stay behind. Keep the door shut behind us," the feral sister grunted at the other. "I'm with you."

The sisters quickly opened the door and Diana, Tae, Gerome, and a band of ten sisters raced from the keep with a howl loud enough to warn the archers of their presence. They streamed outside, immediately finishing off the burned men around the battering ram, silencing their howls of agony.

There as a cry of support from the archers at the windows as they ran as a team. Tae drew his spear from his back with a flourish and lashed out at one of the raiders on horseback. Four had dismounted before they'd left, running to grab the ram from their fallen comrades. The sisters launched at them in force, avoiding their horses and taking advantage of their surprise attack to either stab the raiders or distract them enough that the archers could pick them off.

Diana went for one of the mounted riders. His horse danced nervously at the new wave of violence and Diana parried the raiders blows while using his mount's fear against him. After a few exchanges, she swung up onto the horse and slit the raider's throat just above the collar of his armor.

Everyone fought viciously and valiantly. Once the element of surprise had worn off the battle became more intense. These were trained warriors. Without the help of the archers, Diana and her entire party would have been massacred.

Once they were down to six attackers, more sisters ran from Madrisah, overwhelming the raiders and killing all but one, who they intended to take prisoner. When Diana approached him, however, he pulled a knife from his sleeve and drove it into his own neck. Diana watched in horror as he fell to the ground, dead.

They weren't just a hired force, they were a force ready to kill themselves before they could be questioned. They either cost a fortune, or these were legitimate members of the Order. That implication was darker: were they building an army?

Diana turned to the gathered crowd as the sisters surveyed the damage. The sand was stained with blood and covered with bodies – raiders and sisters alike. The surviving sisters fell over their fellows in mourning while others warily examined the damage to Madrisah. They had saved their abbey, but barely. They hadn't been ready for an attack at such a scale.

Diana's breath caught in her throat at the loss of life. It had been so sudden. She glanced up at the windows where she knew Elana and Taisa would be waiting and tried to steel herself for whatever came next.

Elana waited in a small prayer room for Di'Nay. She looked out over the desert from the small window. Night had fallen hours ago, but the sands were still lit by the bonfires used to burn the dead – soldiers and sisters alike. Elana didn't know what to expect from the Order anymore. She hadn't wanted the bonfires to be built right away, but Sister Rose was insistent. It was unholy to leave the body of a sister to decay.

Elana knew it would take time before word of the Order's defeat could reach their leaders, but she couldn't know if there were messengers assessing the battle from afar or if another band of warriors was waiting to sweep in as a second wave. As the day progressed, however, she started to relax. The bodies were gathered and searched. They found amulets and little else. They didn't even carry their orders. They were burned in a separate fire from the sisters – each of whom were given their own ceremonial fire.

Elana felt a touch of guilt at the deaths, but she would never know if the raiders had followed her party to Madrisah or if they had been after Gerome. It seemed like overkill for a single escaped Blue Sight, but she didn't know how they could have been spotted without being seen in return. Either way, they couldn't stay in Madrisah for long. Gerome's visions about the Order growing seemed to be true.

Elana heard footsteps and felt Di'Nay approaching. She closed her eyes and tried to let go of everything but her lover for a moment. She was a touchstone. A presence that helped Elana escape the stress of Aggar. By the time Di'Nay entered, Elana was smiling.

"Tae and Taisa will be here in a moment. Gerome wants to

talk to us as well.”

“Makes sense. Have you spoken with Sister Rose?”

“No. She’s still attending to the fires. I doubt she’ll come in tonight.”

Elana looked back out at the fires crackling in the distance. “It must be a harrowing vigil.”

“Elana.”

Elana turned to Di’Nay and frowned. She was obviously upset. “What is it?”

“Last night I met two Marshals here in Madrisah.”

Elana’s blood ran chill and her eyes narrowed. “Marshals? Here?”

“They were looking for Gerome, but approached me. They’re not here anymore.”

“You’re sure?”

“I asked multiple sisters. They were invited in as guests a few days ago. The sisters were looking for them after the fight, but they seemed to have disappeared.”

“That can’t be a coincidence.”

“I’m not sure what it means, but there has to be a connection.”

“Like they led the Order to us?”

“Or they left to send word about the attack to Tristan,” Di’Nay responded, her tone cautious.

Elana grit her teeth for a moment, fighting back her frustration at the organization. Di’Nay was right – they didn’t know what the Marshals were doing, but they needed to find out.

Di’Nay opened her mouth to speak again, but shut it as the door opened and they were joined by Tae and Taisa. It was a wise decision. Taisa already had enough reasons not to trust the Marshals.

Gerome followed close behind. He was solemn and contemplative.

“Gerome?” Di’Nay questioned with concern. “Did something happen?”

He thought a moment, then shook his head. “Not anything new, no. But I’ve decided I need to come with you when you leave.” Elana relaxed slightly, nodding her head. She figured it would come to this. “This happened because of me. Sisters died because I was being tracked. This is a holy place. It would be blasphemous of me to put it in further danger."

"Will they stop attacking if we leave?" Tae questioned. "Are they vengeful?"

"We don't know," Di'Nay remarked, her arms crossed over her chest as she strategized. "We don't know how extensive their information system is. If they think we're still here, they'll come again."

"Their informant network is extensive and swift," Taisa stated. "They wouldn't have launched an attack like this without witnesses to send word of the result. There were probably a half dozen men watching from afar when we defeated the Order."

"Then we need to make sure they see us leave," Tae remarked.

"That would be dangerous in the desert. We wouldn't have a way to hide or lose them in the sands. We want to move undiscovered until we reach the lowlands in the north," Di'Nay commented.

"I should pray about it," Gerome mumbled. "We can do as the Mother wills."

Taisa turned to him sharply, her face tense with incredulous anger that was about to explode. "That's a good idea." Elana stopped the argument before it began. "Anything will help."

Gerome nodded solemnly and slipped out of the room.

"His faith will get him killed," Taisa grunted. "He still doesn't understand what it means to be hunted by the Order of Blindness."

"Yes, he does," Di'Nay argued gently. "This is the way he copes with it. We could use his help."

"Perhaps he really does have a connection with the Mother," Tae interjected. "Prayer is powerful."

Taisa snorted. "I prayed every night from the day I could talk and the Mother didn't save me from the Order. If prayer works, the Mother is fickle."

Tae regarded her warily, his expression a mix of hurt and confusion. Taisa's face softened a bit as she read his amarin, but she squared her shoulders and refused to show him mercy. Elana watched them and felt the touch of a headache forming behind her eyes. This was going to be a long trip.

"We now have a party with three Blue Sights. Whether through prayer or vision, we should be able to make a decision.

And if the Sight doesn't offer any guidance, we'll still have to act. We know the Order will attack again if we stay. There's a chance they'll be spared if we leave."

"But where do we go next?" Taisa questioned.

"North, back to the Ramains. The Order is becoming more of a threat there. This army wasn't a coincidence. We need to stop them before they attack anywhere else. We need to get a step ahead of them instead of constantly being three steps behind," Elana stated.

"Drawing them after us may be the only way to do this," Di'Nay muttered to herself, taking back her previous statement. "We know a couple towns where they have a presence. If we make an appearance near the Ramains border we could draw the Order after us and away from Madrisah. Once we know we're being tracked, we can turn the tables on our attackers. Get some answers."

"That may be the only way to go about this," Elana agreed.

"How far are we to the border?" Tae questioned.

"Some time," Di'Nay remarked.

"We'd have to move quickly or another band could be mobilized before we're spotted elsewhere," Tae cautioned.

Di'Nay nodded slowly, now lost in planning.

"Whatever happens, we should leave in the morning," Elana recommended. "We know where our final destination is, and we know we need to move quickly – whether we're followed or reveal ourselves eventually."

Taisa and Tae nodded. "We'll meet by the horses at dawn."

"Thank you. Good night," Elana whispered and they left. Elana rested her hand on Di'Nay's shoulder. "We'll figure this out."

Di'Nay lifted Elana's hand and kissed her fingers. "I know we will. We always do."

Elana stood still, relishing a moment of closeness between them. The wariness of their long journey hung heavy on both of their shoulders. She'd felt it in Taisa, who was growing more easily fatigued due to the baby. She'd felt it mingling with Gerome's sadness and in Tae's confusion. They all needed to be careful not to overextend themselves. To walk the narrow line between caring for themselves and doing the work that needed to be done.

"This will come to an end soon, one way of the other," Elana announced.

"I know."

"When it does... I want to leave with you."

Di'Nay turned to look at her. "For Yemaya?"

"Yes. I think I'm ready to go."

Di'Nay smiled and Elana felt her heart warm, partly from her own happiness and partly from the swell of delight from Di'Nay. "You made up your mind."

"I made up my mind long ago. It just took a while for the time to be right. Once we return the missing seers – once we're able to cripple the Order, either by giving enough information to the Keep or the Marshals to hand the fight to them, speaking to the king of the Ramains, or even just killing the heads of their organization I'll be done here. I just want to be with you."

Di'Nay swept her into a deep kiss and held her tight, all her hopes and dreams for their future overwhelming Elana's senses until she laughed aloud in joy.

"Spend the night with me. One more night before we're stuck in the wild with companions again," Elana whispered. "Please."

Di'Nay kissed her again, this time slowly, passionately. They returned to their room, trying for a few hours to put the pain of the day behind them. Whatever happened at the end of their journey on Aggar, they would always have each other.

FACILITY 3023

Elana closed her eyes and smiled as the landscape shifted from sand to dirt, the brush growing thicker into grass and shrubbery. It was the first taste of home in such a long time. While the southern Ramains was very little like the forests around the Keep, there was a distinct difference between the desert, jungle, swamps, and seaside towns that had made up most of her journey. There really was no place on Aggar quite like her home.

It had been so long. The journey through the Southern Desert had taken longer than she'd liked, a constant mix of traveling as quickly as possible, hiding from caravans and travelers, and, near the end, making strategic appearances in small towns in an attempt to draw the attention of the Order away from Madrisah. It had been handy for gathering supplies – Di'Nay had leveraged the last of her relationships with various trading outposts to secure food, proper horses, and basic supplies for everyone in the party. They'd even found clothing for Taisa and Tae, who wouldn't be used to the north's colder climates. But the stop and go pace of their travels had been surprisingly rigorous.

Di'Nay noticed her joy and Elana felt the softness of her lover's smile even with her eyes closed.

"We should reach real forests in a couple days," Di'Nay reminded her.

"It will be nice to be surrounded by silverpines."

Elana turned as she heard a scuffle and Taisa led her horse off the path and dismounted. She held up a hand and the party paused as Taisa stumbled into a thick cluster of brush, fell to her knees, and vomited. Di'Nay slid from her horse and went to kneel beside Taisa. As their journey became more turbulent and it became harder for Taisa to hide her pregnancy, Di'Nay had become her most trusted companion. Perhaps it was their time healing together in Cheongu or their talks in the swamps, but Taisa didn't want anyone else near when she was sick.

"We should find her a healer," Tae grunted softly, frustrated that she wouldn't let him help her. "She's not getting better."

Elana and Gerome exchanged glances. Taisa would have to tell the truth sooner or later.

Di'Nay rubbed Taisa's back as she took a moment to wipe her mouth and gather her composure. She was trembling with both emotion and nausea. Elana frowned. If both Taisa and her child had the Sight, it wasn't good for either of them for Taisa to be so upset.

Di'Nay glanced at the sky. "Do any of you have a problem with making camp early?"

Taisa stood. "I'm fine."

"You're really not," Di'Nay rebutted.

"Di'Nay."

"Taisa."

"I wouldn't mind," Gerome announced, his voice soft, gently breaking the tension. Elana glanced at him out of the corner of her eye. He had changed so much since they'd met. "We rode so hard yesterday I'm still a bit tired."

Di'Nay and Taisa exchanged glances and Taisa finally relented. She crossed her arms over her chest and clenched her teeth. "Fine."

After a bit of scouting they found a spot surrounded by brush and a small copse of trees. It wasn't much cover, but it would do for a night. They made camp quickly and, despite stopping primarily for Taisa, it seemed everyone appreciated the rest. Elana caught herself yawning the moment she sat on her bedmat.

"It always catches up the minute you let yourself rest," Di'Nay remarked as she sat beside her. "Are you all right?"

"Fine," Elana commented. "Just feeling this hopefully coming to an end. We'll sleep for a tenday when we get to Yemaya."

Di'Nay laughed. "We'll be in hyper sleep for a while. You'll be plenty rested when you get to Yemaya."

"It won't be true sleep."

Di'Nay rested a hand on Elana's knee. "You can do

whatever you want when we get to Yemaya."

Elana and Di'Nay were interrupted by a cry of outrage as Tae shouted in his own language. Elana leapt to her feet. She didn't know enough of the Cheongu language to understand everything he was saying, but she recognized a few explitives.

Elana, Di'Nay, and Gerome reached him as he stalked deeper into the forest, leaving Taisa behind. She watched him go, her face red and her fists clenched.

"You told him," Elana whispered.

Taisa turned and pushed her way past them, heading in the opposite direction. Di'Nay moved to go after her and Elana grabbed her arm. They locked eyes. "Are you sure?" Elana asked.

"She shouldn't be alone," Di'Nay remarked and Elana released her.

"I think I might take a vow of celibacy," Gerome muttered and Elana couldn't bite back a laugh.

"To avoid pregnancy or domestic disputes?"

"Do I have to choose?"

Elana smiled softly and watched Di'Nay as she comforted Taisa. She held the younger woman in a tight hug, letting her rage and cry against her chest. Di'Nay's face was sure and calm – always a rock when things became chaotic. Elana was happy she wanted to be a parent. Di'Nay would make a strong, stable mother. "Not all relationships are so volatile."

"But all of them are more complicated than worship."

"You're very young."

"Even more reason not to think about children." Gerome glanced over his shoulder. "Should I go after Tae? We aren't close, but he may be more receptive to me than-"

Gerome was caught off by a ragged cry from Taisa. Di'nay's peaceful expression turned to shock and Taisa trembled violently in Di'nay's arms. Di'Nay lowered Taisa to the ground as carefully as she could as the younger woman thrashed and stepped away to give her space.

Elana and Gerome rushed to Taisa's side as she seized, her eyes rolling into the back of her head. Her muscles twitched and jumped, contorting her limbs. She started to bleed from dozens of scratches from thrashing over the rough forest floor.

Elana tried to see into her amarin, to understand what had caused the seizure, but Taisa was completely blocked to her. Even after his rage, Tae ran to them, his face twisted with terror and concern. He reached out toward Taisa and Elana stopped him.

"This has to run its course," she warned. "She'll hurt herself if we restrain her."

"Did I do this?" he questioned, his voice trembling. "I never lose my temper. I never... I didn't mean to –"

Elana shook her head. "You walked away. You did the right thing. This is something else."

After nearly a minute of seizing, Taisa started to calm. Her thrashing grew weaker and finally she was still. It took her another long moment to return to herself.

She gasped and her eyes opened and focused on the people standing around her. She scanned each of them, then her eyes locked on Elana's. "I had a vision."

Elana raised her eyebrows in surprise. She had never seen such a sudden and violent vision. "What did you see?"

She closed her eyes and brought one shaky hand up to cover them. She drew long, intentional breaths and attempted to calm herself. "I saw... White walls. Impossibly white. And smooth. I've never seen anything like it. There were lights without fire. A... sharp sound. Like a horn but higher and sustained. I saw the forest floor open like a door."

Elana glanced at Di'Nay in surprise and they shared a moment of understanding. She was seeing Terran technology.

"What else did you see?"

Taisa started to cry. "I felt them. Children. Seers. They're so scared. More scared than they were in Saranthis. They're awake. How are they awake? Why can't they free themselves?"

"Calm down. Please. Just breathe," Di'Nay intoned, her voice gentle and reassuring. "Come back to us."

Tae knelt, but didn't approach her any further. "Taisa."

"I'm fine," Taisa grunted, but then she softened her tone. "I'm fine."

"She was loud," Gerome whispered, his voice so low only Elana could hear him well.

Taisa lowered her hand and stared in shock up at the sky. "Look out!"

Elana leapt aside in shock as two men dropped from the trees and drew knives from their belts. She couldn't sense their amarins. They might as well not exist to her Sight. They were supported by the Order of Blindness.

In a moment, Di'Nay had drawn her short sword and charged their attackers. Elana was frozen a moment longer, her eyes locked on the cast of their skin, the shape of their features. They were Terrans.

Diana raced at the assassins and in a couple parries was able to kill the first. She turned to the second and fell back in shock as Tae threw his spear, catching the attacker in the stomach and pinning him to a tree.

Diana took a deep, ragged breath, a shock of relief flooding her body. She had good senses and reflexes, but every time she had to use them she was well aware of how lucky she was that she was faster than her opponent.

Everyone moved toward the pinned attacker. He gasped for breath and struggled against the spear – his shock numbing some of the pain. He wouldn't survive. Tae's aim had been true, the spear piercing multiple organs. But they had a few moments to ask questions. She opened her mouth to speak and paused as the man beat her to it.

"You won't find them," he growled, his voice deep and guttural like a wild animal. "We're too well hidden. And there are more of us patrolling. They'll take you down."

Diana hesitated. He wasn't a mercenary, he was a scout. They had to be close to something. "We've gotten this far," Diana countered.

"We outnumber you." His voice was ragged and fading.

Diana grabbed her knife from her belt and cut the cord to the man's amulet, removing his protection. His eyes widened in terror and flicked between the three Blue Sights in the party. "We won't find them," Diana repeated his words, thinking over her next move. "Where are the children?"

"Where not even they can find them," he growled, nodding to Elana. Diana smiled. Victory.

"I know when you're lying," Elana warned, taking her own chances.

"I'll be dead before you can do anything to me."

"I can keep you alive."

"And I can keep them from hurting you," Diana countered, playing off Elana's ferocity to earn the man's trust. "Tell me where you're keeping the seers and I'll let you go to the afterlife in peace."

He hesitated. "Your kind should be wiped off the planet."

Diana raised an eyebrow. "Mine?"

"Terrans and blue-eyed demons. Interlopers. Invaders. You're corrupting our world."

Diana indicated the dead man nearby. "Your companion there was a Terran."

The man curled his nose in disgust. "He was being cleansed." He coughed, leaving a splatter of blood in the dirt and coating his lips. His face was losing all color.

"We'll save them," Taisa warned, her lips curled in a fury.

"You can't even save yourself," he countered boldly. "I saw you. You're sick."

"And you're dead."

"Not for long." Diana raised her brows in shock.

"What do you mean?"

He slumped forward and Diana grunted in annoyance as she watched him die. Tae pulled his spear from the dead man and the corpse hit the ground hard.

"We wouldn't have gotten answers out of him so quickly anyway," Elana stated, her voice full of disappointment. "We should bury the bodies. Hide our trail a bit longer."

"We have to be close. That wasn't a mercenary," Diana pointed out.

"We are. And if the scouts expected us, this must be a powerful stronghold. They assume it's out end goal." Gerome added.

"We need to move more carefully. We should hide the bodies then find real protective shelter."

Everyone nodded at Diana's suggestion and started working to move the bodies. Elana stopped Taisa with a hand on her shoulder before she could join in. "You should rest."

"I'm fine."

"You're not. This stress is hurting the child."

"I'm not going to be left behind," Taisa hissed. "I can't."

You're not being left behind," Diana replied. "But you're still ill right now. You need to stay strong. Rest a bit. We can handle the bodies."

Diana saw the now-familiar flame of opposition in Taisa's eyes, but it was no match for Diana's surety and calm demeanor.

After a moment of mental battling, she sighed and nodded. "I don't want to be a hindrance."

"You won't be as long as you take care of yourself," Diana assured her. "You're the one getting the visions. For some reason, your Sight is what we need to find these children. You're a help. Just maybe not a physical one for a while."

Taisa met her eyes defiantly once more and stalked deeper into the forest, lingering just within sight. Diana sighed and returned to helping hide the bodies.

She started with the first attacker that had been killed – a Terran. She studied him for a moment, trying to think if she'd ever seen him before, but he was a mystery. His face was generic – wide jaw, small eyes, no scars or marks. Blonde hair and beard. He could be any Terran soldier.

She searched his pockets quickly, removing his amulet and finding nothing but some pocket change and basic weaponry. He bore no marks of his base or allegiance to any party save the Order of Blindness.

Diana frowned. She had heard of Terran soldiers making trouble on Aggar, everything from verbal harassment to petty crime. There had been individuals accused of horrible crimes, but rarely a party more than two or three. But this man had likely deserted his post, and Taisa was having visions of Terran tech – possibly even a Terran base. How many deserters were aligned with the Order?

The Terrans were only able to exist on Aggar with any layer of peace because most of their presence was hidden. The people of Aggar knew what some Terrans looked like. They knew there were outposts and might have seen shuttles in the sky, but the space station and the larger bases were hidden through holograms and force fields. If the people of Aggar suspected they were being invaded – that, in many ways, they already *had* been invaded – their peace would disappear.

This could be dangerous. It could go beyond disappearing seers or cults. If Aggar actively revolted against the Terran presence on Aggar, there would be a massacre at best. Diana had to figure out how the Terrans and Order were linked and find a way to sever the tie as quickly and quietly as possible.

Elana led her horse into the cave as night fell outside. It was a wonder they'd found the shelter in the first place – a small, stone cavern built into the side of a rocky outcropping. It was more of a hollow than a full cavern, but it would protect them on three sides and provide some shelter while they planned their next steps.

"I'll start a fire," Tae offered as he swung down from his saddle and walked back out into the forest. He had barely spoken on the journey and had opted to ride as far from Taisa as possible. Gerome exchanged glances with her and followed Tae. Elana understood the man's frustration and felt it was warranted, but if Taisa and Tae's tumultuous relationship was going to cause a rift in the party, she needed to know.

"I'm fine," Taisa grunted as Di'Nay helped her to the ground.

Di'Nay smiled softly. "I didn't say anything."

"I know your expressions." Taisa steadied herself on Di'Nay's shoulder as she became nauseous again. The hand on Di'Nay's shoulder balled into a fist but Di'Nay pretended not to notice. She understood the rage of suddenly feeling helpless.

Elana looked out the mouth of the cavern into the woods, her hands on her hips. She scanned its depths in the fading light and considered their options. Once Taisa was settled on her bedmat, Di'Nay moved to stand beside Elana.

"We have to be getting close to something," Elana muttered. "Not close enough I can feel anything. You'd think I'd be able to sense a disruption in the tree line if anything."

"Taisa's having visions of Terran technology and one of the scouts was a Terran."

"Do you know of anything Terran built in the area? Do you have mobile settlements? Missing ships?"

Di'Nay shook her head, her mouth set in a firm frown. She drew a slow, frustrated breath. She was talking about warning signals, white walls, and a door opening in the forest floor. It might not be a small space. She might be seeing a base."

"A base in the southern forest? I thought the Terrans were primarily posted in the north?"

Di'Nay shook her head. "They're spread farther than anyone on Aggar knows. Most of their settlements are very hidden."

Elana's stomach turned at the thought and she suppressed a shudder at the thought of a more of a Terran presence than she'd thought. She tried not to let Di'Nay see, but her lover knew her too well. Di'Nay smiled almost sadly. "I don't particularly like it, either. But for the length of time the Terrans have actually been here, I'm glad they originally hid their bases. They were here long before the people of Aggar knew it."

"Do you know of any bases that were built in this area?"

"Di'Nay shook her head. I was primarily settled in the desert. I've never heard of anything here, but that's not necessarily a sign that there's nothing here."

"Maybe Taisa's seeing something else. Somewhere else. Visions aren't always about the near future."

Di'Nay laughed softly. "Do you think we have that kind of luck?"

"It doesn't make sense that the Terrans would be supporting the Order of Blindness. While individuals might get involved with people from Aggar, the leadership is more interested in their space battles than anyone on our planet. And they would need some kind of leadership involvement if the Order had control of an entire base."

"I don't think this is a Terran issue. Our attacker had no sign of his base and no technology. He was a deserter."

"I don't understand."

"The base could have been abandoned or seized. It wouldn't be unusual for an old, small settlement or bunker to be hollowed out and left for a larger location."

"They've been here that long?"

Di'Nay looked at her apologetically. "We won't know anything for sure until we find whatever the scouts were protecting."

Elana nodded slowly and turned to Taisa and sat beside her on the bed mat. Taisa's tattoos on her face seemed to somehow glow softly in the growing darkness, reflecting a hint of the depths of her blue eyes.

"I need to know more of what you saw," Elana said softly. "Anything that might give us a clue of what we're looking for."

"I didn't see anything specific," Taisa remarked. "And I don't remember everything." She hesitated a moment. "Are they often like that? The visions?"

"No. But the dreaming is different for everyone. Most don't even have it, just those of us with a closer connection to seer abilities.”

“I don’t want it if it’s going to be like that.”

“It may be the pregnancy.”

Taisa frowned. “Does that mean visions will be like that for her?”

“You’re so sure it’s a girl?”

Taisa nodded slowly. “I’ve started to feel her. Or maybe I’m feeling what she’ll become. But she’s there.”

“She’s trying to help you the best she can,” Elana responded. “She must be very strong.”

“And a seer.”

Elana nodded slowly. “She’ll have at least some seer ability, yes.”

Taisa ran her hand through her short hair, her fingers raking across her scalp. She bit back tears and the muscles in her jaw twitched with her anger and fear. “She’d be safe in Cheongu.”

“Yes.”

“You know I love him.”

Elana chose her words carefully. “I had considered it.”

“Don’t. I know you know.”

“He’s a good man. He’s not upset that you’re pregnant. He’s upset you left without telling him.”

“The last time I loved a man I let him lead me into the Order. I locked myself away – I wore one of those damn amulets – for years. What will I become this time?”

Elana smiled softly and touched one of the lines of the tattoo across her cheek. “You’re more your own now than you were then.”

“It was easy to be myself when that was all I had.”

“Then don’t lose yourself again.”

“What if I can’t?”

“You have to. And you have to trust that he isn’t Nile.”

“He’s nothing like Nile. But maybe it was never Nile. Maybe it was me.”

“You can’t take all the blame for what happened to you. The Order of Blindness is a cult. They excel at brainwashing. You were abused.”

“I made my choices.”

“Then make them again. You don’t have to be with him. You don’t even have to raise this child. But you need to make your own choices and I think you're better able to do that now. The world isn't as black and white as you thought it was."

Taisa rested a hand on her stomach. "Do you think she's doing this to me so I can't fight?"

"To protect herself?"

Taisa shook her head, her eyes still on her hand. "To protect me from my rage."

"I think you're close enough with her that whatever you suspect is most likely real."

Taisa sighed. "I don't want her to have to take care of me."

Elana squeezed her shoulder. "Think about it. Di'Nay and I will support whatever you choose."

"Thank you."

Elana stood and rejoined Di'Nay. "We have all we'll ever have. We should do our own scouting."

"We can't leave her alone."

"I'll stay with her," Gerome called as he and Tae returned with wood for a fire.

"No." Taisa's voice echoed from deeper in the cavern. "If there's a base in the forest, the Sight will find it. Gerome should go with Elana." She turned to the mouth of the cavern, her eyes wide but sure. "Tae, will you stay with me?"

A silence settled around them as they all understood. After what felt like an eternity, Tae pulled his spear from his back, rested it against the cavern wall, and started building a fire.

"We can navigate well in the dark," Elana whispered. "It doesn't affect us, but it might affect the scouts."

"A short sweep of the area?" Gerome questioned.

"Let's go," Di'Nay agreed, and they left Taisa and Tae to their own conversation.

Elana navigated through the forest with the help of her Sight. Her eyes were decent on their own, but the constant projections of amarin from the trees and flora – even the scattered amarins of small forest creatures moving through the underbrush – made the forest as bright as day.

She used to find the feeling comfortable, but surrounded by the Order of Blindness she knew how false her Sight could be. She was thankful once again to have Di'Nay by her side. Her reflexes, senses, and experience detecting threats was invaluable.

"Do you feel that?" Gerome whispered as he moved up behind Elana. "That darkness?"

Elana narrowed her eyes and tried to sense whatever Gerome did. "I don't feel anything out of the ordinary."

"It's like... something is missing. The forest is unsettled."

Elana tried once more, and in the far distance she could start to feel some of the chaos Gerome did. "It might be the Order. They can ward small areas against the Sight."

"What Taisa explained... That's not a structure of Aggar."

"No, it's Terran," Elana admitted.

Gerome's face twisted into a grimace of anger and frustration. "They're with the Order?"

"No. But the Order might be using Terran technology," Di'Nay responded. "They're probably underground."

"The forest wouldn't like that," Gerome stated. "A foreign object splitting the root system, interrupting the fungus networks."

"That's what I was hoping," Elana admitted. "We can't trace the Order, but sometimes we can trace the effects they have on the amarin around them."

Di'Nay tensed, putting Elana immediately on guard. Her hand went to her crossbow, where she had already loaded a bolt. She had just glanced up into the trees when a dozen scouts pounced. She was able to fire a single bolt before one pulled out a small, metal device and Elana screamed as it was pressed against the small of her back, emitting a sharp electric shock that knocked her to the ground. Her muscles jumped and her strength fled. She heard Di'Nay and Gerome cry out in surprise at the attack. She tried to push herself back up and was instantly knocked over the head with the butt of a sword.

She wondered why the attacks weren't lethal before she was struck again and knocked unconscious.

Diana woke slowly. Her head pounded. Her mouth was dry and her eyelids were heavy. She focused on her breathing and tried to gather her memories. She remembered the forest. The scouts. Elana. The realization that she couldn't feel her lover knocked all other thoughts from her mind. Her lifestone felt cold in her wrist. Where was Elana?

She forced her eyes open and squinted against the light. They were bulbs, their soft electrical hum droning to her pounding head. The yellow light reflecting off the white walls. The cot she'd been laying on creaked as she sat up. Her room was narrow and small – a holding cell or isolation chamber. She fought to remain calm, but her heart pounded in her chest. She knew a Terran space when she saw it. Where were Elana and Gerome?

She stood and heard a sharp beep. She glanced down at her arm and noticed a metal bracelet. A tracker. There were footsteps by the door and a metal slot opened. A tray of food was pushed through. "Eat. You've been out for days."

Diana tried to glance through the hole to see her guard, but she only caught sight of his hands. They were definitely Terran. "How many?" she questioned.

"Two." His reply was sharp and matter-of-fact.

"I'm a representative of the Empire. They'll notice if I go missing," she warned. There was no response. "My companions will be missed as well. Elana is an emissary from the Keep. Do you understand what that means? What kind of people you'll upset by kidnapping her?"

"The Keep doesn't scare any of us here. Their witches are useless against the Order of Blindness."

"Is that what they tell you?"

The metal slot slammed shut and Diana's lips pressed into a tight line. Maybe she'd shaken him. She had no way of knowing. All she knew was she needed to find a way out.

She investigated her meal – soup, bread, a bit of butter. It was richer than she'd expect to be served to a prisoner. Besides being trapped, she didn't seem to have been touched. She was still in her travel clothes. She didn't feel any severe injuries. Perhaps some of the Terrans were genuinely nervous about her station in the Empire. They were unsure of what to do with her. She might be able to use it to her advantage. It was a long shot, but it was a bit of hope.

Still, she inspected everything before eating it and she only ate small bites. It wouldn't take much to lace the meal with sedatives or poisons. She hid the rest under her bed even as her stomach grumbled. She needed to make a plan, and she needed to act soon. There was no telling what had happened to Elana and Gerome. She was certain she'd know through her lifestone if Elana was dead – at least she hoped she would – but that didn't mean much when she felt her lover was so far away.

She looked around the room. Her cot was simple and bolted to the ground. There was a small toilet built into the corner. A camera was suspended from the ceiling in the right corner of the room near the door. There was nothing she could use as a weapon and no marks to give her any sense of place, type of bunker, or time.

After what felt like hours of silence – but for all she knew could have been minutes or days – she heard footsteps again. The slot opened. "Dinner." It was a different voice. Diana didn't take the offered tray. "I want to speak to your leader."

The man laughed. "You're a prisoner. You're lucky you're alive."

"I'm a high-ranking member of the Terran fleet. People will be looking for me. People who can find a Terran bunker. I don't know the size of your force here, but I doubt it could survive against a Terran army."

There was a short pause – long enough for an unsteady breath. When the man spoke again, he was less confident. "We'll deal with the Terrans."

"You *are* a Terran."

"I'm an apostle of the Order of Blindness."

"You're a traitor."

"The Terrans are invaders!"

Diana smiled at the outburst. He was easier to manipulate than she thought. "Pathetic. Forget the Sight, the seers will be able to smell your fear."

"I'm not afraid. Especially not of seers."

"Saying it won't save you when they scramble your mind."

"Stop it."

"Do you think they'll save you? When everything falls apart – when the Terrans attack or the seers rip this bunker apart – do you think the Order won't throw you away? That they'll risk their own for you?"

"I'm a full member of the Order."

"You're laser-fodder. A front-line stupid enough to think that a cult dedicated to attacking anyone different would accept foreigners with open arms."

"You don't know what you're talking about."

"Then why is your voice quivering?"

Diana was ready for him when he threw open the door and

charged her in a rage. In two quick motions she punched him in the stomach and pushed him to the floor. She kicked him in the head, knocking him out.

She let out a sharp breath. It had been so easy. Almost too easy. Still, with a quick glance to the camera in the corner of the room, she knew she had little time to spare.

She raced from the room, shutting and locking the door behind herself in case the guard woke up. She held her breath, holding onto the fact that no alarm had sounded yet. Perhaps the camera wasn't working or wasn't manned. As she moved through what she could now clearly tell was a very old Terran bunker she spotted multiple lights and electrical panels that were down. The electricity had to be routed to more important areas. The fact that anything in the bunker would be deemed more important than a camera monitoring a prisoner didn't sit well with her.

She made her way through the halls as swiftly and silently as she could. She monitored the ceilings for more cameras and moved around them whenever possible. She hid around corners and in empty rooms whenever members of the Order passed.

From what she could see, the inhabitants of the bunker were fairly evenly mixed between people of Aggar and Terrans. It was likely the Terrans were only allowed into the Order in exchange for information about and use of the base. There didn't seem to be many – Diana only counted a dozen or so as she moved through the halls – but she suspected there were more populated sections of the bunker.

As she moved down a particularly dark and narrow hall she saw a door half-open with a dark, blue light emanating from deep within. She crept up to it and stared inside in shock before stepping inside.

It was a security room. A wall of cameras revealed different sections of the bunker. Half the cameras were off. The cameras that were on covered some kind of medical ward. White rooms with security plastic walls were filled with people of Aggar in medical gowns. Most were young. Diana assumed they were seers based on the ways they clustered together or screamed and pounded against the walls. All of them were wearing amulets.

She saw Gerome in one of the rooms. He fought against four Terran doctors. They were holding him down, strapping him to his cot. A shot of tranquilizer left him unconscious.

Diana knew the security room wouldn't be empty for long. She must have somehow escaped in the few minutes between shifts. She needed to find a way to get to Elana. She needed to hide. But she was frozen in place, her eyes locked on one of the cameras.

It showed Elana, dressed in a Terran medical gown, strapped to a table. She was unconscious. A nurse meandered through the room in the early stages of a procedure. Diana spotted a small tracker on a metal table nearby. Her stomach twisted as she realized what was about to happen. They were going to implant a tracker in Elana. They were going to operate on her.

Diana's shoulders tightened and she clenched her fists. She had to get to Elana. Fast.

Elana could hear children screaming in the darkness. It felt like a part of herself, the sound more in her mind than in reality. Was she dreaming? Was it a vision? She couldn't tell.

She caught a flash of light and whispered, "Silver?" The girl didn't appear. She was alone in a void, nothing but herself and the screams. For a moment she thought she might go mad.

Elana shifted and the void started to fall away like a dream. her vision was clouded. She felt trapped somewhere between dreaming and reality. Every muscle burned. Her head pounded. She tasted blood in her mouth. She was wearing an amulet and the realization made her nauseous.

"Don't bite down." The woman's voice was sharp and unsympathetic. An order. She felt hands on her jaw and she clenched her muscles, refusing to open her mouth. She was too weak or too disconnected from her body for her muscles to respond to her commands and she felt her mouth forced open and a tablet placed on her tongue. It tasted like metal and salt.

"Don't swallow it. It will dry your mouth out, that's all." Elana found just enough strength to spit the pill out. She felt the woman grab her face not hard enough to hurt her, but firm enough to get her attention. "You will not do that again."

"It's no use. She's waking up."

A second woman. Elana blinked hard over and over, trying to clear her vision but she couldn't. She was defenseless. She didn't know where she was. She couldn't see and her Sight was bound. She was an infant in a lions' den.

"They won't want her awake for the procedure."

"There are things they can do with her awake."

"Not this. We don't have the supplies to keep bringing them down from shock."

"She isn't a random kid snatched from the capitol. They'll keep her alive."

Elana's vision started to clear and her chest tightened in a panic. She was in a small, circular room. It was completely white. Sterile. Two women stood over her, their faces covered in masks and their gloved hands reaching out for her. She heard the sharp bursts of an electrical device and it took her a moment to realize it was beeping to the rhythm of her speeding heart.

Elana started to shake, her limbs pulling at the thick leather straps holding her down to the bed. The strap around her right wrist started to come loose and she fought against it in a primal need to be free.

"She shouldn't be this awake!" the first nurse growled as she pinned her arm down. The second nurse drew a liquid into a small plunger with a needle and stabbed it into Elana's arm.

Elana cried out, more in fear and surprise than out of pain. Instantly her heart started to calm and her head swam. She felt delightfully warm, as if she was floating on a puff of steam high above her own body. The first nurse released her arm.

"She's strong."

"You've heard the stories about her, haven't you?" the second nurse countered. "How many of us she's killed?"

"Blue Sight witch," the first spat. "Maybe they'll get more out of her. She's the oldest one here."

"You think they're like snakes? The little ones are the most poisonous?"

"Anything's possible."

Elana gasped but the breath wouldn't escape her lungs as her jaw was grabbed once again and another metallic tablet pressed to her tongue. She was too weak to spit it out. She couldn't even find the muscles in her face to move them. "It won't hurt you, just dry your mouth." the first nurse repeated, more out of annoyance than in any attempt to reassure Elana. "The tools the doctors will use are very expensive. If they're going to break, it won't be because of your saliva."

This must be the Cellar. The thought came to Elana unbidden. She couldn't be alive. She must have died and ended up in the darkest reaches of the Fates' domain. She was violated. She couldn't do anything to save herself. What were they going to do to her? Could she still die in the Cellar?

As promised, her mouth started to dry. It burned and she couldn't feel anything but her thirst.

"Do you think she's unconscious again?" The second nurse studied her closely. The first shined a light in her eyes and she couldn't look away.

"Close enough."

Elana wanted to scream. She wanted to feel her heart pound and her body burn with fear. But she didn't feel anything. Her body ignoring her emotions felt more violating than anything the nurses had done to her.

She was awake. The knowledge repeated over and over in her mind. She was awake and they didn't know it. Whatever happened to her, she would feel every second of it.

The door to the facility opened and two more masked people entered. Elana couldn't even move her eyes to follow their movements and with her Sight bound she couldn't feel their intention or emotion.

"Is she ready?" a man questioned.

"We had to sedate her," the second nurse warned. "She woke during preparation."

"But she's calm now?"

The first nurse indicated one of the monitors. "Her heart rate is stable and her abilities are contained."

"Good."

Elana tried to feel if there was any part of herself that she had any control over anymore. Some muscle she could move, some bit of her Sight she could still sense. All she felt was a small warmth – a warmth in her lifestone. Di'Nay was alive. She couldn't be far. She held onto the knowledge and focused on that warmth. She tried to sense some kind of heartbeat or lingering bit of Di'Nay's emotion.

She didn't know if it was wishful thinking or dissociation with her body out of fear, but as she heard the nurses and doctor moving through the room, she narrowed her entire focus onto the feeling in her lifestone. Her world narrowed. Her focus became a pinpoint. She felt like the warmth was getting stronger. She thought she could sense a light pulse – evidence that Di'Nay was near and thinking of her. There were no alarms, no sense of urgency in the building. How could Di'Nay be moving closer?

Elana felt the doctors moving toward her and she inwardly flinched at their presence. One of the nurses rested her hand on Elana's shoulder, the pressure solid, like holding her down. She closed Elana's eyes with a gloved hand. She had to have some idea that Elana was still awake, locked inside a paralyzed body.

Elana strained to hear everything around her. Without either form of her vision, she felt more lost than ever. But then she heard the shift of the door opening again and a gasp of shock. Elana held to the noise as she heard running, the crash of the metal cart, the heavy thud of something solid against flesh. The lifestone in Elana's wrist was all but burning.

Elana felt a familiar hand on her arm and she wanted to cry out. She wanted to call for Di'Nay and throw her arms around her. But she still couldn't move. She couldn't even quicken her own breath.

She felt a sharp sting in her neck and her body exploded back to life. Her muscles spasmed violently and she strained against her bonds, but after the initial violent awakening she had control of her body again. She curled her fingers, feeling her palms. She drew deep, intentional breaths. And she opened her eyes.

Di'Nay stood over her, pale and terrified, but her mouth broke into a wide smile when Elana woke.

"I didn't know what they did to you," she whispered, her voice trembling but regaining strength.

"Nothing yet," Elana responded. "Help me?"

Di'Nay unstrapped one of Elana's wrists and they both freed the rest of her limbs. Di'Nay removed the Order amulet and threw it across the room. They kissed, and Elana savored the touch, letting it soothe away the fear and claustrophobia of being imprisoned in her own body.

Elana pulled herself to her feet and stumbled once, but found her footing. An alarm started blaring through the facility.

"We have to get out of here," Di'Nay remarked, her eyes darting to the speaker blaring the alarm.

They moved as quickly as they could. Elana silently cursed her lingering weakness, but she was able to keep up with Di'Nay as they found a darkened room and slipped inside.

"There are a few places like this that don't have electricity," Di'Nay spoke quickly. "The facility is only partially functional."

"How did you find me?"

"There are cameras. I saw Gerome as well. And seers."

"We need to help them."

"How?"

Elana glanced at the door. They wouldn't stay hidden for long. "We'd never make it out anyway. You saw what a few seer children did to the outpost in Saranthis."

"The twins broke free from their amulets. If any of the children here had that kind of power, they would have freed themselves."

"Then we remove their amulets."

"They would kill us, too!"

"I have faith in them."

Elana could tell Di'Nay was uneasy, but Elana was right – they wouldn't escape with an alarm already sounded. They would have to fight their way out."

Di'Nay reached out and grabbed Elana's hand. "I'm with you."

Elana nodded sharply, squeezed her lover's hand, and they headed back out into the hall.

Diana tried to remember the video screens she'd seen and piece together some kind of map. They barely avoided the teams of scouts and Order guards streaming through the main hallways and searching every room. Diana expected the seers would be better guarded than ever. Gerome had probably been moved. Every minute they hid or had to slip away from the main path made their chances at success plummet.

Diana never let go of Elana's hand. She had been able to push her fear at seeing Elana strapped to a Terran surgical table to the back of her mind, but she still felt sick thinking what would happen if they were caught again. Diana had no doubt she would be killed and her body dumped in the desert, where the Empire would think her the casualty of a raiding party. Elana would become a lab rat. Perhaps their separation would kill her by way of their lifestone, if she was lucky. Diana had no doubt Elana would rather be dead than live in an endless stream of surgeries and medical testing.

"How far do you think we are from the seers?" Elana

whispered as they hid behind a large cabinet.

"Not far, but they're going to be guarded. We might not be able to remain hidden much longer."

"How many do you think there are?"

"I have no idea."

Elana held Diana's hand tighter and Diana knew what she was going to ask. "Should we fight? Should we charge them? Even setting one seer free could start a chain reaction."

Diana's strategic mind spun. She searched desperately for other options, but they were out of time and out of resources. She clenched her fists and refused to let tears come to her eyes.

"I wanted you to see Yemaya."

"Don't. We won't die."

"If we do, I'm happy it's at your side."

Elana smiled softly. It was genuine, even in the depths of impending tragedy. "I'm just happy I found you."

They kissed and the touch gave Diana more courage, lit a fire under her skin. She was determined, and that made her a force to be reckoned with.

Together they left the safety of the cabinet and moved back toward the main hallways. Right before they reached it, however, Elana paused.

"What is it?" Diana questioned.

"Something... come here."

Diana let Elana lead her down a narrow side-corridor. She crouched beside a corner and peeked around to a door guarded by two members of the Order. They held crossbows at the ready.

Elana looked at Diana. A dozen thoughts spun through the Amazon's mind. The door hid something worth guarding, but either it was low priority, or there were no significant stockpiles of Terran weapons on the base. Perhaps their force was even smaller than she expected. It would make sense – a larger force would have discovered them by now.

Elana wanted to investigate. Diana didn't remember seeing a corridor like this on the monitors, but she trusted Elana's Sight. If Elana wanted to charge the two guards, she thought there was something worth dying for behind the doors.

Diana drew a deep breath and nodded. They sped around the corner, catching the guards by surprise. They fired. Diana avoided one arrow, but took the other in her left shoulder. She cried out in pain, but didn't let it slow her. The hallways were short. They wouldn't have time to reload. If they both aimed at her, Elana was safe.

They clashed and Diana grabbed one guard's face, slamming his head into the metal wall. He fell unconscious as Elana grappled the other, grabbing one of his crossbow bolts and stabbing him in the throat before he could pin her to the ground.

She stood and wiped the blood on her hands on her hospital gown. "Your shoulder..."

Di'Nay drew a deep breath and pulled the arrow from her arm. She bit back a cry of pain as it came free. Her arm burned. Thankfully, it didn't go through the entire joint. She must have been dodging when it hit.

Elana used one of the guard's knives to cut cloth from his shirt and bind Diana's shoulder. "That will have to do for now."

"I'm all right," Di'Nay promised, but she knew Elana wasn't fooled. At least it wasn't her dominant arm.

They quickly gathered the crossbows, bolts, and Diana took one of their daggers.

Elana started stripping one of the guards, weighing his measurements against her own. His clothing was too big for her, but offered more protection than a medical gown. She chose to remain barefoot.

"Better," she commented as she secured the quiver of crossbow bolts and took Diana's hand once more. She opened the door that had been guarded and they both stepped inside.

It was a small room, a digital board with statistics and readouts along one wall and a small control panel attached. It hadn't been manned in some time, but it was functional. Diana studied the charts and her brows knit at the levels of power the program was using. "No wonder the base rations electricity."

"What is it?" Elana questioned.

"A signal. Powerful. It doesn't seem very complex. It will reach a long way."

"As far as Onethis?"

"Maybe."

Elana moved around the room, opening the two cabinets and finding only a handful of empty folders. "Why would they guard this room but not work to monitor the program?"

"It may not be needed," Diana responded. "It doesn't seem

particularly complex or volatile. Or perhaps they moved the operators to a safer location until we were found."

"What's this?" Elana pointed out a small wave in the corner of the screen.

"The signal's frequency?" Diana guessed as she took a closer look.

"This room makes me sick."

Diana glanced at her in confusion. "You feel something?'

"Like touching an amulet."

Diana suddenly understood. "You think this is some kind of power source for them?"

"I think there's nothing on Aggar that could block the Sight like those medallions. But the Terrans are technologically advanced. They could have found a type of metal that will react to this frequency."

"How would they be able to calibrate something like that?"

"They must have been experimenting for a long time."

"Unless they were very lucky, they would have to have been testing since this base was in Terran use," Diana argued.

"What's a medical facility doing in the middle of a Ramains forest?" Elana countered, her voice deeper and darker than before. "Do you think the Terrans wouldn't be curious about our Sighted from the moment they landed on Aggar?"

Diana bristled slightly at the accusation, but she knew Elana was right. She would be more surprised if the Terrans hadn't looked into the unusual abilities on Aggar. "They must have abandoned the project when relations with Aggar proved peaceful."

"But it wasn't abandoned by everyone."

"No."

Elana touched the wave. "I think this is the wavelength where the Sight exists."

"Can that be quantified?"

"It must have been for a signal to be able to block it."

Diana was fascinated by the idea, but felt instant shame. It must have been the same curiosity the Terrans felt when they started their testing. "Then we can turn it off."

"If the amulets no longer work anywhere on Aggar, the Order will fall," Elana agreed. "They can't hold us without protection."

"I can try to figure it out," Diana offered.

"Does this machine control the signal or just study it?"

"It appears to be a control panel," Diana remarked.

"What it the machine was destroyed?"

Diana smiled. "Easier than hacking."

Diana pulled out her knife and proceeded to cut every cable and cord she could find. Elana grabbed one of the small cabinets and threw it at the machine, busting the monitor and control panel with a flurry of sparks.

Elana let out an audible gasp and nearly doubled over. "Elana?" Diana questioned, wrapping her arms around her.

"It's down. They're all down," Elana whispered. "I can feel all of them again.

The halls were suddenly filled with screams.

Diana couldn't make sense of the chaos that followed. Her head swam and her ears rang at the noise. She felt as if she were hallucinating. Was there really fire? Really smoke? Really the pounding of thousands of feet echoing through the metal halls?

Through it all she held tight to Elana's hand. It was her touchstone. The one thing she knew was real.

When the smoke started to clear and her senses returned, she found herself in the main hall, being led by Elana against a flood of fleeing members of the Order. They barely seemed to notice them, all their attention on escaping. They reached the medical wards, where the seers were clustered together, sitting on the floor and holding each other as their powers and fear rippled out of control.

Diana stumbled at the intensity, but she knew she should be dead. They had to have some idea of who she was and were trying to protect her. Hallucinations fled across her eyes again and she thought she could see waves of power like ripples on the sea. She saw Silver, standing over the seers. She saw the seers from Cheongu – the twins, Janis.

There was a sickening sound like bending and twisting metal and Diana realized they were tearing the building apart.

"Wait!" she cried. "We're underground! You'll kill us!"

Elana dropped to her knees and tried to get their attention, but they were locked in on themselves. "You're safe now! You're safe!" Elana begged, but they couldn't hear her anymore.

The smell of smoke grew stronger. Diana coughed on it, the

heat tearing at her throat. "Elana, we have to leave!" her voice was barely audible even to her own ears. She felt arms around her shoulders and she turned, ready to fight.

"I'm not with the Order!" the man called, indicating a mark on his red, quilted jacket. He was a Marshal.

"What are you —" Diana barely got the words out before he pulled at her arm. There were dozens like him moving down the hall, cloths over their mouths to help ward out smoke. "We'll help you out."

Diana was torn. She didn't trust the Marshals, but she trusted the collapsing building less. She pulled on Elana's arm, squeezing her hand, and Elana turned in shock. Her eyes flicked between the seers and the Marshal, but she didn't fight as Diana pulled her forward and they ran with the Marshal through the winding hallways, past the rubble, out the main doors back to the forest.

Elana stood before the Keep as if for the first time. It hadn't changed since she'd left – it had barely changed since she'd arrived as a child. She could feel the warmth and the distant hum of seer songs as they welcomed more of their own. She felt the amarin of the students and Council. She could smell the silverpine and fresh, chill scent that seemed unique to the Keep's grounds.

If she had ever had a home, this was it. But now there was a rift in her heart. A change. She didn't belong here anymore. A part of her life had ended. But she found, as she felt Di'Nay approaching from behind her, that she didn't mind. She was ready to let go. To go on with her life off Aggar.

"He should be here soon," Di'Nay announced. She clapped her gloved hands together to ward off the cold. Despite the stress and danger of their travels, Elana knew her lover's first thought upon returning to the Keep was mourning the warmer desert climate. Elana was just happy to see her arms so mobile. She had healed well from her crossbow bolt injury, but it had been far too long for Elana's liking.

"He shouldn't keep us waiting so long," Elana groused.

"In all fairness, we're alive because of him."

"We're alive because Taisa overcame her pride and reached out to the Marshals again."

"Elana."

Elana reached out to take Di'Nay's hand and sighed softly. "I know. I'm just ready for this to be done."

Di'Nay kissed her softly. Her face was lit with a gentle smile. "Are you really ready?"

"The shuttle arrives tomorrow," Elana commented with a laugh. "I can't back out now."

"You can back out whenever you like."

Elana shook her head. "I'm ready. I promise."

Di'Nay pulled her into a tight hug and rested her head on Elana's shoulder. They existed in the moment together, peaceful and filled with the warmth of new beginnings. Soon there would be no more hiding or lying. Soon they would only live for each other.

"About time." Elana and Di'Nay turned as Gerome approached. "I never liked you pretending you were just travel companions."

Elana smiled softly at his brazen attitude. "No point in pretending anything anymore. We won't be here long."

"Sometimes I think you're the lucky ones," Gerome stated with a sigh.

"The Order isn't a threat anymore," Elana reminded him.

"And if they become one again, I'll be here."

"Are you going back to Madrisah?"

Gerome glanced away. "I'm not sure yet. Maybe I'll take some time to travel."

Elana frowned. "But Madrisah was becoming your home."

"No. It was a place I could study and pray, but I'm starting to think perhaps my calling lies elsewhere. Somewhere I can serve the other Blue Sights as well."

Elana smiled. "I'm sure you'll find your way."

"Perhaps I'll spend some time in Cheongu."

Gerome glanced over his shoulder as Taisa and Tae approached as well. In the time since their return, Taisa's pregnancy had become impossible to hide. While they weren't a couple yet, their friendship had seemed to return.

"I can't wait to get out of here," Taisa grumbled as she hugged her arms close to her chest. She wore a thick, fur-lined coat but she had spent so long south of Karatan it barely helped.

"It's not so bad," Tae observed.

"You like it here," Taisa grunted.

"How are you this morning?" Elana questioned.

"Good enough. I've stopped getting sick every morning," Taisa answered. She rested a hand on her stomach. "Don't know how long she'll give me a break."

"She didn't get her fury from me," Tae remarked with a mischievous glance.

"As long as she can stay calm until we get back to Cheongu."

"So you did decide to leave?" Di'Nay questioned.

"Might as well," Taisa replied. "The Marshals hid me there. The Order won't find me and no one would dare threaten the village with the seers there now."

"And your child will be cared for," Elana agreed. "I think it's a good course of action."

Taisa sighed. "Now if Tristan would stop dallying we could start our journey back."

"I rushed so quickly to answer your message I think a little waiting won't hurt you now, Taisa."

Everyone turned as Tristan arrived from the forest, unwrapping a woven scarf from around his lower face. The mysterious leader of the Marshals stood before them, confident and even smug. Elana looked him over and tried to get a read of his amarin, but even his spirit seemed mixed. Even after his forces had saved her life, she didn't know how much she trusted him.

"That isn't funny," Taisa argued.

"It amuses me," Tristan remarked. "Nice to see you again, Taisa. You've... changed. I can't send you on assignment anymore with those tattoos."

"Good thing I don't work for you anymore, then."

"Quite right."

"You asked us to meet you here?" Di'Nay stated, breaking the argument before it became heated.

"Yes. I wanted to thank you and Elana for the information you sent, as spotty as it was, and the work you did to protect the Ramains from the Order of Blindness. I thought you'd like to know the Terran bunker has been completely demolished. Reports say all the amulets have stopped working as well. Order outposts are going up in smoke as we speak. I doubt the cult will be able to recover in any significant way."

"And any seers discovered?" Elana pressed.

"Will be sent to the Keep, as I promised your Mistress. She

and I agree that your mission was a rousing success.”

“I’m sure you didn’t act out of the kindness of your heart?” Taisa stated.

“I acted in the best interest of my country. A country that is no longer threatened by a war between extremists and the Council. I couldn’t want much more than to know the Ramains is safe again.”

“Much more?” Di’Nay raised an eyebrow in question.

Tristan turned to Elana. “I have one thing to ask. Something I’ll need your help convincing the Council to accept.”

Elana was instantly on guard. “What is it?”

“I don’t have to tell you that there’s constant question in the royal court about the true loyalty of the Keep. You’re in the Ramains, but you act as a nation of your own.”

“We keep to ourselves.”

Tristan chuckled. “Like I keep to the Ramains, yes?” Elana cocked an indignant eyebrow. “I’m not asking for the council to answer to the court of the Ramains. I’m not even sure if that would make the Ramains safer. But I don’t think so many secrets benefit either of us.”

“It’s in our best interest to remain a mystery,” Elana countered.

“I’m sure it is, but I deal in mystery. I want an agent in the Keep. Someone who will report back to me alone.”

“Your brother is a Shadow here.”

Tristan waved his hand. “Frisk doesn’t listen to me. He left family bonds behind like every other Shadow. I need someone loyal to the Ramains first.”

“No.”

“I don’t think you understand how much you owe me.”

“I might owe you my life, but I’m not the Council.”

“What about a compromise?” Di’Nay suggested. “An agent who works for both the Keep and the Marshals. Trained by both. Answering to both.”

Tristan considered. “I suppose trust should be mutual.”

Elana instantly thought of dozens of ways such an arrangement could go awry, but she also knew the existence of the Marshals was a potential risk to the Keep, especially if Tristan was so set on learning its secrets. “A Blue Sight.”

Tristan shrugged. “I could do with a few Blue Sights in the

Marshals."

"And I think there's a better chance of neutrality and less chance of corruption if the shared agent can sense intention."

Tristan's smile turned more flippant, the hint of a challenge in his eyes. The idea interested him. "I can count on your support, then, when I appeal the Council tonight?"

"Will you forgive Di'Nay and I our debts to you?"

"Instantly."

"Then yes."

He pulled his scarf back around his shoulders. "Then I suppose that's all until later tonight. It was pleasant doing business with you. All of you." He glanced at Gerome. "You have any interest in being Elana's go-between?"

"I don't work for anyone but the Mother."

"Ah. Still a holy man, then. Pity." He turned to Taisa. "I suspect you'll do your best to make sure the growing colony of seers on Cheongu keeps its influence below the Southern Desert."

"I see you on Cheongu and I'll spear you myself," Taisa threatened.

"Pleasant as always." He nodded to Tae. "Good luck with her. Keep her out of trouble, will you?"

"I don't keep her anywhere."

Tristan drew the scarf up over his nose with a laugh that was soft enough it was almost a sigh. He waved to them once and returned to the gardens, disappearing from view as if he'd turned to mist.

"You sure that's a good idea?" Taisa questioned once he was gone. "He'll try to sway anyone who might be able to get him Keep secrets."

"Or perhaps the Keep will finally learn who the Marshals are and how they operate. Any Blue Sight chosen by the Keep and loyal to the Council is a match for him."

Taisa held her stomach again. "It just makes me happier to leave."

"Keep an eye out. He may turn his attention to Cheongu soon, as Jisoo's temple grows."

"He can try," Tae announced, a smoldering ferocity in his eyes. "We've defended ourselves since the beginning of time. His force is strong, but we own the sea."

Elana smiled. Perhaps he was right. Perhaps she wouldn't

leave Aggar on the edge of ruin. For the rest of her life she'd imagine everything working out as brightly as they imagined. "I'm sure he doesn't stand a chance."

Di'Nay's communicator started to beep and she squeezed Elana's hand – a silent message that she'd be right back. She moved deeper into the garden to speak with Cleis, probably about the shuttle coming the next day.

"Are you scared?" Taisa asked quietly, trying not to be overheard by Di'Nay. "You saw what their world is like in that bunker."

Elana shook her head. "Those are Terrans. I'm not going to a Terran world. I'm going to Di'Nay's world."

"I don't think I could do it," Taisa countered.

"I hope not. I like thinking of you here, keeping Aggar safe."

"The Mother protect you wherever you go," Gerome blessed her. "Even off Aggar, she'll care for her own."

"Thank you."

"It will be a great adventure." Tae sounded jealous.

"You would have made a good Shadow," Elana remarked with a smile.

"A great compliment."

Di'Nay returned. "Everything's cleared for our pickup. Cleis is excited to see us."

"And I her," Elana returned. "I'm excited for whatever's to come." She smiled at Di'Nay and saw her future reflected in her lover's eyes. "I'm ready to go home."

The End of Book Six

DICTIONARY OF AGGAR TERMS

amarin: The amarin is the essence of life, the empathic imprint of animate existence which results in a cumulative pattern of feelings, thoughts and reflexes. It is one's aura.

basker jackal: a sleek, scavenger canine, native to the Ramains' plains and renowned for its blood lust; semi-domesticated by militia for chase and guard chores

black glass: a ceramic-glass compound of especially durable strength that hones to a sharp edge; commonly used in making knife blades

blackpine: A valuable hardwood conifer with a black, barkless trunk and green-black needles which is common to Maltar's lands.

Blue Sight: The Sight or Blue Gift is a sixth sense genetically linked to blue eyes; an awareness of and ability to manipulate life auras and amarin. The terms also refers to a person possessing the Blue Sight.

bondmate: any eitteh, human, or sandwolf who has been empathically bonded into a sandwolf's familial unit (see pack bond; sandwolf)

boko: A food native to the Ramains, boko is a vegetable-meat paste wrapped in boiled leaves.

braygoat: a short-horned goat native to Ramians' southern districts

brushberry: an evergreen bush with a sweet-tart berry; a Ramains wine

bunt: A tall, stemmed grain which yields red-brown seedlings and whose husks are often used for animal fodder. The term also applies to the grayish flour produced from the seedlings.

buntsow: a carnivorous, hooved mammal; a scavenger native to the northern forests; a non-venomous cousin of schefea

"By the Mother's Hand": (idiom) "Done with the Goddess' blessings."

Changlings: Sentient half-human, half-feline beasts native to the Northern Continent, Changlings are a race of people known for their amoral selling and reselling of information. They are also miners of lifestones.

Circle, The: The elite soldiers of the Core, bands of bandits and warriors who do the Twins' bidding

Clan, the: people of the Clan's Plateau; descendents of off-worlders who were stranded on Aggar at the fall of the Galactic Terran Empire; renowned for their weapons technology and raiding activities

Clan Lead: legislative representatives chosen by and from among the Clan folk; (plural) a governing assembly; civil servant

Clantown: the governing settlement and militia corp of the Clan's Plateau; a village in the ancient Terran Quadrant, located at the edge of the eastern plateau adjacent to the Ramains' Great Forests

commons: A Ramains' term for a tavern housed by an inn.

Core, The: The nation risen from the ruins of the Clan's settlement, once the Maltar's realm.

Council of Ten: A collection of ten Masters and Mistresses educated in the history and humanity of Aggar who are guardians of the planet's integrity.

Crowned Rule: the designated heir of the Ramains' Royal Family; usually chosen for skills of statescraft rather than warfare

cucarae: A small, extremely poisonous scavenger, this crustacean is found in the wastelands of both the Northern and Southern Continents.

cucarii: A group or nest of cucarae.

Desert Peoples: Also known as The Southerners, the Desert Peoples are loosely organized nomadic tribes native to the Southern Continent and renown for their distilled liquors and merchant ventures.

Diblum: a small Ramains' village southeast of Khirla

dracoon: A governing marshal appointed by the Ramains' King.

Dumauz: (plural: — en) a kind-hearted individual; a concerned friend

early moon: The first of the twin moons to rise on any given evening.

eitteh: A sentient feline native to the Northern Continent. The term eitteh usually refers to the winged females of the species as males are never seen. See also winged-cats and men-cats.

Eldest Prepared: These individuals are the best of the Shadow trainees at the Council's Keep and are the preferred choice for assignments and lifebonding. They also instruct the younger recruits.

Fates, the: The male deities of evil mischief, the Fates are mystical rulers of the dark underworld. Their primary figures include Malice and Ambition while their secondary figures include War, Ire, Greed and others.

Fates' Cellar: The legendary home of the Fates, Fates' Cellar is the mythical place where evil souls go after death to suffer in a punishing afterlife. Also known as hell.

Fates' Jest: (idiom) A malicious turn of events attributed to the Fates.

Firecaps: These intersecting, volcanic mountain ranges comprise the northeastern third of the Northern Continent. They are uninhabited and controlled by Seers in order to stabilize continental land masses.

grubber: A generic term for ground rodents in the Northern Continent. Grubber generally refers to smallish, nasty-tempered mammals.

harmon: a soul-spirit; self-image projected by a Blue Sight to another

honeywood: a deciduous hardwood with rough, red bark; yields a golden grain of decorative value; common to the southern Ramains

Jezebet: Usually given to a woman, this title is bestowed upon someone who is a resident of the Council's Keep and is trained in the arts of lifebonding Shadowmates.

jumier: a fowl native to the Ramains' northern districts

Karatan: a jungle region in the southern-most continent of Aggar

Khirla: Dracoon's capital in the Ramains' southeasterly district Khirlan

lexion: A domesticated fowl common to farms of the Northern Continent which is raised for its meat.

lifestone: An opal-like energy stone often found in limestone deposits in the Northern Continent and used by the Council in the practice of lifebonding Shadowmates.

mala': A female slave or bond-servant of the Ramains whose duties are restricted to the household and the bedroom.

Maltar: The ruling family of the northern half of the Northern Continent. The term may refer either to the ruling family member or the country itself.

men-cats: The male of the eitteh species, these cat-like savages inhabit the mountain ranges on the Northern Continent.

mesta: A thick-skinned, amber fruit with a tart, meaty pulp in the seed pods that is cultivated by farmers in the Northern Continent.

midnight moon: The second of the twin moons to rise on any given night.

Min: A generic title given to free-born women in the Ramains. It is comparable to the Terran term ma'am.

milkdeer: middle-sized, long necked mammal native to the Ramains; frequently domesticated for its milk

monarc: A standard calendar division, roughly equivalent to a Terran month, which is comprised of four, ten-day periods.

Mother, the: A nurturing female deity who is seen as the birthmother of the universe. Aggar's twin moons are associated with her watchful light.

mumut: a spice leaf grown chiefly in the lower districts of the Ramains

pack bond: empathic understanding of personal commitments; empathic bond of sandwolves used to define familial units (see sandwolf)

pripper: A small, tree-dwelling mammal known for its comical antics and bushy coat.

Purge, The: The last attack on Aggar by Terran forces that culminated in the use of biochemical warfare that massacred nearly every Blue Sight. The battle also destroyed the Council's Keep and Valley Bay, scattered the seers and Amazons.

Ramains: The southwestern third of the Northern Continent which is united beneath a liberal monarchy and shares a border with the Council's lands.

Royal Marshall: special emissaries of the Ramains' Royal Family; originally banded to protect travelers; duties expanded to provide districts with legal and military resolutions, to supply the Royal Court with information from outlying districts

sandwolf: sentient canine, originally native to the Southern Continent, which instinctively imprints at birth to one or more sentient others to provide an emotional, empathic bond in developing protective behaviors and communication skills (see pack bond)

schaefea: A hoofed scavenger of middle size native to the northern mountains. The schaefea has protruding tusks and venomous saliva glands.

Seers: Those individuals gifted with the Blue Sight who are bound to Aggar's lifecycles and no longer capable of individual thoughts or actions. They are directed by the Council of Ten and are the crafters of Aggar's landscapes. Sometimes referred to as mystics.

silverwood: A hardwood conifer with a smooth, silver-green bark and gray-green needles which is common to the Ramains foothills and mountain regions. Also called silverpine.

single moon: The night at the end of each monarc in which only one of the twin moons is visible. Term is synonymous with monarc.

Songs: the unseen force that allows the Choir to manipulate the minds of the people of Aggar; named for the mournful tune that drifts through the air whenever they're near

Tad: Generic title given to free-born men in the Ramains which is similar to the Terran term sir.

tinker-trade: a traveling merchant member of the Traders' Guild

ten-day: A division of days within a monarc, roughly equivalent to a Terran week.

tenmoon season: A period of time roughly the same as two Terran years. The name comes from the fact that ten single moon nights will occur during the time it takes for Aggar to complete one orbit around its sun.

torin: An edible, broad-leafed fern commonly found in the wooded rangers of the Northern Continent.

Traders' Guild, the: a merchant union supported by membership dues that promotes the fair exchange of market goods; endorsed by the Desert Peoples, Ramains, Council and Valley Bay the union may provide arbitrators, bonded transport agents, and travel lodging to supplement regional resources

twin moons: Two planetoids orbiting around Aggar's globe. The term is also associated with the Mother's watchful care.

Twins: The tyrannical, magical rulers of the Core

Unseen Wall: An unidentified energy field which was ordered by the Council of Ten and is controlled by the Seers; the Unseen Wall comprises the border around the Terran Base Quadrant.

Valley Bay: the settlement of the Sisterhood; located near the White Isles, isolated from the Northern Continent by the Firecaps; governed by the Ring of Valley Bay and bound to the home world through the Blue Sighted gifts of the Ring's Binder.

waterferret: amphibious ferret with both scales and fur; often used to aide fisherman and common along coastal towns; very intelligent, but often sneaky and prone to theft.

White Isles of Fire, the: The group of volcanic islands off the eastern Firecaps of the Northern Continent. Sometimes called the Archipelago, it is the native homeland of the Council and the Seers.

Wine of Decisions: A spiced wine containing a natural drug which prompts the visions of the Blue Sight.

winged-cats: Generally used as another term for female eitteh.

DICTIONARY OF SORORIAN TERMS

Amazon: a Sister choosing to work/settle outside of the Sisterhood's jurisdiction

ann: (idiom) A word used to emphasize thoughts or ideas and function as a verbal exclamation point. Ann might also be translated as "Take note!" Other meanings include to be far away or distant.

be: far, distant

beasties: Large, hoofed mammals, these horned animals have copper-colored, wooly coats and are descended from the Highland Cattle of old Terra.

bin: A preposition meaning between. Sometimes means to or from.

Cee: A word that refers to the customs or ways of any given people.

cheroan: to make safe, to protect

Coramee: daughter

corean: A verb meaning to find precious, to treasure.

crone: a wise elder among healers n'Shea

dey: This word can be used as either an article as in "the" or a pronoun as in "we" or "our" and is meant to connote respect.

duen: to do kindly; to act with concern

Dumauz: (plural: —en) a kind-hearted individual; a concerned friend

Feast of Helen: This anniversary celebration of unity and independence marks the birth of the Sisterhood's firstborn child.

felan: A verb form meaning using, doing or creating.

Founding, the: the original planetary colonization of dey Sorormin under the Galactic Terran Empire; settlement of the home world

Helen: This name refers to the Red star of dey Sorormin's solar system, the firstborn of dey Sorormin's original settlement and the leader of n'Sappho during early negotiations to retain Sorormin independence. The word means "light."

Houses of dey Sorormin: surnames of Sisters, designating family and/or skills; six of Seven Houses recall ancient goddesses of Terran lore (n'Athena: guardians (Greek), n'Awehai: crafters (Iroquois), n'Hina: agricultural providers (Polynesian), n'Huitaca: artists (Chibcha), n'Minona: historians/teachers (Dahomey), n'Shea: healers (Irish); First House of dey Sorormin (n'Sappho: legislative leaders) recalls a Terran stateswoman of Greece

Kahmee: little daughter; a very young girl

kahn: A noun meaning sunrise or dawn.

kamak: A verb which indicates something is brought to completion or finished. It may also be used in place of is made.

kau: A pronoun referring to the second person singular (you).

ki: A word indicating possession (yours).

kumin: A verb meaning to join together.

m': A preposition denoting as or of (from).

m'Sormee: birth mother; (literally) from the woman's life

mae: A word indicating that something is dear or precious.

"Mae n'Pour": (idiom) An expression which means "Give me strength." This term is often used as a curse to express frustration or anger but can also be used as a genuine prayer to the Goddess.

mau: A noun meaning heart.

mauen: The plural form of mau (hearts).

mee: A noun which denotes life.

minmee: A word meaning birth, minmee also carries the connotation of the sacred connection of life-giving or creating.

n': This expression denotes possession. It is usually used to indicate an individual's House.

n'Athena: One of the Seven Houses of dey Sorormin, members of this house are traditionally the guardians of the Sisterhood. The term also recalls a Terran goddess from ancient Greek lore.

n'Awehai: One of the Seven Houses of dey Sorormin, members of this house are traditionally the builders and craftswomen of the Sisterhood. The term also recalls a Terran goddess of Iroquois (Native Northern American) lore.

n'Hina: One of the Seven Houses of dey Sorormin, members of this house are traditionally the agricultural providers of the Sisterhood. The term also recalls a Terran goddess of Polynesian lore.

n'Huitaca: One of the Seven Houses of dey Sorormin, members of this house are traditionally the treasurers of music and arts of the Sisterhood. The term also recalls a Terran goddess of Colombian Chibcha (Native Southern American) lore.

n'Minona: One of the Seven Houses of dey Sorormin, members of this house are traditionally the historians and teachers of the Sisterhood. The term also recalls a Terran goddess of African Dahomey lore.

n'Sappho: First House of the Seven Houses of dey Sorormin, members of this house traditionally make up the legislature and leadership of the Sisterhood. The term also recalls a Terran stateswoman of ancient Greek citizenship.

n'Shea: One of the Seven Houses of dey Sorormin, members of this house are traditionally the healers and earthwitches of the Sisterhood. The term also recalls a Terran woman-deity and/or the white witches of ancient Irish lore.

n'Sormee: parenting mother or guardian; (literally) of the woman's life

nehna: (idiom) A prompt for more information meaning and then, then it happened that or so then.

Niachero: Daughter of the Stars; descriptive of Sisters who genetically resemble those n'Athena who negotiated the settlement of Valley Bay; Amazons who led the space protectors to save Aggar during the fall of the Galactic Terran Empire

nor: An word that indicates an event happened in the past.

puor: An word meaning strength, stability or virtuousness.

quinn: A word denoting peace, tranquility or the absence of violence.

quitan: to nurture; to tend with compassion

ret: A word meaning cruelty or harm.

sae: Another term for please, this word denotes a request.

sak: This word means intelligence or cleverness.

shea: This noun refers to a healing witch from the House of n'Shea. A member of this house will frequently be one who is closely bound to nature. She may also be a mistress of love potions and possess the evil eye. See the term n'Shea.

sheaz: A noun meaning the earth or world, this term may also refer to the components of a nurturing Earthmother Creator.

Shekhina: The moon of Helen's second planet. This moon is home to Helen's high-tech base where diplomatic contacts between the dey Sorormin and the Galactic Terran Empire occur. It is also the home of the Immigration offices and the orientation/screening facilities for new Sisters. Historically, the term refers to an ancient Terran goddess of Judaic lore and sometimes connotes the divine image of a woman.

sor: The noun meaning woman.

soroe: The noun denoting friend or dear companion.

Soroi: loved one; lover; beloved

Sororian: The woman-made language of the Sisterhood. The term derives its root meaning from the ancient Terran word which refers to sisters.

Sorormin: A noun that is synonymous with the word Sisterhood.

Sorormin, dey: The word which represents the proper name of The Sisterhood. The term also refers generally to the culture of women who settled on Helen's second planet. dey Sorormin are recognized members of the Senate in the Third Galactic Terran Empire.

sueht: A past tense form of the verb to lose or to misplace.

tau: A pronoun denoting me.

ti: A word that indicates possession (my).

tizmar: A verb which means to remain, to settle or to unite and/or join together.

vu: A term meaning very little, a small amount.

z': A term indicating for or with.

"Z'ki Sak, Diana": (idiom) An expression of regret or disbelief which translates as "By your wits, Goddess."